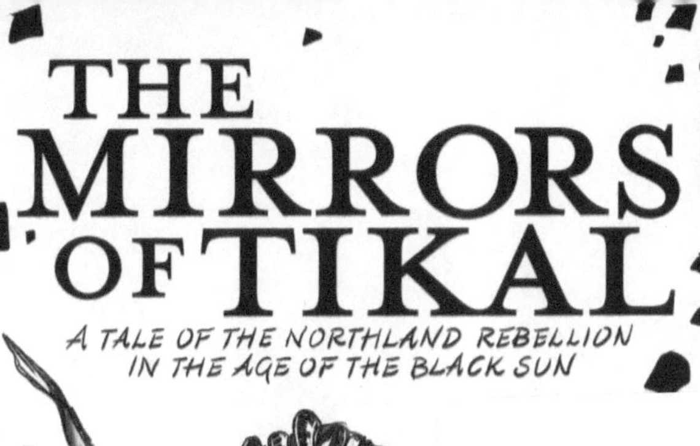

THE
MIRRORS
OF TIKAL
A TALE OF THE NORTHLAND REBELLION
IN THE AGE OF THE BLACK SUN
I0645477

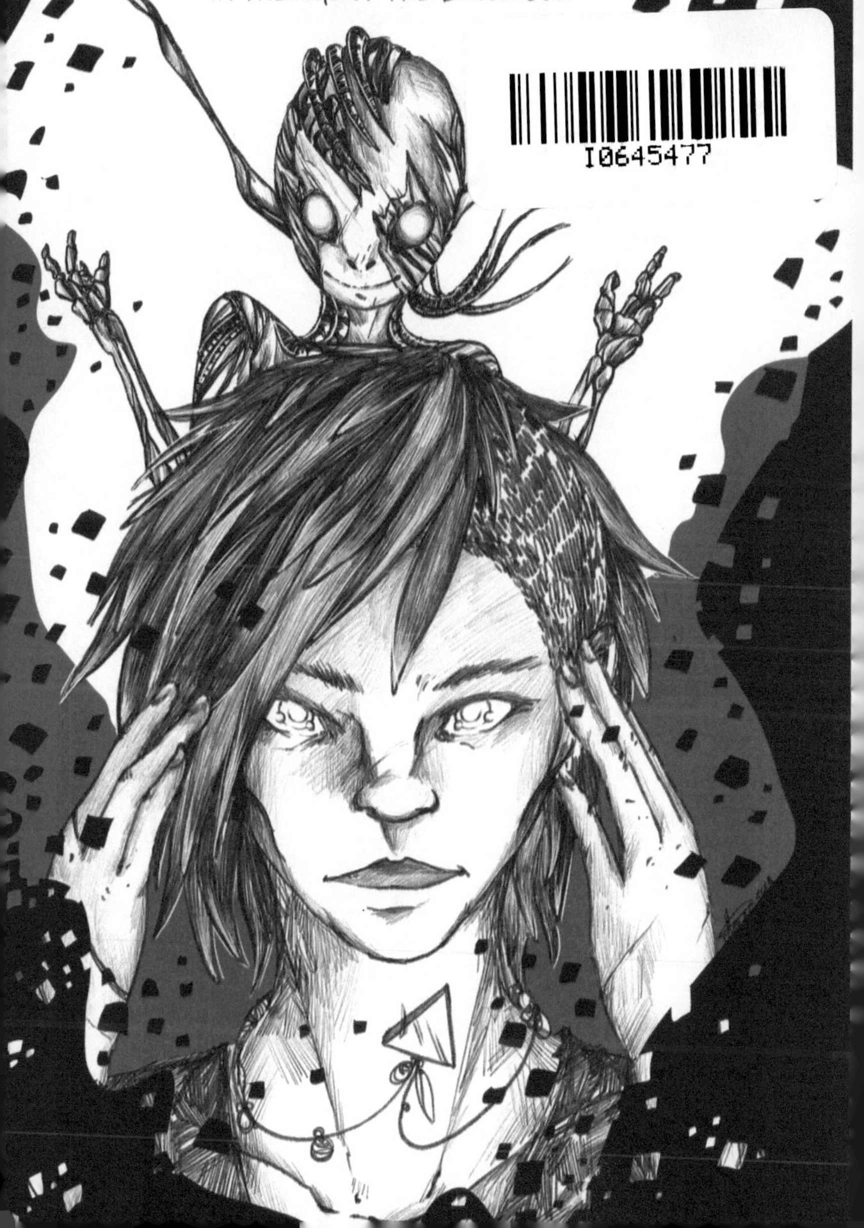

THE MIRRORS OF TIKAL
A TALE OF THE NORTHLAND REBELLION
IN THE AGE OF THE BLACK SUN
Book Two
Northland Rebellion
Without direction we
are left to wander.
We can only weather the Storm,
Climb the Mountain.
Trail through the Valley.
We trust that someday
Hope will shine true.

PUBLISHER
Kylie Leane

COVER ARTIST
Jorge Jacinto

COVER LAYOUT
Kylie Leane

MIRRORS OF TIKAL
Northland Rebellion: Book Two

ISBN: 978-0-9944382-5-6

For information address:
authorkylieleane@gmail.com

Kylie Leane can be found online at
authorkylie.com

Other Works By Kylie Leane

Chronicles of the Children
KEY: Book One
Protectors: Book Two

Northland Rebellion
Orphans & Outcasts: Book One

Thank you for all the evenings
you spent trying to teach me how to spell.
I appreciate the effort you put in to give me
such a love of words when
I could not even write them.

Scribe's Note

Here we are again, Dearest Readers, another book!

Thank you so much for your continued patience throughout this journey we've embarked upon. I am so grateful for all your support over these years. I know I've taken the really, really long road to bring these stories into existence but I truly hope you find this next adventure worth the wait.

This book is a continuation of the *Northland Rebellion*—which started with *Orphans & Outcasts*—and together they fit in-between *KEY* and *Protectors* from *Chronicles of the Children* as a sub-series. You're going to find, as the two series gradually progress, that characters and events from *Chronicles of the Children* will be shared with the *Northland Rebellion*. They're meant to be read side-by-side. I know, I know, *MORE* stories Kylie! Don't you have enough to write? Hah, hah, *NEVER!*

While writing can be a very lonely experience, it does not mean that a novel is written without a myriad of aid. Thank you to Katie, Matt, Karen and Alex for being such great, supportive author friends—I really appreciate having gotten the chance to know you guys over the years.

I must thank the new management, Steve and Pete, of *The Hub Café* who have graciously continued letting me sit at my favourite table in a welcoming, comfortable environment – and supply me with my favourite croissants – no – seriously – they're the best in Adelaide. Thanks guys!

Thank you to Elle for editing another one of my books. I have been so grateful for her input, wisdom, understanding and knowledge over the years. I honestly could not have done what I've done without her. Mere words cannot express my gratitude.

A massive thanks Jorge Jacinto for some really beautiful cover art. It is always exciting to see covers come to life. I really appreciated Jorge's creative input. Thank you!

As always, my parents have stood beside me as a constant support. Even when I waver, when my pain gets to much, or my loneliness to overwhelming, they'll tell me to just keep moving forward because what else is there to do.

When all else fails –

Just hope.

Hold onto hope and keep moving forward.

And a huge thanks to Popa and Nana.

Thank you, dearest readers, for picking up my books, finding my haunts on the web, coming to see me at conventions and your encouragement.

I really, really do appreciate all of it. You're all a part of this adventure!

Enjoy this tale!

Your scribe,

KL

THE BLESSING

Sometimes it feels like the tide is rising,
And you are drowning under the weight of the burdens upon you.
You cannot possibly discern the sunlight through the murky waters
as you are pulled deeper by ribbons of great currents.
That is why, my friend, I tell you:
don't travel alone upon your journey.
Tread your path with a friend who can
pull you through times of great storms.

But, if you must take the lonely road,
If you are a Lone Wanderer,
A Pilgrim of Begotten Paths,
A Companionless Hero,
Remember to stop a while here, and rest.
Linger and listen
To tales of those who have gone before.
So you may know
You are never truly alone.
For every road that has ever been,
Has been walked at least once before.

The Lonely Bard

KEMET
Coltarian
Thonrae
Pennadot
Mondraina
Utillia
Sin'musk'qu
Shroq
Ryrllot
Awunot
The Northlands
DANGER
All this place STAY AWAY ALL HERE
Gifu DoNOT go Here
Don't go Here
Not here
Don't go Here
I FIXED IT FOR YOU GIFU!
Yes, I can see that, San, thank you. I will endeavor not to enter Kemet.

Pennadot
Pass of Stairs
Bkapl
Glass Lake
Flats of Tykatida
Krrirren Tree
Forest Bamgnep
Yrra Kru "Lost Death"
Mt. Thoth
Krrirren Tree
Uti
Forest Dreard
Nishragra
The Three Little Kings
Pipeline
Nanir
Cyrnbyrin Iles
Manjinarra (Abrial)
Nirajsa Cluster
Dyna Island
Ishabal
Thrunthton "City of Ash"
Anatea Isles
Prince's Nest
Hiagran Isles
Queen's Eyes
MorMor
Utillia
Land of the Burning-Sea

CHAPTER ONE

"Seal it off!" Sekhmet screeched as he tore down the corridor, pushing past his confused children. He yelled into the commlink attached to his chin. "Disgleirio! Seal off the Observation Deck, right now! Our orbit dropped too low! They're inside!" He skidded to a halt as a shuddering groan vibrated through the metal sheets of the walls. His body twisted as he stared back down the corridor. Lights began rupturing. Philepcon liquid spewed across the floor. His commlink crackled in his ear, Disgleirio's voice distorted. The eyes of one of his children sought his and Sekhmet instinctively reached out.
"No!"
The Zaprex was ripped away with a shriek.

Jarvis gripped the wheel of the *Silver Slasher*, feeling a dune rise beneath them. He was still uneasy at the controls. Aaldryn considered him adorable and short, unable to see over the helm of the sand-ship without standing on a box. It was the most annoying thing to be teased about. He was a Wynnila; he was always going to be short, and around Titus and Aaldryn it was ruthless hair ruffling all day. As the sand stabilised, Jarvis relaxed and rolled his aching shoulders. Inside, he felt the satisfied hum of his protector bot, a charge of energy vibrating through his limbs, spreading out through the philepcon liquid invading his organs. He curled his toes at the sensation. At least part of him was happy about the Sun. He had never before in his life suffered scorching burns to his skin due to the heat of the Sun, even at the peak of Pennadotian Summer when the temperature was near unbearable and his skin went Sunstone gold. He had thought his sister beautiful, those pristine summer months, when she wove her rusty-toned hair and wore fabrics shaded in yellows, reds, and blues to match her bright eyes. Her footsteps still haunted his dreams. Some nights he startled awake, panting, delirious, thinking she was beside him.

She never would be.

Father, mother, sister and her husband—gone—all taken.

"Don' yeh scratch at it!" Master Titus slapped at his wrists. "Yeh'll make it worse, Sonny."

Jarvis blinked. He stared down at himself. He had not even realised what he was doing. He sheepishly ducked away from Titus' hand.

"Why am I burning like this? This doesn't happen in Pennadot."

Titus looked at the Sun, low in the sky-sea. "I ain't a Zaprex genius but I think it be something ta do with the sky-sea. They be different in each land."

"Oh." Jarvis frowned. "The turrets must be calibrated differently. The poor Kimwyns. No wonder Jythal lost his sight."

That was not something he should have known. Jarvis shook his head, clearing it of the protector bot's influence.

Aaldryn leant over him, pulling a few levers. "When we next dock for supplies we'll have to get you some treatment for your burns."

"I really thought my bot would have healed them by now."

Aaldryn lifted one of Jarvis' arms, studying the skin thoughtfully. "It's possible it isn't registering the damage because it happens so slowly. Can't you tell yourself it's a wound?"

"I'm in constant complaint. Isn't that enough?"

"No, I mean log it as a complaint. Have you tried to access the protector bot at all?"

Jarvis cringed at the thought of connecting to the protector bot again. It tended to sit, somewhere—he imagined it lurking in the background, humming away—only rising to the surface when provoked or if he called for it. To access it was like touching a torrent of energy, being drenched in information he had no ability to comprehend. Would he ever be ready to allow the protector bot control of everything, all his limbs, of the whole of his mind? Would he cease being Jarvis of the Plains People the moment he let it free?

Was that why his skin was burning? Because he insisted on clinging to a piece of himself that was still Human?

"Maybe I am scared of letting it take over," he murmured. "I don't want to not be me."

"I can understand," Aaldryn offered. "I felt that way, too, when I first began to realise who Khamsin was. And I am sure your Master would understand."

That much was true. He had never been bold enough to ask for the story of how his master had become consumed by a Twizel, and, in the end, overcome the Dragon's minion and regained control of his body.

Jarvis laughed. "How odd." He looked up at the prince. "All three of us are hosts to something."

"We were all touched by the Secondary Realm, little brother, and we're alive to tell the tale."

Jarvis released the controls to Aaldryn, but he remained resting against the prince, reluctant to move away with the Sun waning and the chill of winter's evening falling upon them. Aaldryn was a heat bag, like the kind full of rice that his mother would use on cold nights to warm his bed. Sometimes Aaldryn even smelt like rice, but that was because he worked with their Mist engines so often. Mist smelt like rice. Maybe it actually was rice—it would be no surprise if something so simple, mundane, and abundant in Pennadot was magical and coveted in Utillia.

Jarvis watched as a rush of Mist swelled through the sails, the engines of their little dhow thrumming from within. He breathed in the aroma from the glistening Mist flaking off the sails like fire embers.

The scent was a small piece of home in a foreign land.

"Aaldryn…"

Aaldryn's ears flicked back. "Yep."

Jarvis rubbed the back of his neck. "How did Khamsin come to be bound to you?"

Aaldryn held out a paw, wiggling the claws. "What do you see?"

"Errr." Jarvis frowned. "Your paws."

"Anything different about them?"

Jarvis leant forward. Nope. They were normal paws—oh—

"You have an extra claw," he whispered. How had he never seen that before?

"That I do." Aaldryn tapped the claws on each paw.

"They're a mutation," Titus interjected. "We've seen it crop up in the House of Flames, from the interbreeding that occurred in our dwindling population. Mind yeh, it tends ta be lack of limbs, not extra."

Aaldryn lifted a foot-paw, revealing the same extra toes.

"Do they bother you?" Jarvis murmured.

"Nah, not really. Don't know any different. I went through a phase in which I despised them, and I did try to cut them off. Mother was very upset at me for being so ungrateful."

Jarvis shuddered.

Aaldryn looked at him fondly. "You'll hear the phrase 'misfit-born' thrown around a lot in Utillia. We misfits are the children of the sands. The cast-offs, the outcasts." He tapped his extra digits on the wheel. "A Zaprex mistake, some would say. Some of us are born very ill, for there is a sickness rising out of the burning-sea. It is why the life-span of Humans and Kelibs in Utillia is so short. They fall ill."

"The crystals in the Zaprex technology." Jarvis looked out across the dune-waves. "They've broken out of their containment fields and started leaking."

Aaldryn nodded. "It is my belief, and Khamsin's, that those who dwell in Utillia have been gradually changing every generation due to the exposure. My example is a small one. So is Nixlye's. She was born with malformed legs—the bones too mangled to function. Yet somewhere, out there, the Iposti must be keeping secrets we know nothing about."

It was the way Aaldryn's air-gills frilled out enough to show the emotions behind his words, though his tone was still soft, that Jarvis found most intriguing. The Kattamont could reveal his intense dislike without raising his voice, but his shimmering gills could say so much.

Aaldryn rubbed at his growing mane. "I know it is difficult to believe, but I was born a very small, very weak cub. The healers said I was sickly with the illness they could not cure. Mother hid me from the Iposti and smuggled me out of the Silvertide docks. For many days and nights, she roamed the burning-sea weeping, begging the Rythrya Stones to spare me. Khamsin says he heard her voice on the wind and felt compelled by her compassion, for it was so like his own. His sorrow for his children, bound in chains by the Iposti, drew him to her."

"Yer mother made a pact with an Elemental Titan?" Titus interrupted.

Jarvis stirred. It was difficult for him to picture the Kattamont queen in such despair that she would make a pact with an Elemental being. Yet it was in their bleakest moments that a person discovered who they really were. He had not known who he was until he was released from his boxed prison. Maybe Queen Zafiashid had found herself in a promise to save her son.

"Did she realise what she was doin'?" his master continued. "'Tis serious stuff ta bind yer life ta a Titan."

Aaldryn's brow furrowed. "I suppose she really didn't." He laughed, then, and Jarvis wondered if Khamsin had made a comment they could not hear. "But here I am, the embodiment of the Northern Wind."

"Yah." Titus clapped his head in mock play. "Wee laddie, I know the Titan of Fire and I have even encountered the Titan of Shadows. Seems ma lot in life is ta be bunked with Elemental forces."

Aaldryn's whole demeanour changed. His back straightened, and his ears flicked upright. It was as though a tight string had pulled on every one of his limbs. He looked eerily like a puppet.

"Oh? So, the little Shadow survived the war too? How did he do that?" Khamsin's voice was a low whisper. Jarvis looked away, wishing he could turn off his visual display so he did not have to be reminded constantly of the second life inhabiting his friend. As much as he wanted to believe Khamsin was not a threat, it was too similar to the Dragon's silky, frightening touch sliding against his firewalls.

"The Titan of Shadows sided with the enemy."

"Ah." Khamsin sighed. "I suppose that does make sense."

"Didna turn out so well for him, though," Titus mused. "His kids are in just as much trouble as yers. Maybe worse."

"Seems to happen to us." Khamsin frowned. "Our punishment for accepting the Dragon as kin. What about Prometheus' children?"

"Dying out." Titus shrugged.

That seemed to startle the wind-god. "But surely…? That makes no sense. They can become corporeal. When Prometheus took physical form so did all the Thyrrhos. They have a Life Nest, with the fleshlings as fuel. They should be breeding fine."

Jarvis covered his mouth, trying to hide the laugh that bubbled up. "You do realise, Khamsin, that you're stuck in a fleshling body, too, right?"

He received a heavy whack over his head for his gibe.

"This body is a willing host. Prometheus' children became bound to the soil of this world. They are trapped here. They are not free, no matter what they think. They are prisoners of the Primary Realm. I grieve for them."

Titus brushed a hand through his hair. "That's true enough, I s'ppose. It's possibly the reason why they're dyin' out. The population of the House can't even maintain its own growth. Those who're chosen as partners of the Thyrrhos are referred to as Souls and were excluded from the Breeding Program until a few decades back. A lot went down when they started forcing the Breeding Program onto the Souls." The Hunter sighed. "Practically shattered the House into two factions. Now the poor Souls get called 'Leeches'. Lovely new term for 'em, heh?"

"That doesn't sound very nice." Jarvis wondered how the conversation had taken such a dark turn.

"It's derogatory." Titus sighed. "Seems ta be the thing these days. An Elemental must get energy from somewhere ta survive in the Primary Realm, so the Thyrrhos Nation, being already corporeal, partner with Souls, from whom they draw emotions to survive. Rather like Khamsin has taken Aaldryn as a host to survive, but less drastic."

"So, they're like each other's soul-mates?" Jarvis grinned.

"Oh, yah, I suppose it be something like that. I don' know how much longer the House can sustain itself before the population collapses entirely. Like I mentioned before, interbreeding started a while back due to our limited numbers."

"That wouldn't be a problem for Kelibs, though." Aaldryn was back. Jarvis felt himself relax.

"Their clans are big family networks, like Kattamonts. I'm pretty sure that Nixlye is of the Jezumatu Pride, as is Jythal, and it is likely that by the time we return they'll have cubs."

"Are you sad about that?" Jarvis asked.

"No. I am the Alpha; I protect the Pride. If my actions now save my family, then I am content." Aaldryn's long, thick arm folded around Jarvis' shoulder. "Besides, you are part of the Pride."

Titus was smiling. "We're very similar souls, Aaldryn. Yeh're right, though. Kelibs would be fine in our small population, but we have very few pure-blooded Kelibs left."

"Seriously?" What did the House of Flames look like then? Jarvis wondered.

"Our Kelibs come from Pennadot. We save them from the prisoner caravans being taken over the Pass of Fire to fuel the Dragon's Army, but it is hard to balance loss and gain saving those caravans."

Aaldryn hung his head. "I suppose it is to be expected. Messengers have been fighting a war for a very long time."

"Do you think we'll reach them in time, to warn them?" Jarvis whispered.

His master looked at him, and his smile was one of reassurance. "Yeh let me worry about that, Sonny Jon. Your job is ta get that special crystal ta the Key."

Jarvis was beginning to think that if he stared out into the sand-dune waves long enough he would be swallowed by the tide. The days and long nights had blurred together on board the *Silver Slasher* until months became a single stream. If it were not for his protector bot's ability to perfectly recall the time he would have thought himself in a dream of never-ending golden horizons. He brushed his darkening skin. It was burning less often, becoming more golden Sunstone metallic than enflamed red. Even though the Sun barely touched the sky-sea for a few hours a day, it still scorched the earth with a harshness he had never known in Pennadot. The sky-sea was immense, wider, further, and more magnificent than it had ever been on the moors of his forefathers. The gradual enhancing of his senses, the flicker, click, and whirr of the mechanics taking over inside him, the philepcon liquid slurping, was becoming less terrifying and more invigorating. The endless horizon made it even more thrilling. The little voice within him had thoughts he would never have considered and it longed for things—Zaprex things—he would never have longed for.

Like the sky-sea, and what lay beyond it. He wanted to fly. He needed to fly. He was a Human who craved the return of his wings.

Jarvis breathed in sharply, touching his cheek as a single tear trailed down, catching on the edge of his chin. He brushed it aside. Was it triggered by his own feelings, or by the protector bot within him?

Or were they the same person?

Titus joined him at the railing. Jarvis looked up, smiling at his master. The sky-sea was dazzling with pre-twilight stars. This was his favourite time of the evening, when the colours reflected from the burning-sea mixed with early stars in the sky-sea and everything was like the jewellery his sister had worn on her wedding day. Titus crouched and pointed.

"That's the Black Wall, the caldera of Coltarian."

Jarvis blew a rasp. "That's the Black Wall? It doesn't look very imposing."

"It mightna look imposing now, but wait until yeh see it up close, Little Weasel." Titus cuffed him over the head. He tried to dodge it but was met with more hair ruffling and a fist twisted into his skull. Surprisingly, his yelling and squawking worked for once as Titus dropped him slowly back onto the deck. He dusted himself off, settling his hair-jewels back into place. His master had lifted himself onto the rigging and was peering out across the sand-dunes, scanning the darkening area. Jarvis felt his defence program shift into alert.

"Master Titus?"

"Get up here. Tell me what yer eyes see."

He scrambled to obey, joining the Hunter on the rigging. He leant out over the sand and scanned the horizon, zooming in and out at various levels. Alarms blared in his skull and he pulled back, almost losing his footing.

"Aaldryn!" Jarvis yelped out. "We're heading straight for some rocks! Really sharp rocks. Right over this—"

He was about to say 'dune', but a sudden bounce of gravity sent him flipping up with a shout. His gravity-bubble settled him down upon the deck where Titus was swearing loudly, having landed on his rump.

Jarvis ran for the controls. Aaldryn unlooped a spyglass, peering out through it and across the sand-dune waves. The prince released a high-pitched cry of alarm.

"Not rocks!" Aaldryn spun the dhow's wheel. Jarvis felt the *Silver Slasher* jerk beneath him and he thumped heavily against the banister. Wind rippled through the Mist sails, tossing sand across the deck as the small vessel fought the gravity currents.

Not rocks? What, then, had spooked Aaldryn to such a degree that he would summon Khamsin's wind? Jarvis blinked, clearing his lenses of sand, slowing his racing heartbeat. He focused through the darkness. The floodgate opened the moment he allowed it to, the protector bot accessing his optical lenses, expanding his sensor arrays. He had been fighting it since the Dragon's attack in the Secondary Realm, but now he let the sensation overtake every inch of him. The world filled with lines of colour, all in grid format across the burning-sea, the sand particles tossed by wind slowing as his sensors adapted and scanned the area Aaldryn was so intent on avoiding.

He gasped. Not rocks. A swarming layer of gleaming, rock-shaped creatures burst onto the burning-sea's surface like boiling bubbles. They were gnawing and feasting upon a vessel the size of their own dhow. Jarvis shrank back. The screams. He could hear them now.

"Aaldryn! There is a sand-ship." He grabbed the prince's arm.

"There is nothing we can do for them."

"No, we have to save them."

"I'm not stopping for anything caught up in a swarm of azhaw." Aaldryn heaved on a lever and their sails expanded, rippling across the sand-waves. "If they catch even a whiff of us, we're goners."

Jarvis' gaze lingered on the sinking sand-ship in the distance. His gut clenched. A distress signal flickered on the edge of his optical lenses. The protector bot within him urged him to move, to aid those screams. He felt the surge of power injected through his limbs, building up between the cracks of his hull to trigger the metal exoskeleton and send him charging forth.

He had almost cleared the railing when Aaldryn's full weight connected with him, pinning him against the deck. Air was forced from his lungs before he had a chance to initiate his gravity control and flip the heavier Kattamont. Instead, he wrapped his legs around Aaldryn's torso, tightening in a vice. He struck out with a clenched fist but missed, cracking the deck with the force of the strike.

The prince's air-gills flashed out, rattling.

Warning signals flared in Jarvis' receptors, blazing over all sectors of his optical lenses and he braced himself, knowing exactly what it meant. He flung up his arms, crisscrossing them, barely feeling the shield of pulsating energy polarize from across the hull of his metal exoskeleton as Khamsin's wind struck him. No amount of training could have prepared him for the full force of the Titan's rampage. The rush felt like knives, hundreds of them, beating against him.

His shield cracked. Jarvis watched the fissures form in the invisible field, before it shattered into flakes of energy and his body snapped back across the deck, striking one of the masts of the *Silver Slasher*.

CHAPTER TWO

*The metal Zaprex and Human corpses that surrounded Sekhmet
had been torn asunder. It was almost impossible for him to make out
what had originally belonged to either. In death, the two races had
finally become one. It had not been a battle—it had been a slaughter.
He covered his face as oily tears bled down his cheeks. There was not
enough strength remaining in him for rage, the rage that had once
burned in him, allowing him to obliterate entire planets without mercy.
Losing so many of his children seared with such a deep, agonising
pain there was no room left to feel anything else. This war had taken
everything from him. His country, his siblings, his partner, his Dynasty,
and, someday, Eternity willing, it would take his life.*
"Disgleirio, how are you?" Sekhmet murmured.
The soft voice of a child crackled over the intercom. "I'm cold, sir."
*"I'm sorry. I'm sorry to ask this, but do you think you have enough
energy to take us into a higher orbit? You can rest then."*
"I think I can, sir."
*"It's Gibo, Disgleirio. Please, just call me Gibo again. You're all I have
left."*

The room was eerily familiar from a childhood that had long passed.
An echo of a memory. A slight haze softened the sharp edges
surrounding Denvy, but it was The Room. Denvy had known no other
name for the terrifying chamber full of bright lights, cold floors that
soaked the warmth out of his foot-paws, and stark metal walls. He
stepped softly over the frozen floor. It felt as it always had: sterile. It
was home, though, for it was a Zaprex room, with blinking holograms
lighting every corner, shimmering off glass panels. No matter how
repulsed he was by finding himself in The Room, it still overwhelmed
him with a sense of familiarity and comfort. He had once spent days
within the starkness, being rebuilt, piece by piece. The Zaprexes who
had worked on him were kind. Their hands always gentle. It was the
pain between his eyes, and the sensation of floating beyond himself,
lost in the void of the Secondary Realm, the fear that he would never
return, that he associated with this place.

Hazanin had visited him often—because Gibo was trapped in the
Tower. The Time Master's beautiful voice had filled The Room with a
sweet song. Though he had never believed himself to be either strong
or courageous, he had been told he was, and the Time Master assured
him it was true. So, it had to be, right?

Denvy brushed his paws over a long bed. This was where he had
been remade, reforged, into a timeless being of data.

A voice startled him. "Denvy, where are we?"

Denvy jerked around. In the corner of The Room, Ryojin's avatar stood in a swirl of glittering flakes, a whirlpool of indigo, mimicking the hue his fur had taken in life. He should not have been surprised by the young prince's presence inside the dreamscape, after all, with the yoke still binding his dreamathic mind, Ryojin was his only connection to the Data Stream—a foot-paw jamming open a door for him to shuffle uncomfortably through. But the invasion of his privacy was still disconcerting.

"This is a nightmare," Denvy murmured.

"A nightmare?" Ryojin glanced around, hesitating in his corner.

"Indeed. I have not had this one before." Denvy gently caressed the bed he had lain upon eons ago. The metal of its arches was warped and scorched. The walls that had encased him within The Room had visible heat marks. Glass panels were shattered, and his foot-paws crunched them as he walked. It was the glistening blue liquid leaking between the scattered mosaic of crystals that caused his fur to stand on end.

Blood.

Zaprex blood.

There had been a battle here, in The Room.

His ears flicked rearward as cries echoed beyond the slightly ajar door. Footsteps approached and four Zaprexes stumbled through, dressed in stained white lab coats. The eldest, skin a pale turquoise, staggered back against the door, ripples of his metal hull straining as he slammed it shut and slid against it, panting heavily.

Denvy's lips parted. "Gifu."

It was Nefertem. His Creator. The Zaprex who had spent so long with him in The Room, with a smile of silver and a voice of honey. He made to move, but Ryojin grabbed his shoulder in a sudden vice grip. "You'll disrupt the data sequence. Let it play out."

Tears collected on the edges of his cheeks and he covered his mouth, holding back his sob. This was a dream, and he could not interact with it. It was a code long ago logged into his files that had never surfaced, perhaps because he had never before set foot in Utillia for the upload to run its course. Now he was trapped here, in an execution process he had no desire to watch.

Anything but this—

He did not wish to dream this.

"Go!" Nefertem turned weakly. "Get into your pods, quickly. Go!" He gestured at the three lingering Zaprexes.

"But, Pharaoh—"

"Go! I will hold them off for as long as I can! The facility is sinking. There is no other way."

"What about self-destruct mode?" one Zaprex piped up, trying to struggle out of the grip of another as he was dragged away.

"It is impossible now." Nefertem looked pained. Denvy had never seen such an expression cross his Creator's usually calm features. "Without Sekhmet."

Denvy sucked in a sharp breath. What was this? Sekhmet was gone?

"Please go. Begin stasis. Hurry. Just hurry."

None of the Zaprexes wanted to leave, but they could not disobey the head of their Dynasty. How Denvy wished even just one of them had remained, to stand by the frail fairy, who was now alone by the door. The lights of their antennae faded from view as they vanished through an entrance that clipped tightly shut behind them. Nefertem visibly relaxed for a moment before turning on his heel. His delicate, illumed boots chimed against the floor as he moved around the room, pulling open drawers, searching through equipment. Denvy and Ryojin turned, missing the Zaprex's movements as he glided around them. The fairy was weeping softly. It was barely audible, but the tears glistened like jewels down his cheeks.

"I was never supposed to be a warrior. I am a scientist! A scientist!" The thin chest heaved. He pulled a weapon from a shelf.

Denvy stepped back, shaking his head in denial.

"What is it?" Ryojin asked.

"Nefertem swore an oath to never wield a weapon," Denvy whispered.

The Zaprex continued, "I never wanted to join the cycle like this. Why, Sekhmet, did you have to go and die first? We are terrible apart—"

A crack reverberated through The Room. The door at the entrance buckled. Denvy and Ryojin reared back, both ducking behind the bed. Denvy's air-gills and tail frilled in alarm. Beside him, he heard Ryojin's low, territorial hissing as a profane stench of heated metal tainted the air.

This was familiar. He bit his bottom lip. This smell filled him with a dread and a weight that had lasted eons before it had finally begun to ease, and now, suddenly, it collapsed back onto his shoulders like a fallen beam. The sight of the door glowing, leaking into liquid, a terrible reminder of the days of the Thousand Sol-Cycle War when Zaprex metal had become breakable.

Nefertem breathed, seeming to steel himself.

"I hope you made it, Hazanin. Find Osiris. Please. Restart the cycle. Please. Don't make everything I did be for nothing."

He trained his weapon on the remaining crystal terminals. Denvy curled his paws against his ears and Ryojin burrowed into his chest with a cry as the laser shattered through the devices. The door erupted with a deafening crack, slamming into the nearest wall at the force of the blast. Swirling golden chains swept around Nefertem creating a cage, throwing the tiny Zaprex against the broken displays, pinning him down. A golden hand, burning crimson from within, formed layer by layer over Nefertem's neck, until a smirking female face stared down at the cyborg.

Denvy felt his paw automatically reach for his water-sword. It came up short and he growled, heaving to his feet, claws lengthening. All it would take was a few strides, and he would be upon the hellish fiend pinning down his Creator.

"Denvy, stop! Your program is going haywire. You need to calm down. I can't contain you." Ryojin clawed at his shoulders.

"Then don't!" he snarled.

"She isn't real! You have no control over your dreamathic mind with the yoke on. I'm the only thing between you and burning out the minds of everyone on board the *Lawless Child*. Please. If we are going to free you from the yoke, we need to do it together. Calm down!"

The distortions within the dream crackled around him. He glared at each vein of looping data, drawing on the hypnotising swirl to quieten the thundering roar of his mind. She was familiar, but he could not place her, it was as though she was from a delegation somewhere, her face in a crowd, and yet he could not pick the memory from amongst the millions.

But she was an Elemental.

Denvy seized Ryojin's paw on his shoulder, grasping it for support as a burning desire surged through him to roar forward and rip apart the being of the Secondary Realm. This was a dream of the end of the Thousand Sol-Cycle War—a war he had run from.

"It appears you have left yourself without protection, Programmer," the Elemental said mockingly to Nefertem.

"I'll have to add that to my list of things to fix after my death," Nefertem wheezed out.

The woman of molten-gold laughed, bending forward slightly. "Whoever said anything about your demise? I need your unique skills."

"I am afraid you lost all hope of negotiating a truce when you attacked my bonding partner."

"I had a chance?" the Elemental purred.

"No." Nefertem spat out blue liquid.

Wiping the spittle aside, the Elemental retorted, "It was enjoyable watching the imp melt."

"You sicken me!" Nefertem cried. "You are nothing more than a lowly Earth Elemental wanting to be a Titan! You will never be what your siblings are, you child! Whatever the Dragon has promised you, to corrupt you so, he cannot give you."

Golden chains filled The Room, burrowing into the walls, melting whatever they touched. Denvy and Ryojin pulled away from them. The Elemental's skin blazed hot, before solidifying into diamonds. "I will be spring, the smell of rain, the beauty in dawn! I will be like my siblings. When this world is made anew, I will be the only one you will use to seed this world. The Dragon will make it so!" The woman's shape distorted briefly as it reformed in flames. The golden chains rooting it to the floor rattled in fury.

Nefertem sniggered wearily. "Child, you are so blind. I am a scientist; I am not one of the Tower Keepers. You killed the last one!"

"But you are the Programmer. You brought life to a barren world. You created the server-gods—"

"Do you think I did it alone? We are Zaprexes! We work in Dynasties! You destroyed mine—"

"Make me a server-god!" the Elemental shrieked.

Nefertem gradually raised his weapon. In that moment, Denvy caught the gaze of the Zaprex. It was piercing, and it stared at him, not through him as though he were bystander, watching a sequence run its course. His hearts raced. The cyborg he had loved as a father looked so old, so broken, and so very alone.

"You are not alone," Denvy whispered. "I am here." He reached out a paw. "I am here..."

The Elemental walked forward, the chains around Nefertem dropping away as the diamond body pressed up against him. The weapon he held in his trembling grasp indented into the being's waist.

"You cannot kill me," she sneered. "I know you are from the original cycle; you cannot harm another living being. It is your weakness."

"We are physically opposed to violence against other races, my dear. Not each other. Not ourselves. Always remove a weapon from a Zaprex's hand. You never know what we will do with it."

Nefertem swung the laser around, lodging it against his chin and fired.

Denvy fell backwards, tumbling through a stream of chaotic numerals and the pressure of collapsing information crushing into him as the sequence folded in on itself. Ryojin's voice was lost in the roaring chaos until he landed roughly in a sea of stars, dispersing the nebulae as he rolled. He heaved, wanting to vomit, but he was having a physical reaction within an avatar, and the action only worsened his distress. It had been centuries since he had found himself this lost, this unbridled inside the Data-Stream he had once so easily manipulated.

Ryojin's avatar drifted down beside him, his indigo hexagon an abnormality within the space surrounding them, revealing how unique the young prince's drifting data was. A driver left to slowly decay, too corrupt to move through the Osiris Gate, but pieced together enough to form a coherent stream of consciousness—for now, at least. He felt like a trembling cub before the far younger prince as he dragged himself upright, sitting slumped forward, weary shoulders sagging.

"I'm sorry, Denvy." Ryojin knelt, brushing his air-gills gently.

Denvy closed his eyes. No one was as sorry as he was, for abandoning those he loved during a war. His family had needed him, and he had not been there. He could not tell when the transition between sleep and waking took place, but he found himself blinking away tears as he huddled amongst tangled blankets on the floor of his cabin. He wanted to sleep, but sleep was no longer an escape, so he lay awake, staring through the small porthole window, wondering about paths never taken.

Ki'b scrubbed at her eyes, trying to rub away the blur of exhaustion. Adapting to the coming of the Long Night was tiring. Her body was never sure when she was supposed to sleep. It was made worse by her feet never touching soil, no longer being grounded. And Khwaja Denvy. Since Ishabal, his sleep state caused vibrations that often startled her awake.

Her fingers brushed against the loops of rocks and roots around her neck. They were her connection, now, to home, to the soil—to Pennadot. Would the Kelibs of Pennadot know how to survive the desert land of Utillia without their trees? She sought to be near Queen Zafiashid as much as possible, finding her overpowering but respectful manner as soothing as being close to her Mor-Mors. As captain of the sand-ship, the queen moved around her vessel with pride, her air-gills and fan-tail glistening with an inner glow Ki'b could only recall seeing in the darkest parts of Pennadot's forests. Kovlrok, the ship's First-mate, was another whose company brought Ki'b relief. The half-breed Kelib smiled down at her, his tattooed cheeks crinkled with age. He had his own necklace of rocks and carved dry wood, replacing the one he had given her upon their first meeting. He was always warm and jovial, despite the disconcerting way the Humanness of his blue eyes distorted his natural Kelib features. His skin was such a pale jade when compared to her emerald that his tattoos stood out jarringly, and hardly needed the illumined ink within them.

"Ah, little mountain flower," he greeted her.

Ki'b returned his smile. "Rythrya's blessings, Kovlrok."

"What are you doing down here at this hour, lassie?"

She clasped her hands in front of her dress. "I'm trying to find Clive and Penny. You haven't seen them, have you?"

He hummed low in his chest, producing a rattling that sounded uncomfortable. Ki'b squeezed her hands more tightly. Jythal had explained late one night how Humans and Kelibs should not have been able to breathe the air of Utillia. It was only because of the processing of Mist by the ancient Zaprex machines that they could, but the toxins remained, always surrounding them, and it gradually ruined their insides. It was frightening. She wondered if eventually she, too, would die because of the air she now breathed.

"I do believe I saw Volcano-Boy outside, top-deck, love. I think he is trying to learn the art of Swords and Runes from the Doctor."

Ki'b bowed low. "Thank you, Kovlrok."

He stepped to one side, allowing her to pass. "Careful on the way up, little mountain flower. Don't slip on the Mist. It's been a thick cloud day. Winter's good for the Mist Farmers, but not good for our old lady. Her decking gets a bit wet."

Ki'b moved past him. "I'll be careful."

She loved the burning-sea-sailors, how they cared for the *Lawless Child* like it was a beautiful lady, frocked out in the most stunning of gowns. They called her wings and sails a dress, and truly it was when all four wings and all eight sails were released with Mist. Without Aaldryn the crew said they no longer had a wind-tamer, so they relied entirely upon the Mist engines deep in the belly of the *Lawless Child*. Though it was not as a powerful as the song of Pennadot's soil, the engines thrummed with a beat that she sometimes felt she could dance to, were her heart not so heavy.

The sweet-flavoured smell of burning Mist grew even richer as she ventured outside. Top-deck was lit with the erupting light of the sails and lanterns hanging from ropes of spun rigging dangling everywhere she turned. Crew were busy washing sand from the deck. She was about to offer help, when she caught sight of Clive, surrounded by a ring of stones, with Jythal standing beside him. Jythal had been trying to teach him to access his birth elemental gift with Runes, because his abilities would become dormant when the Sun went away. Although there appeared to be little progress, she could feel the change of energy in the rocks echoing through the necklace she wore. He was so very close to succeeding. Her face lit up and she hurried across the deck.

"He's getting there," she said to Jythal.

The weak pulsation Ki'b felt from the Runes died away. Clive ducked his head and loosely touched the goggles hanging around his neck before kneeling and collecting his assortment of small rocks, each with a fire rune drawn wonkily on their surface. He stowed them away in a small pouch.

"Same time tomorrow," Jythal said kindly, and Clive nodded his response though his disappointment was evident in his face. "I'm going to learn the language of Livila, Ki'b," Clive said to her as he passed.

Ki'b took hold of Clive's hand and looked at Jythal.

She wished he could see her smile to know how grateful she was. Clive needed praise. He needed someone to believe in him. "You will," she answered. "I know you will."

"Do you think that Jarvis would be proud of me?" Clive asked, a blush reflecting his mop of red hair.

Ki'b clapped. "Oh, yes. I think he would be very happy. The Temple Brothers would be happy, too. They must see you working so hard, from all the way up in the Sun." She did not know much about the strange Sun Faith, only what Jarvis had told her. But Jarvis had not known much either, since he had been a farmer's son, and had surprised her with knowing more about trees and soil than sky-gods.

She gently wrapped her arm around his middle, remembering not to hug too tightly.

Jythal crouched down beside them both. "You did very well today, Clive."

"Penny doesn't think so. She never comes to watch."

"Penny is hurt still that she cannot go home," Ki'b offered.

"But we are home!" Clive looked around the deck, his arms spread wide. "Wherever family is, is home, right?"

"Something like that," Ki'b said.

Clive struck a pose. "I will make the best Sun Monk in Utillia."

"Might even be the first," Jythal responded.

"I'll be a missionary, then!"

Jythal stood. "Then, your next mission should be to find Penny and the two of you can help with the rigging."

"Aww, but—"

"Ah, nope, no buts. That was our deal. I teach you and you help the crew. Now, off you go, lad." Jythal made a shooing motion and Clive stuck out his tongue at the blind Kattamont. Ki'b covered her mouth. Clive might want to be a revered Sun Monk, but he had a long way to go before he even started to grow up.

Jythal let her take his paw. "He really is doing better," she commented.

"I think so, too." He smiled. "Have you broken your fast yet, little one?"

Ki'b shook her head, and then remembered to speak aloud for Jythal's benefit. "No, I haven't. I was about to ask Penny to join me, so, no, I haven't."

"Then come along." Jythal almost swept her off her feet as he stepped out. "Let's find Nixlye and Denvy. I am sure they have forgone breaking their fast."

Her heart fluttered with worry. "Khwaja should not be missing breakfast. He is too skinny." They had gone through such a terrible ordeal when the city of Ishabal had collapsed into a null-zone. She had almost lost Denvy. Since that time, her awareness of his presence had changed and it unsettled her.

"He is not doing it on purpose," Jythal said gently. "They're very absorbed in looking at maps at the moment. I am, alas, quite useless when it comes to that area." He laughed, but it was a sad laugh.

Nixlye and Jythal's cabin had become a refuge to Ki'b, and, while she always did try to be near Clive and Penny, she found herself more often drawn to the quarters of the young queen and her second mate. As Jythal bumped the door open with his hip, she smelt the warm aromas of Jythal's special blend of tea leaves. The stove was already lit to chase away the frigid winter, and her stomach grumbled at the sight of scones and butter waiting on the table.

Suddenly the world upturned.

Nixlye and her wheelchair slid and tumbled as the cabin turned on its side. Jythal bellowed in his confusion as he, too, was tossed against the wall. Reacting on instinct, Ki'b grabbed onto the bolted-down furniture and scrambled to the stove, jamming shut the little oven door before more than a handful of blistering hot coals could escape. These she quickly smothered with her hands, without time to protect her skin.

When the *Lawless Child* swung right side up once more, Jythal managed to find his way to Nixlye and help her right her chair. "We're under attack," he murmured. He handed her the Mist prosthetics she had not worn since Ryojin had died. Ki'b caught the momentary hesitation in her movement before she grabbed them from the prince.

The queen gave Jythal a fierce look as she began to crank the mechanical legs into life and said, "Go. Stop them. Take Ki'b. Teach her. I'll catch up with you."

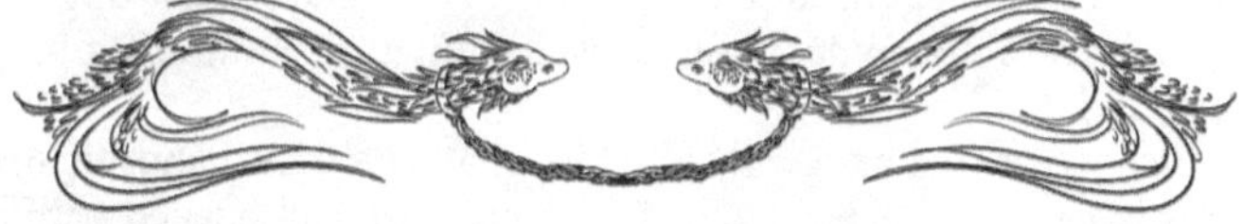

Denvy placed his head in his paws. This morning was particularly brutal with a pounding headache refusing to lift. The ache had been gradually increasing since his dream. Clive burst into the large cabin, almost bouncing off the walls, unheeding of Denvy's state.

"Clive!" Denvy begged. "Enough. Please. Surely you are meant to be helping on deck at this hour, little *aiv'a*."

Clive flung himself into his cot. "I came to get Penny. But I don't want to go back outside. It's sad out there. The Sun is only up for a few hours now and I don't like it, Khwaja. It makes me weak."

Denvy massaged his brow. It was a concern, the decline of Clive's birth elemental gift with the coming of the Long Night. The lad had been dropped off at a Sun Temple, due to his father's wandering lifestyle as a bard, and being raised so young by Sun Monks had strengthened his connection to the Sun.

"You're being silly, Clive," Penny snapped.

Oh. Bother. Denvy's shoulders sank in despair as Clive erupted. Titus had rightly named the lad Volcanic. He could burst like a volcano blowing its top and then simmer for days afterwards. His Retennan accent, twanging like a bass gong, grew more pronounced the angrier he was.

"You don't know nothing, Penny! I am a Warrior Sun Monk! I can't do anything without the Sun!" Clive stormed out the door again, slamming it shut behind him. Denvy winced. His ears folded as his skull echoed with the sound, causing a vibrating pain down his spine. He did not need this right now. His gaze shifted to Penny as she set aside her knitting and readied herself for deck work. How many scarves had the little dear finished now? She had almost made something for the whole crew, it seemed. It was her eyes, though, that told of the turmoil that her cloudy expression withheld. Her mask was not entirely set in the stones of the city she called home.

He crouched beside her.

"Petunia, dear one, I know you miss your home, but Clive misses the monastery and the Monks who raised him. The Sun is his connection to those brave men and women."

Penny's hands trembled. Tears leaked down her cheeks as the cracks in her stone mask began to show. Denvy reached out, stroking the tears aside with a claw.

"That's just it, Khwaja." She threw herself into his arms, hiding in his fur. "Clive has the Sun, his prayers, his rituals. Ki'b has her green skin, her bare feet, her herbs and spices. I don't have anything!" He felt her small hands curl into his air-gills. "I don't have rocks, or gold, or jewels from my home. I don't have anything to remind me of my Papa or Mama."

Denvy gathered her gently into his lap and held her hands tightly in his large paw. His head ached, and his chest still burned with a Human illness that never seemed to fade away, but the power of his dreamathic ability thrummed within him like a lute being strummed, though he was not the bard composing the songs. He would have to trust Ryojin's compositions, no matter how difficult a sensation it was.

"I want you to picture in your mind something very special, something so special to you it is as clear as you can make it," he whispered.

Her eyes widened.

He chuckled and touched her nose with his moist one.

"With your eyes closed, love."

She giggled and did as instructed, snuggling against him.

Denvy placed a paw to her head. With the yoke's heavy presence around his shoulders like an iron gate, he forced his way forward, envisioning a battering ram hammering against the walls of his mind. The throbbing pain in his skull spiked, and he tasted copper in the back of his throat. Many dreamathics described their art as colours in paintings, emotions becoming intricate, beautiful designs they could paint within their waking daydreams or their sleeping hours. Penny's emotions were still heavily grey and deep blues, sorrowful colours of grief and shame, but they parted in slow swirls of yellows and pink, creating flower-like patterns until a clear image bled through the pain thundering in his head. Denvy smiled weakly. A little dove necklace made of diamond. He breathed in a shuddering breath and tugged on the image and the yellow emotion that had birthed it: love. The yoke fought him, its ruthless enchantments clawing down his spine, spiking his tail feathers, until Ryojin's crystal against his chest cooled the heat and a sudden weight pressed upon the palm of his paw. The release of his dreamathic mind was intense, flooding him with a wave of exhaustion. Denvy looked at the necklace, glittering brightly. It was a small thing, but worth every daydream.

He carefully slipped it around Penny's neck. Her eyes opened, and she gasped, holding out the necklace in disbelief.

"How?"

"Dreams are special things, my dear. Hold onto them, always." He kissed her forehead.

She hugged him tightly before leaping off his lap. "I am going to say sorry to Clive."

Denvy inclined his head. Penny rushed out the door, squeaking as she bumped into Zafiashid. She bowed to the queen before scooting down the corridor.

Denvy raised an eyebrow as Zafiashid leant against the doorframe of the cabin that belonged to her. Her tail flicked playfully.

"Are you going to stand there, or are you going to offer me a paw up?" he grumbled.

She scoffed. "You're fine. If you can bring into being kegs of Mist, I think one little necklace will not kill you."

He snorted, holding his head. "If only that were true."

She nibbled her bottom lip. "You have not seemed yourself this past week."

Denvy rubbed his air-gills, flipping them back. With a grunt he heaved himself up and grabbed his heavy jacket from the nearby chair. "They are only dreams."

It was an ambiguous answer, because he knew she despised them and seeing her brow furrow with displeasure amused him, until she noted his perked lips and snarled. He winced as she stomped into her cabin, and he side stepped her swinging tail.

"You should not wear those Human clothes, they cover your fur!" Her paws pressed against his shoulders, plucking at the offending fabric. "Nixlye is half-Human; she I can understand, but you are a Gold Lion prince, so why must you hide such a magnificent coat? Do you feel ashamed? Your health has improved."

Denvy chuckled. If that was her roundabout way of apologising for calling him a sack of bones, he would accept it. It was likely as close to an apology he would get. "I have worn Human clothing for a very long time, my dear. I find it comforting."

Her face twisted in disgust as she pawed at the fur on his chest. "You ruin your coat. If I asked, would you wear Kattamont attire instead?"

"Probably not. I am too old to change now."

Her paws against his chest clenched. "But Utillia is the land of change—"

The *Lawless Child* lurched to one side. The floor beneath them veered. It was not his aching head playing games. Everything had suddenly vaulted. It took several moments for Denvy's mind to catch up with his body as the cabin around him swayed. His shoulder impacted the hard edge of the cabin's wall, and his side thudded upon his bed. Zafiashid connected with his middle. He grunted at the force, feeling the air shoved ruthlessly out of his lungs. Zafiashid's air-gills pressed tightly against her back, fur stiffening at the sound of the hull groaning. Wood and metal creaked. The wall visibly buckled under intense strain. The *Lawless Child* continued to tilt, and he flung out an arm to break his impact. The nearby porthole hissed and he was horrified to see sand scratching the glass. There should have been no sand anywhere near his window; he was in one of the highest cabins on the vessel.

He grunted. "We're on our side. We need to get right side up."

Zafiashid smacked the wind out of him as she collided with him. The glitter in her eyes froze him in place. "The weights will swing in a minute," she reassured him.

Denvy cringed as the cabin tilted once more and they both rolled from the wall, landing roughly on the bed before thudding to the floor. He wrapped his arms tightly around Zafiashid as the floor shuddered. Screams echoed through the corridors beyond the swinging door of the cabin.

"The cubs!" he spluttered out.

Zafiashid scrambled off him, crawling for the door as the floor shook. He followed her tail as she vanished into the dim light of the sparking lanterns. The cubs—where were his cubs? Ki'b would have been with Jythal and Nixlye, but Clive and Penny? They had just gone out on the deck—they may even have been top-deck.

"Dear Sun," he choked out, "please, please let them have been tied on!"

Clive was forever disobeying the deck-master's orders to tie himself down with a rope to the masts. The boy wanted a pair of gravity-boots like half the crew. If he had not tied himself down—

Denvy burst out into the bitter winter air, following Zafiashid into the chaos of the upper decks. The Mist rolling from the sails lit the murky world in a hazy glow. Sand-sea sailors dashed about in a panic, some dragging limp bodies over the edges of the banisters. Denvy's hearts leapt into his throat.

"What's going on?" Zafiashid roared out.

First-mate Kovlrok swung down and swiftly tied a rope around her waist. Denvy blinked as the process was repeated on him.

"We've been sighted by a Jezumatu vessel. They blasted us with a grav-cannon. Threw our magnets out of sync. I'm still counting the crew."

Zafiashid swore, snatching a spyglass from Kovlrok's belt. She hoisted herself onto a railing. Denvy turned to Kovlrok. "The cubs, are they—?"

"Clive went overboard but I got him. Silly little *totu* learnt his lesson about tying himself down. Penny's tongue lashing him still."

Tension drained from his tight shoulders. Denvy relaxed against the stairs leading to the helm.

Zafiashid clicked shut the spyglass. "Kovlrok, get two of the crew to take the cubs below deck."

"Why?"

"It's the *Queen's Mercy*."

"Princess Pohehi?" Kovlrok made a small curse sign with his fingers and spat on the deck.

"Princess Pohehi, the *Queen's Mercy*?" Denvy frowned, following Zafiashid as she leapt down from her perch.

"A sand-ship and a princess known for their speed and ruthlessness in chasing down their prey." Kovlrok tugged on an earring. "Though, no one has ever actually seen Princess Pohehi."

"Jythal has." Zafiashid spat out. "And he won't, ever again."

Denvy frowned as he took in the double meaning of her words.

Kovlrok looked at their sails. "Without Prince Aaldryn it is unlikely that we'll be able to outrun them on Mist alone. The *Lawless Child* is no match against the *Queen's Mercy*."

Zafiashid swept up the stairs to the helm. "We can try."

She disappeared behind the controls and the *Lawless Child* lurched. The sails burst with a radiant shine of Mist. A sensation Denvy had not felt in sol-cycles almost knocked him from his feet, emotions so strong they slammed through the barrier of the yoke, bleeding through the cracks Ryojin was chipping into the enchantments. Hope rose up from the crew. It burned in their eyes, a fierce fire of determination. Denvy's paws went to the yoke. The Kattamont queen at the helm claimed not to believe in curses, and he was starting to wonder if that was all it took to break them.

Ki'b had never seen the white lion in such a state. Jythal's air-gills frilled about his head in a territorial display, and he moved as though he were not blind at all. Ki'b followed him. Nixlye called her a princess, and so she would obey the orders of the young queen. She would never forget how the wheelchair-bound Kattamont had saved their lives with her arrows. And since joining the *Lawless Child*, Ki'b had heard stories from the crew of the fierce pit-battles fought and won by both Nixlye and Zafiashid. Without such a reputation, they would likely be confined to the other-sectors like most pirate vessels. The trading their vessel managed to do rode on the strength of Zafiashid's name.

Ki'b's heart pounded faster the closer they came to top-deck, for the sound of battle rang in her ears. Jythal paused behind the double doors. He held out a paw, motioning to her. "Stay near me."

He drew four stones from his pelt pouches and threw them lightly into the air. Ki'b gasped as they morphed in mid-flight, forming elegantly-crafted blades that the blind prince snatched swiftly. She fumbled for her tiny dagger. It was not much, but Jarvis had given it to her. It felt weighted in her grasp, weighted with the reality that it was a weapon and not a sewing knife.

Jythal slammed the doors open. Ki'b tracked his tail's movements across the deck like it was a lifeline. The transformation within him was frightening. He was no longer the gentle blind doctor who served her tea, but a ferocious slayer.

Wayward Mist from the sails lit the world in a murky glow, barely enough to see Jythal's tail in front of her, and it made the scene all the more chaotic. There were strange Kattamonts mingling with their crew, Mist-powered weapons sparking energy. She cried out in alarm and sidestepped as a blade hissed past her, almost taking off her ear. Jythal's shadow fell over her, the deck rumbled with the force of his weight, and she stumbled. Blood from his blades slopped over her skin. She heard them hiss as they sliced the air and ripped through a Kattamont behind her. Rune stones hummed with crackling heat, surrounding the doctor in a halo. He surged forward, taking out another two Kattamonts with quick, successive strikes. An enormous sand-ship loomed beside them, far larger than the *Lawless*. Its metal hull was tinted black but filled with veins of blue philepcon liquid. Its threaded Mist wings rippled out, mimicking the appearance of merciless teeth. Wood splintered as the *Lawless Child* rocked against a forceful blast.

"Gravity-cannon? A gravity-cannon! Is that the *Queen's Mercy*?" He tilted his head to one side, listening to the thrum in the air. "We're being chased by the *Queen's Mercy!* By the Rythrya!" Jythal staggered, cursing as his foot-paws slipped on the deck. All around them the crew scrambled to find a hold, or to clutch tightly to their lines.

"Ki'b! Ki'b, where are you?" Jythal reached blindly for her as the *Lawless Child* groaned. The masts shuddered, burrowing into a sand wave billowing up against the hull. Ki'b was flung from the deck. She bounced across the rough wooden surface, scraping her skin. With a shout she thrust her dagger into the wood, clutching at the hilt. Her bloodied hands slipped, the grip loosening as the sand-ship continued to tip over. Crew dangled from their lines; crates not buckled down tumbled into the burning-sea. Ki'b squeezed her eyes shut, biting her lip as her fingers clawed at her dagger. Tears leaked down her cheeks. Her nails gave way. She had not wanted to scream but it burst from her lungs, only to be cut short as Jythal snatched her roughly from mid-air. The prince bounced, catching hanging ropes, slowing his own descent before landing with a shattering crack against the banister of the deck, his legs impacting the rails.

Ki'b scrambled into his arms, clutching his neck as she held back the cry in her throat.

"Hush, hush, dear, it is all right. The magnets will swing back soon."

It felt like forever. Wood and metal continued to splinter, cannon fire still echoed in the background.

"Why are they doing this?" she gasped out.

"They need to expose our sand-ship's under-belly. If they rupture it, we'll sink."

She stared down into the depths of the burning-sea she had almost fallen into and her heart raced. It looked so alive in the glow of the tattered Mist sail swirling amongst it. It seemed to boil and bubble, like a cauldron upon a fire. Her fingers dug into Jythal's fur in a panic. It was not right—something was moving, something shiny and reflective against the glittering of the sails.

"Jythal! There is something down there, something in the burning-sea."

Jythal tipped his head to one side, his ears flickering.

"Kovlrok! Is there someone overboard?" the doctor howled out.

Ki'b's stomach was beginning to sway. The same sensation had come just before the *Lawless Child's* great magnets had swept them upright. She kept her gaze on the waves of the sand and the eerie little shapes surrounding their sails. Kovlrok swung down beside them on a rope. He frowned at the sight of her but twisted to look into the burning-sea. She caught the sudden widening of his eyes as the sand-ship tipped and they rolled over the decking. Kovlrok was on his feet instantly.

Ki'b gulped down vomit in her throat as she crawled out from under Jythal.

"Captain!" Kovlrok waved his arms. "Azhaw swarm ahead! We have an azhaw swarm!"

Ki'b looked at Jythal as the prince stood, swaying.

"Azhaw?" She curled her tongue around the foreign word.

"Ship-eaters," he translated. "Perfect. They'll have no idea what hit them." He twirled his blades as he spun. "Dump the dead *Mercies* overboard," he called out. "We're tarring the sand-ship. Move it! They'll catch up to us on the next wave. Half-power to the Mist-shields!"

All around her the crew scrambled to obey the prince. She darted through them, running to the nearest banister, heaving herself over it. Wind caught her hair and she blinked against the stinging sand. The *Queen's Mercy* was roaring towards them, cresting the sand-wave. A gravity swell would send it hurling their way. Heat from the cannons down its side burned starkly in the night, reminding her of the piercing eyes of a dozen vipers, poised to strike. Kovlrok's hands grabbed her around the shoulders and she was pulled away from the banisters. One moment the *Queen's Mercy* was on the edge of the sand-wave, the next it was side-by-side with them, sparks of energy bolting across the gap between their vessels.

"Their Mist-shields are up!" Kovlrok bellowed. "Full power! We're going to feel a hit. Prepare for their fire."

Ki'b scrubbed at her eyes, blinking away the bursting lights of the two shields smashing against each other.

Zafiashid's voice shouted from the helm. "Never mind their shields. Pummel them with cannon fire! Keep them interested in us. Drive them into the azhaw swarm."

Kovlrok released Ki'b. Moving towards the nearest deck-com, he yelled into it, "Open fire at your leisure."

Ki'b curled into a ball as the world became noise. The deck danced under her bare feet. A stench of hot, sizzling smoke surrounded her. She peered up, daring to sneak a view of the sand-ship bearing down on them. The *Queen's Mercy* was almost beautiful in the crackling power that sparked off its shields, in the rippling waves of the cannon fire ricocheting off its hull. It was majestic compared to the patch-work quilt that was the *Lawless Child*. She was suddenly flung back. She rolled over the deck as the *Lawless Child* launched upwards. She thought they were going to fly, high into the sky-sea, like a bird over the Ovin-tu Mountains. She heard what she thought was Queen Zafiashid laughing maniacally as they sailed over the ridge of a dune-wave.

Jythal wrapped himself around her, pinning her to the deck, and she hid against him as everything rattled. She braced for the impact of their landing. It sent a vibrating shock through the sand-ship. A wave of sand plumed around them.

Jythal sprang up. "Tar the sides!" he bellowed.

The crew scrambled to obey, throwing thick, foul-smelling tar over the banisters. Jythal flung out his arms and the rune stones surrounding him flew forth in a circle, igniting in flames. The edges of the *Lawless Child* erupted with fire. Painful squeals caught Ki'b's ears, and she covered them, crying at the thought of the dying azhaw burning in the heat of the flaming tar now soaking their bodies. Jythal's paw settled on her head, gently stroking her hair.

"It is all right. We are safe."

She peered up. The deck was full of foul black smoke, but she could see the ruins, the splintered wood through the flames, and their stores all amuck—and, worse, their wounded crew. Her chest tightened.

She scrambled up, stepping out. "No, no, that sand-ship, it will catch up with us!"

Jythal snatched up her hand swiftly. "They got caught up in the azhaw swarm. Mother made sure our sand-ship seized the gravity-wave first."

"Then they are gone?" she whispered.

Jythal sighed, shaking his head. "The *Queen's Mercy* is not the type of vessel that goes down to azhaw, I am afraid. Princess Pohehi can match me in the fighting pits. She would never let the *Queen's Mercy* sink that easily."

Ki'b frowned, hugging Jythal's leg tightly. She had thought princes only fought other princes, so why had Jythal been fighting a princess? She had been told it was Nixlye who had won Jythal's freedom.

Kovlrok crouched down to match her height, his wrinkled, tattooed face bloodied from the fight, but managing a reassuring smile. "We're the better sailors, Little Mountain Flower." He coughed back the black smoke swirling around the deck.

"We just don't mind burning our own sand-ship to save our skins. This is going to cost a bit in repairs, I imagine," Jythal said.

Kovlrok ruffled her hair and Ki'b grinned at the half-breed as he guffawed. "It always does. It always does, but it is better the cost in repairs than the cost in lives."

Ki'b nibbled her lip, pressing herself closer to Jythal as he nursed her burned and scraped hands in his large paws. Her gaze trailed back to the *Queen's Mercy*, slinking away across the horizon like a defeated plains lion without prey. She shivered. They had lost no lives—but would it continue to be so? Resting her head against Jythal's chest as he lifted her, Ki'b held in a sob, closing her eyes against the stinging smoke and her tears. She needed to become a part of Utillia, a part of the wildness, to survive the untamed, ever-moving land. She had to forget the forests of her Mor-Mors and learn to drift without roots.

This was her new home, a home where the foundations were their loved ones and not the earth or the trees.

All she missed—

Was Jarvis.

A cheer rang out and Ki'b opened her eyes to see a ring of burning stones twirling around Clive, his face shining with elation.

"He did it," she said weakly to Jythal. "Clive. The Runes."

Kovlrok rattled out a laugh. "A bit late for today's attack," he said, but not unkindly.

"There will be plenty more battles," Ki'b heard Jythal say as she nestled into his fur.

Ki'b

CHAPTER THREE

Sekhmet's trembling hands pawed at the activation pad, slopping philepcon liquid across the surface. He stumbled through the door as it wheezed open and the medical bay lights blinked awake with a crackle. With a clunk he went down on his knees, metal hull seizing in pain.

"Sir! Sir! Oh, Sir! Please stop moving. You're damaging yourself."

"Why are you out of your containment chamber?" Sekhmet murmured at the blurry figure of a white-haired child who was sorting through the cabinets, tossing useless items onto the floor. Pale, glowing eyes turned in his direction. Cool air vented against his hot hull from the overhead medical bed. His hand cupped the split plates of his abdominal armour, so long ago weakened, and now damaged beyond repair.

"Sir. We're all that remains. I know I am becoming a black hole, sir, but, please, let me help you until the very end."

"Disgleirio."

Sekhmet reached out weakly for the slender hand of the Starborn child and held it to his cheek. "My brave little black hole. No one believed in us, and, look, we are all that is left—a dying star and a broken fairy."

"I may be a dying star, sir, but I can still keep this station powered. All you need to do is stay alive."

Sekhmet managed a weak smile. Children. They had such faith.

Jarvis jerked upright, weapons systems activating instantly, the charge spiralling up his spine. His optical lenses blurred before crystallising on his surrounds. The bow of the *Silver Slasher* beat heavily against rising dune waves, and a thick layer of Mist coated a dark night sky-sea. He was still on the deck, exactly where Khamsin had thrown him. The wooden planks beneath him had cracked in several places, the information flashing across his optical lenses as they completed the scan. There was pain, he noted, a pain he had never processed before; a stressing of his metal hull. He felt as though he was a town thief after a public beating. His lips parted in a whine as he raised trembling hands to clasp his hot cheeks. The failure to fulfil his function filled him with an immense sense of horror.

"Yeh still with us, laddie?"

Jarvis stirred as the hem of Master Titus' coat brushed the deck nearby. The Hunter slumped down beside him, an anxious knit to his brow.

"I could have saved them," Jarvis muttered as a tear ran down his cheek. Steady at the helm, Aaldryn was lit by the glow of the Mist in the sails, but it was the eerie echo of Khamsin's slithering form, distorting the Primary Realm with cracks and dislodgments of data that made Jarvis' hull tighten.

Titus sighed. "He shouldn't have taken yeh down like that. We had words; don' yeh think I didna give him a tongue-lashin' for yeh. Yeh're a true Messenger, Jarvis. We don' go back for our dead; there is a danger in that. But if there is someone to save ahead of us, we do what we can."

Jarvis ducked his head. He felt so limp, so useless, so much like the day that his family had been taken from him. Master Titus' hand settled on his shoulder.

"Sometimes, laddie, yeh just canna save everyone."

It was not a single tear that leaked from his eyes this time, but a stream of them. No, he could not save everyone, but a part of him wanted to try.

"Promise me one thing, Jarvis, laddie."

He struggled to get the words out through his weeping. "Yes, sir?"

"If yeh get the chance to choose between returning to yeh sweet lass or going away on some foolhardy task, yeh go back to your lass. Don' yeh give up on being happy. Sometimes we Messengers sacrifice too much." Titus sighed and squeezed his shoulder firmly. Jarvis looked into the hooded features, waxen pale, with black, unblinking eyes that could never again stare into the blessed Sunlight. Even now, in the gentle twilight of the Twin Winter months, his Master was cursed to remain under his cloak of pure darkness. He wondered what Twizel it was that had consumed him—had it been a strong one? Surely it had been someone important in the Twizel Army if that ugly thing Aaldryn had called 'Torka' was so intent on chasing them.

"It isn't as easy as that," he sobbed. "I don't know if I will ever be able to control my programming enough to be the one to make that choice, when it comes to it."

Titus groaned as he heaved himself to his feet. Jarvis could have sworn he heard the rattling of chains as he did, his cloak rippling around his ankles.

A kindly smile was sent his way. "Jarvis, ma sweet Sun-kissed boy, if anyone can control a Zaprex bot it'd be yeh. And if anyone was going to help yeh take that control, it'd be me. Yeh're goin' ta make a great Commander of War someday."

His chest swelled with gratitude. "You think?"

"Oh, aye. I do."

An eerie reflection of the Sun's blessed rays off the burning-sea's shimmering surface lit the sky-sea in a constant twilight. Jarvis was hesitant to call it beautiful. It reminded him too much of the times the wooden box's doors would creak open, admitting just enough light to silhouette the decomposing bodies of children who had died beside him in that box. The last time the Long Night had fallen across the Northlands he had been six sol-cycles old, and it had lasted two sol-cycles. Now, whenever he turned his eyes to the sky-sea, to watch the dance of the stars, something in the pit of his stomach churned. It might have been the same unseen pattern in the glittering specks of light that the protector bot was tracking, or the effect of the unnerving yellow twilight glow, but he was certain there would not be a spring for some time to come. Still, even if there was no shifting of the seasons to track his age it did not alter the fact that he had grown as Khamsin whisked them across the burning-sea.

He breathed out, watching his breath fog the cold air. "How are we supposed to gauge when Coltarian will erupt if we don't know the changing of the seasons."

"The celestial calendar, laddie," Titus retorted. "Read the stars. Don' they teach yeh Plains kids these things?"

Jarvis grimaced. "That sort of sky-sea nonsense is for Sun Monks. I'm a Muddy. I watch the seasons."

"Oh, yeh're still such a Pennadotian." His Master swung back and forth in a hammock, eyes closed, seemingly at peace with the world. But Jarvis was well aware of the crackle of tension that had replaced the easy friendship between them all since the day Khamsin had changed everything.

Jarvis gazed at the horizon. His vision cleared, pixels fitting into place to make a perfect gloss. A gentle hum vibrated up his backbone as philepcon liquid flooded through links, flushing into his cheeks and eyes as he scanned the horizon.

Yellow circles formed over insignificant rock formations, green circles shifted over sand-dune waves where gravity was building, and the blaring orange of warning blinked around rising spires far in the distance. Orange—not yet sufficient danger to warrant red. Jarvis puckered his dry lips, still prickling with sunburn. He cocked his head towards Aaldryn and pointed.

"Somewhere over there are some ruins—" He frowned as the *Silver Slasher* rose over a sand dune wave, capping it, and he gasped. Suddenly the ruins were visible atop the dunes. The tops of high-rise buildings and crystal spires, haphazardly poking out of the burning-sea, spanned miles in either direction, like a blockade across their path.

"Oh! Wow! It's like a glass forest."

"Must be Yrva Krv, then." Aaldryn steadied the wheel against the tug of gravity as the small sand-ship dived down the wave.

"Yrva Krv?" Jarvis inquired.

"Means 'Last Breath,'" Aaldryn said. "As in the last breath you'll take."

Jarvis pulled a face. "Sounds delightful."

The Kattamont sighed. "To get out of Utillia we must pass through Yrva Krv. There is no going around it."

Sitting back on the nearest seat by the controls, Jarvis switched off his vision, blinking a few times as his optical lenses returned to their usual, dimmed state. "Why the ominous name?"

"Aside from the ghosts and the spores," Aaldryn scratched his chin, "bandits have been known to use them as hideouts."

"I don't get it. You are scavengers who burrow deep into the burning-sea to dig up metal from buried Zaprex cities below the surface. Why don't you scavenge that first?" Jarvis waved his hand at the ruins ahead of them. "Wouldn't it be so much easier?"

Aaldryn's shoulders sagged. "Many have tried and failed. The air is too thick with spores from the uncontained crystals. I have seen Kattamonts and Humans melt from breathing them in. Some aren't so blessed. Some take months to die. It gets into your skin." Aaldryn rubbed at his arms. "Burrowing in like little blades, and slowly crystals grow out of you." He looked back at Jarvis. "You look pretty after you die, though."

Jarvis snorted. "I'm sure that's a really big consolation."

Aaldryn sniggered. "Trust me, little brother, it's an improvement for some."

"Don't call me that." Jarvis jerked up and began to climb to the crow's nest.

"I'm not your enemy," Aaldryn bellowed over his shoulder. "And Khamsin saved your life."

The closer they drew to Yrva Krv, the more tense Aaldryn grew. Jarvis had the sinking feeling Aaldryn had been in the ruins before, and that it had not been a pleasant experience—not by the way his air-gills were spreading in alarm around his neck. He could see every muscle under his fur twitching with anticipation and anxiety. Jarvis gripped his colour-blade's hilt, wishing he could not hear the thudding of Aaldryn's two hearts. It was immensely distracting, and he had not yet figured out how to prioritise sounds. He kept spooking himself with the heightened noises surrounding him. Creaking metal against metal, the groan of the sand-ship's bow against the dune-waves, the hiss of Mist through the engines. It all made him think he was under threat of attack at any minute.

Even Master Titus seemed wary. He stood, alert, as they sailed amongst the tall, foreboding shadows of the ancient buildings, eyeing the towers in concern that they could collapse upon them at any moment.

There was a deathly stillness in the air, behind the noises and the dune-waves. It prickled along Jarvis' skin like a chill. The structures were untouched, silent—at peace as though they had been frozen and locked in time. They grew out of the burning-sea like trees from the soil, forming a canopy of interlinking bridges of glass and sparkling diamonds.

"My Creators really knew how to build cities," Jarvis whispered. "They remind me of the wood ants' nests—the ones that ate through our wood piles during the summer months. They made the most amazing, intricate designs."

Aaldryn looked back with a half-smile.

"Still," Jarvis kept his voice soft, "why here in Utillia, more so than Pennadot?"

Aaldryn shrugged. "I think the Kattamonts were one of the few races that actually forged a friendship with the Zaprexes, at least that is what our research has led us to believe. We Kattamonts were heavily attacked in the Thousand Sol-cycle War for our refusal to take the Dragon's side. But, in return, the Zaprexes protected our land. Somehow." Aaldryn looked around.

"It doesn't seem protected," Jarvis muttered.

"Ah." Titus held up a hand. "Yeh only see the destruction of the surface. Yeh be comparing it ta Pennadot, laddie—all pretty and green. Sure, yeh'd say Pennadot appears much better off but what happens when the Borders all crack away and rotation stops entirely? What happens when Coltarian erupts?"

"The sky-sea will fall." Jarvis looked past the high towers, to the dark, glittering canopy of night above them.

"But not here in Utillia." Aaldryn breathed out. "All the power that once sustained our land's surface now powers the sky-sea. We are like an island, alone, standing against a great tide."

A pang ached sharply in his chest and Jarvis reached up, brushing a hand over his leather vesting, frowning at the remnant of the old bullet wound that still bothered him. The protector bot had not fully converted the flesh of his lungs. Was that what the Zaprexes had tried to do with Livila? Convert it like the protector bot was trying to do with his Human body? Had they desperately tried to convert Livila into something else entirely—and failed? Had it all been too late?

"Do Kattamonts blame the Zaprexes for what happened to Utillia?"

"Many do, yes." Aaldryn's air-gills flipped rearward. "That is what the Iposti preach, that the Zaprexes caused the calamity after the Thousand Sol-Cycle War. I certainly don't think so, and I'm not the only one." Aaldryn gripped the wheel tightly. "I hear the voices of the wind, and, if you listen, they will tell you what truly happened. They echo the tales down through time, carving it into the mountains and the cliffs." He raised a paw, holding it above his head, catching the Mist as it streamed through the air. "There are others who can hear the wind. They know the truth."

"That they tried to save us."

Aaldryn nodded.

"Everything they did, they did to save us. Sometimes, Jarvis, good intentions or not, things go wrong. Yet you must believe that, in the end, it will turn out all right. If you don't believe that, then why keep going at all?"

Jarvis curled his fingers into his coat pockets. His protector bot was vibrating a soft, lonesome song along his backbone, and it was so sad. It chimed off the walls of the skyscrapers. It was doubtful that Aaldryn or Titus could hear it, but it was a call—a call for others like him—lonely, lost machines, abandoned by Creators who had long faded into history.

"I really hope we make it to the House in time." He continued to stare at the alien sky-sea and the stars whose dances he knew not.

"We will, laddie," Titus responded. "Yeh have to trust in our unseen path."

Jarvis smiled. He almost turned his eyes from the stars, only to pause as his optical lenses caught a brief flicker of a shadow blinking across the bright lights between the buildings. His chest tightened. A cloud perhaps. No—the sky-sea had been crystal clear; the storms were coming in from the East and they were travelling West. The command was automatic now, shifting his whole body into protector bot mode. Energy surged through the philepcon liquid between the plates of his metal armour beneath his skin.

"Jarvis!" Titus whipped around, positioning himself protectively between Jarvis and Khamsin.

"Something is out there." Jarvis narrowed his eyes, ignoring the sense that the Titan was looming threateningly over and around his Master, and forced himself to focus on scanning the skyscraper tops. Infrared showed nothing. Echolocation, perhaps? He sent out a soft song, hearing it bounce back in gradual circles around them, then it caught on something. Something that flickered for a moment before vanishing. Jarvis gasped.

"It's the Twizel!"

"What? That's impossible. I'd know if it was nearby." Titus suddenly released a string of curses. "Of all the Generals I must battle, it has to be him. It has to be him! *Thraki*! This is just my cursed luck."

"Master, what is it?"

Titus gripped his shoulder and Jarvis winced. "Don' ever let him know yeh can sense him. Jarvis. That's yer one advantage. It may very well save yer life." Titus crouched and looked hauntingly into his eyes. "He's only ever consumed vapour elementalists as fuel. This means he's gained the ability to blend in and out of the Primary Realm, without fear of being drawn back into the Secondary Realm. It makes him impossible to track."

Jarvis stared at him. Titus was never one to admit there was something out there that could be dangerous to him. His Master was strong, brave, unbreakable—like his rock giant blade.

"Master—"

The *Silver Slasher* ruptured. Metal and wood burst into the air as the vessel was torn apart from beneath. Glittering beak and talons splintered through the hull from below. Jarvis was propelled backwards, flying over the banisters. His gravity control swung into action as he collected the sand, skidding across the surface. Aaldryn landed beside him, wind spinning around his form as he twirled out a pistol.

"Master Titus!" Jarvis howled. "No!"

Aaldryn snatched him around the middle, hefting him up despite his protests. He could not tear his eyes from the vicious fight of coiling shadows, a bright beak of iron, clashing against his master's blade of stone. He called out, begging.

"Please, please. Dear Sun, don't die. I still need you!"

It was the same numbness Jarvis had felt when the Twizels had burst through the door of the farmhouse. Mother had been serving dinner. He had been telling his sister and brother-in-law of his trip with Father into the nearby town. How happy and perfect the picture had been until the foul-smelling shadows had shattered the wooden doors and the windows. Screams and blood—then nothing.

It was as though his body refused to accept reality and withdrew into itself. In the dark-cold box a gravelled, warm, gentlemanly voice had drawn him slowly back—to feel pain, but also hope. Khwaja Denvy had been there, in the darkness.

The voice breaking through now was unfamiliar—it was not Khwaja Denvy, who he knew was far away, and had not the forceful strength of Khamsin. It was no more than a droplet pinging into the pool of his consciousness and echoing in the vast nothingness of his blank mind.

Wake up, little protector. Wake up.

Though the voice was soft, like a child whispering in a game of find-go-seek, there was no doubting the immensity behind it of the entity waiting to be released. A surge sparked up his spine, spreading out through the connections of his interface. His eyes blinked open, light flooded his lenses in a flare before calming as information processed swiftly and he assessed his position. He was folded over Aaldryn's back like a sack of grain, being carried over the sand-waves towards one of the great spires.

Instantly he was pummelling the back of the Kattamont, screaming at him though his voice was a dry rasp.

Aaldryn paused and set Jarvis down.

Jarvis swelled up a sphere of gravity, allowing him to float atop the burning-sea. Quickly he scanned the horizon. The *Silver Slasher* was gone, and so was any sign of Master Titus and the Twizel.

"Titus seems to have drawn Torka away from us—"

"Sure!" Jarvis muttered. "You let him go after a dangerous Twizel but you won't let me fulfil my function—"

"Jarvis." Aaldryn sighed. "Your 'function' is to get the Map Piece to the Key. Not sacrifice yourself…"

Jarvis repressed the urge to curl into a ball. The thought of Master Titus—no, he simply could not allow his mind to follow that path of thought unless he wanted to be overwhelmed into a shut-down. He blinked rapidly, scrubbing at his eyes to clear away the salty build-up of tears.

"Where are we?"

"Our supplies are gone." Aaldryn dug at his hip-bags. "Other than those we keep on ourselves for emergencies."

Jarvis drew a shuddering breath and glanced at the nearest skyscraper, its silver sheen bright in the darkness of the Long Night. He shielded his eyes from the intense glow that burned his night-vision. Ever since Ishabal he had not taken for granted his ability to tap into Zaprex technology. Though if he struggled to understand and comprehend it, surely the more he allowed himself to analyse it the easier it would be to grasp? No symbols of warnings were showing, only red sectors within the buildings themselves.

"I think parts of the skyscrapers have been contaminated."

"You can see it?" Aaldryn raised his brow.

"Sure." Jarvis pointed. "When I scan the area, it is rendered like a map. Parts are red, parts are orange, others are purple and blue. I think the purple and blue mean they're good, red and orange mean bad."

"Know a way in? Usually I wander around until I find a broken window or a hole."

Jarvis focused on the structure rising above them, unharmed by the tossing waves of the sand battering it. The shimmer of a force-field dimmed by ill-maintenance reflected in his vision.

"Aye." He gestured. "I think I see an entry portal. It's a few storeys up, though. We'll have to scale those broken beams."

Their going was slow against the pull of the burning-sea without a sand-ship to propel them across the dunes. Jarvis felt sweat gather at his temples and the nape of his neck. The intensity of his gravity manipulation combating the force of the sand was unbearable. Without the aid of the protector bot within his system he would not have had the strength to remain afloat. His eyes were drawn to the lording structures above them in the darkness. Whatever unseen horrors awaiting them were hidden behind those glistening walls. Every so often Jarvis heard the distant clatter of battle—the roar of a monster, the clang of blade on talon, but if he turned back he only encountered the darkness and the sheen of the burning-sea swelling in its rhythmic beat.

They came to the broken beam, collapsed against the side of the skyscraper protruding from the sand-dunes. Jarvis stared up at it. Remains of a devastating battle had warped the metal and superheated glass into odd shapes. Every inch of him wanted to turn away and flee the scene of destruction, but he followed Aaldryn, step by step and hand over hand. Aaldryn was adept at scaling old ruins of Zaprex machinery, and he moved swiftly over the smooth surfaces, finding nooks and crevices with impressive ease.

Crawling over the last edge, Jarvis blinked at the stinging hiss of the wind from so high above the world. Then it abruptly stopped, and he looked at Aaldryn, bristling, aware that Khamsin must have calmed the weather around them.

The Kattamont whistled. "Will you look at that view!"

Jarvis turned. His breath caught in his chest. The splendour of the waiting city was undeniably beautiful. It looked like it was moving, as though they were moving with it, when it was, in reality, the ocean of sand beneath them that moved. With the glint of the dancing stars reflected in the surface of the glass skyscrapers, the effect was infinitely mirrored. Jarvis closed his eyes. How he wished—how the philepcon liquid within his veins and the metal his bones were becoming wished the world was not dying, and the beauty he saw was not fleeting.

"Come on." Aaldryn urged, and the moment was lost. "Where is the door?"

Jarvis swivelled. He hopped over the large, dimly blinking lights attached to the collapsed beam, Aaldryn following him in puffs of wind. They reached the edge of the spire. The surface was smooth to the touch, but warm. Warm and still so very alive.

"I don't see a door."

Jarvis scoffed. "That's because you don't have my eyes."

Smoothing his hands over the surface of the spire, he focused, sensing the seams that made up the portal. His voice-box had not yet developed to the point where it could make the notes to sing activation tones, but Zaprexes had not designed their technology only for themselves—they had always included a way for others who sought their aid.

He tapped, his fingers seeking patterns for a code, moving as though they were shifting over the keys of an instrument like a bard might have played in a province lord's hall. A whine made Aaldryn's ears pin back and the Kattamont stepped away. They both watched with bated breath as the door above their heads wheezed open.

Jarvis grabbed the edges of the doorframe, heaving himself up and into the darkness of the corridor. Aaldryn followed him with more grace.

"There don't seem to be any spores around. I think we're safe, for now," Aaldryn murmured. "A bit dark, though."

Jarvis gently pressed a hand to the wall. The ceiling lit with a dim glow, trailing down the long hall like a blue snake.

"It recognises you as a Zaprex machine. Interesting."

The prince's tail flicked back and forth, his back arching in curiosity as he made his way down the corridor. Jarvis rubbed his arms. He was trying not to let it show; alerting Aaldryn to his situation would be embarrassing, but he was unsure how long his façade would hold, and he was only a few feet inside the spire.

It surrounded him like a shroud, encasing his body in a thin sheet of particles that he doubted even Khamsin knew about—the data of so many dead Zaprexes, lingering in the air, stagnant, without a melody. Something awful had transpired here, and it was terrifying to the very core of his underdeveloped matrix crystal.

He clutched at the nearest wall, emptying the contents of his stomach.

Aaldryn was at his side, but he barely felt him. The panic was sharp in his skull. An invasion, an intrusion, something battering against his firewalls.

The Dragon?

No. Not the Dragon.

A soft, echoing voice through the numbness. The voice that had pulled him out of his unconsciousness.

Everyone is gone. They could not escape. The Darkness came. Everyone is…gone…

Jarvis looked up sharply, staring at his faint reflection in the gloss of the wall. His eyes were alight with their rainbow hue, bright, alive, and eerily mechanic as their lenses clicked and swirled.

We are alone. Alone. Amongst the Angels.

"Jarvis." Aaldryn's voice stirred him from his daze. "Are you all right?"

He sat back on his heels, slowly nodding. "Yeah. I think so." Looking up at the Kattamont he winced at the bitterness in his mouth and reached for his water-skin, taking a long drink. "This place is a graveyard. There are ghosts in here."

"We can turn back—"

"No. We need to find a safe place to wait for Master Titus."

The silence between them was heavy. Neither of them wanted to speak of the unbidden worry that the Hunter might not return. Of what that would mean when Jarvis could no longer trust Aaldryn and the Elemental he was host to. Jarvis heaved himself to his feet, wiping his sweating palms on his trousers.

"It appears there is an observation deck a few floors up. We'll be able to see more from up there if we can get the panorama filters working."

"How far is 'a few floors up'?" Aaldryn cocked an eyebrow.

"You don't trust my navigation skills?"

"This place is huge, Jarvis. A few floors could easily mean a few days of hiking."

Jarvis frowned. "True. Best get started then, heh?"

If he had not been infected with the protector bot, Jarvis would have thought they had indeed travelled for days, drifting through the eerie silence that was broken only by their footsteps and the occasional groan of metal upon metal in the distance. However, he could hear the songs of the still-growing crystals alive within the walls and, even further beneath them, somewhere below the burning-sea, a larger force not even his protector bot could pin-point.

The song was beautiful, and so lonely, it made his chest ache with the intensity of it. What felt like days was really only hours, but time seemed non-existent within the castle of the fairies.

Jarvis paused, as a ping caught the edges of his scan. The song dimmed into the background, fading away. He heightened his senses, allowing them to expand around him, further out beyond the metal walls surrounding them.

He could sense Aaldryn's hearts beating and the swishing of his blood, though it was the creaking of the Kattamont's muscles that often distracted him the most. He pushed past the pressure of Khamsin's powerful hum, into the tainted corridors that he had been consciously avoiding due to the crystals there having burst like unfurling flowers, releasing their toxic spores.

"What is it?" Aaldryn turned to him.

"A disturbance in the shield. Something ripped through it." Jarvis touched his temple. The action was not needed to activate his optical lenses, but it made triggering the programs easier when he attached a motion to them. "About a hundred clicks away." He gasped sharply as the images flickered. A blurry smudge, swirling with heat. Master Titus' cloak!

"Master Titus! It's Master Titus!"

"How can you tell?"

"His cloak is made of nano-bots. Its technology is different to anything else anyone has. Quickly!" Jarvis burst down the corridor, skidding around a corner. He made to jump through a force-field, into a sealed section beyond.

"Hold it!" Aaldryn snatched him out of mid-run, winding him as he landed on his rump. "Jarvis, that area is contaminated with crystal spores."

Jarvis groaned, rolling onto his side. He glared up at the Kattamont standing over him, air-gills ruffled in alarm.

"Don't do that!" Jarvis spat out.

"Holy Rythrya, Jarvis! Spores are deadly. They'll kill you—"

"I'm a machine. The crystal spores can't hurt me."

Aaldryn went slack before pulling a frustrated face.

"Just stop trying to protect me. I don't need you." He pulled himself up, panting, and plunged a hand through the force-field.

"This could be a trap."

Jarvis stopped.

"The Twizel could be immune too."

That had not occurred to him.

Aaldryn tugged out his mask, slipping it on, attaching its tubing to his air-gills. Jarvis crossed through the force-field, a charge racing down his spine as the energy cleaned his systems. He stood blinking against the toxicity of the air, filled with the thick glow of tiny crystal particles, all whispering a lonesome tune, wanting to attach themselves to something so they could liquefy once again.

Jarvis breathed, sucking in a mouthful of the spores. He cringed as his vision blackened for a moment, before his systems processed the lingering remnants of the degrading city. Everything was clearer as his eyesight returned, as though the crystal spores had already begun to merge with his own processor core.

"Master Titus!" The words ripped from his mouth, and he vaulted over the edge of the stairs.

The skeleton sat propped upon a wall, unmoving, his broken giant stone blade scattered in pieces around him.

Ryojin

CHAPTER FOUR

Silence. It was the silence that was driving Sekhmet slowly mad. He had always known that their symphony would fade. He had never expected to live to witness it. So many cycles. So many universes. So many worlds they had nursed. This was their last. This was the world that had defeated them.

He clutched his hand against his burning midriff, the sharpening pain of his wound scorching more deeply with each breath.

Gentle footsteps approached from across the central control room. Disgleirio's bare feet paused several paces behind him. The pressure of the child's intense gravity, though contained by the unique suit he wore, was overwhelming, even with all the precautions his bonding partner had put into place to keep the ill Starborn from collapsing into a black hole. Sekhmet snorted. Here they were. The remnants of a fallen Empire. The banished warrior no one had listened to and the black hole his siblings had been too scared to handle.

"Oh, the irony," he muttered, "that you all burned in nuclear fire and I am still here."

"You should sleep," Disgleirio whispered.

"Sleep?" Sekhmet frowned. "I can't leave you alone."

"I am going to go home, Gibo."

Sekhmet turned sharply in his seat, facing the boy in surprise. "What?"

It was easier to know he was dreaming this time; his body felt disproportional. He was staring out of younger eyes, from a youthful body. The world around him was not a simple, indecisive dreamscape, pieced together from drifting thoughts and shapes crafted from events of the day; it was a world he had once been familiar with.

This was a nightmare.

All the instructions he had once given young dreamathics at the House of Flames on how to deal with the devastating effects of insidious nightmares were suddenly utterly useless. In the middle of the screeching alarms, the overwhelming smell of burning philepcon liquid, nothing but fear gripped him. He was swept up in the horror. His foot-paws met with a warm metal floor as he ran. Zaprexes dashed past, some wearing suits, leaping over the edges of the boulevard he rushed down. Denvy watched as the small cyborgs vanished into the cockpits of star-gliders. Through intermittent windows the world outside was revealed—he was in the sky-sea.

Flying.

He was on board a sky-ship.

A light flared sharply in his vision. A bomb.

It shattered against a window. The force threw him backwards against the railing, onto his tail, and he cried out, cowering.

Strong hands gathered him up and he peered through his air-gills at the person kneeling by his side. His younger-self gasped out in relief at the woman's familiar face but trapped within the nightmare he could only stare in horror.

How long had it been since he had seen a Starborn Human alight in all their glory? He had not been there when young King Delwyn had awakened his starblood—though he had seen Zinkx stir his once on the battlefield. It had been beautiful and frightening for him. Now he was faced with a woman from his youth, with a constant glow pooling from her black hair, framing obsidian skin that shone with starlight. A flight suit coated her from shoulder to toe, but still the glow permeated the fabric.

"Navigator Denvy? I thought we sent you home."

"D...I tried...calling through my mic...but no one was... answering me," Denvy heard himself stutter. "What...what's going on?" He had no control. He wanted to scream, to warn the woman in front of him—danger—they were all in danger—but this was a nightmare, a memory; he was trapped inside events he already knew.

Ástrídr continued to strap on her boots. Zaprexes ran past them. One slowed, pausing at Ástrídr's side. Denvy wanted to gape at the delicate little imp in shock. It was Sez-hat; they had been siblings. He had always aspired to be like the fusion Zaprex, who took after Nefertem in eerie, ethereal beauty but Sekhmet in unbridled ruthlessness. Sez-hat was a Zaprex without inhibitors, a fusion, a deadly, terrifying being who had been robbed of continuing the Nefertem-Sekhmet Dynasty by the Dragon. The wrath it brought upon Elementals was swift and merciless.

Why was he seeing Sez-hat, now, in this nightmare? His older self wanted to flee from the very sight of him, while his younger self felt only revered respect and childish adoration.

"We're losing altitude, Ástrídr. Those last few missiles were aimed too near to *Lord:_Leaves_on_the_Wind's* turbines. If we're going to do this, we need to do it now." Sez-hat knelt, finishing her boot for her. The gaze they shared, Denvy knew, was one he would never have understood as a kitten, but witnessing it with older, wiser eyes, the love was apparent in that simple gesture.

"What squad have we been assigned to?" Ástrídr asked.

Sez-hat flicked his wrist, activating a hologram. "Squad Origin. How original."

"Sez, what's going on?" Denvy gasped out.

The Zaprex's illumed pink eyes turned upon him. How he had ever coped with the intensity of that stare he could not fathom, the irises such a brilliant pink within the emptiness of pure black. It was enveloping. He was not greeted with a smile, or a pat on the arm, or a jesting joke about their parent's newest book; instead Sez-hat looked suddenly exhausted.

"Kemet is under attack, Denvy. You shouldn't be here. You're not programmed for combat. Go back to the bridge and get yourself home. That's an order."

"You heard your brother." Ástrídr stood. Denvy winced as his youthful mane was ruffled. "I'll add to that order, though. Get *Lord:_Leaves_on_the_Wind* back to *Tikal:_of_the_Rainbows*. We're going to need backup."

"Please, I can help fight." Denvy stepped forward.

"No." Ástrídr, though far shorter than he, gave a sharp, barking order that made even his older self wince at its tone. Ahead of them Sez-hat had turned to look at them both impassively.

"Denvy, you have barely begun your flight training. You are too important to risk in this battle." Sez-hat frowned. "I am not going to be responsible for you being shot out of the sky—"

"But I'm immortal!"

"No one is immortal when their insides are splattered over a dashboard. No one is immortal when the Dragon eats their data. Negative-Parent would never forgive me if your program was lost. You're all that remains of our Dynasty. Don't you ever forget that." Sez-hat's voice was cutting. "Ástrídr, we have to go. The platoon is waiting."

Ástrídr nodded. "Get this Lord back to Utillia, Denvy."

His shoulders slumped in dejection. A swelling pain was rising in his chest. This—this was the last time he ever saw the Starborn, and his sibling. Slowly he approached the nearest window, clasping tightly to the ledge for support, though he knew his younger self was filled with the frustration of watching the star-gliders depart without him across the Ovin-tu Mountains towards the shine of Kemet. Over the intercom his name was being repeated. He would need to return to the CCR to begin the defragmentation-merge, but his foot-claws could not move from their position. He was wedged firmly at the window, watching the star-gliders vanish over the horizon.

A glitter shone in the distance.

Denvy felt his hearts race.

Within the youthful body of the nightmare there was naught he could do but watch the memory and feel the terror of the dreadful moment in time. The horizon burned bright, lighting up in a flare far more intense than the Sun itself. The shields of his dreamathic mind ripped apart, torn to pieces in a blink of a second. The pulse of agonizing pain ruptured through the Secondary Realm, and he was knocked back from the window as millions of minds died.

Denvy covered his mouth, collapsing to his knees at the sight of the mushrooming clouds rising from Kemet. Screams echoed down the hallways of the sky-ship. Zaprexes, all the Zaprexes within the vessel, their connection severed from their home. Pain. It was too much pain.

Panic surged through him. Denvy snagged hold of the strands of the Secondary Realm, pulling on the defragmentation-drive and yanked it roughly, dragging the ship through the Data-Stream without a merge.

His younger self knew not where he was going, but anywhere was better than watching a whole land burn—or so he had thought then.

He knew so much better now.

He was cold. Alone. His breaths came out in deep, long, foggy puffs. Time was irrelevant when trapped within a nightmare. The dreamscape surrounding him was beginning to splinter and collapse, breaking into flakes of data as his emotions frayed. *Lord:_Leaves_On_ The_Wind's* CCR surrounded him in a pale, dull glow of a gradually dying life-support system. Crystal terminals were shattered from the impact of the crash, and philepcon liquid had spilt across the floor, only to form intricate patterns as it grew and froze in the chill.

Ryojin's avatar settled gently beside Denvy in the frightful ice that layered his coat. "Denvy…" the stray-data whispered. "Denvy, please, you need to focus on me. I'm losing you in this nightmare. Denvy."

The avatar fizzed, discarding its shape briefly. Denvy squinted through the frozen air, biting his cold bottom lip.

"Denvy, this isn't real. You aren't here."

"I know…" he murmured.

"You're punishing yourself needlessly. Come on. Stop this." Ryojin held out a paw.

"Didn't you see it? Everyone died, and I ran away."

"The past has happened, Denvy. You can't change it."

Denvy rubbed at his eyes. Ice particles melted slowly, releasing him from his prison. *Lord:_Leaves-On-The-Wind's* CCR surrounded him like a silent frozen tomb. Bodies of fallen Zaprexes and their Human counterparts lay where they had fallen, sprawled out like delicate, sleeping children. Outside the panoramic windows the darkness of an ocean, so deep and dark, rippled against the force-field still encasing the vessel.

Ryojin had floated to the nearby entrance, waiting for him, and he gingerly picked himself off the floor. The dreamscape rippled at his movement. It was held together by his raw grief and shame, and if he let those emotions go, the dreamscape would crumble.

"Where are we?" Ryojin looked around the CCR, before drifting between the frozen bodies. He crouched beside two, a Zaprex and a Human, wrapped around each other, even in death. There was a peacefulness to them, with ice having captured the last moment of life, their last breath. Denvy joined him, steadying the emotions within that threatened to shatter the dreamscape surrounding them.

"After the Calamity of Kemet, I made an un-directed defrag. The result was disastrous. We found ourselves here, at the bottom of a frozen ocean, without propulsion and with failing shields. All lifeboats had been used during the war. We were trapped in a tomb. Life-support systems slowly collapsed. The Zaprexes who had not been linked to Kemet during the Calamity went into hibernation and their Human counterparts…" Denvy raised a paw. "Well, you can see they did not survive."

"Could you not have defragged them out again?"

Denvy's shoulders sagged. "I had no idea where we were. I had not yet learnt how to defrag without the aid of a machine or a song. What I had done was a fluke, the first of many, I will admit, until I mastered my skill. It did not take long for the Humans to fade."

Ryojin gently settled a hand on Denvy's arm, pixels scattering at the touch, but Denvy smiled at the reassurance from the wayward data.

"I wanted to die, but I couldn't. So I went to sleep, here, for several hundred sol-cycles. Everything I had known, everyone I have loved, was gone, and I had run away. I was a child…" Denvy sighed. "I had no idea what to do."

Ryojin's paw rested on his shoulder. "Denvy, none of this is your fault. It was war."

"I still ran, when I could have helped—"

They both heard the cries—from outside the dreamscape.

"Something is wrong." Ryojin gave Denvy a shove, logging him out with a jolt. "*The Lawless* needs your help now!"

Denvy woke with a start. Shouts of alarms caught his ear from beyond the closed door. It was jarring, the sudden shift from dreamscape to reality. He made to leap up, only to feel Zafiashid's paw smother his mouth, pushing him firmly against the pillows of his bed. Her eyes were wide, her air-gills fluffed high around her neck as her fur plumed.

"Iposti," she whispered. "They have us. They are drawing us in to one of the Wind Cities."

"Wake up, little one," Jythal whispered. Ki'b wrinkled her nose. She raised a hand to push away the thick blankets. She wanted to snuggle back down between the prince and Nixlye, but now that she had opened her eyes she was aware of the light.

Ki'b frowned.

Light—there should not have been such a bright light in the Long Night.

"I sense danger," Jythal continued in a whisper. "Tell me what you see."

She carefully clambered over to the porthole and the eerie light creeping out under its little curtain.

As she tugged back the curtain, a gasp of alarm escaped her at the scene outside the small round window. She had become so accustomed to the toss and roll of the floor beneath her feet she had never thought about how it changed, but it was gentler this morning, and now it was obvious why.

"We've docked. I don't know where we are, though. It is huge. There are windmills." Hundreds, perhaps thousands—she could not fathom the number—of Mist lanterns, lined street upon street, going ever onward and upward, through twining windmills and towering walls of shambled metal and ancient wood. It was so bright it made her eyes water.

She looked at Jythal. He pulled a face, wiggling a claw into one of his ears.

"Ah, that would be the thrumming in the air, then."

Ki'b frowned. Thrumming? She could not hear anything. Jythal leant forward, cracking open the window and she winced, expecting a rush of noise. Only it never came. She blinked. Jythal was right. It was a strange background hum that made her skin tickle.

"One of the Wind Cities." Jythal sniffed the cool air, before easing the window shut again. He bowed his head. "Threnthton. City of Ash."

"City of Ash?" Ki'b rubbed her nose. The air had a thick, roasting flavour to it that adhered to her palate.

"Threnthton?" Nixlye's voice was high-pitched with shock. Ki'b looked around to see the young queen launch herself from the bed to her wheelchair in one fluid movement. She began gathering weapons. "The air smells like ash in Threnthton because the Iposti burn bodies in the Haven Hall. Though no one will admit it. Aaldryn might have met his fate here had Mother not intervened."

Ki'b twisted her lips.

"What about you?"

"Me?"

"Well…" Ki'b pointed to her own legs.

"I was useful to the Iposti. They never dispose of useful things, but a misfit prince like Aaldryn—no, not good to have one of those running around. Princes need to be moulded to their will."

With a loud knock that did not wait for a response, Khwaja Denvy burst through the door. "The Queen says the two of you are in great danger. We have to get you off the ship."

Nixlye looked affronted. "She expects me not to fight for the *Lawless*?"

Denvy urged them into the corridor. Zafiashid paced, her tail coiling like an agitated snake. Ki'b squeezed herself between Jythal and Denvy. The corridor was tight, with the two towering princes and both queens forming a circle under the glow of a Mist lantern. There was commotion on the decks above, and she hoped Clive and Penny were safe.

"We've been forcefully docked at Threnthton," Zafiashid said.

"I noticed," Nixlye snarled.

"We need to get you both off the ship before the Iposti board us. They must not find you here." Zafiashid was speaking to Nixlye, but Ki'b noticed she was looking at Jythal.

"Mother, if they call a pit-fight, I will fight—"

"I do not doubt you would!" Zafiashid snapped. "But since we have been forced into this situation, I would far rather take the burden of that for you. I am still Queen of this Pride."

Nixlye eased back slightly in her wheelchair, but the tautness in her shoulders hackled her neck fur, even as she spoke. "What do you wish, Mother?"

"We seek the location of the Rythrya Stones, yes?" Zafiashid spoke urgently. "Then we must first find a Haven Hall. Threnthton has one."

Nixlye sighed heavily. "Are you sure? We are going off dreams, here."

"Dreams are the greatest conduits of untold knowledge," Denvy answered.

"We are actually considering breaking into a Haven Hall? I know we've often joked about uncovering a City of Gold, but…" Jythal frowned. "It would be your greatest achievement and Aaldryn isn't even here."

Nixlye reached for Jythal's paw, squeezing it tightly.

"I am sure he is having adventures of his own," Ki'b piped up. "After all, Jarvis is a Changeling. Imagine what that could mean here in Utillia with all the Zaprex technology."

Denvy's paws settled on Ki'b's shoulders and she looked up, studying the creases of his aged brow. Sometimes she forgot how old Khwaja Denvy was, that he had sol-cycles of memories, not all of them happy, to sift through. And it must have weighed heavily on his shoulders, perhaps more so than the yoke did.

"How do we get into the Haven Hall?" Nixlye's chest fur fluffed. "And back out again. Ryojin and I fought tooth and claw when I fled from the convent. We barely escaped with our lives."

"We need a diversion," Zafiashid said. "Therefore, I will force them to call a pit-fight. Though I hardly think they will need much of an excuse."

Nixlye straightened in her chair. "You barely survived the last one. You are mad, utterly mad!"

"Yes, but it does allow her current prince to accompany her," Denvy said.

"By the Rythrya, this is insane." Nixlye shook her head.

Jythal spread his paws. "So, while you're pit-fighting one of the Jezumatu princesses—Four Winds forbid it is not Princess Pohehi— we sneak in?" He frowned. "I suppose it could work. Clive is becoming rather good with his Runes and the two of us might be enough to create an illusion sphere. Nothing on the level of a Batitic concealment conduction, but enough to throw off those with low level auras."

"And I will pull away during the pit-fight and meet up with you." Denvy added.

"Ryojin would be horrified to know I'm going back into a Haven Hall by my own free will," Nixlye muttered.

Denvy took her paw. Something shone in his eyes, that distant look again that worried Ki'b so much, as though he was staring into a horizon that had no end. "He wanted you to be free to make your own choices, dear. Whatever you choose to do, I am sure he would have accepted."

She sighed and forced a weak smile. "This is a bad plan."

Ki'b turned her gaze towards the window and the glow of the street lamps beyond, with the whirling windmills churning the sky-sea in a haze of Mist. She heard Khwaja Denvy's low rumble as his chest rose and fell.

"All the best ones tend to be."

She rubbed her shoulder, feeling the keloid scarring that marred her flesh and ached sharply from time to time, reminding her of the wild, crazy plan Khwaja Denvy had come up with in the darkness of the box. Even now she could still recall the feeling of his claws cutting her flesh, like hot blades to her even hotter, fevered body.

Looking up at the old gold lion, Ki'b wrapped her small hand around one of his claws, squeezing it firmly. "If we do it together, it will all work out. Right, Khwaja Denvy?"

"I hope so, Little Mountain Flower. I do hope so."

Zafiashid crouched suddenly and Ki'b gasped as the queen's bright blue eyes faced her. Those eyes were sapphires glistening out from her inky pelt, and Ki'b had to clasp her hands tightly to resist the urge to smooth her fingers through the rich fur. From her belts, the queen tugged free two elegantly curved Mist blades, their scabbards the simplest of blackened wood, engraved with lines of gold, while the hilts hummed with twisting balls of Mist. She twirled them expertly, smiling with a wistful gaze of recollection, before holding them out. Ki'b blinked at the weapons.

"You are a princess of a Pride now. These are appropriate to your status."

"Oh, I could not, Queen Zafiashid," Ki'b choked out.

In the paws of Zafiashid they were daggers, yet to her small, trembling hands, they would be swords.

Zafiashid shook her head, pressing the weapons into her grasp. "They were my first blades when I shifted from a neutral to a princess. You have become a princess, thus it is time you take up arms. May they serve you as they served me."

The queen stood and Ki'b bowed her head. "Thank you," she murmured.

Zafiashid's tail coiled. "Thank me, Little Mountain Flower, on the day you win your first pit-fight."

Ki'b covered her mouth, nodding quickly, trying to hold in her jubilation. She was not sure if the tears that wanted to well up within her and burst out came from the trust and acceptance of the queen before her, or the wish that Jarvis could see her now. She looked up at Khwaja Denvy and caught his tender smile. She fitted the new short swords to her belts. Their weight felt right on her hips, like she had been missing them and now that she had them she was complete. Her fingers curled around the pommels of her new blades.

I will survive. I will fight. For Home. For Jarvis.

The sound of small feet beating against the corridor floor turned their heads. Clive burst around the corner, waving his lanky arms above him. "Queen Zafiashid! Quickly! Kovlrok said the Iposti are boarding us! He's going to try and stall them. Penny is getting the ropes ready. We need to go."

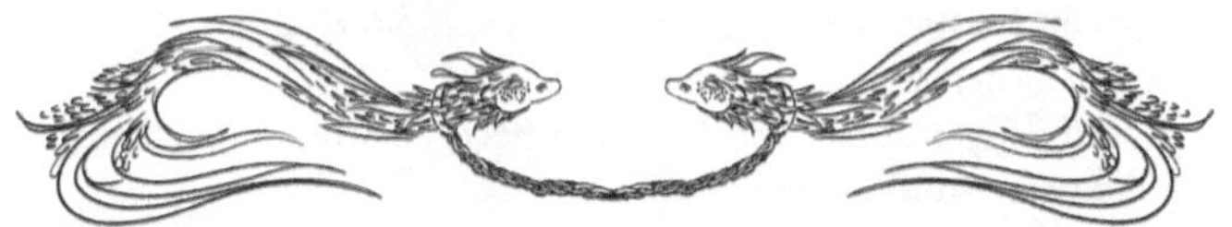

Ki'b slipped her arms into the heavy coat Nixlye had made for her. The feathers that decorated the sleeves were a mixture of both Nixlye's and Jythal's tails woven together. She felt as colourful as a Kattamont, even if she did not look anything like one. She hoped she would blend into the patch-work rug of the harbour that awaited them. From the balcony at the stern, where Penny and several of the crew were lowering ropes to a floating jetty, Ki'b could see the bustling streets of Threnthton. A ball of anxiety knotted itself tightly in her chest, and she inched closer to Nixlye. Jythal flung their pack of supplies over with the last rope, and began to loop both Clive and Penny in a complicated series of knots to lower them.

"I sometimes forget that he is blind," Ki'b whispered.

"He knows the *Lawless Child* very well," Nixlye answered. "Jythal is very skilled at Runes," she added, noting Ki'b's look of concern. "You have only seen very little of what he can do with them in battle. With

Aaldryn gone, Jythal takes alpha status in our Pride so he will force himself to act accordingly, even if it is difficult for him."

They joined Zafiashid at the railing. "I don't see any sign of the *Queen's Mercy*."

"Nor the Silvertide Pride," Nixlye added.

"Oh, the Silvertide would hardly come near the stench of Threnthton. This place reeks of Iposti." Zafiashid covered her nose and mouth.

"It does have a rather pungent scent." Denvy looked up, towards the towering windmills.

Zafiashid turned to a member of the crew, her brow furrowing. "Do you think you can complete the necessary repairs without drawing too much attention?"

"Aye, Captain. Kovlrok believes so."

Zafiashid's tail flicked. "I am certain we will need to leave in a hurry."

"We'll be ready to hoist anchor the moment of your return."

She tugged on an air-gill, looking at the crew member. "Kovlrok is still in contact with his extended family, yes?"

"You mean the Evergreen Tavern, Captain?"

Zafiashid waved a paw. "Yes. That place. The one that hates Kattamonts."

The sailor gave a sheepish rub of his neck. "I, ah, well, I believe so."

"Tell him to get in contact with them. Let them know Outcast Zafiashid may need a quick rendezvous point."

"Will do, Captain." The salior saluted and darted away.

Zafiashid settled a paw upon Nixlye's shoulder. "Be safe."

"You're worrying far too much."

"This is Threnthton, not the Outer Sectors. Your wheelchair may as well be a beacon to the Iposti."

Nixlye frowned. "I can't use my prosthetics. They won't last long enough, and I need them primed for an emergency. Trust the Winds, Mother. There will be enough trading going on for me to be inconspicuous. Threnthton is still the heart of commercial deep burning-sea diving."

Zafiashid sniffed. "I trust in very little but myself."

The lack of the rough toss and sway of the deck unnerved Denvy. To control the vast power of the burning-sea, the Iposti were showing their strength, and it was intimidating to him. The *Lawless Child* was a mere speck against the enormous backdrop of Threnthton. Zafiashid waited in the shadows amongst the crates on the upper-deck, though undoubtedly the Iposti that stood patiently by the gangplank knew of her presence. Denvy sidled across to Kovlrok, eyeing the Iposti with a frown. He had been expecting more than a single heavily-robed neutral with a black, polished mask.

"That's an Iposti?"

"Don't be fooled by their innocent look. However, something is not right," Kovlrok whispered. Several of the crew behind him murmured in agreement. "They would not send a novice to meet a Queen, even the Queen of an outcast Pride such as ours."

Denvy nodded. He could only trust Kovlrok's judgement. The Iposti had not existed in his era. They were a fascinating mutation of the culture of his race. "Would you expect them to make such an obvious blunder?"

"If they are stalling for time, then, yes." Kovlrok drew his Mist-pistol, the action echoed by his crew.

"Get on your knees, Iposti."

The defiant eyes of the neutral glared through the mask. Kovlrok fired, the warning shot popping short of the Iposti's foot-paw.

"Knees. Now!"

"You are too late; the Winds have already spoken. Those who are born of the burning-sea must return to it," the novice finally said.

Emerging from the shadows, Zafiashid snarled, "Get this scum off my ship, Kovlrok."

The novice continued, "The Wind hears all, the Wind knows all—"

Zafiashid curled her lips as several of the crew dragged the novice aside. "Denvy, it appears I have become far too reliant upon Khamsin and forgotten how slimy the Iposti truly are. I have paid dearly for this. Let's go." She marched down the gangplank. Denvy followed her swiftly onto the steady harbour. Her tail rattled in contained fury.

"Find Nixlye and Jythal. Do your dreamathic thing," she ordered.

"What did Nixlye and Jythal do to be hunted so?" he murmured.

"They survived. Now find them."

He focused, drawing his mind through the cracks in the yoke, sensing the warm presence of Ryojin's crystal beside the nexus gem beating against his chest. The next moment sharp sparks of panicked yellows, like lightning bolts, caused him to stagger backwards.

Nixlye was broadcasting an alarm.

"This way!" He followed the flashes within his mind, just as he had taught countless Messengers in the search for trapped comrades in the Trenches. Zafiashid urged him to slow down, a paw on his shoulder, pulling him back against a large freight container. Denvy looked around the side.

His chest tightened at the sight of armed neutral Kattamonts, decked in the pale blue holy attire of Iposti. Four of the neutrals were hissing as they pinned Jythal to the harbour. The position they had locked the white prince in looked painful, but not as painful as Nixlye dragged out of her wheelchair, her arms held down, so she was unable to activate her Mist prosthetics. Ki'b was snarling. She looked as though she had punched one of the nearby Kattamonts, and now had her short swords out, having positioned herself in front of Nixlye, along with Clive and Penny.

Clive was a furious little righteous fire.

"How dare you! Do you like going around hurting people who can't walk, heh, or see? He's blind, yeh big bullies! It's not like he can see you to hit you!"

Denvy winced, forcing himself not to step forward as an Iposti turned towards Clive.

"Foolish Human, this is the Sword of the Jezumatu. He is far more dangerous blind than he ever was with eyes."

Jythal snarled, spreading his air-gills. The prince suddenly reared up, smashing back the neutrals holding him down. It happened so fast, Denvy almost missed the Rune the white prince threw into the air, but, in the moment between Jythal leaping up and casting out his paw, a blade formed out of pulsing hot air. It settled against the neck of the Iposti that had spoken.

"I am not owned by the Jezumatu anymore. You will do well to remember that, Iposti. One word from my queen and I will remove your head."

The Iposti smirked. "I think not."

Denvy felt his fur spike.

A surge of wind ripped through the planks of the dock. He could not see them wrap around Jythal, but the impression against the prince's fur was like ropes encasing his body, sucking all breath from his lungs.

Jythal's paw released his Rune weapon and it vanished into vapour. Denvy tensed. So, this was why the Iposti were called wind-tamers. They had control over the Simoon.

He narrowed his eyes. This made them dangerous. He had to wonder if they had all the skills of those born under the element of wind, or whether they could only control the Simoon like a snake tamer charmed a snake.

His spiking fur was slowly calming. Now it was time to act, while he still felt he could.

Zafiashid's paw caught his arm and he glanced down, facing her. He had teased her so often, calling her young, but never had she looked so much like a cub now, in the darkness, so frightened and alone.

Denvy brushed a paw over her cheek.

It was scandalous of him, the soft kiss he pressed to her lips, but her smile was worth the ache in his chest.

"You are strong and brave, my dear. I have no doubt you will win," he whispered.

"If I do," she held his paw against her chest tightly with her own, "will you be my prize?"

"I am an immortal Ancient One—"

"I do not believe in curses." She shoved him roughly out from behind the freight container.

He stumbled slightly before righting himself. Willing forth his water-sword, Denvy drew up, facing the Iposti, noticing their momentary baffled expressions at his sudden appearance.

"If you would, Master Iposti, please release my blood-brother. I can assure you he will not attack your pride members."

The master Iposti's robes rustled as he moved, tail shifting dangerously. Denvy cringed as Jythal groaned, the ropes of wind tightening. Fingering the hilt of his water-sword Denvy stepped forward. He might not have returned to the fully muscular force he had once been, but he was still far taller and broader than any neutral Kattamont could ever be and the Iposti surrounding him all appeared to be neutrals. It left him wondering if their whole order was constructed entirely out of neutrals. What if none ever became princesses or queens? It made no sense how their pride could function if it was a pride of neutrals.

"Release him. Immediately." Denvy snarled, fanning out his air-gills and fan-tail. "Or do you desire to test your Simoon against my Merkr[1]." He swept his blade through the air, letting droplets of water freeze upon the floor.

A whisper stirred through the neutrals. "That's impossible. The Merkr no longer exist."

Denvy chuckled low within his chest, raising an eyebrow at the head Iposti. "You are ill informed."

Despite the mask the Kattamont wore Denvy could see the eyes of the neutral clearly. He was being studied, judged and gauged, and no doubt the Iposti was attempting to gather the truth of his words. It took every ounce of his self-control not to shudder at the soft brush of wind that tickled against his air-gills. The fur around the nape of his neck settled as the Iposti waved a paw, causing those around him to shift away from Ki'b, Penny, Clive and Nixlye.

Jythal slid to the harbour decking as the wind ropes dissolved. The prince panted heavily, his air-gills expanding in gasps. Penny rushed

---

1 The Titan of Water was one of the Elementals cast into the Unknown Realm by the Dragon. Water Elementals, and all derivatives of water, suffered considerably from the loss of their Titan. Few Water Elementals remain. Those that do tend to be found bound to ancient weapons, particular sites, or an individual family-line that they've remained attached to down the centuries.

to his side, glaring at the neutrals as they backed away. Denvy shared a glance with Nixlye, catching the barest nod of her head. Gradually he lowered his water-sword. He heard murmurs behind him, and caught the words "Gold Lion", but a glare from their master silenced them.

"If you promise to behave with respect, then I will allow you to see our Queen. I will try to overlook how you have abused our princesses and neutrals if you refrain from further insult."

"They are half-breeds! A Kelib and Humans! They are not Kattamonts."

"They have chosen to live in Utillia and therefore they have accepted the life of the Pride. They will be treated as Kattamonts." Denvy growled low.

Clive shouted. "Yeah! What Khwaja Denvy said—"

Clive was quickly muffled. Either Ki'b or Penny had clamped down on him. The lad had such a feisty heart, and he meant well. Inclining his head in an honourable bow, Denvy stepped to one side, allowing Zafiashid to slide forward from her position behind him. The scowl she wore was one of fury. If she had been adorned with a crown, no other Kattamont in Utillia would have better owned the title of queen. Her fur was stiff, and her tail swept out in toying frustration.

"This is not how I expected you to treat my Pride, Master Iposti. I am an outcast, not a criminal to be dragged into dock and boarded without warning." Soft and deadly, her voice was perfectly even.

Denvy noted the very slight shift in the Iposti's expression— entrenched submissiveness warring with a much fresher taste of power—and he smothered a snort. A neutral was still a neutral no matter the robes they wore or the masks they put on to cover their faces. Eventually a queen would come along strong enough to command them. It simply was the law of their race.

"Princess Uyrilk has summoned you to the pits."

"Uyrilk? Really?" Zafiashid glanced at Jythal and Nixlye. "Interesting. I had presumed she would become the next queen."

The change to the Iposti's smirk under the mask was unnerving, and the way his eyes settled upon Jythal and Nixlye like a hungry bird-of-prey. Denvy tightened his grip on his blade once more as his skin prickled.

"No. The new Queen of the Jezumatu Pride is Agatoish. I crowned her myself."

Jythal loosened a string of curses.

Nixlye's rage was barely contained. Were it not for their greater plan to infiltrate the Haven Hall, Denvy was sure she would have lunged upon the master Iposti with a dagger and dealt with him then and there. "Who thought it a good idea to make that mad little xenophobe queen!"

The Iposti sneered. "Dear princess, she won the pit-fight."

"With one paw?" Nixlye snarled. "I made sure she would never use that sword arm again. She couldn't even get it replaced with a Mist prosthetic when I was finished with her."

The Iposti shrugged. "She had another paw."

"What of Princess Pohehi?" Zafiashid's tone was still measured. "I find it difficult to believe she allowed another to take the place of queen."

The barking laugh of the master Iposti startled Denvy. "We of the Iposti have warned those who dive the burning-seas of the madness that lies therein, but our warnings fall on deaf ears. Princess Pohehi has been cast out. She is mad."

Nixlye hissed. "Then I guess the next time I fight *Queen* Agatoish I will have to rip out her eyes for Princess Pohehi."

"You do that, princess, and I will happily add a bonus to your winnings." The master Iposti made a gesture and they were surrounded and bound none too gently. "Enough prattling. I am eager to watch a decent pit battle. Or more than one." The half-crazed look he sent around their motley group made Denvy's hearts thud.

Sekhmet

CHAPTER FIVE

Home. It was a word that clanged with such clarity. Home. It was also a painful blade, cutting Sekhmet's wound deeper. How long had it been since his mind had lingered on the Little Blue Planet that had cradled them—not all the variations they had passed through, but the precious first they had failed to save?

Home. Their home. He was sure that failure had been what had shaped their prime directive.

Had it also shaped their eventual demise?

He watched as Disgleirio packed his precious treasures into a box. The child had come to him with next to nothing and was leaving with little again.

"Disgleirio, you do understand that if you leave you cannot return? The Data-Ways have been sealed and I do not know where Maahes is."

"Then, after I have returned home, I will search for my brother." Disgleirio swung his pack across his shoulder.

"I also cannot give you an estimate on how long you have before you grow unstable and collapse."

"I trust your failsafe, Gibo."

Sekhmet smiled wearily, reaching out. He drew Disgleirio into his trembling arms. "I raised my children to be far too brave. You've all outgrown me."

"Master Titus!"

Aaldryn watched as Jarvis ignored the stairs and instead leapt over the railing. He tossed up spores as he landed amongst the crystals, betraying how much of a boy he still was as he threw himself onto the Hunter. The remains of Titus' giant stone-blade lay around him. It had been shattered into shards by a tremendous force. All that remained was the impressive hilt in the Hunter's lap. Black tar, like thickened blood, splattered the railings, floor, and ceiling. The battle had been ruthless. Khamsin's wind fluttered against each remaining entail. Not all of it was Titus' alone; the Ki'rayh, too, had been viciously wounded.

Under his mask he studied the Messenger, whose limp, bone hand gently cupped Jarvis' cheek. The skull looked down at the boy with what Aaldryn read as warmth and fatherly pride. To withstand the might of such an ancient Shadow Elemental… Aaldryn knew he had underestimated the Hunter. He sensed a shift in Khamsin's attitude, too. Wind was a fickle element. It changed rapidly, without warning, but when it did change it was with profound consequences, that much he did know. Gradually he descended the stairs, careful not to disturb the spores of the crystals stirring around his foot-paws like thick milk. He shivered. One breath and his lungs would melt. He would not even know he had died, it would be so swift. Yet, ahead of him, Jarvis sat on his knees able to breathe the air without concern.

How he envied the Changeling.

Titus looked up at his approach. So much emotion conveyed through the black depths of the eye sockets that studied him.

"Yeh look hilarious in that thing." Titus pointed awkwardly at his mask.

Aaldryn shrugged. "You're in a contaminated zone. Didn't have a choice."

"Ah, guess that explains the shiny crystals everywhere, and my current state." He touched a bone finger to his skull, clicking it idly.

"Are you all right, Master?" Jarvis held onto the bones of his arm.

Titus dipped towards the boy. "Tired, laddie. I ain't as young as I use ta be, yeh know."

"Don't say that, Master. Whatever happened to dying in a blaze of glory?"

Titus laughed, causing his jawbone to rattle. "Still enough time for that, son."

Oh—how that single, simple word resonated through the air between them like one of Jythal's runes. Aaldryn watched as Jarvis' thin chest heaved sharply. Khamsin caught the subtle shifts of the boy's cheeks, revealing both happiness, overwhelming affection, and the ever-present mixture of sadness left by the gaping hole that had once been filled by the lad's family.

Humans. They claimed they needed no one, they claimed they needed no prides, no brotherhoods, and yet they needed far more connection than any other race upon Livila.

After all, Khamsin whispered from within, *they are the aliens. They need us more than we need them.*

Like lost children, still searching for a home. They will have a home in Utillia. Utillia is home to all, Aaldryn replied.

He sensed Khamsin's amusement but was drawn back to the conversation outside of his mind. Jarvis had inquired after the Ki'rayh. The beast was nowhere to be seen.

"Oh." Titus waved a hand loosely. "Don' yeh worry, laddie."

Jarvis grinned with relief, collapsing against Titus' lap.

Aaldryn frowned. How elegantly those words had been used to ease his little brother's fears, without confirming the eradication of the Twizel. Titus' black stare turned slowly towards him and the Hunter wearily shook his head as his hand settled upon Jarvis' shoulders, gently patting the boy in reassurance.

Aaldryn nodded. If this was Titus' wish, then he was not going to intervene. Their truce was too shaky as it was. He would need to win back Jarvis' trust. He looked again at the black blood on the walls, shimmering in the glow of the crystals around them. No matter how beautiful their world looked, it was still dangerous.

Titus could not protect Jarvis forever.

Jarvis clung to Titus. The relief of seeing him made his metal gears move more easily, as though the happiness bubbling up inside him created an electric charge that ignited the philepcon liquid, enhancing his propulsion.

The Ki'rayh was gone.

Now they could concentrate on their task without worrying about being tracked to Coltarian. Jarvis sighed with relief. He flinched as Titus' skeleton hand ruffled his hair suddenly.

"Yeh all right there, Little Weasel?"

"Yup." He pulled away from the strange touch of bone. He had not realised how attached he had become to the Hunter. It was somewhat alarming, and the knowledge unsteadied him. He tried to centre himself on the task at hand, finding a pathway through the maze of the Zaprex ruins, and hopefully a safe place to camp out for time—at least until Titus was well enough to move at a swifter pace.

As far as he could tell, his master was putting on a brave front. The loss of his giant stone blade made him look eerily older, and it was frightening. Seeing the huge weapon broken into pieces had sent a sharp jab of fear through his stomach. Titus had the hilt slung over his shoulder like a baton, trying to make light of the situation. Though, if all his master had lost to defeat the Ki'rayh was his sword, it had to be considered a good outcome.

Jarvis shivered, turning away to focus his attention on the schematics of the turret they were currently in, scanning for safe zones. Yellow blurs appeared on his lenses and he froze, sucking in a sharp breath, taking a moment to crystalize the shapes and analyse their compositions.

"Aaldryn!" Jarvis turned, drawing his colour-blade. "We've got company. Two princes."

Aaldryn sprang into action, dodging to one side and flattening himself against the wall. Jarvis froze, picturing himself becoming part of the surrounds. He merged with the colours. Master Titus slunk into the shadows. Jarvis glanced at Aaldryn, noticing the small twitch of the prince's ears.

"They're heading this way," he murmured in reply.

Paw-steps approached.

Jarvis focused on the beating of his heart, the rhythm a calming sensation as a figure came into view of his optical lenses.

A Kattamont prince with fur as bright as fire, and tail-feathers like rippling flames. Jarvis tensed as eyes suddenly snapped his way. No—it was not possible for the Kattamont to have sensed him.

Wait.

He could hear Aaldryn hissing.

Bother, he cursed inwardly. Kattamonts and their territorial instincts.

In a single fluid movement an arrow was nocked in the bow of the prince and released. The arrow skimmed Aaldryn's arm, spraying blood across Jarvis' face. He stiffened, staring in disbelief at the enormous shaft of the weapon protruding from the wall. It had pierced Zaprex metal. Aaldryn swept forward, his Mist pistol firing down the hall. He rolled, dodging another arrow. Springing to his hind legs, the prince spun, using the tight confines of the corridor as his shield.

"Jarvis, run! Come on!"

He needed no further urging to burst into a mad dash and vault down a flight of stairs, across banisters, and through more twisting glass chambers. Aaldryn and Titus were hard on his heels.

"Titus, we need to split up. I don't think they've seen you," Aaldryn called out.

"All right. I'll be close by."

"Jarvis, whatever you do, do not let the protector bot come out," Aaldryn shouted.

"What? Why?" They skidded around the nearest corner, Titus vanishing into the folds of darkness. Jarvis' chest tightened at the sudden disappearance of his master. He dropped and rolled as a bullet whizzed past and he swung back his sword, releasing a scattering of rainbow light in a haloing shield.

Aaldryn reloaded his pistol. "Your protector bot is an advantage we cannot reveal yet. You still pass for Human. If they think you are, they might let you live, if you convince them to keep you as a slave. That should give Titus enough time to come back around and fetch you."

Jarvis hesitated, but there was too much to be said. He pounded down a set of stairs, halting abruptly as a Kattamont-sized arrow burrowed into his shoulder, snapping off as it hit a metal plate. He collapsed, gravity control lost in the alarm from the pain before it realigned, and he surged to his feet. He felt for the wound, but it was already healing over.

"Jarvis!" Aaldryn called to him from the other side of the room, his paw outstretched in panic.

Jarvis made to run, but he was hoisted off his feet, his chest constricted by powerful arms. He looked up into the ferocious glinting eyes of a prince twice the size of Aaldryn. This, he imagined suddenly, was what Khwaja Denvy should look like—a powerful beast, skin taut with muscle, air-gills spread in a halo of power, colour displaying pride as a warrior. The first prince moved into his vision, shorter, with fire-fur, and fan-fail rippling in yellows and blues.

Aaldryn snarled at his appearance. Alphas. Aaldryn and the fire-fur were both alphas, facing off in a small room, and both very, very angry.

Aaldryn lifted his pistol, Mist hissing against the air as it powered up in a burst.

"Drop my brother!"

Jarvis squeaked, "I'm fine!"

It was holding back the protector bot that was taking the real strain on him.

The prince holding him tightened his grip and Jarvis tensed as the tender metal of his hull began to shout alarms through his mind, blaring red across his vision. He cursed aloud as well as his breathless lungs allowed him to. How frustrating it was to still be part-Human—and he was not sure which side of him was annoyed by that fact: the Human, or the machine.

Aaldryn's fan-tail and air-gills spread in fury, a sight that was stunning to behold. He was frighteningly beautiful as he stalked forward, eyes narrowed. His fur rippled, readying for the pounce on the alpha prince.

"You're in our pride's territory." The red prince matched Aaldryn's stalking. "Leave before I cleave your head from your shoulders."

Aaldryn growled. "I do not take orders from bandits. Release my brother or I will slit both your throats and leave you to the mercy of the crystals."

"You talk high of yourself when you are but one prince."

Aaldryn threw the pistol aside. "Not all things can be seen clearly in the Primary, bandit."

Tension between the two princes grew. Their muscles pulled like springs ready to release. The ruthlessness was shocking. Jarvis stared in horror as the princes clashed in the centre, claws and jaws ripping through fur. Blood sprayed across the silver floor. They rolled, locked in a deathly embrace, both struggling to gain the upper position. He had seen the plains lions fight; his father had often taken him out on misty mornings to watch the territorial display of the mighty beasts, to remind him how deadly they could be. This was as unbearable as those times. Only now he could smell the blood up close and hear the ripping of flesh and yowls of pain. His protector bot eyes caught every twist and turn of the princes—the moment the lashing tail of the red Kattamont began to split. It was so natural, so fast, Jarvis had no time to shout a warning.

Aaldryn leapt aside, barely missed by the new appendage and the keen blade buried within its fanned feathers. He crouched, panting heavily as he stared at the two-tailed prince.

"You are misfit-born."

The red prince spat out blood. "Yes. Do I disgust you?"

Aaldryn snorted. "I would have to find myself equally as disgusting." Standing to his full height, Aaldryn held out his paws. He wiggled the extra digits and smirked.

"It would appear we are kin." The red prince raised his brow.

Aaldryn laughed. "I think you got the better deal. An extra tail is far more interesting than an extra claw."

"It is more cumbersome than it appears, brother."

"Great!" Jarvis shouted. "Now that you are best friends, can I please be put down?"

Both princes turned his way and Aaldryn shifted sheepishly. "Sorry, brother."

"Yes! Be sorry!" he sniped. He bit back the retort about not being Aaldryn's brother. Now was not the time.

The red prince waved a paw, and the heavy-set Kattamont holding Jarvis loosened his grip. He slid free of the brute's arms, glaring up at the Kattamont. "I would say thanks, but, ah, no."

His head was given a solid pat. "Sorry. Just following orders," a surprisingly mellow voice flowed from the large prince's chest. "You're pretty strong for a little Human."

"I get that a lot." Jarvis tugged on the collar of his shirt.

Across the room, Aaldryn was offering the two-tailed prince a paw up and he rolled his eyes at the situation. How easily things could be pacified by simply identifying as a particular group. He recoiled, wondering what would have happened if Aaldryn had not had extra claws to show them.

"I am Aaldryn of the Misfit Pride." Aaldryn inclined his head.

"Outcast Zafiashid's offspring? Should have seen that; your coat alone is clearly Silvertide heritage." The prince stepped back, towards his larger companion. "I am Eloiko, and my blood-brother is Dayts. We are princes of the Dwellers' Pride."

Jarvis craned his neck to look up at the tall Kattamonts surrounding him.

"You dwell inside Yrva Krv?" He scratched his chin.

"Indeed, we do, Little Human."

Jarvis frowned. "That'd explain the mutations, then, if you are living so close to the contaminated sectors. His must be extreme muscle density." He jutted a thumb at Dayts.

Eloiko's eyebrow lifted curiously, his tails curling.

"How did you know?"

Jarvis thrust out his hand in Human greeting. "Jarvis of the Plains People, Pennadotian-born Messenger. That's my Master, stalking in the shadows over there."

Eloiko stepped back in alarm. "There is another?"

Titus landed with a thud, his cloak swelling in an inky ripple. Jarvis breathed a sigh of relief at the sight of his master's cocky smile and pale cheeks blazing with freckles. They were far enough away from the eerie glow of any Zaprex crystals that the Hunter's skin was unaffected. Though he still looked deathly pale, and his eyes vacantly black, he at least passed for a Human.

"How?" Eloiko spluttered out. "How did we not sense you?" He looked around, up to the ceiling in bafflement.

"Battle tactics, laddie. I come from a warzone. Hunter Titus Timothy Telvon, Commander of Second Base, Sector Eight-Two."

"Messengers." Eloiko looked at them both, his stance relaxing further. "We have met a few of you travelling through Yrva Krv before but you have become fewer over the sol-cycles."

"Nice ta know there are kindly people still left in the world." Titus shrugged.

"Our apologises for attacking you. We are usually not so unwelcoming upon first sight."

"Really?" Aaldryn laughed. "From the tales, you folk are rather horrid."

Dayts inclined his head. "The bandits are difficult to deal with, but we have staked out our territory. This tower is ours. Our…queen…and princesses and neutrals were quite ruthless when it came to defence."

Jarvis blinked. *Were?*

"I'd believe that." Aaldryn rolled a bloodied shoulder.

Eloiko waved a paw. "You did rather well. We are evenly matched."

"Well, if you'd stuck your blood-brother on me, it might have been another story." Aaldryn glanced at Dayts, who smiled warmly.

"He does not let me fight unless the situation is dire."

"Pulling the arms off guests is not a great way to start a conversation." Eloiko clapped his brother-brother on the arm.

Titus barked a sudden laugh. "Ah, yes, I can see how that would be a problem."

Dayts rubbed a paw behind an ear. "I can be helpful."

"Don' doubt it, laddie. Fellow like yeh would be mighty handy in a tight spot."

"That wound though," Jarvis motioned to Dayts, "it looks recent.

Dayts glanced briefly at the bandage wrapped tightly around his forearm. Jarvis could smell the festering odour of the wound: Twizel venom. What did Twizel venom do to Kattamonts? Were they, perhaps, immune to the toxin of the Dragon's fiends like their Batitic bestial cousins?

It seemed they were not entirely resistant, but at least they were not as helpless as Humans and Kelibs.

"Aye, it is recent." Dayts touched the bandage. "I met my match."

Jarvis raised an eyebrow. What if he faced the muscular mutant in his exo-skeleton? How would that battle turn out? It was unlikely he would get the chance to learn.

"We were in this area tracking the movements of a…monster…" Eloiko frowned. "A fiend from Coltarian. It caught us off guard on a hunt."

"A Twizel?" Titus offered. "Don' worry about it. I dealt with it."

The tension that Eloiko had been holding melted away and he staggered back against the railing of the stairs. "Then we owe you much gratitude, Messenger. The beast killed our queen and our princess."

Jarvis felt Aaldryn's tail wrap protectively around his waist, pulling him against his leg. He had no choice but to follow the movement and bump against the prince, to feel the low purr of mourning from the Kattamont.

"I am so sorry," Aaldryn murmured.

Eloiko bowed his head. "Truly, only fellow princes can understand the sorrow and grief of losing our mates." He shifted closer to Dayts as if seeking the comforting protection of the larger prince. "Tell me, Prince Aaldryn, what takes you from your queen's side?"

"I am on a mission for her." Aaldryn touched a paw to his chest.

Eloiko studied them. "To involve Messengers in the ways of the Prides, this can only mean…"

"War be coming, laddie," Titus offered. "There ain't gonna be an end to this Long Night for a long while."

"Is it him? The one the Messengers speak of whenever they come?" Dayts asked.

"The Dragon?" Jarvis curled his fingers around the small prism under his shirt. "Yes."

Eloiko sighed. "The Iposti would have us all believe he is but a myth of the past, like the Zaprexes. And, yet, here we stand, amongst the ruins of their civilization. How can you not believe it?" He waved a paw, motioning them to follow him. "Come, come, you are misfit-born. We are of the same stock, born of the crystal flowers. We are all brothers here. Our Pride is your Pride."

It was strange to see homely Kattamont tents scattered around the large observation decks of the Zaprex turret, with overarching windows stretching out around them in an enveloping view of the cityscape. Above the tent village, like a small lording sun, the ebbing glow of a crystal shimmered in a constant watch. It made Aaldryn's skin crawl, though he was unsure if it was Khamsin's reaction or his own—it was difficult to tell these days.

"Mebbe yeh shoulda brought Jythal along if yeh're gonna get yerself ripped to shreds by every Kattamont we encounter." Titus hummed in amusement as he made an exaggerated inspection of Aaldryn's wounds. "Shame Khamsin doesn't help yeh with that."

Aaldryn flicked his tail irritably. "It's not his area of expertise. Unless it's life threatening, he won't really do too much. He never cared about mortal fleshlings until I came along."

"He should maintain his host, surely? Was that not part of yeh deal to allow him access to the Primary Realm?"

Aaldryn shrugged. "The pact was only to take away my illness when I was born, but in doing so he—"

"Removed yer immune system and replaced it, so he now has to make sure he acts as part of yeh body. I know." Titus waved his gloved hand. "I've been around Elementals ma whole life. Prometheus practically raised me. I was intended to be the Soul of Eros."

Khamsin stirred and Aaldryn's fur spiked down his spine as the wind god's interest rose from a bored background hum to a piqued buzz.

Eros survived? Well, I suppose Eros was never truly a Titan.

How can a Titan not be a Titan? You're either something or you're not.

Complicated family matters. We Titans are all direct offspring of the World Tree. Eros is a…how do you put it in fleshling terms? A half-sibling, or, perhaps, a bastard?

That makes no sense. How can elementals have bastard children? That's a Human concept.

Khamsin gave the equivalent of a mental shrug.

"Yeh and Khamsin need to be prepared for what yeh find at the House. The tension between the Thyrrhos Nation and the Messengers is probably much worse than when I left. While I trust Prometheus…" Titus sighed.

Aaldryn relented as Khamsin took over the conversation. The ancient wind-god spoke through his lips, but was still not at home with using his body. His voice sounded uneven.

"I was there when the Zaprexes designed the Obelisk System," Khamsin warbled. "Prometheus was willingly shackled. Prometheus knew what was at stake."

"Yes." Titus frowned. "But for the Obelisk System to collapse, Prometheus' hold must also be weakening."

Khamsin sighed. "Despite the old tales of us, young Shadow, we are not invincible. We gain our energy from the flow of the Secondary Realm, which in turn is fuelled by the spin of our world. And as the rotational spin of the Northlands fades with the breaking of the Borders, it is only natural that the Elemental races will either continue to die away or find ways to escape into the Primary Realm and form more contracts with mortals, like you have, and like I have."

Titus brushed a hand through his curls. "Tah, we really messed up."

Aaldryn blinked a few times as Khamsin released control and sensation returned to his limbs. He smiled at the Hunter.

"At least we have a chance to possibly, maybe, help fix it."

Instinctively, Aaldryn shot up moments before he scented the return of the alpha prince. He hissed out a breath of pain at the sharp movement, ignoring Titus' smirk.

Eloiko spread his paws as he approached. It was a small relief to note that he was limping. Aaldryn would have worried for his dignity before the Dwellers had he appeared weaker than their alpha prince.

You Kattamonts have the oddest way of thinking, Khamsin's murmur stirred in his mind. *You fought well. You did not even need to summon me.*

I do fight my own battles, sometimes.

He sensed a scoff from the wind-god. *It is not like I lower myself to fight little mortal princes.*

No, no, you're saving yourself for Coltarian. Aaldryn mentally rolled his eyes. *Remember my weak mortal body when you meet your sibling in battle, please.*

Khamsin only hummed in reply, but it was a warm, amused hum and Aaldryn smiled faintly at the wind-god's seemingly content state.

"Your arrival has caused much excitement in our pride," Eloiko told them. With a swing of his tails he motioned for them to follow him down a path.

Aaldryn studied the small village as they wandered through. It reminded him of the *Lawless Child*. Though there was no toss of the deck beneath him, which was still unnerving, the environment was warming and cheerful. The colours of the tent skins reminded him of the *Lawless Child's* brightly painted walls. Misfit-born seemed to express themselves freely, making up for the lack of the ancient coral reefs of their ancestors by crafting them from whatever could be found.

The village was lively, smelling of food, and his stomach constricted tightly, reminding him of how long it had been since he had eaten a decent meal. His eyes swept around the faces of different Kattamonts, freckled with half-breed Humans and a mingling of Kelibs—all with mutations, some as small as his own extra digits, others unbelievably severe, and not all would survive long outside in the conditions of the burning-sea. He could see now why they lived in the confines of the Zaprex ruins; they simply could not leave.

It is likely due to living in the Zaprex ruins that has caused the mutations to grow so bizarrely. I have not seen the like before, Khamsin said.

The Iposti tend to get to those who are worse off than I. Nixlye said *she saw folk like this in the convent. And to think I never believed her or Ryojin's stories.* Aaldryn looked up at the domed ceiling and the overwhelming glow of the great crystal above them. It was terrifying, and he had no idea how anyone could live with it glistening overhead like an omnipotent god. It made his fur curl thinking about it. He glanced at Jarvis, who had been unusually quiet for the entire tour of the tent village, and noticed the young man's generally pinkish-brown cheeks had turned a pale tinge of iron. He frowned. The centre home-tent they approached was much like those his Mother had often vanished into for negotiations with lesser-queens of the smaller prides of the Outer Islands. His gaze settled on the entrance, and what it was that had Jarvis so tightly wound.

Strung up, dangling like trophies from bound-together driftwood and glittering metal woven into hexagons, hung the limp exoskeletons of two Zaprexes.

CHAPTER SIX

Denvy peered out of the rattling carriage's window. His skin was crawling. No matter how much he told himself he was not in the boxed wagon, his mind kept wandering to the smell of decaying dead children, and rotting hay filled with faeces and the stench of urine. They had been split up. Nixlye and Jythal had been sent ahead in a smaller carriage with the Master Iposti eager to collect the bounties on their heads. In actuality, it suited their plan perfectly. Across from him Clive looked pale, beads of sweat pooling at his jawline. But at least his practice of the Runes was paying off. He clutched at Penny's wrists, carefully forming an illusion of the bonds that he had just removed. Denvy sighed in relief as the Runes hung in place and the illusion held. It would take more than rope to hold his cubs captive again. The noise from beyond the door kept his ears twitching. Denvy nudged back the small curtain and peered out into the streets. They were bustling with all manner of folk, deeply tanned Humans in strange attire, Kelibs looking decidedly foreign so far from the forests and soils of their ancestors, and Kattamonts tall, proud, and aloof.

He looked up. It was impossible to see the stars. The pollution rising from the Haven Hall in the centre of the city, and the constant lights that made the Long Night blaze like day, cast out a greyness over the sky-sea. It surprised Denvy how much a lack of stars unsettled him. Threnthton was not on the scale of Palace-Town, or the House of Flames, yet it made him feel incredibly tiny and if he had been able to see the stars perhaps he would have been able to remind himself that the city itself was part of something greater.

Centuries of Kattamonts collecting Zaprex vessels and metal from beneath the burning-sea and piecing together the ruins like a puzzle had given the city a tartan appearance. It creaked and groaned as the motors of wind turbines churned deep within its underbelly.

Denvy flattened his ears against his head. Even with the yoke about his neck, his sensitive dreamathic mind could feel them: thousands of Simoon bound in agony.

Scratching a claw through his slowly growing mane, Denvy heaved a sigh.

"Now I see, Khamsin, what has forced you to become so docile, when you were the most terrifying of the Four Winds." His gaze trailed back to the starless, grey sky-sea, to the memories of battles from within the cock-pits of gliding machines, against the very wind elementals he could hear screaming.

"In the end, just like the Zaprexes, it is to save your children that you have become what you feared: a tame wind…"

"Talking to yourself, old one?" Zafiashid asked.

"No, no, I was talking to Khamsin."

He caught the queen's raised eyebrow in the dim Mist lantern light. "Aaldryn is not here."

"You truly do not know who it is that you gave your son to, do you?"

"A Wind Elemental."

Denvy sighed heavily, rubbing his temples. "Back in the Era of Forging, there existed the Elemental Race, the Olympians if you prefer their Zaprex title. They dwelt within the Secondary Realm and forged our planet. Without their existence, our world's surface would not have the elementals needed for our survival. Some of them were the Titans—I suppose the Kattamont equivalent would be their queens. Of those, you have the Four Winds, the Corners of Livila." He raised his paws, making a square. "The windmills outside are a perfect representation of their Pillars."

"The Four Winds worshipped by the Kattamonts of the outer-sectors?" Zafiashid whispered.

Denvy inclined his head. "Khamsin is the North Wind of the Northlands. You gave your son and your allegiance to the Titan of the North Wind, a being from the Forging of the World, even older than I am." He touched his chest lightly. "And that is saying something."

She snorted. "If he is such a being, why is he skulking around Utillia of all places? And why would he not have told me who he is?"

Denvy frowned. "The Thousand Sol-cycle War was devastating, my dear. It is difficult to describe the sheer ruthlessness of what transpired, but the Elementals suffered incredible losses for siding with the Dragon. He betrayed them, consumed them for power. The Zaprexes had to create artificial systems to replace the Elementals, otherwise we would not be breathing the air we are breathing right now."

"The myth of the Dragon throwing the Elementals into the Unknown Realm, then, you are telling me, is true?" Zafiashid glanced towards him.

"I am afraid it is."

"Why would he do it, if we need them to live?"

"The Dragon does not like rivals."

"Hmm. Considering I was thrown out as a rival, I can, in part, understand that. Kattamont queens detest rivals."

Denvy snorted. "One does not understand the reasoning of the Dragon."

"Old one, if you do not understand your enemy, then you will never win your war."

That was something he could not refute, but his stomach turned at the thought of ever being able to comprehend the Dragon. Hazanin-*sama* had battled the beast for so long, and he had watched the Time Master decay into nothing but a shadow of a great warrior. He never wanted that, not for himself, not for Khamsin, not for Zinkx.

The Dragon had taken far too much—

"Zafiashid, can you not hear them crying? The Simoon are in pain…" His eyes turned to the window once more. "Utillia has become a den where Elementals are held captive, Kattamonts fight in pits, and someone can buy a child for a barrel of Mist. This, this is not my home…"

The queen's paw startled him as it cupped his cheek, bringing his attention towards the glow of her blue eyes. "Then you should never have left," she whispered.

"It was more complicated than that," Denvy grumbled. "It was war. I had to go."

"And what about those you left behind?"

He wanted to look away, to hide the shame he was sure was reflected in his furrowed brow and sagged shoulders, but her stare was too intense. It was as though she was dreamathic and able to pierce through the barriers erected in his mind. Of course it was impossible for her to do so—yet there she was, capturing his attention as though he were once more a cub.

"It wasn't as though they couldn't look after themselves."

"I simply ask, old one," Zafiashid lowered her paw, smiling tenderly, "because I want to know if you have the habit of running away when someone needs you."

Denvy frowned, aware suddenly of the attention of his cubs to their conversation. Zafiashid's question was one he was sure many had wanted to ask him for centuries: young Lord Jarid Telvon, little Chance of Palace-Town, Healer Raphael of the House of Flames… Zinkx. Yet he had never gone back, never had to face those he had left behind to confront their questions, their anger, their frustration at his abandonment. Denvy raised his paw, clutching it against the yoke, choking back the pain as his skin met the metal and the enchantments therein. If only it was not binding his mind so tightly, he might be able to know where Zinkx was, whether he had found his way back to the House of Flames. He could have found out what was happening there and learnt the fate of those he loved, like Titus' dear wife and children.

Squeezing shut his eyes, Denvy held back the swell of tears.

Mayhap the young queen sitting beside him was right. He did run from those who needed him, but fear had been following him for as long as he could remember, like the echoing blast of the nuclear bombs erupting in the distance. He could still feel their heat. Still feel the horror, the terror, the utter shock from centuries ago.

It was enough to make him want to turn tail and run, even now.

He bowed his head, looking down at the queen tucked against his side.

"I truly hope I don't," he muttered.

Zafiashid took his paw, gripping it firmly. "Think about it, Denvy, and tell me someday."

He startled as the carriage eased to a halt. Beside him Ki'b unfurled herself from the little ball she had huddled into, her wide eyes staring at the carriage door. The meagre light that bled through the curtains no doubt reminded her of the bleak trickles of sunlight they had lived by within the wagon.

Zafiashid's paw rested on his jittering leg. "This is it," she murmured.

"Indeed, it would appear so." Denvy frowned. He looked at Clive as Ki'b slid into the seat to join Penny. "You three know what to do. Find Nixlye. Stay with her."

Clive nodded. "I can find Jythal anywhere." Denvy slapped open the door as he heard the key turn in the lock. He lunged out, startling the Iposti escorting them. Zafiashid smirked at the neutral. "We are ready. Do lead the way now that you have accosted us into this nonsense."

The robed Kattamont turned sharply, snapping out orders, but the neutrals surrounding them seemed unwilling to touch them. They slowed to a saunter, much to the annoyance of the petite little priest.

"Is that the fighting-pit?" Denvy frowned as he looked up at the lording building they were heading for. "And here I was expecting something grander."

"Whatever do you mean. This is magnificent!" Zafiashid's tail flicked him sharply.

Denvy snorted. Magnificent was hardly the word he would have used to describe the welded together, shambled structure reaching towards the darkened sky-sea. Wood and metal bent into cruel shapes, making the circular construction, highlighted by glittering flags under Mist lanterns. A stark difference to the lush, oceanic coral world his people had once inhabited. Always it had been moving and dancing with the swell of thick air. He could still picture the schools of fish weaving through rows of streaming grass, cubs playfully chasing after them, fan-tails and air-gills shimmering brightly. This monstrosity was hardly a reflection on the beauty his people had once called home, but perhaps if he tilted his head to one side—Denvy smiled slightly.

Yes, he could see it. The wood sticking free of the metal structure had once been carved and joined together to create the illusion of a coral tree, growing around the metal.

They had tried, at least for a time, to hold onto the past.

"Just because you are old and have seen many things does not give you reason to criticize our fighting-pits." Zafiashid huffed beside him.

"Oh, no, my dear." Denvy followed the Iposti through the crowd. "This world is simply very new to me."

"It is like you have become young again, old one."

He looked upwards, to the great opening of the fighting-pits they strolled so casually through, and his fur spiked up his spine, loosening the feathers of his tail. Blood. He smelt blood. The sensation in his stomach became a terrible, twisting snake. Glancing at Zafiashid, he breathed in deeply, steadying his nerves. He was not the only one going into battle. He had to figure out a way to give her enough incentive to return, unharmed. Alive.

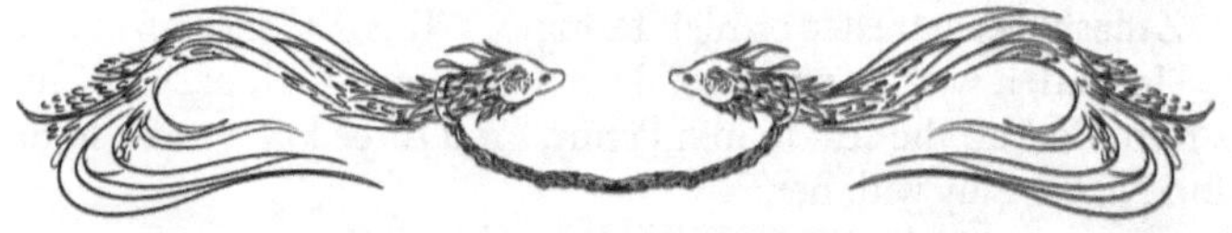

The sound of the crowd chanting vibrated the panels of the floor as Zafiashid paced before the pit doors. They were the flimsiest of barriers between her and the arena. Her body burned in its anticipation for battle, an anxious thrill weaving its way up her spine, tingling across her skin to spike her fur and fan out her air-gills. How many sol-cycles had it been since she had fought in a pit? Too long. The very idea now—it brought back memories of who she was: a warrior, a queen, a rage of fury across the burning-sea.

Zafiashid breathed in deeply, blinking in the light bleeding through the wooden panels of the doors. Distantly, against the chanting, she could hear the Iposti speaking the rules of combat to the crowd.

This was a waste of time. As if those who enjoyed the sport of watching two Kattamonts fight did not already know the rules. When was she to fight?

Her nose twitched. Denvy's calming scent—sweet wet grass and moist, ancient forests—drifted over her. She closed her eyes briefly, lingering in the comfort it brought, before turning towards the prince.

He stood in the small entrance of the fighting-pit's waiting chamber, smiling with his cocky grin. How his smile made him look like a cub she had no idea, but it was as though the sol-cycles vanished from him.

An Iposti appeared behind him in the shadows and her air-gills flattened. Denvy had managed the impossible to see her. No one was permitted in the presence of a queen or princess before battle, and yet here he was, with a single coerced Iposti watching them.

He chuckled, gesturing to the young Iposti.

"This neutral thinks my fur is pretty."

The Iposti gasped loudly. "I never said that!"

"You did not have to." Denvy smirked. "I know you think it."

"Fine! You…you have a few minutes. Make it quick." The Iposti scampered away, tail between her legs. Zafiashid watched in amusement.

"Nixlye is right," she murmured. "If left alone, you would conquer all Utillia by standing there, showing off your air-gills."

"Perks of being fairy-born." Denvy shrugged nonchalantly, then his demeanour shifted, his eyes glancing to the entrance. He reached for her paws, clasping them tightly.

"You will be careful, won't you?"

She smiled. "This is different, having a prince concerned about me."

"Yes, well, this entire situation is unfamiliar…" Denvy muttered.

"Listen, Nixlye and Jythal already know, but our rendezvous is a Kelib Tavern called Evergreen. Head for the back door. The woman will ask you your name—tell her it is *Krrirren*."

"Queen…" Denvy chuckled. "Of course."

"If you run into difficulty, they will be accommodating." Zafiashid squeezed his paw and released her grip, only for him to tighten his paws around hers.

"You are right, dear. I have been running away for a long time."

Zafiashid bit her lip. "Denvy, you don't have to explain—"

He shook his head and gently wrapped a string of silver around her wrist. Her chest clenched as she fingered it. Tears lingered on the edges of her lashes as she breathed in sharply. It was so beautiful, more beautiful than all the jewels she had ever bartered for, or fought for, or won herself.

"I saw something terrible, love. I saw those I considered my people, my creators, my family, burn, and I was afraid. I was afraid of the pain of losing those I loved, so I decided to never love again, and I only ever ran and kept running."

She dared to look up, into his emerald eyes, set in the golden fur of his gradually returning mane. Her paw moved on his own accord, brushing aside the beads Ki'b had woven through strands of fur. "Are you still afraid?" she whispered.

"I doubt I will ever stop being afraid."

"Will you keep running?

The crowd had begun chanting beyond the gate, a constant beat, but she only felt the thudding of their hearts, racing against her rib cage as Denvy pressed his forehead against hers.

"No. You have shown me how to stand firm."

She smiled. "Then I will win." She swung away, grabbing her blade. "And you shall be my prize."

Zafiashid looked back as the gate creaked open, letting in the blinding light of the outside world. The prince leant against the wall, arms folded wearily over his chest, still wearing his smile. Her chest expanded with immense joy.

He shook his head. "No one has ever tried winning me, you know."

Zafiashid grinned. "Then I shall be the first and I shall break this foolish enchantment upon you."

Ki'b looked around, hopping about on her toes. She had thought Ishabal was huge, that the *Lawless Child* was a wonderful world of its own, but nothing could have ever prepared her for the size of Threnthton.

The Wind City ran in endless streets that built upon each other like links in a chain, with the thrum and beat of windmills singing a lonesome, aching tune she could feel deep within her chest. It did nothing to ease the fear eating at her stomach. Ki'b curled her toes, wishing she could feel soil, just this once, and know its comforting, grounding touch, to reassure her that Queen Zafiashid would be fine.

"Ki'b…" Clive's hand gently settled on her shoulder. He had grown stronger over the months on the *Lawless Child*, most likely from all the strenuous work he did. Callouses now covered some of the scars that would never go away.

"Ki'b, it will be all right. Queen Zafiashid is very strong."

"I know." She twisted her fingers around her necklace. "These pit-fights sound so very scary."

"Scary, yah, but don't Kelib men do something similar?" Clive brushed back his curls from his eyes.

She frowned. Perhaps they did. Somewhere in her mind she had a recollection of people fighting, but it was all so dim. Everything before the darkness of the box and Khwaja Denvy's voice was shadowy.

"I don't really know. I never really met any Kelib men in Pennadot."

"Is that normal for Kelib women?"

"I don't…really…know that either."

"Well, you're brimming with information, aren't ya?"

"How about you try it!" She swung a punch his way and he nimbly ducked, laughing.

"Shhh, you two!" Penny hissed from the doorway she hid behind, keeping watch.

The world outside their small hideaway busily moved on, the large bodies of Kattamonts thundering past, some with whirring and hissing Mist limbs clanking as they hit the metal road. Humans scurried between carriages, bearing heavy burdens, looking like pack-mules.

Ki'b crouched down beside Penny. "Do you see them?"

"No." Penny shook her head. "Wait." She paused. "There! It's Nixlye!"

Ki'b felt the immense relief upon catching sight of the young queen wheeling through the chaos, skilfully missing the carriages and moving bodies, Jythal beside her, swinging his stick side to side. The urge to dash out and greet them was strong, but their order to remain in the small vacant shop had been very strict and she bit her tongue, waiting patiently as they drew closer.

Nixlye swept through the door, swinging her chair around. She dumped a bag on the floor and Clive dived for it, sorting through the confiscated weapons they had been stripped of.

He whooped in glee. "How did you get them back?"

Nixlye smirked. "Twisted some arms, broke a few jaws."

"We asked. Nicely. Drawing attention to ourselves would not be beneficial to the plan, would it?" Jythal chided his mate.

Ki'b smiled as she refitted her daggers beneath her coat. Jythal dangled something in front of her nose, a sweet little wooden necklace. She looked up at the prince as he passed others to Penny and Clive.

"What are these?" Clive held up the wooden amulet.

"They're Haven Hall market passes." Nixlye slipped on her own. "You need them to get through the Haven Hall gates. Cost a few coins. They'll allow us to blend into the market crowd today, which, I must say, is rather busy." She frowned in thought. "Hopefully my wheelchair won't be too noticeable. I'd rather not use up the Mist in my prosthetics before I have to."

Clive scrunched up his face. "Threnthton is really different from Ishabal. There were lots of disabled people about. Why is it so different here?"

Nixlye's voice was gentle and even, though there was a hint of a deep sorrow. "The Outer Sectors live beyond the reach of the Iposti. Here, in the Wind Cities and the Clustered Isles, the Iposti frown upon anything they judge as misfit."

"But then what about you and Jythal? Doesn't that mean you're in danger?" Clive looked from one to the other anxiously.

"Usually, yes. But deep burning-sea divers quite often lose their limbs and they must sell their wares somewhere. Threnthton is still mutual territory between the Ruling Prides. It is the major centre of trade."

"So, basically, you're hoping you'll be safe because money is really important?" Clive frowned.

"If all goes well, then, yes." Nixlye chuckled. "I think I heard something about a large haul coming up from Sector Eighteen, Level Six. Must have everyone excited." Jythal leant on his cane. "No one has been that deep in that sector before. It will work to our advantage today."

Nixlye whistled. "Indeed, that is a feat. Pity Aaldryn isn't here. He would have loved a chance to check that out. Ah, well, we have a mission. Come along, my little snoops, let's go treasure hunting!" She clapped her hands together. "I have always wanted to break back into a Haven Hall, ever since I broke out of one."

Ki'b covered her mouth before laughter erupted. Nixlye's mischievous grin was contagious.

"Sounds like you are conspiring merrily in here. Did I miss anything?" Khwaja Denvy's low rumbling tones startled Ki'b. She twisted, catching her breath. The old lion stood in the doorway, waving a paw to fan himself down. He looked hot, and a bit flushed, as though he had been running to catch up with them. The heavy yoke still weighed him down, making even simple things so hard for him.

"Khwaja Denvy! You made it." Ki'b hugged him tightly. She was heaved off her feet and set on his hip as he moved through the door, glancing back outside to inspect the crowd.

"How is Mother?" Jythal inquired.

"Her usual intimidating self." Denvy accepted his water-sword and the wooden amulet. "Come. We may not have much time. I doubt Zafiashid will be able to resist finishing off the fight for long."

"Yes. Mother is never one to let anything linger." Nixlye sighed.

Ki'b watched as Denvy's lips drew back into a warm smile. "She is rather forthright." He motioned with his free paw. "Lead the way, my dear."

The young queen gripped the wheels of her chair. "Right, let's do this."

Clive leapt into the air, cheering loudly. Ki'b shook her head as the boy snatched hold of Penny's hand and charged out the door, leaving them to follow into the mayhem beyond their hideaway. Her eyes could not rest on a single sight. She was glad to be high in Khwaja Denvy's arms otherwise she would have been so small and lost amongst the ankles of the bigger folk around her, unable to see anything.

Nixlye lead them towards a beautifully sculpted building, with many windmills rising from the metal framework of its woven roof. It was alight with Mist fires, glittering brightly under multi-coloured glass. Her breath caught in her chest and she leant against Khwaja Denvy's shoulder.

"Is that the Haven Hall?"

"Indeed, it is. While Kattamonts appear to have long forgotten the days in which we swam the great forest oceans of Utillia, building our homes amongst the corals, something remains within the depths of our memories. All the buildings I have seen seem to pay homage in some way to the beauty of what once was."

"It must have been so different," Ki'b said. She studied the market surrounding the skirts of the Haven Hall. She had never seen a Temple of the Sun in Pennadot, but Clive loved to describe the one he had come from, in a tiny town along the Spider Road. He had said it was smooth and round, with glowing rocks inside a big circle, and people would gather inside the circle to feel safe.

"Haven means safe, doesn't it?" Ki'b tugged on Denvy's earing. "Are all these people selling here because they feel safe?"

"Haven has a few different meanings in Basic. Since I have not been in Utillia for such a long time, I am not sure, my dear, about the changing role of the Haven Hall in the culture of my people. Haven is also a word for port, anchorage, harbour…Kattamonts have always been sailors. It is why we found such kinship with the Zaprexes." Denvy looked towards the sky-sea. "They sailed to places we could only ever dream of." He glanced back, his bushy eyebrows lifting. "Should be interesting to see what the Iposti are up to, heh?"

He let her slide down from his hip-bags and Ki'b jogged to join Jythal and Penny beside a wall. It was smooth and metal, inset with panes of coloured glass, and she peered through one. There was a courtyard beyond, void of people, with a path leading down into darkness.

Jythal rested a paw on her head. "Keep watch for me. This is going to require a bit of work on Clive's and my part. Denvy, think you can stand there and look intimidating along with Nixlye?"

"I did not know Nixlye knew how to be intimidating," Denvy joked.

She huffed, clapping him firmly on the tail junction. "Please. I was born with this ferocious look on my face."

Ki'b shook her head, half trying to keep watch on the passing patrons, while her curiosity kept her glancing back, catching sight of Clive placing Rune-stones against the surface of the wall. Warmth tickled her bare feet as Jythal and Clive held out their arms, channelling the energy. The surge of heat spread up her ankles, catching a breath in her throat. The wall shimmered faintly, losing its solidity and Ki'b began to feel oddly ill in her stomach.

Jythal motioned to Clive. "Go through and hold it open on the other end."

With a bounce to his step, Clive leapt through the opening they had formed.

"All right," Jythal urged, "Penny, you next. Hurry, hurry, I cannot keep these open long even with Clive's help." He pushed her through with the butt of his cane and Ki'b dashed up, ready to lunge across after Penny.

"Hurry. Guards," Nixlye hissed.

Ki'b flung herself through, feeling a pop before she landed on the other side, rolling across smooth pavement. She landed beside Penny. Khwaja Denvy looked cut in half as he poked through the opening, then all of him stepped out. His fur was spiked, hinting at his cautiousness. He thrust his arms back, heaving Nixlye, wheelchair and all, through the wall, settling her down gently.

Nixlye did not wait. "Penny, Ki'b, come with me. Quickly, this way. Jythal and Clive will follow. Come." She sped down the path. They dashed after her swift wheels, meeting a set of stairs. Ki'b covered her mouth before she could cry out in alarm; Nixlye did not stop at the edge, simply spun her wheels expertly, taking the stairs as though they were no obstacle at all.

Penny pushed Ki'b sharply, urging her to take the lead. She followed Nixlye into the enfolding, cool darkness of the tunnel. Lights, dim at first, lit their way, growing sharper the further they advanced. Ki'b rubbed at her arms, assuring herself she was not in the box. Besides, the air was so cool and refreshing, it tasted almost sweet on her tongue. She focused on the scent, letting it linger against the palate of her mouth.

"Ah, there it is!" The damp air muffled Nixlye's voice. "This is the back door into the kitchens. It's always in the same place." Her tail flicked. "Penny, have you a light on you?"

"Oh, yes, wait a minute. Clive gave me a Rune."

Ki'b blinked against the shiny rock Penny held up, attached to the tip of a small stick. She released a strangled scream at the sight appearing over the shoulder of her Human sister—a towering Kattamont prince. He lunged. Nixlye shoved Penny to one side. The light skittered over the pavement as Penny dropped it.

Nixlye ducked a swing from the Kattamont's fist. Armour rattled in the murky light as the scuffle continued. Ki'b dashed forward, running around Nixlye's chair. The Kattamont loomed over them, air-gills spread in a haloed rage. She dived for his ankles, forcing him to stagger away from Nixlye. He snagged her hair, claws dragging through the skin of her scalp.

Ki'b cried out. She tossed in the Kattamont's grip, all thought of her daggers forgotten in her panic. The jolt was sudden as Khwaja Denvy's golden fur blurred past and she was dropped, landing roughly on the ground. Nixlye snatched her up and held her against her chest. Ki'b turned, eyes wide, staring at Khwaja Denvy. He heaved the guard off his foot-paws. The Kattamont's skull met the wall as Khwaja Denvy gripped him around the throat. His legs dangled in the air and air-gills slapped, but slowly they sank limply over his neck and his body slumped.

Denvy set the guard down gently. Jythal stepped forward, checking beneath his air-gills before setting a stick upon his forehead, carved with faintly glowing Runes.

Jythal sat back on his heels.

"This is a prince. I thought male Kattamonts were not permitted on Iposti grounds." While he could not see Nixlye, his full body turned towards his mate.

"Maybe something has changed since I was in the order. I hope they're not trying to turn themselves into queens; that would be disastrous. The balance would be entirely thrown out."

Denvy scratched his chin. "I imagine there are barely enough brotherhoods to go around."

"Princes are already in high demand," Nixlye agreed.

Jythal stood. "He should be no problem now. The Rune will keep him sedated." He slapped out his cane.

"Thank you, Khwaja Denvy," Ki'b murmured, tugging on his sleeve.

Denvy smiled. "Keeping you all safe is my duty, dear one."

"Whoa, Kattamonts run fast!" Clive suddenly appeared, heaving for air. "Did I miss anything?" He bent over, holding his stomach. "Argh, cramp. Hey. Nixlye, do all Haven Halls have these passages? They're awesome!"

Ki'b rolled her eyes. Typical. Clive missed all the action and now fired off questions like an erupting volcano.

Nixlye answered patiently. "They are for ceremonial purposes during the Festival of Winds. The layouts of Haven Halls tend to remain similar overall. They follow the Wind Flows. This tunnel, though, leads to the kitchen."

"Oh, a bit like the Temples back in Pennadot are plotted to the Celestial Calendar."

Nixlye shrugged. "Something like that. Now. Let's see if I can still remember my training." She rolled her chair forward, feeling the surface of the door with her hands.

Ki'b admired the coiled maze of twisted, branch-like netting, woven together to craft the shape of a door. Her fingers itched to reach out and feel the tiny little hairs on the soft, barky surfaces, tinted bright yellows and pinks, for, just like the drums of the forests in Pennadot, she was sure an instrument whispered to her.

"Astounding…" Denvy muttered, his whiskers twitching. "You are communicating through touch, like we used to. You are speaking to the coral."

Nixlye stirred at his words. Her long lashes flickered in the dim light as she blinked, looking his way with a slight frown. "This is coral? All the doors in the Haven Hall are made of this. It is one of the first things those born into the Iposti Order must learn."

"How were you ever allowed to leave?"

A shadow of a smile graced Nixlye's lips. "Despite what Mother may think of them, the Iposti are not all murderous scum. Some are simply kindly scholars who desire only to live in peace, away from the riffraff of the world. The neutral who saved me was one of those; she wanted for me to be able to live freely the life I wished, to forge my own path, as she would say." Nixlye sighed. "She liked to tell me that the Element of Wind was the element of freedom and the Iposti had forgotten that."

"Ah," Denvy rested his paws on his hip-bags, "there are those who still speak gems of wisdom even in the darkest of places."

The young queen nodded. "Something like that." She hummed a soft tune in the back of her throat. Ki'b tapped along with the melody, losing herself to the flow. She gasped, alarmed at the sight of the door's knotted rivets curling back on themselves. Nixlye withdrew her wet hands and rolled away. An entrance into a warm, Mist-lit room welcomed them. Ki'b curled her toes as the heat brushed past her, tickling her skin. Denvy poked his head into the ingress. His claws chipped at the wooden texture of the doorframe as he anxiously drew back, breathing out steadily.

"Seems we are clear. Let's go."

They moved as one group into the Haven Hall. Ki'b rubbed her fingers against her necklace.

Her stomach knotted. Flicking her gaze around the hallway, Ki'b bit her lip, tugging on dry skin. The tiny seed of bravery growing within her had not yet bloomed; it felt as though it was wilting with each step she took, and her trembling hands slid away from her necklace, latching on to Khwaja Denvy's paw, squeezing it.

Her shaking breath caught in her throat. The rocks that made up the warm floor were uneasy against her skin, whispering unsavoury things; telling her to walk back the way she had come. Had her feet been on soil, and not artificial ground, she was sure she would have felt it screaming.

Khwaja Denvy Maz - Dream Master of the Northlands

KEJOEN -TROQ - ELOIKO - DAYTS
THE DWELLER PRINCES

CHAPTER SEVEN

The warmth of the inn's crackling fire chased away the chill of the rain battering down outside. Since his return to Pennadot it had been near constant, the rain. The ash-cloud from Avalon's crash would take several decades to dissipate. He was grateful that the sky-sea of Kemet had contained the nuclear fallout from the Cataclysm otherwise he would be dealing with an entirely different disaster.

"When the folks of this town started talking about a Starborn staying here, my hope was not high..." A melodious voice stirred him from his tumbling thoughts.

Disgleirio turned in his seat. A Kimwyn man stood in the doorway, drenched in black rain, with a young Obilb lad clutching at his coat.

"Selwyn, it is good to see you. Is that your son?"

"Yes. This is Ewyni. Ewyni, this is your uncle, Prince Disgleirio."

"I am not a prince, Selwyn, any more than you are. We both abdicated the throne."

He studied his brother. Gone was the Starborn shine that had once haloed him. Replaced with the humming melody of data that fed through the ambience of the Secondary Realm surrounding them. "I see that you went through with Gifu's procedure."

"I see that you are still a White Star."

Disgleirio bowed his head, glancing back at the flickering flames. He reached out, letting them play across his bright skin, much to the wonderment of the inn's other patrons.

Selwyn crouched beside him. "Disgleirio, you may very well be the only Starborn left alive. Not only are you a prince, you are Pennadot's future."

"Dead and alive at the same time." He chuckled. "Call me Schrödinger's Cat."

Jarvis felt like he was floating in clouds.

Are you lost, Protector?

Jarvis was vaguely aware of Titus calling his name.

"I think my receiver is picking up something."

That was strange. He was on his back, staring up at the eerie light of the giant Zaprex crystal that loomed over the Dwellers' tent village on the observation decks of the skyscraper. Its glow had long ago changed from natural blue to an unnerving purple tinge with veins of red. The protector was alarmed by that. He knew what it meant—gradual contamination. The entire system needed purification. His fingers twitched, wishing he could do so but he could not; he had no programming for such a task.

Are you lost, Protector?

Jarvis rolled over.

"No," he spoke softly, "I am not lost."

He yelped as the world tipped suddenly. He flung out his arms, expecting to land sharply on his head as everything turned upside down. Jarvis gaped in confusion, his processor core spinning madly as it whirred with alarm. A blinking image flickered in front of him.

His heart constricted, as though a hand had seized it, tightening it in a vice grip. If he had never seen the tiny Key before he would have panicked at the sight of the dainty, static Zaprex image.

You first have to be lost to ever be found.

"Who are you?"

I am the mirror upon which you walk, child-bot, the many hues of a single sunbeam.

The apparition smiled through the static. He could barely make out its image as it blurred.

You heard me.

"All right, so I heard you. I'll ask again. Who are you?" Jarvis held out his hands.

I am the creator of currents, the great shield of Atum-Ra.

Something shifted within his mind, files being accessed, rifled through and analysed as he stared at the wavering apparition. The protector bot had blocks of memories, names, places, and concepts he could not comprehend—at least not yet. The flickering of images across his lenses halted on a sky-sea scene, filled with immense clouds that slowly shifted to reveal the pristine gleam of a flying city, coated in glass. Jarvis blinked slowly. A crackle sparked down his spine, making him step forward, reaching out automatically.

"*Mothership:_Tikal_of_Rainbows,*" his voice warbled, "have you come to take me home?"

There is no home, child-bot. Home burned. We are alone.

"No! We aren't alone." Jarvis clutched the Map piece under his shirt. "The Key is here, and he is going to save the world. I need to get this crystal-tech to Coltarian and meet him!"

The apparition cocked its head to one side. *So, the Creators have returned.*

Jarvis slumped back. "Are you angry that they left?'

Angry? No, child-bot. I am sad. I know the cost of restarting engines; all ships know the cost. You, too, in time, will come to know the true cost for our Creators. The weakening image shifted away.

Jarvis stepped forward. "Wait, please, wait. If you are Tikal then can't you help me?"

I told you, child-bot, you first have to be lost to be found. My mirrors are everywhere; eventually one will find you. I tire. This direct line is dying. It looked down briefly, creasing its brow as it studied the glow of the crystal beneath them. *You should inform these fleshlings that their home is becoming unsuitable for them. I am unsure how much longer the shields will be maintained in this sector. It might be another few generations, or a few days.*

"Something tells me they're not going to leave no matter what I say."

Irrational creatures, living here. Do they not see what it is doing to them?

"To be honest, I don't think they care."

The apparition's image suddenly sharpened, and he saw clear, white eyes, surrounded by twirling pink hair, set amongst rich crystal jewels. It was breathtaking, the sweet impish features, wearing such rich, formal attire, fit for royalty.

They should care, child-bot, if they knew what was happening further inland, to the forsaken children! They should care! My mirrors are many. I know what is happening and I am disgusted. Fine. I will solve this myself! I cannot promise they will approve of my actions!

Jarvis' stomach flipped as the world swung right-side up.

"Oof." He landed roughly in Titus' arms, fighting to wake up.

"Jarvis! Laddie, there you are. Back with us again."

"Sorry. Sorry."

"Rythrya, what happened to you?" Aaldryn asked beside them, air-gills ruffled.

Jarvis rubbed his face. There was no strange, pink-haired hologram, and the world was back on its correct axis.

Except—Jarvis turned his gaze back to the Zaprex skeletons.

Eloiko waved a paw, concern on his face. "How long has it been since the child has eaten a decent meal? Please, we would be honoured if you would break fast with us."

Aaldryn inclined his head. "Thank you. Jarvis, come, let's get you inside where you can rest. It is all right."

"No." Jarvis remained rooted to the spot, despite the tug Aaldryn gave his shoulder.

"Jarvis. Please. Eloiko is right. You probably fainted from hunger."

"I refuse to enter this abode while my Creators' bodies hang over their door."

Eloiko paused at the entrance, looking up with a surprised glance as though he had never given the ancient relics a passing thought. "We mean no disrespect towards the Zaprexes," he said. "We did our best to preserve them in a manner befitting them. We honour them. They protect us." He motioned to the entrance and slowly Jarvis allowed himself to be led inside.

"What do they protect you from?" Jarvis glanced over his shoulder.

"That's actually a very good question," Titus said.

"Monsters."

"Monsters?" Aaldryn spluttered out.

"Indeed. Whenever the monsters come, the pride gathers in this tent." Eloiko waved his paws. "They cannot get in because the Zaprexes protect us."

Jarvis sat where he could look out of the tent doorway and see the crystal hanging over the village like an artificial sun. The song it released was more vibrant now; it coiled through his philepcon liquid like an urging call, drawing him towards something—only he could not understand what. His fingers wrapped tightly around the map piece, cold to the touch.

Aaldryn felt uneasy. He had seen strange behaviour before from those who dived the Burning-Sea, only this was more than being witness to the disturbing fit his little brother had just experienced. Was it just hunger, or a reaction to the Zaprex skeletons?

Jarvis still sat close to Titus, his whole body trembling. Aaldryn knew his brother was trying to control the protector bot within him—or perhaps it was more than that. He had seemed terrified of the Zaprex skeletons. Perhaps because they were so perfect they almost looked like they were still alive.

They are indeed in perfect condition, Khamsin commented. *Have you any idea how rare those are?*

Titus murmured beside Aaldryn, "Have you ever found any Zaprex skeletons in your archaeological digs?"

"No," he whispered back. "But it is possible I have never dived deep enough. As far as we can tell from the records, half of Utillia was covered in Zaprex cities. That was a lot of Zaprex population."

Titus' brow furrowed. "Yah, that be what's worrying me."

"I've only ever reached level three, the ship-level. Level thirty is the city-scape level, level fifty is the bottom. It's a very deep sea." He hoped his words were reassuring, but Titus' frown only grew deeper.

Eloiko re-entered the tent, followed by Dayts, who bore platters of bread and meat, butter and milk, which he placed on a low table. Jarvis remained motionless, eyes bright and sharp. Aaldryn was sure he could hear the boy's body whirring and clicking as it processed everything around them furiously.

A shrill voice suddenly cut the air. "Papa! I want to see our new brothers!"

Aaldryn turned sharply, his tail unfurling and his air-gills lowering around his neck at the high-pitched squeal. A blur of yellow whizzed past them, leaping into Eloiko's arms. The prince staggered back, steadying himself on his tails.

"Sorry, brother, he got away from me." Through the entrance a young half-breed prince appeared. He greeted Aaldryn with a smile that glinted in pale blue eyes. Aaldryn stared. He had never thought it possible to look at a half-breed version of himself, albeit a few sol-cycles younger and without a mane, but a Silvertide half-breed nonetheless. The prince held out a paw. Aaldryn accepted the odd Human greeting.

"Troq Silvertide."

Aaldryn grinned. "You have our pelt."

"Nice to meet you, cousin." Troq's tail bumped his playfully. "Thank you for aiding my brothers in dispatching the fiend that terrorised our pride."

"Ah, well." Aaldryn ruffled his air-gills. "I had little to do with that. Titus is the Hunter amongst us."

"At least you let our alpha come back in one piece. He tends to get a little carried away."

"Just a little?" Aaldryn turned to Eloiko with a raised eyebrow. "I'm sure I'll feel an ache or two myself for the next week."

Eloiko laughed. "Serves you right." He approached, swinging the cub over his shoulders. "This is my son, Kejoen." Eloiko released the cub, who tore around the rugs across the home-tent floor on all fours in a blur of fiery colours and twin tails. He was a replica of his father, yet the colours that tipped his air-gills and fan-tail had to have reflected the queen who had mothered him.

Aaldryn could feel the echoing hollowness within the home-tent. There was no one to replace those who had been lost with both queen and princess killed. He studied Eloiko, wondering how it was that the alpha was maintaining order in such a large pride without the influence of a queen or a princess; there surely had to be several neutrals within the pride fighting for the positions. He had never heard of a pride ruled by a brotherhood alone, though it was not impossible.

Troq sent him a smile. Aaldryn puffed out his air-gills, glad he did not have to play diplomat within a brotherhood. Had this been any other situation, with a queen or princess, he was sure he would be failing terribly—but then again he had to wonder what sort of queen the Dwellers Pride's had been. She must have been a vagabond like his mother and she might have been just as accommodating.

"Please," Eloiko said, gesturing to the food laid out before them, "eat with us, brothers."

"Out of curiosity," Titus began, "what do these monsters look like—the ones the Zaprexes protect yeh from? Are they anything like the one that killed yer queen? It would be helpful to know if yeh're having trouble with Twizels."

Silence. Aaldryn pinned his ears against his head. The silence was awful. He should have warned Titus not to mention anything about the deaths, especially in front of the cub; they were still in mourning. Messengers had no shame when it came to speaking of death, but

Kattamonts took great care and honour in respecting those who did pass through the Osiris Gate.

Eloiko breathed out slowly and gently shook his head. He smoothed a paw over his son's head. "No, Titus, they are not Twizels. Our queen and princess would be alive today if we could have hidden from that fiend you killed. These monsters are from the depths of the lower levels of the cities."

Aaldryn's eyes widened. "Machines?"

"We're not sure." Troq shrugged, tearing a piece of meat apart and passing it to Kejoen. "We've never actually seen them."

"And those who do venture down into the lower levels of the city rarely return with their minds intact to tell us anything but nonsense." Dayts shuddered. "They go insane."

"We only lead Messengers beyond the safety-zone. You folk are foolhardy enough to try and reach your homeland." Troq sipped his drink. "Which I presume you are trying to do. I mean, you would not be trying to cross Yrva Krv were it not for a dire reason."

Titus sighed.

"Please." Troq leant forward. "Tell me, is it to do with signs we have seen in the distance, of the missing Obelisks of Coltarian?"

Titus' shoulders slumped. He set down his mug, rubbing his gloved hands wearily against his eyes. "That bad, is it, that yeh can see it from this far away?"

Eloiko rested his elbows on the table. "We are dwellers. We live in the ancient ruins of the Zaprexes; we know a little of how to use their technology. Enough to make the windows see-far. We can track much of what happens beyond Yrva Krv. It has been troubling, observing from a distance, yet not knowing what the cause of such unrest has been."

"When the great monuments of the Zaprexes fall, it can only mean ill for the Messengers." Troq wrapped his tail around his neck as if warding off a chill. "The war, it would appear, is not going well."

"It has not been going well for a long time. We win few battles these days." Titus drew back, closing his eyes. He settled his hands in his lap. "I was sent to Pennadot in search of my former Commander. He had been directed by the Dreamers who Dream to seek out the Key. I was unable to find him, but he did leave a message. It was full of ill news for the Northlands." He glanced towards Jarvis and pointed at Aaldryn. "We are hoping to reach the House of Flames with a warning. Coltarian is destabilising. Its eruption is due on the Summer Solstice, if any more of the Obelisks fail. When it erupts it will destroy the Borders. We will lose the system the Zaprexes created to sustain life within the Northlands."

"By the Four Winds." Eloiko choked out.

Jarvis lifted his head. "We think Utillia will be the only land that will survive the eruption. The Creator who oversaw Utillia did something to this land that, while it destroyed the whole surface desktop grid, did save the sky-sea." He made a dome shape with his arms. "Coltarian's eruption cannot harm Utillia because its sky-sea remains active. We must get to the House of Flames and tell the Messengers to evacuate. Pennadotians should already be coming over the Northern Border."

"Pennadotian refugees?" Troq breathed out heavily. "This will not bode well for the tentative peace between the prides. Kattamonts are territorial beasts."

"That is going to be the least of our troubles, I believe, but it will be something we will need to deal with in time," Eloiko muttered.

"Yes." Troq nodded. "For now it would seem your mission is of utmost importance." He smiled, curling his paws together. "We can take you as far as the safety-zone. After that, you will need to be on your own. It is the only way that we know of through Yrva Krv."

Aaldryn shook his head. "I cannot ask you to risk your lives—"

Eloiko raised his paw. "You helped us, we now shall help you."

Titus inclined his head. "Point us in the right direction and we will walk forward. We're Messengers; it is what we do."

Eloiko rose. "After you have eaten your fill, and rested to your desires, Troq and I will see to your supplies and take you down into the city's depths. We're the best at burning-sea diving. Hopefully the way hasn't caved in since last we went through. Dayts, you've got the pride until we get back."

Dayts flopped back dramatically. Eloiko threw Kejoen at the larger prince. "Attack him, little warrior."

Aaldryn smiled at the scene and the laughter from both prince and cub. He wondered whether, by the time he returned, he would be welcomed by the same laughter of cubs in his own pride. His air-gills spread with hope at the thought and he turned to Eloiko, bowing his head to the young prince. "Thank you, Eloiko."

Jarvis shrugged into the thick coat, wondering what foreign animal had provided the skin for such fine work. It was warm and comfortable, reminding him of his wonderful bed on the *Lawless Child*. He wondered if he would ever return to it. He sighed through his teeth. Master Titus was conversing with Troq over their hip-bags of supplies and he kept finding his gaze trailing back to him, unnerved by his presence.

It was off-putting, and he was unsure why, when Aaldryn and Jythal had made him feel so safe. Troq was not at all threatening and he seemed rather nice, perhaps too nice.

But they had recently lost their queen, and their princess—so maybe he was reading into the prince's hidden grief a little too much.

He almost squeaked when Aaldryn's paw settled on his shoulder and a pulse of wind rippled past him. "You all right, little brother?"

"Don't call me that," he growled. He busied himself rechecking his hip-bags: fresh water, Mist, and salt-dried food, the deep burning-sea city-diving equipment that Eloiko was donating. He had a sinking feeling it had once belonged to the princess but none of them had argued with the generous offer. By the whispers following them, they were going to need all the aid they could receive. Aaldryn knelt to buckle up his own equipment, making the process look easy from all his sol-cycles of practice.

"You are a member of my Pride now, whether you want to be or not," Aaldryn said quietly. "We are about to embark on a very dangerous dive. I have to be able to trust you. And you have to trust me." He looked into Jarvis' eyes. "Don't you feel it? Distrust towards other Prides—" He pointed his chin towards Troq, raising an eyebrow. "That feeling is natural, Jarvis, even as a Human." Jarvis gaped at Aaldryn as he continued, "I really do not know what causes the phenomenon. Perhaps it is the air of Utillia, but Humans who become integrated into a Kattamont Pride find themselves under the same influences as the bestial race."

That was more fascinating than Aaldryn could possibly have known. Jarvis touched his chin, rubbing it. The first few days Clive, Penny, and Ki'b had been in Utillia they had suffered terribly from the toxic air, and even he had struggled to adapt to it despite his changing physiology. Yet gradually his orphan siblings had improved until the nightmare of being unable to breathe was nothing but a hazy dream.

His eyes shifted towards the panoramic windows surrounding the observation deck, opening to the skyscape view. Hexagons shimmered in patterns across the windows. Faint though they were, he could make out their form, and within the large hexagons smaller ones repeated over and over. He could time his breathing with the looping pattern they made with the swell of the burning-sea sand brushing against the outside surface of the calibrated force-field.

"Do you think it's possible that the sky-sea has been programmed to…" He frowned. No, even the protector bot within him was refusing to accept such a thought. But—was he not proof it could happen?

"Jarvis?" Aaldryn's paw settled on his shoulder. "What is it?"

"Do you think the Creators could program the turrets across Utillia to purposely change Humans and Kelibs to be more like Kattamonts? I mean, it'd make sense, right? You breathe entirely different air to us, so

Humans would have to change physically in order to breathe your air."

Aaldryn rubbed at his air-gills. "If they did, the foresight of such a plan would have been incredible, considering it would not have any effect until now, centuries later. But, also," the prince paused, his gaze turning to the crystal high above them, its ominous glow a foreboding presence, "they would have had to intentionally alter their creations for such a malicious purpose, and I do not think even the Zaprexes could have done that."

"They would have if they knew it would preserve life."

Aaldryn shook his head. "Ah, but how would they have known? Look around, Jarvis. We're mutants. Sure, Humans and Kattamonts can interbreed, Humans and Kelibs can live in Utillia, but can you truly say the results are good? I highly doubt the Zaprexes would have wanted this…"

Jarvis' brow furrowed. "I suppose."

It troubled him, a nibbling feeling in his stomach. If it had not been done on purpose, then was it simply an accidental fluke of creating such a powerful sky-sea that could be sustained beyond the collapse of the Borders? Whoever had diverted all the power from the desktop to the sky-sea could not have known the future results of their actions—and if they had, they had accepted the consequences.

"I guess they really wanted to protect the Kattamonts."

Aaldryn laughed. "Look around, little brother." The prince spread his arms wide, spinning around on his heels. "Is it not obvious that we were good friends with the Zaprexes. They built cities alongside ours."

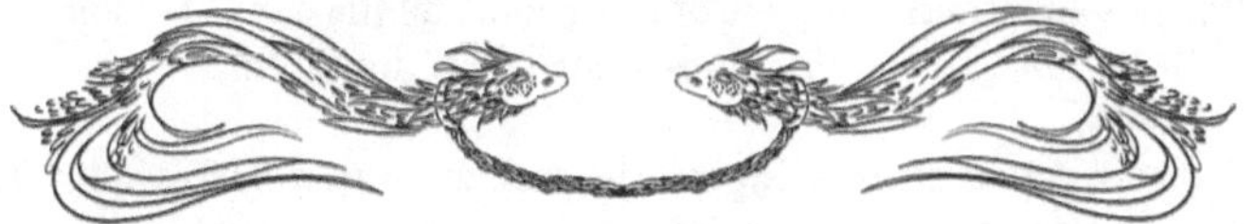

Dayts and Kejoen were waiting at the edge of the village. Jarvis forced a smile as Eloiko swept his cub into his arms, throwing him high into the light of the ever-glowing crystal sun that lit their little world within the walls of the fairy-castle.

"Be good, my little cub, for brother Dayts, yes?"

"Yes, yes, Papa."

Troq and Eloiko bumped tails with Dayts.

"We should be back in a week or so." Eloiko leapt over a fallen beam, calling back, "Keep everyone safe."

Dayts nodded. "Will do."

Jarvis followed the princes over the collapsed metal. He glanced back at the tall Kattamont, holding the fiery little cub in his arms.

"Jarvis. Come along now, no dawdling. We don't want to lose you." Master Titus called out. "I know yeh get easily distracted by things that are all shiny and pretty."

Jarvis rolled his eyes, but he knew the hunter's lightness of tone was an act for the benefit of the Kattamonts. His Master would do all in his power to protect him, so he could get the Map Piece to the Key.

He followed the others into the dark maintenance tunnel. His optical lenses adapted swiftly to the change in the light, latching onto the specks of flowing energy surrounding them. It was nowhere near the level of volatility, and he highly doubted the others would notice it, other than as faint static tickling their skin, but it made his philepcon liquid sing as he absorbed the fuel. As they reached tighter spaces where they were forced to crawl, the air became dense and thick, and it was like he was drinking it instead of breathing. Were it not for his internal positioning system he would have entirely lost track of their whereabouts, not knowing if he was moving up or down, left or right.

"Sometimes we have to come and fetch cubs." Eloiko was speaking to Aaldryn ahead of him, their voices muffled by the tight walls. "They have the Misfit Dream and think themselves capable of uncovering great wonders. I cannot tell you how many times Troq and I have been through here looking for the foolish little things."

"We have lost a couple," Troq spoke from up ahead. "It is quite terrible being unable to find their bodies for proper burial, no matter how well we look."

"Guess you get rather good at navigating your way around after a while," Aaldryn answered. "I've been doing it since I was old enough to put a mask on. Mother was unable to convince me it was dangerous. I had to know what was under the burning-sea after I had the Misfit Dream. I am afraid I was one of those foolish little cubs." He sighed.

"Have any run-ins with null-zones?" Troq inquired.

"A few."

Jarvis gaped at him. Right. The null-zone that had swallowed Ishabal was not worth mentioning?

"Fifth level," Troq announced. The words were barely out of his mouth before Jarvis felt the jolt of connection buzz through his mind. Across his optical lenses, a world opened, panning out in hues of blues, greens, reds, and oranges as levels and layers built upon each other in hexagons. A grid-map of the buried city expanded around him, far clearer than he had been shown before.

"Holy Sun…" he murmured, blinking at the schematics. He stilled, allowing the flood of information to assimilate fully into his systems.

"We're dropping down into a larger section now," Troq continued. "I'm not sure if things are stable down there, so I will go first—"

"Wait!" Jarvis shouted. Troq froze, looking back at him. Jarvis tensed at the reflection of his eyes staring at him through the murky light. Aaldryn inched forward.

"Jarvis, what is it?"

"The whole skyscraper—it's being held up by that crystal in the observation deck. The structural integrity of the building has been compromised. I think it grew rapidly and expanded around the damaged sections to protect the building."

Troq set down his Mist lantern. "You can see it? You are more than you appear, aren't you?"

"A little." Jarvis breathed out. "It's incredible, and terrifying. I don't know how much longer it's going to last against the burning-sea currents. There is no way to tell how many skyscrapers it's linked to."

"What do you mean?' Aaldryn frowned.

"It is like a fungus, growing and growing. It has spread every-where there is damage, invading everything it can hold together, but eventually it will crack under the pressure of the burning-sea. I can't tell how much of Yrva Krv is infected."

Titus placed a hand on his shoulder. The solidity of his Master's touch was grounding, pulling Jarvis out of the overwhelming expanse surrounding him. He relaxed, grateful for that supporting presence.

"Sounds like yeh might need ta consider moving soon, laddies." The Hunter looked at the ceiling in concern, as though it were about to collapse.

Eloiko flicked his tails dismissively. "Perhaps." The way he said the word—Jarvis knew with a sense of dread that it was highly unlikely they would ever consider moving. They would rather die here. Eloiko took up his Mist lantern. "Let's keep going. We can, can't we?"

Jarvis nodded. He could not speak, his mouth felt dry with the vibrating currents surrounding him. Whatever the Crystal contained was powerful, like an entity in and of itself, and there seemed to be no end to the song it radiated. Titus' hand on his shoulder squeezed tighter. He breathed out, realising he had been holding his breath. There was a sheer drop between them and what seemed to be a large open chamber far below. Troq and the Mist lantern vanished into the depths. It felt like eternity until the prince's voice echoed up to them, distant but alive.

Aaldryn attached his diving ropes around his waist, following Eloiko down. Jarvis glanced hesitantly at Master Titus before leaping off the edge. He surged his gravity-bubble around himself protectively, gradually sailing downward. Light slowly began to flick into life, like specks dancing across his vision at first. He blinked rapidly, trying to clear the spots from his optical lenses. The glow filled a wide valley, shining with the limbs of hundreds of crystals, all different shades like a field of wild flowers over the moors of his father's farmlands. His optical lenses were not showing any signs of danger. The crystals, while they had outgrown their containment fields, had not yet bloomed. He smiled, having a sudden urge to run through them, with his arms spread wide in glee. Jarvis delicately settled himself beside Troq, wincing when Master Titus landed with a thud, then began to stretch, the clanking and clicking of bones sounding under his thick cloak.

Aaldryn and Eloiko soon joined them, rolling their ropes around their waists.

Aaldryn whistled. "Level five, heh?" His voice reflected a warble of awe. The prince peered around. Jarvis had a feeling he was resisting the urge to explore all the fallen panels and broken working stations they could see around them.

"I've only been this deep twice, and I ran into spores both times. Wasn't able to see much."

"As far as we can tell, these crystals haven't shattered yet." Eloiko knelt beside a protruding arm of a glittering gem which had burst through the metal wall like a tree branch. "As long as we don't touch any of them, we should be fine."

"Ah, oh lovely…" Master Titus muttered beside him and Jarvis winced on behalf of the Hunter. He could already smell the distinct odour of cooking skin emanating from the man.

"This way." Troq waved.

Jarvis followed Eloiko and Aaldryn. It was difficult to contain the delight of his protector bot. It felt so at home it made everything within him buzz. Somewhere in the distance he could hear the songs of machines, like the chirping of birds in the morning. Protectors like him—ancient, twisted, waiting. They were calling, their songs stretching out in a pattern, hoping to reach someone, anyone, to awaken them from their long slumber.

The light of the crystals danced over his skin, creating patterns that looked like star-charts. The scattered gems were like a meadow of mushrooms, growing in the darkness. If they were not causing so much devastation in the world above them Jarvis would have called it all beautiful—perhaps it was still beautiful, in some twisted, cruel, ironic way. The further onward they travelled, the worse the environment grew, as though the pressure of the burning-sea above them was crushing the metal, caving it in despite the best efforts of the crystals.

Signs of war was obvious all around them. Warped sheets dispersed, decay where it should not have been. The Creators' work should have been incorruptible, and yet under his feet pixels crumbled away as he moved, leaving gaping holes. They were forced against the sides of corridors where floor after floor had dropped away into endless caverns. He had never felt so terrified and thrilled all at once, for the world was both dying and alive, a contradiction that could only have worked for the Creators.

"We're almost there." Troq paused to take a drink from his water flask. "I hope we can still reach the entrance, otherwise this will be all for naught. The other entrance was lost in the cave-in a few months back."

Jarvis shouldered his packs. The deeper they dived into the

underworld of the burning-sea the more difficult it grew for his location system to place him in any sort of grid within Livila. The distortions were irritating, but he was growing used to the bursts of static down his spine whenever he lost connection to whatever immense network surrounded him. It troubled him, though, that when they did eventually find this entrance into the depths of the ancient city, without Troq and Eloiko, he was all the navigation they would have.

Jarvis shook his head, clearing the thoughts. For now, he needed to focus on the dangers surrounding them. Aaldryn and Eloiko had paused by a ruptured entrance way, the door blown open by a force so hot and strong the metal had melted into odd shapes. Jarvis ran his fingers over the sculptures, trembling at the ghost songs that lingered therein. War. Such terrible recollections of war within the data that remained trapped in the tiny crystal particles forever melded into the blasted metal.

"Ah…" Jarvis frowned at the two princes unbuckling their ropes. "That's an elevator shaft."

Aaldryn and Eloiko looked his way, puzzled at his alarm.

"What's an elevator?" Aaldryn laughed.

Titus emerged from the shadows. "They're boxes or panels that carry you up and down levels of skyscrapers. We have them at the House." The Hunter peered into the shaft, holding out his Mist lantern. "Can't see the elevator."

Jarvis cringed. "Hopefully it's not somewhere above us. Imagine if it dropped. I don't want to end my life squished by a falling piece of Zaprex technology."

"Yeh are not painting a nice picture, laddie. Not how I'd like ta go out either." Titus pulled away.

Troq finished tying the ropes to a nearby metal stake. He pushed past them, flinging the ropes over the edge. "Haven't got a choice. The entrance to level six is down there."

Jarvis blew a long rasp. He tried to shove aside the imagined visions of how badly this could go wrong as Aaldryn vaulted over the edge of the long drop with their diving gear. With a glance to check that Master Titus was following, Jarvis took a run up and leapt into the gloom, jerking his body's gravity-bubble. This time his stomach turned uncomfortably as he sailed downward, past the three princes climbing down.

A warning glow in his optical lenses caught him off guard; a deep orange filled his vision. He sucked in a breath, catching sight of a platform suspended in the elevator shaft, held firmly in place by an overgrown crystal. He cursed loudly.

"Jarvis, what is it?" Aaldryn shouted.

"It's a contaminated crystal."

"Spores?"

"No, not yet. It hasn't bloomed."

"Do you see a doorway?" Troq's yell joined in the conversation.

Jarvis settled on the platform. It did not jolt against his full weight. It felt solidly braced—for now. He walked slowly between the crystals, many of them cracked and bursting through the metal of the trapped elevator. Despite their unsavoury hum, they were still stunning. Likely the elevator had become wedged by the cave-in, and its gravity-drive had burst at some point, causing the crystal to expand beyond its containment-field. A doorway was sealed shut to one side and he studied it. Nothing dangerous beyond it showed on his optical lenses and he shrugged, slapping his hand on the activation panel, keying in the right notes to open it. It slid aside. Darkness. An opening to seemingly nowhere. Cold air of a long-disused environmental system breathed past him and his protector bot stirred, the metal of his hull dancing at the sudden invitation. He was being urged forward, by some alluring undercurrent in the energy surrounding him.

"I opened the door," he yelled up the shaft.

So, this was beginning of level six. Aaldryn had not dived any deeper into the depths of the cityscape ruins than this. From this point on everything they saw was new.

Be found.

He shook away the whisper against his receiver.

"I'm not lost," he choked out.

You first have to be lost to ever be found.

The others finally reached him, though it took an age in his opinion. Master Titus dropped down only when there was no danger of the ropes the princes used snapping from above. He had been wondering why his master had not joined him right away.

"Right." Eloiko lead them to the open corridor. "We'll take you as far as the next entrance, and then you're on your own." He waved his Mist Lantern into the darkness. Jarvis peered down the corridor, annoyed that none of the usual lights were activating at his presence. Did this mean he was going to struggle to use any of the buried technology this far down? Was it all contaminated from here onwards?

He puffed out in frustration, glancing back towards the sea of glowing orange coming from the open doorway. Troq was bundling up his ropes and pack patiently, in a methodical and organized manner.

He blinked. Red flared across his vision. His body moved, suddenly compelled into action. He felt as though his whole mind had been left behind, and he was watching himself in slow motion.

"Spores!" Jarvis shouted. "Troq! Watch out!" He was not going to make it in time, though his legs carried him forward in a frantic charge, bursting down the corridor. The prince looked back at his shout, staring at the crystals surrounding him. One shattered, its sudden bloom causing a chain reaction and others began erupting. Their bursting light was momentarily intense, like a flashing of sunlight and the loud pops vibrated inside Jarvis' skull. Troq threw up his arms, slapping paws over his mouth, nose and eyes.

Jarvis spun at the sound of Eloiko's cry. He stared at his Master, Aaldryn, and the Dwellers' alpha with wide eyes as he smacked his hand to the surface of the activation pad. The door slammed shut, cutting off the swirl of contaminated spores.

He barely heard Titus banging on the door, his attention swinging towards Troq. The Kattamont prince was trembling as he held his breath, curled into a ball. The air was thick with spores, already coating the prince in a cloak. Jarvis crouched, tugging out his knife from his belt.

"This is going to hurt, but it will be worth it if it you live through it. Keep holding your breath."

He had no idea if the half-breed could hear him, but he moved to the nearest wall panel, running his fingers over the seam. It cracked open and he dug his knife between the metal sheets, tearing them apart. Like veins, thin pipes of philepcon liquid, dozens of different shades, lay therein. His fingers brushed hesitantly against one, wincing at the surging song that pulsed through his arm. His protector bot was far out of its league in this area; he was simply going to have to guess which one was a branch to the core.

"Finc, you'll do," he muttered. Snagging the cord he had touched, he pulled it free, feeling it splinter in his grasp. Philepcon liquid dribbled down his arm as he dragged it towards Troq. With a swing of his knife he stabbed the Kattamont prince in the leg, gripping him tightly as he reared up in pain. Jarvis slapped a hand over Troq's mouth.

"I'm sorry. I'm really, really sorry and I hope this works. I hope it accepts you."

He drove the cord into the wound, releasing the philepcon liquid. He cringed at the recollection of being contaminated by the protector bot, how everything had sped up to such a pace he had been unable to comprehend the world he had once known. He had thought his mind would erupt from the pain and his body would fail him in trying to contain such an immense presence.

Jarvis gradually released his grip on Troq's mouth and whispered. "Let it live in you."

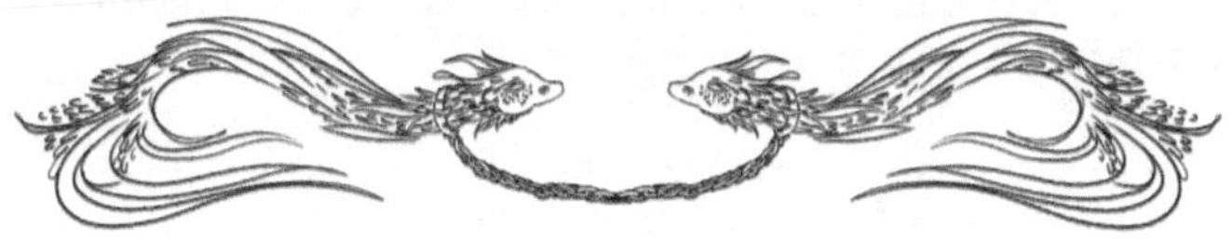

The banging on the door had finally died down, though every so often Jarvis caught sight of either Aaldryn or Eloiko peering through the window. He had the sinking feeling Master Titus was off searching every nook he could find for a breach to reach him. How long had it been? He crinkled his brow, trying to bring up some type of time code. Perhaps two days. Master Titus would be beside himself. He felt awful for causing such distress, but he knew he had been unable to control the reaction of his body to Troq's immediate danger.

It felt as though something had seized control of his protector bot, and, for that moment, compelled him into action. The hours he had spent running over the sequence of events had led him to one conclusion—only an AI far more elite in the hierarchy could have provoked such a reaction. He was no longer sure if such a notion frightened him.

Was it like the Dragon invading his mind?

No. I moved you. I did not touch your mind, child-bot. These are two different things for us. Someday you will understand.

Jarvis wiped back his hair, resting his head on the wall.

"Hello, *Tikal_of_Rainbows*."

The spores still contaminated the air surrounding him, seeping out of the blooming crystals protruding from the lid of the trapped elevator. It was mesmerizing, the ebbing glow, playing patterns across his skin. He reached out a hand, waving it through the spores, distorting their pathways.

Interesting choice of actions, child-bot, to create a hybrid like yourself.

Jarvis frowned at the soft voice whispering in his receiver, reminding him of the melodious harmony of his sister and brother-in-law when they had sung together for the Spring festivals. It was Tikal, he was sure of it, but how and why the Mothership was speaking to him he could not fathom. He stared around, through the haze of glittering spores, wondering where the Mothership was—was it all around them? He blinked rapidly—had he contaminated Troq with the Mothership's philepcon liquid? Holy Sun on High!

Ah, now you are thinking, little child-bot.

"Wait? Did I actually make him a hybrid of you…?"

His only reply was a sweet chuckle. Jarvis sat up straighter as he heard a soft groan. He scrambled over to Troq and carefully lifted his head, cradling it gently.

"Hey."

Troq's eyes fluttered open; tears had caked around their edges. Jarvis brushed at them. Troq smiled weakly.

"I'm not dead."

Jarvis shrugged. "Depends on your definition of alive, I suppose."

"What did you do to me?" Troq winced, and Jarvis felt the echo of his sharp pain. He reached for his water-skin, untying the tip and carefully offered it to the Kattamont.

"It's going to be painful for a while. The integration of philepcon liquid into your system takes a long time, and, to be honest, I don't think it works on everyone."

"So, you had no idea if this would work?" Troq breathed out, causing spores to dance around them.

"Philepcon liquid tends to reject the host it infects, that's why," he stared around the thick sea of spores surrounding them, "the adverse reaction to the spores happens."

"So… why me?"

"I guess the AI of Yrva Krv liked what it saw." Jarvis shrugged. "I can only go off my own experience, and I know the protector bot that infected me wanted to live and experience life. It decided to continue existing within me, so it could continue its role as a protector. Perhaps the AI of this city has a task it needs a Changeling for."

Troq closed his eyes.

"You're just going to have to figure it out. I was compelled to do what I did, so that has to mean that something more powerful than my protector bot wanted to create you."

The prince blinked slowly, several times, and Jarvis was sure he was adjusting his optical lenses. If he remembered correctly from his own transformation, the first thing to be altered had been his eyes, and the incredible change had been startling.

"This is so beautiful…" Troq whispered.

Jarvis sat back on his haunches. The ocean of spores swirling around them was truly incredible and being amongst it without a mask was an experience few could have. The air itself glowed and hummed with life—an impossible life—a new form of life.

"It's like stardust."

"Probably is," Jarvis murmured as he lifted himself up, wincing as the blood rushed to his numbed feet. He shook the feeling back into his limbs, much to Troq's amusement. He headed towards the sealed door, trying to work up enough saliva to wet his dry throat. This was what he had been dreading. Slamming his fist against the door, he listened to the echoing drum through the shaft.

Aaldryn's face suddenly appeared at the small window, startling him into stepping back. The prince's eyes were large with panic. Jarvis tried to wave cheerfully, but his stomach was spinning loops. He pointed to his face, indicating a mask. Aaldryn frowned at first, then nodded in understanding, pulling out his spore mask. He vanished and Jarvis waited, tapping his foot on the floor. This was going to be a very interesting reunion.

"Is Eloiko all right?" Troq enquired. He was trying to raise himself onto his elbow but kept slipping.

"I think so." Jarvis urged the frail prince back down. "I have a feeling both our alphas are furious at me."

"They're over protective. Being cut off from us—they would imagine the worse-case scenario. A clean death is better; at least they would know we're dead."

Jarvis was drawn back to the window, noticing both Aaldryn and Eloiko were wearing their masks. He shifted to the control panel and reactivated the release song. The door wheezed. Jarvis winced, hoping it was still open. With the bursting of the nearby crystals, the whole section had become unstable, and power was unlikely to be distributed evenly. Grabbing the door, he pushed a surge of energy through his hull into the mechanics beyond and it gradually creaked open. He barely had time to comprehend the three figures in front of him before a blast of wind burst past him, clearing the air of most of the spores, enough to see clearly.

He was grabbed roughly by Master Titus' bony hand and dragged forward.

"Little Weasel! My stupid little Weasel, what in the name of the Paladins were yeh trying ta do?"

Once he would have been terrified of the fury in the face that glared down at him, but now he was aware it was not anger that Titus felt; it was fear of loss.

"I just reacted. And I am not sorry!" Jarvis straightened his shoulders. "I had to do something or Troq would have died and so would Aaldryn and Eloiko."

Titus clapped a hand over his face. "Gah! Yeh're making me age beyond ma sol-cycles with worry."

Aaldryn was patting him down, checking for any wounds. Jarvis slapped him away. Sun Above, it was not like he had been in a fight. They were acting like he had been to another land, not on the other side of a locked door. "I'm fine, honestly. I'm fine! The crystal bloomed suddenly, and I reacted on impulse to save Troq. That's all."

"What did you do to him?" Eloiko's strained voice was hollow. "Did you make him mad?"

"What?" Jarvis spluttered out. He spun around sharply, staring at the Kattamont in shock. "No! I integrated him with the systems of this city—the one you dwell in. Sun on High. He is not insane! He's a Changeling. Like me. You should be honoured he was accepted."

Eloiko collapsed suddenly, as though his body had simply given out. He slumped beside Troq, wrapping himself around his blood-brother. Jarvis blinked, realising the alpha was sobbing inside his mask. Troq lifted a trembling hand to settle it on Eloiko's mane.

Jarvis relaxed and allowed Aaldryn to draw him away, further down the corridor, towards the gathering of Mist lanterns surrounding their packs.

"Eloiko's in shock," Aaldryn explained. "We alphas, we get

protective. You could have let us know. Eloiko had no idea if his blood-brother was alive or dead, and you let him wait for two days to find out. That amount of stress is immense."

"Oh." Jarvis sulked as a bowl of stew was shoved into his hands and from the stark glare Master Titus gave him, he was aware he was being ordered to sit and eat. "I'm sorry."

"Don't be. The shock of losing his queen and princess, and then maybe a blood-brother as well in such a short amount of time, would very likely have killed Eloiko. You saved two princes."

Jarvis stared up at the Kattamont. "You really do survive through your prides, don't you?"

Jarvis ate his stew, amused that his protector bot was humming in satisfaction as if it was utterly pleased with itself.

CLIVE AND PENNY

CHAPTER EIGHT

Disgleirio dug his shovel heavily into the damp soil and wiped away a thick mixture of sweat and dirt. He loathed this muggy weather that the thick ash-cloud channelled. In the fifty sol-cycles he had been slowly restoring the land, the ash-cloud had not yet dissipated to the point where sunlight could filter through properly. They were left with Sunstones to light the darkness and restore the forests. How the Sisters Three despised him. He was surprised the Kelibs had not risen to conquer Avalon—yet. But they had their own troubles.

"Uncle!" Ewyni ran towards him across the thick purple grass, the skirts of his royal gown tangling around his ankles. The boy skidded up to him, handing over a missive. "This came from the Province of Telvash. Father thinks the Batitics are finally willing to trade!"

"Blessed Suns," Disgleirio muttered. He reached for the missive, only for a sudden spasm to send him to his knees. Blood erupted from his mouth. The shock was more alarming than the pain. He had not had an episode in nearly a century, not since he had been a mere boy and Gifu and Gibo had contained his collapsing energy field.

Ewyni's pale silver eyes were wide with horror. He could not blame the lad.

Disgleirio stared at the glistening blood staining his shimmering hand. He gulped back the thick iron taste in his mouth. He had been living on borrowed time. Finally his containment field was collapsing. It was not fair. He had so much to do. He had not yet found a wife, not yet had children. Avalon was still in such disrepair. The clouds that coated the sky-sea had not yet dissipated. He was still Pennadot's great Sun. Forcing a smile he smeared the blood across his chiton and heaved himself to his feet, clasping Ewyni's shoulder for support.

"I'm fine, little snake."

"Please don't die, Uncle!" Tears filled Ewyni's eyes and the boy flung himself into his arms. He sighed as he listened to the sobbing. Death came to everyone, eventually, even those who tried to outrun it.

Denvy shivered. He had not expected the Haven Hall to be so cold. The frozen air caused his jaw to ache. Instinctively he rubbed at the twinge as he gauged his surroundings. There was nothing overtly ominous about the corridors themselves. Indeed, they seemed comforting in a rather homely manner, harkening back to Pennadot's rustic Human halls, filled with tapestries and long rugs. If it were not for the bitter air biting at his skin beneath his fur, he would have shaken off the foreboding wariness lingering in the corners, where the shadows played. His fur simply refused to settle.

A song wavered in the background, not one his ears could capture, but his dreamathic mind was aware of it, and it urged him to run like a frightened child—escape now, while he had the chance.

He was a foolish little fish, swimming into the hungry mouth of a predator waiting in the coral reef.

Swim.

Swim away.

The song echoed in a constant loop. He shook his head, trying to clear it. From the pale look Nixlye was casting his way, it was likely she too was catching at least a tail end of the dreamathic whispers.

He focused his attention on the small collection of stones and sticks Clive and Jythal crouched beside. The creation of concealment Runes had to be cast in the place one wanted to be hidden in, and therefore took a considerable amount of time exposed within enemy territory. Clive finally pulled away, wiping sweat from his brow. He gathered up his few rocks and sticks, glittering Runes etched into their surfaces, and passed them out.

"Keep these on you at all times. They should last us an hour or so. We need to move quickly now. They won't keep us entirely concealed, just not noticeable, so try not to make too much noise."

Ki'b nodded. Denvy' neck fur puffed as he accepted the small stone from the lad. Clive was maturing, and it was wonderful to witness. His chest felt tight and he gave it a small pat, trying to settle down the surging warmth of the pride within him. He motioned to Nixlye.

"You know the layout. Any idea where we go from here?"

"Each Haven Hall has a Records Room." The young queen wheeled on ahead of them. "We were only permitted inside during the Wind Festivals, but you might be able to get inside."

"Can't you open the door like you did the other one?" Ki'b queried.

Nixlye shook her head. "Not the Records Room. It's a unique door. You'll see when we reach it."

The Haven Hall's corridors grew increasingly darker the deeper they explored. While it was not a problem for him, Jythal, or Nixlye, leading the cubs around grew difficult and he had not expected that something so small could become such a hindrance between races. Kattamonts' natural ability to see in the dark was something he rarely thought about. In a home designed for his people, the lack of light would not be troublesome. Indeed, in the days of old, they had dwelt in the coral reefs below the touch of the Sun.

Clive and Penny lagged behind, with Penny's laboured breathing and panicked mind betraying what she was struggling with in the darkness and tight corridors. The terrors of the Twizel box haunted her. He sighed through his air-gills. Clive was doing his best to comfort her, trying softly to urge her forward.

Denvy glanced back at the two, Penny kneeling, clutching her cheeks, and Clive, with his small Monk hat sitting wonky on his mop of hair, urging her with kind words. The sight was endearing. How he wished he could have captured it in an image forever.

"Dear Sun!" He moved swiftly, his tail sweeping out, latching onto both children, sweeping them off their feet and into a small nook in the wall beside him. The wall hanging fluttered. He touched it lightly, settling it back into place as two figures strolled into view, speaking in hushed tones. The Iposti robes rustled more loudly than their foot-paws thudded. Herbs hung around their necks, and Denvy hoped that would be enough to mask the Human scent in the air.

They glided past, leaving through the open doorway to the side, their voices fading into silence. Denvy uncurled from around Clive and Penny. Their trembling bodies tumbled out. Penny panted for air, holding her cheeks tightly.

"That was too close," Denvy muttered.

"I am so sorry," Penny whispered.

"Never mind," he reassured her. "No harm done. Come along, let's catch up with the others. This way."

They nodded and scurried after him, this time keeping close to his heels. The group had stalled in front of an arched door. Nixlye's under-standing of it being used in ceremonies seemed correct. It appeared quite magnificent within the immense, lonely chamber it was situated. Their steps echoed. Denvy's ears perked back in concern. Faint lines of glittering coral lit the ceiling, but the light was barely enough for the children to see by. They were simply vague, blurring lines, tracking a web across the domed roof. He doubted it had seen enough sunlight for sol-cycles to emit sufficient glow to light the entire chamber.

"We're alone. I cannot hear anyone else," Jythal offered at his approach.

"Is it odd, Nixlye, for there to be no guards here?"

"Who would rob a Haven Hall? All Kattamonts have been raised under their banner, and those who are Misfit-born like us simply have no reason to. And if they did, well, you would need a convert like me to get in and there simply aren't that many of us who diverged from our life on the Isles of Ricrove."

There was a story behind her words, but it was one that would have to wait. What had led to the young princess becoming a queen, mated to the son of an outcast. Denvy frowned, turning back to the door blocking their path. It did not sit well with him. The emptiness of the domed hall surrounding them, and the single door. It was, indeed, no ordinary door as Nixlye had indicated. It was not formed out of wood, or coral, though coral had grown and hardened around its edges, creating a beautiful frame over the Zaprex metal. Denvy studied it with a deepening scowl.

"So…" Nixlye touched the sleeve of his tunic. "Do you know what type of door it is?"

Denvy pursed his lips. "Yes. I do. It is troubling."

"What is it, Khwaja Denvy?" Clive piped up.

"This is an entrance into a Zaprex Archive. However, I do not believe this actually is a Zaprex Archive. I think this is only a door of one." He brushed his paw over the surface. "And it has been jerry-rigged into this building. Rather impressive, though I suppose not surprising considering what I have seen done with the sand-ships and the cities now." It did seem Kattamonts had become rather skilled at scavenging the Zaprex wonders below the burning-sea and putting them all to marvellous use.

"Can you open it? I doubt I will be able to perform a Rune cycle to get us through that. I wouldn't be able to hold the runes long enough on Zaprex metal." Jythal pressed forward, urging Penny to one side.

Denvy scratched his skin. "If I make a mistake, the alarms will go off. Let me think on this for a moment. I need to work out where this door is from."

"Why?"

He blinked. That was a very typical Clive question.

"Most Zaprex Archives have a secret code that opens them." Denvy looked down at the boy. "One thing I learnt from being raised by Zaprexes is how to open their doors and sneak into places they never wanted me to get into."

Clive grinned. "You must have been so very naughty."

Denvy chuckled. He reached out and tweaked the boy's chin fondly.

It was impossible for the door to have come from Tikal's main HUB itself, so that was entirely out of the question, but the markings across the top were uncannily similar to the Rainbow City. If it was not Tikal's central HUB itself, then what else had carried the Matrix Crystal of Tikal? He squeezed his eyes shut, massaging his temples. Memories were jumbled from sol-cycles of time. While he had been created by a Zaprex, he was lacking the advantage of a Zaprex mind, capable of the straightforward process of accessing desired memories.

His chest swelled as Ryojin's crystal under his tunic grew warm. The barest whisper broke through the cracks in the yoke's binding.

It reminds me of your nightmare. The Room. The markings are similar.

Ah. Of course. Thank you, Ryojin.

He flattened his air-gills. The Room. The laboratory of his creator, Nefertem, had been stationed within a separate arm of Tikal, but had still been linked to the city's HUB. That was where he had seen this door: somewhere within the maze of corridors that had been Nefertem's Laboratory. In a swell, like a wave hitting him, hard enough for him to stagger, the memories flooded back. Denvy covered his face with a shaking paw, unsure if he was supposed to smile or weep at the images of his creator's kind face, and Hazanin-*sama's* sweet voice calling to him out of the darkness of non-existence.

"So, what is the code?" Clive bounced on his heels.

Denvy breathlessly thanked the boy's enthusiasm for pulling him out of his reminiscences.

"Patience, child." He shifted forward, waving a paw over the surface of the door. A soft glowing hologram flickered to life, revealing a panel of numerals and a screen of hexagons circling them. He felt the group crowd around him, stiffening his fur by their proximity as they peered up in curiosity.

"It is in Zaprex." Nixlye sighed.

Denvy raised his brow at the young princess and spoke slowly, translating for her.

"We glitter in sun, but are not precious gems,

We grow old, die, but live again,

Some of us smile in winter, some in summer.

What are we?"

He looked around, amused by the startled faces in the light of the holograms. "Any ideas?"

"A riddle?" Nixlye spluttered out. "The code is a riddle?"

"They're fairies. Were you expecting something else?" Denvy smirked. "I actually know the answer, but come…come…Ki'b, dear, you might know this one, or perhaps you, Clive? Someone from Pennadot?"

The two children shook their heads. Denvy pouted. "Really? I always thought this one was rather easy."

"Leaves." Jythal lifted his paw. "The answer is leaves. Leaves glitter in sunlight, they grow old, die, but regrow. Some are evergreen, some are only around in summer and spring."

"Well done." Denvy purred.

"Just remembering what leaves looked like." The prince shrugged.

Nixlye reached for his paw, pressing her lips to his palm.

Into the holographic display Denvy typed the word and, barely a moment after, blue light spread through the links in the metal, creating intricate designs that split apart, peeling back to reveal the room within. Clive whooped, dashing in before anyone could stop him.

"Books! Scrolls!" The boy had entirely forgotten his own words about keeping his voice down.

It was a wonderful sight to behold. Lining the Records Room, almost to its high arched ceiling stood row upon row of shelves, stuffed with books and sweet-scented cotton scrolls.

"Where in all the Sun did they find these?" This was unfathomable. What was such history doing here? Denvy looked at Nixlye as she rolled past. "Each Haven Hall has one of these?"

She nodded. "This is where information from every exhibition, every exploration into the sectors below the burning-sea is stored. The Iposti are keepers of the knowledge that came before us. It is why they believe the Zaprexes caused the great calamity. It is how they have interpreted everything they have gathered. However, there are those in their ranks who understand it vastly differently; I am the result of one such Iposti."

"Whoa!" Clive's voice rang out. "Khwaja Denvy, you have got to come and see these! They're amazing!"

Denvy pinched the bridge of his nose. Here he had thought Clive was finally learning some restraint. Alas, it seemed it would take some time for such an achievement. He smiled faintly as they moved through the rows of the library, finding the boy bouncing around a glass table that floated above the ground. It was an observation-eye; display desks that had once sat on the main decks of Zaprex galactic-ships, used to observe over long distances. Seeing one here, in such a strange environment that was not suited for it was jarring, made worse because he could recall the pristine white and blue ships in which it had sat, contrasting so starkly now with the earthy browns of the Haven Hall's dying coral floors and walls.

"Ah, yes." Nixlye heaved on her wheels, joining Clive beside the gently humming table. "These are what we're here for. Excellent job, Clive."

The boy puffed out his chest as the queen gave his cheek a pat.

Denvy wandered around the holographic table. It explained the eerie light that lit the room now. It was likely that Zaprex terminals were stationed across the vast library, emitting a constant glow. A chill crept up his spine as Nixlye tapped the table, activating it with practiced ease. Likely, then, that this was not the first one she had accessed.

Denvy chewed on the inside of his cheek. Not even at the House of Flames had he allowed himself to activate the Zaprex technology that had lingered in slumber therein. He had tried desperately hard to keep away from it, for the ache of what he had lost in the Thousand Sol-Cycle War was still so raw, despite the centuries that had passed. There was no running away from any of the wounds now, no matter how he felt. He would have to face the memories and accept what had transpired. What he had lost—and run from.

Instead of images of other Zaprex vessels, air-currents, and docking stations that he would once have expected to see through the observation-eye, the table lit up to reveal the gridded sections of the burning-sea, tossing with sand-dune waves. Nixlye whistled in approval.

"I knew it! I knew they would have one. The Iposti always have one of these to make their maps from." She wagged a finger. "You must be right, Denvy. These all have to be linked to Tikal." She looked to him for confirmation, her eyes shining, her little round ears perked back.

"Yes, this is very likely Tikal's navigation system. If we want to locate your Rythrya Stones, and, therefore, Tikal itself, this would be how," he agreed.

Nixlye grinned, her neck fur hackling. "The maps in this section will have a numbering and level section. They'll be the current charts," she looked around, "and they will work in real time. We should take a few of them, so we can create a table rather like this one for ourselves." She waved her hands over the observation-eye.

Penny poked her head over the rim of the table. "Yes, but, if we take them, won't the Iposti notice?"

Jythal nodded. "She has a point, Nixlye."

The young queen frowned, studying the movement of the holograms shifting across the surface of the table. They watched as a small sand-ship came into view upon the rise of a sand-dune wave. Ki'b giggled at the sight of it, her nose barely poking over the observation-eye. Denvy was tempted to lift her, so she could wave her hands through the diagrams.

"Is it possible to transfer and duplicate the holograms onto a new parchment?" Ki'b queried. "There are so many of them, so they must do it, mustn't they?"

"True, true. It is worth a try." Jythal felt through his hip-bags, pulling out some folded sheets. Denvy smiled. Typical of the doctor, coming prepared for every situation.

"Do you have your holographic inker in there as well?" Nixlye raised an eyebrow.

"Never leave the *Lawless* without it, dear."

Ki'b and Penny aided Jythal in placing the parchments across the observation-eye.

Nixlye flipped the holographic inker Jythal gave her, the slim silver cylinder glowing a gentle warm hue against her palm. "This should only take a few minutes. Then we can leave."

Denvy tried to ease the tension in his shoulders. The longer they remained, the worse his air-gills ached with worry, not only about where they were, but also about Zafiashid in the fighting-pit. His ears flicked back. Something was missing. Noise. It was Clive's near constant chatter. Clive was missing.

"Oh, dear Sun," Denvy grumbled, "Clive's run off again." He pointed at Penny and Ki'b. "Stay with Nixlye."

The two girls bobbed their heads. Denvy trudged through the library rows, searching for Clive's emotional signature. He could feel an amusement that was not his own irritation bleeding through the cracks of the yoke's binding enchantments.

Cubs are a handful. Ryojin's dreamathic thoughts were shaped like wiggling lines, almost as though they were being shoved through the gaps in his mental walls. Difficult to visualize with the yoke's presence, but a comforting change to the pure silence of a lonesome mind he had endured within the dark box. *He's to your right. No, next right. Yes…through there.*

Thank you, he replied.

It was easy to spot the red-haired boy, and he had at least not gone too far. Clive's attention had been caught by one of the glass Zaprex terminals, like a moth to a glowing flame. The holographic display lit the boy's freckled cheeks disconcertingly, hollowing out his eyes. Denvy paused for a moment, startled by the vision. He shook his head. It was simply showing how spooked he was that he was allowing his mind to play such nasty tricks.

Clive's wrist flicked back and forth, quickly zipping through dozens of displays by tapping the crystal surface of the terminal. Denvy carefully approached, a reprimand on the tip of his tongue, but his eyes caught an image and he threw out a paw, grabbing Clive's wrist before it could move to issue the information away. His hearts felt as though they froze, his chest clenching painfully tight as his air-gills and tail went flat.

Slowly he released Clive's hand.

Clive blinked up at him. "Khwaja Denvy…what is it?" he whispered.

"Run back to Jythal. Tell him I need more parchment and his holographic inker. Go! Quickly!"

"Yes, sir!" Clive dashed away.

He stood, slack, a part of him in straight denial, not wanting to dare believe the information available to him so unhidden it was as though it had wanted to be found. His paws curled around the yoke binding his dreamathic mind. Could he call it a blessing now—a blessing that he had been contained in a box that held his precious cubs and taken back to his homeland—all to face this monstrosity?

Jythal's paw-steps disturbed his growing rage, a rage he was aware could not be contained by Ryojin and it was only the blind prince holding forth a parchment that drew him out of his hissing.

"What is it?"

There was a tentative tone of frustration in Jythal's voice. Of course, he was unable to see anything on the display screens and holographic scrolls surrounding him. Denvy twirled the crystal controls upon the terminal, shifting the light spectrum to tactile levels. Reaching out he took Jythal's paws, feeling his resistance before the prince relented and he pushed them over the hologram.

Jythal froze in alarm as he ran his paws over the images, then across the lettering. His air-gills fanned out in alarm. "What in the Four Winds is this?" He withdrew, shaking his paws as though the residual energy pained him. "No. No. They wouldn't do this. The Zaprexes are sacred. Children are sacred!"

Children and Zaprexes. The words were so bitter in Denvy's mind. Zaprexes and their fight to save their children; that had been, in the end, what the Thousand Sol-Cycle War had centred on after the Dragon had discovered the means to defeating the fairy race.

Killing their children.

Was this some cruel irony? Was he staring at the Dragon's idea of a joke? At least he had uncovered the reason the Dragon had such an investment in Utillia: Zaprex corpses.

Denvy copied the hologram and quickly rolled up the parchment. His shoulders felt weighted again, as if every burden he had ever carried since little Chans Mazaki had placed the body of a reforged, hidden Starborn prince into his arms, had resurfaced. The hope of the Key's discovery had lightened the load, but it appeared his peace was not to be long kept.

"Is nothing sacred in this age?" he whispered.

"Are you two finished?" Nixlye wheeled up to them.

Denvy felt Ki'b brush up against his leg. The girl carried a bundle of parchments strapped to her back, wearing them with pride. He touched a paw to her head, stroking aside her hair, relief flooding through him just for a moment. She had not suffered the terrible fate that she had been destined for—

He had saved her.

"What is that?" Nixlye must have caught the hologram glittering behind him. She curled back into her chair, her lips paling.

Denvy's gaze settled on Clive, Penny, and Ki'b—his cubs, so innocent, so naïve they had once been to the horrors of the war that now engulfed them. They had been stolen from their lives for a single purpose: to become monsters, to become machines.

"This is what the Dragon's new army looks like," he murmured.

"By the Rythrya, what have we done? We should have let the burning-sea keep everything!" Nixlye covered her mouth.

DISGLEIRIO - THE WANDERING KING - THE WHITE STAR

CHAPTER NINE

Disgleirio considered his Starborn body both a blessing and a curse. It aged slowly, in the manner of Humans who had once taken off on the Great Migration. But it was a Starborn body that was decaying, breaking down into a black hole, contained only by the suit Nefertem had designed for him. There were precious few moments when he could be free of the cursed contraption. Alone. Without fear of catching anyone with the pull of his gravity.

He washed blood from his hands as he sat naked on the rim of the rocky pool. The water swirled, caught up in his allure. Another painful cough. More blood. It felt like he was hacking up his lungs.

A sudden touch to his face caused him to jerk around, eyes wide. He stared at a Kelib woman, kneeling, holding the hem of her skirt that was bloodied from dabbing his cheeks. A large terracotta jug sat beside her. Panic seized him. Were they camped near a Kelib settlement? Sun above—he hoped this was not a sacred site!

She smiled, almond-shaped eyes crinkling with faint lines of age as she settled herself down on the pool edge.

"You must be the King." Her heavily-accented Basic was rough, like the bark of a tree.

"What gave it away? The glow?" he muttered.

"No." She turned her head to the canopy above them, and the clouds visible through the leaves. "Do you not see it? You are pulling everything towards you. The leaves, the branches, the rocks, the waters, even the clouds...I followed the clouds."

Jarvis hunched down beside Troq, passing over a canister of water. Nearby, Aaldryn and Eloiko were talking, but he filtered out their conversation entirely, focusing on the new Changeling before him. Troq managed a meagre smile as he accepted the water. His tail flopped about limply.

"They sound like they're yelling right in my ear." Troq gestured to the two princes.

Jarvis pinched the bridge of his nose. "Hm. It will take a while for you to figure out how to departmentalise. I found it helped to focus on another sound, like a heartbeat, or an insect crawling."

"He thinks I'm mad," Troq whispered.

"That decision is entirely yours." Jarvis continued resorting his pack. "Don't let the hybridisation process alter the most important part of you."

Troq looked up. "Which is what?"

"Your Song."

Troq fell silent, no doubt processing layers of information.

Jarvis wondered what difference Troq's Kattamont nature would make to the hybridisation. As a Human it had all seemed naturally straightforward, but the Kattamont culture seemed to add nuances to everything. "Troq, it'll take time. Even I'm still getting used to things, and I only absorbed the philepcon liquid of a protector bot." Jarvis looked around the corridor's dim, flickering lights. "I think you've been made a part of Yrva Krv, which, if I was reading the schematics right, was once a Galactic Ship."

"The schematics? Those would be the map-like lines I keep seeing?" Troq turned his head from side to side. "I can't seem to turn it off."

Jarvis reached out, gripping the side of Troq's temple. A static buzz passed over his fingertips and he sat back. "You're still not developed enough for me to communicate with you. Shame. Ah…Try blinking several times while ordering the schematics away."

Troq's blue eyes flickered brightly and he smiled suddenly. "They're gone. Thanks. They were giving me a headache. Do you have to deal with that all the time?"

Jarvis shrugged. "After a while it becomes second nature. Now it feels odd not being able to see a grid. I lost access, or something, when we passed the sixth level."

"You did?"

Jarvis scratched the back of his neck as he looked down the corridor. "I think I was forcefully logged out. It's hard to explain. How do I say this? *Ano.* My protector bot was created by a different Pride of Zaprexes to those who watched over Utillia. It seems a machine of my calibre is only granted access to certain levels."

Troq's brow lifted. "Zaprexes had Prides?"

"They were called Dynasties. From what I can gather, they were a pretty important part of Zaprex culture. What Dynasty they were hatched into defined what they would be, and if they bonded into another Dynasty, they automatically created a new smaller dynasty." Jarvis sat back on his haunches.

Interest shone in the prince's eyes and Jarvis felt relief settle over his shoulders. He should have known talking about their Creators would have reignited a spark.

"What Dynasty am I then?"

"Nefertem/Sekhmet. Not surprising; it appears Utillia was a territory of their Dynasty."

It was a brief look of recognition that flashed over Troq's features; most likely the mention of the names had flashed up information so quickly he was having difficulty processing it all. Jarvis glanced away, recalling the grim times when he, too, had struggled with the intense bursts of data that had flooded his systems and overloaded him.

"You're of the Thoth/Seshat Dynasty," Troq murmured.

"I am. Well done!" Jarvis grinned.

"How did I know that?" Troq covered his mouth.

Jarvis laughed. "You'll find yourself knowing an awful lot of random things. Not all of them are useful." Tension rippled up his spine, tightening the armour plates of his shoulders and he noted Troq's curious gaze at his reaction to Aaldryn's approach. Eloiko followed, fiddling with his hip-bags and diving equipment, looking as though he was trying to distract himself from the impending conversation.

"You ready?" Aaldryn quipped.

"Always," Jarvis retorted.

"We should go with them, Eloiko, at least for a little while. Jarvis can no longer see the layout and I can." Troq managed to stagger onto his foot-paws. Jarvis noticed Eloiko's hesitant movement to catch him and frowned.

"I have already decided we shall." Eloiko's air-gills frilled uneasily. "I do not believe it will be beneficial to return to the Pride until you are more stable."

"You think I am mad." Troq pulled away.

"I did not say that!" Eloiko smacked a paw against the nearby wall.

Jarvis jumped at the reverberation down the corridor. He glanced hesitantly at Aaldryn, who gave the smallest of headshakes. This was not Aaldryn's Pride, and it seemed Aaldryn would not—could not—interfere. It was Kattamont custom.

Eloiko breathed unsteadily through his air-gills. "I am sorry, Troq. Aaldryn explained that you would benefit from Jarvis' presence, and I need…to adjust."

Jarvis arched an eyebrow, wondering how Aaldryn had so quickly convinced the Dweller's prince to travel further with them. Perhaps that had been a conversation he should not have filtered out.

Troq's tail slid depressively across the floor, his head down, even as he gathered up his packs. Jarvis clapped him on the shoulder. "Cheer up! He'll come around. We just have to get you steady on your foot-paws."

Troq managed a smile. "Thanks, Jarvis."

Teaching Troq the recalibration process was a task requiring patience, but, as the days wore on and the prince's strength returned, his grasp of the schematics increased. There was less danger of him leading them into contaminated zones. Those twists and turns, avoiding the spores, had led them here, to something spectacular. Ships. Sky-ships; they lined the chamber. Darkness unfolded like a blanket, rippled and bumpy only where the light of Jarvis' Mist lamp touched it. He could not tell if there was an end to the empty expanse. He was trembling. A thrill from within his processor core burst out in a sudden shout of glee. The echo leapt around him in patterns, mimicking the bells bellowing out from a Sun Temple. Jarvis burst into a run, whooping as he skidded around the first of the magnificent machines. He trailed his fingers over the vessel, as though he was gently caressing the surface of a pond. These were ships of space, hawkships, designed for a pilot and a navigator. The Human in him wanted his wings back, he wanted to leap into the ship and seize the controls, take flight right this moment and roar through the sky-sea like the great paladins of old. The protector bot hungered for reconnection, it craved the merging with another machine, to feel a part of something bigger, grander, and beyond his small core body.

You cannot, little protector. Not yet, not now. Leave these children of a bygone era in peace. The whisper nibbled against his receiver, urging him to gently remove his hand from the hawkship's hull, and he pulled back, staring wistfully at the masterpiece forgotten in the folds of time.

"Flying Machines? Holy Rythrya." Aaldryn's shout startled him from his daze.

Eloiko was aiding Troq through a splintered hole blasted in the chamber wall, setting the Changeling down on the ground. Both Dweller princes looked around in awe.

"What are they all doing here?" Eloiko's voice carried through the darkness.

"We're in one of the main hangers," Troq offered the information shyly. "It suffered less damage when Yrva Krv crashed, due to its positioning."

Aaldryn turned back, yelling, "Titus! You have to come and see this. Real flying machines!"

Jarvis heard shuffling and grunting from his master.

"Alright, alright. Yeh kids have done nothin' but run me haggard."

He watched as Titus fell backwards through the hole. The Hunter groaned, heaving himself to his feet, dusting off his coat. As he turned, the crinkled lines of exhaustion and frustration aging his freckled cheeks melted away into awe.

"By the Paladins. There are so many of them!"

"Think of the sand-ship engines that could be built out of these." Eloiko waved a paw. "We'd rule the burning-sea."

Troq's tail shifted uneasily and Eloiko coughed, correcting himself quickly. "Not that we would ever destroy perfectly intact Zaprex monuments."

Jarvis rubbed the back of his neck. To think he had been worried about the two Dweller princes. He should not have been; Troq had Eloiko wrapped around his paw.

"I think we should camp here." Aaldryn walked to the edge of the boulevard, tracing the glass panelling with his paw pads. His protective eyelids folded back as his gaze crystallised on the drop below. His whiskers and air-gills twitched as the frosted air tickled against them. Jarvis shivered, pressing his face against the barrier he was too small to peer over. Ice on the glass had formed intricate artworks that the heat of his bare skin ruined upon touching. Chilly, inky depths, lit only by the distant, dancing lights of crystals, singing lonesome songs, welcomed him like an unfolding carnivorous flower, alluring but so deadly. He could smell the scent of broken crystals releasing their toxic spores. Jarvis turned his nose up, sniffing. Data twirled past his optical lenses as he linked with the environmental system. They were safe—for now…unless the air currents changed, but they seemed to be keeping steady thus far. He picked up a discarded piece of metal, spitting philepcon liquid onto it, and it brightened with light. With a heave he launched it over the edge of the boulevard and watched as it vanished.

Aaldryn whistled. "Well, that's deep."

Jarvis crinkled his nose. He placed his hands back on the cold glass surface and scanned the darkness once more, picking up traces of movement. He repressed a shiver caused by the glinting pictograms that flashed across his optical screens. Machines wandered the lonesome layers below them. He could feel their receivers brush his own every so often, all curious of his presence, but not curious enough to make their own presence known.

Titus blew a long rasp, scratching his scalp as he eyed the hawkships. "Bit spooky, heh, for a camp, with these big winged-thingies."

"I think it'll be the safest place for now. We need to rest. I have no idea how long we've been going." Aaldryn shrugged off his packs, letting them clunk onto the floor.

"According to my internal clock," Jarvis twirled a finger, bringing up the holographic symbols only he could see. "We have been travelling for approximately a day and a half, with only two breaks for meals." He could have got more technical, down to the millisecond, but that would be irrelevant to the others. And irritating. He shared a knowing glance with Troq.

Aaldryn spread his paws. "There you go. We need to pitch camp."

"This is beyond the point we've ever gone before. I'm not sure if we can lead you much further," Troq said. "Jarvis, can you help me work out how to recalculate our position?"

"We can rest first." Jarvis loosened his own hip-bags, settling them down beside the hawkship, smiling up at the machine. It slumbered peacefully, and its presence was comforting. He would sleep well beside it himself. It was humbling, in some ways, to explore the deep, great wonders of the world below the burning-sea and realise that the AIs left alone, without the Creators, had soldiered on, suffering in their silence. He had given his protector bot new life and it felt relief that vibrated down his spine. While he grew ever more amazed by the new, startling world of wonders, he could see a tension curve Master Titus' shoulders, and that made a pit form in his own stomach.

"Master, the sky-ships have powered down. The AI systems within them have all been deactivated. They won't harm us."

Titus set out their plates. The Hunter insisted on them being formal and proper in their meals, as though it was some sort of ritual he had adopted from wartime. He was sent a thin smile, and, in the light of the small Mist stove, Jarvis caught the lines of weary stress around the edges of his master's blackened eyes.

"Ah, laddie, I am not worried about the sleeping machines. I be more troubled that so much of the old fairy magic be still waiting down here, yeh know? We Messengers don' know about it all, aye? It's just a bit overwhelming."

Jarvis accepted his plate of hot stew and curled up on his bedroll. "Well, if it puts your mind at ease, Master, unless someone has philepcon liquid in their system, they cannot use the sky-ships, or most Zaprex technology for that matter."

Eloiko's air-gills fanned out. "I've actually been giving that some thought."

Jarvis looked his way, noticing his master had supressed his reply, allowing the prince to voice his concerns first.

"For generations the burning-sea has been producing Changelings. Even if it was perhaps one, or two, who were accepted every hundred or so sol-cycles, that is still a considerable number of Changelings living somewhere down here." Eloiko glanced at Troq. "We've had at least three in our generation, if you include Troq."

"And they've been considered mad and banished into the lower levels," Troq murmured. "Or worse, the Iposti have taken them away."

"Yeh wondering if they'll retaliate?" Titus arched an eyebrow.

Eloiko nodded uneasily.

"I don't think so." Jarvis tapped his spoon on his knee. "AIs were programmed with a strict code of conduct they had to abide by, and, as Changelings, we've inherited that, albeit diluted by our fleshling nature. But we will find ourselves obeying an AI with higher authority. I don't get the feeling Tikal is a threat. I think it's more likely that, Troq, you've been chosen to unite the Changelings that Utillia has produced."

"Yes, I was afraid you would say something like that," Troq muttered.

Eloiko rested a paw on Troq's thigh. "Which still does not answer the question: what if there is a someone, or something, of a higher authority in Utillia that isn't benevolent?"

Jarvis frowned. "Only a Zaprex or a Changeling could operate anything Zaprex-built, so—"

"Nay, laddie, that be not entirely true." Titus raised a spoon, waggling it in his direction.

"Yes, it is."

"Khamsin says your Master is referring to Starborn Humans and

Silverblood Humans," Aaldryn said dully and Jarvis jerked in his direction. "Though he doubts there are Silverbloods alive today with enough of a lineage to work any Zaprex machine—"

Titus snorted. "Don' doubt it. I'm a Telvon."

A glance passed between Titus and Aaldryn, and Jarvis wondered what it was Khamsin was saying in the Kattamont's head.

"What are Silverbloods?" Jarvis asked.

"Paladins, laddie. Myths of Starborn paladins be about Silverblood humans. Humans with diluted Starblood somewhere in their ancestry. Either they had a pure Starborn ancestor, or a Zaprex ancestor."

"Oh, no…no…" Jarvis held up a hand. "No."

"Oh. Aye. Zaprexes were illusionists. Make yeh see whatever yeh want. They were called fairy-born, or pixie-born. Do not look so affronted, lad. Humans and Zaprexes lived together for centuries before they ever arrived on Livila."

"So, you're saying there might be a whole bunch of Humans out there who could still use Zaprex technology?" Jarvis jutted a finger towards the hawkship behind him.

Titus nodded. "Sure, know of at least two at the House of Flames."

"I can see now why you would find it alarming to see all this Zaprex technology lying around, then. I wouldn't want anyone who didn't know what they were doing to get hold of these," Jarvis muttered. "No offence," he said to Troq.

"Aye." Titus sighed. "Our world doesn't need that, not now, not ever."

In the light of their flickering Mist stove, the reflective surfaces of the hawkships gleamed with barely visible hexagon patterns. The soft song of the sky-ships was wistfully lonesome, but ever hopeful of their masters' return, and he had no desire for them to be tainted by anyone other than his Creators. At least they were forever locked within the confines of the crumbling cities below the burning-sea.

But he could hear them, and he let himself softly hum the tune in reply, so that they would know they were not alone in the forested darkness.

So that they would know someone cared.

The Mist stove burned. With aching eyes Jarvis stared into its flickering flames. The warmth upon his bare cheeks fought for dominance against the biting chill. A halo of Mist enveloped their small camp. His mind was spinning with thoughts. It had no desire to release him into the peaceful world of dreams and dancing colours. Even with his eyelids drooping, caked like clay, lashes latching onto each other, he could not close his eyes to fade into darkness. He sighed in protest, irritated by his insomnia. The heavy weight of his bed-roll shifted from his shoulders, and the icy air clawed his skin.

"Canna sleep, laddie?" His master settled down beside him. It was always a little startling to see him without his hood and cloak, his slender frame apparent under a threadbare shirt.

"I thought that being here, amongst these sky-ships, that I would feel safe, but instead I keep hearing their sad song and I feel…scared. I shouldn't feel scared."

Titus raised an eyebrow. "Why not? Being scared is a perfectly fine response to a situation that is out of our control. It is even a perfectly rational response to a situation that is within our control. Just because we're Messengers, don' mean we don' feel scared, laddie."

Jarvis shifted out of his bed-roll, hissing at the freezing temperature that greeted him. To have gone from the blistering heat of the burning-sea to a frozen underworld was rather shocking.

"It's not this place, this moment, I'm scared of. It's later, the future, of everyone dying, and I'm left by myself." He cast his arms out. "Like these sky-ships. I don't want to die alone."

"I see." Titus brought his knees up to his chin. His shoulders tensed before they relaxed. "Yeh're gonna have ta trust that yeh have it in yeh to survive. That song yeh carry, that we all carry, that piece of the Secondary Realm we are born with, it will never leave yeh. Even if we all do."

"But you won't, will you?"

Titus shrugged. "Jarvis, ma own children haven't seen me in sol-cycles. I don' even know if they remember what I look like. I don' know if I'll ever get back ta them. No Messenger can promise anything."

Jarvis hung his head. Like a babe, clinging to his mother, he was being selfishly needy. He had his master with him, when Titus was far away from his own family. A bony finger slipped under his chin, lifting it, and he faced the Hunter's black gaze.

"I know yeh want ta think of yerself as a man, and yeh are, in many ways. Young laddies like yeh lead battles where I come from, but yeh're on the verge of becoming who yeh are. Don' be afraid of being afraid, laddie. Accept it as a part of yeh."

Jarvis bobbed his head, curling up against the Hunter, glad that Clive was not nearby to tease him for his behaviour.

"Master Titus, why do good people have to die? Like my family?"

"Young Messengers often ask that same question. I did, too, when I was a wee bit younger than yeh. I was a little laddie when I was placed into a Squad. Ma family, it be a large one, and it be a bit like…royalty, I s'pose. But not me, I was a failure." His gaze was lost in the glow of the Mist stove. "Ma first battle was out on the First Lines. Shouldna been, but ma brother was not kind ta me. Paladins be Blessed, 'twas awful. Bodies ripped apart right in front of me. Bullets shredded folk. I recall red blood, and red lava. That red, it still burns ma eyes. Sometimes I wonder how I survived, and why? Why did I live, and they didna?" His chest heaved, shuddering with a rattle of bones. "I hated maself for surviving when ma friends didna."

His master laughed, an exhausted laugh, like a clanking of wind carillons in a breeze through his bones. "I was lost somewhere in self-hatred and fear. Fear of the next battle, and dying like they had. I was not a good Messenger, afraid of death." Titus leant forward, reaching for his hip-bags. He sorted through them, pulling out a small, tightly-bound leather book. He carefully undid it. Jarvis' optical lenses flickered in curiosity, catching the glint of glossy paper, crinkled now with age, and faded from the oils of skin constantly rubbing the edges.

"What are they?" he whispered.

Titus held out the sheets of paper and Jarvis blinked rapidly as he processed the images upon them. Not drawn, not painted, like those the Sun Monks had done for his sister's wedding. These were crystal clear lines, so realistic, as though a moment in time had been caught and blinked into the sheets.

"Captured memories." Jarvis dared to touch one, drawing back in alarm at the smooth surface, so very unlike the paintings of his grandparents that had hung above the fireplace. He had loved those paintings, sleeping under them, studying the faces of his forebears, each line stroked with thick globs of colour to make details. These captured memories were nothing like those paintings.

"Aye," Titus agreed. "That they be. Back yon, when I was a wee lad, I found this Zaprex device that captured time. Zinkx had this rule, if yeh found a piece of Zaprex tech, 'twas yers ta keep. So, I figured out how ta use the little time-capturer."

"Do you still have it?"

Titus laughed. "Nah, I passed it on ta Raphael's kid, Tutankhamun. Ah. Let me see. Where is he? Oh, yah, here he is."

With trembling fingers, frightened he would damage the flimsy paper, Jarvis felt the sheet, studying the somewhat faded image of a slender woman standing in a garden. She wore a style of dress that his protector bot instantly recognised, but he himself, had never seen. She was not at all like his sister, who had stood like a thickened wall, roughened by farm work. If anything, the woman reminded him of a delicate flower. She held a boy of perhaps four sol-cycles in her arms, who was dressed in similarly confusing clothing. They both looked happy, smiling for the one who held the time-capturer.

"Yeh'll like Raphael. She's a lot like yeh. She's High Medic now.

At least, I hope she still is. Very powerful position, very annoying position." Titus smiled. "Ah, here's a good one. I almost broke the time-capturer." He passed over another and Jarvis stared at what would not have been an amusing image at the time, but now it showed a fascinating scene of panicked characters as a Twizel rampaged through a small camp.

Titus waved a hand. "We all scattered, screaming our heads off. I happened ta accidently take the shot. Glad I did. Look at our faces. We're a bunch of freshies."

There were faded sections to the image, and Jarvis' optical lenses pieced them together, gradually forming a clearer picture, heightening the bleached colours, giving clarity to the blurred faces.

"You're all dressed weird."

"Tah, they be lava suits and our armour. Very important in the Plains of Blazing Fire. Oh, this is Kaitla. He and Raphael got married. Ah, here is Zinkx."

He was handed a picture of a young Wynnila man, sitting on a rock, drinking from a thin canister, wearing a worn-out smile that seemed purposely put on for the captured memory. They looked almost the same age. It was startling to stare at a picture of a warrior he had been told such incredible tales of, only to see him as a mere boy. Did he look as young, and as innocent, as the great High Commander?

"He looks so young." He stroked the image.

"Told yeh, he ain't some grand hero, no matter the stories Old Man Denvy told yeh." Titus' smile was hesitantly soft. "Zinkx wasn't a Commander back then, only our Squad Cap'in. I was barely nine when I started taking these, fresh outta training. Cap chose me ta be their Squad Crystal tech, out of ten other candidates."

Titus carefully wrapped the pictures back in their leather casing, leaving Jarvis to wonder if he had pictures of his wife and children somewhere in the pile. "Ma older brother was livid. Thought for sure I would be an embarrassment to the great Telvon name if I went into the field. I didna do so well on ma tests. But Zinkx, he thought I was good enough. Yet, after that first battle on the First Lines," lanky shoulders tightened, "I couldna sleep for nights afterwards, so scared I was. Closed ma eyes and all I saw were dead faces swimming all around me. Zinkx would stay in my cabin, would rock me ta sleep each night, no matter how long it took. He would wait 'til I was asleep."

Jarvis hugged his chest. "Father would do that for me, too."

"Messengers don' have parents. We don' tend ta even know who our parents are, or our siblings. We be raised in large groups, start our training the moment we can talk and walk. I come from the Telvon Family, so I knew I was a Telvon. Never sure who was ma Pa or Ma, though."

"Sounds sad."

"Not really." Titus shrugged. "Our Squads become our family. Zinkx became ma father. I would ask him over and over why did I live and everyone else, who were so much braver, so much stronger than I, die? He would settle me down into the blankets and I knew." Titus held fingers to the sockets of his eyes. "I knew by the look he gave me that he didna really have an answer, but he would say anyway, 'Because it is the world we live in.'"

"Did it help you?"

"Messengers get jaded rather quickly." His master sighed. "But we also love very deeply. It's one of the reasons I fought the Twizel that consumed me, because I knew ma Squad was there for me. You keep hope alive, laddie, somewhere inside yeh, and it can do amazing things."

Jarvis nodded.

"So, no, I don' know why good people have ta die." Jarvis snuggled into his blanket as Titus hunkered down beside him, joining him under the thick hide. "But we live in a world that be dying, falling slowly apart. Bad people, good people, everyone is dying, it matters not who you are."

"What does matter, then?" Jarvis murmured.

"Well, as a Messenger, I be supposed ta say, all that matters is how yeh die: valiantly in battle, worthy of a great tale." Titus laughed, and Jarvis rolled his eyes at the Death Cult mentality. "But Zinkx would not approve."

Jarvis crinkled his nose. Titus reached out and rubbed it, as though he were one of his children. His head was too heavy to hold upright and it sank onto the bed-roll, his weighted eyes refusing to stay open. Titus tucked the blanket around his chin, blocking out the bitter air.

"What matters, my son," he felt Titus brush back his hair, "is that you live the best you can, protecting those you can protect, and loving all you can love, for there is no greater joy for a Messenger than to live and die with one foot always stepping forward."

Jarvis jerked awake. He gasped, looking around their small camp. He blinked away pixels from his lenses, scrubbing at his eyes. Nearby, Titus and Aaldryn were curled up by the Mist stove, Troq and Eloiko wrapped up together in a nest on the other side, all lost in slumber. He remembered Aaldryn waking him for his turn on watch, but beyond that…

"I feel asleep on watch," he hissed. "I am so bad at this."

Something had roused him now, though. It had been like a sharp intrusion into his mind and now he was alert, his heart racing, fear crushing his chest. The Dragon—what if it was the Dragon trying to consume him again? He threw off his blankets. Altering his gravity-bubble, he crept carefully past the ancient sky-ships they had camped beside and peered down the long chamber, running various scans. Nothing touched his senses but the pingback of distant machines. Jarvis frowned. He was spooked because he was alone, on watch, in the bowels of a buried ancient city.

As if a breath had puffed against his skin, a finger lightly touched his cheek and he felt it vibrate in his mind as a connection fitted together. Flickering light caught the corner of his vision. He whipped about so fast he almost tripped over his feet.

The figure moved between the lonesome sky-ships like a spectre, drifting without direction, trailing its fingers over the hulls, creating patterns of refracting light and chiming melodies he could hear within his mind. Melodies that shifted pieces of data back and forth, slotting in new information, clearing hazy sections. Jarvis blinked back tears. It was beautiful; the sound filled out the images of high clouds scudding across blue skies, and wings taking the air currents, banking and spinning playfully and dangerously in a dance, going higher and higher into a frigid world until heights were reached and stars were mapped. He choked on his breath, falling to his knees. Had he been back in Pennadot, on the river banks of the Cor, he would have thought the beautiful creature one of the legendary water sprites, said to inhabit the reeds, for all around it, every reflective surface seemed to glint with colour.

His own skin adapted, his birth element soaking in the rays, shifting from hue to hue. The figure turned towards him, blinking with large glistening eyes, shimmering with rainbows, akin to his own.

Hello, Jarvis-of-the-Plains-People.

"You know my name?"

It ducked under the nearest sky-ship, becoming clearer as it approached. Jarvis stepped back in shock. A Zaprex corpse, misshapen, without the green liquid skin, jerking with the movements of a puppet. It was missing one antenna; the one that remained was buzzing rapidly, as though scanning and receiving in overdrive.

Of course, Little Protector. We watch from above and below. It touched its chest. *We are* Mothership:_Tikal_of_Rainbows. *This body became dormant, empty, open, so we did take, we did use, as we use many. We are many. We see you.* It drifted forward, landing in front of him, bowing low. *We help. We navigate.*

Tikal. The Mothership. The protector bot within Jarvis reeled in awe and confusion, so much so that his vision began to spin. Pictures flashed across his lenses of a glorious blue sky-sea, with hawkships dancing between thin clouds, drawing close to a gleaming, bright glow in the distance that hummed with the song of a thousand birds on a sweet spring morning. Jarvis scrubbed at his eyes, wiping at the tears. It was a flying city. Almost invisible in the sky-sea, for its exterior was gilded in a surface so reflective it mirrored the world surrounding it.

"You're one of them." He clutched at his rapidly heaving chest. "You're one of the Cities of Gold. You're still here? You still exist, after all this time?"

What is Time but a lonely wandering fairy, seeking its lover? Large eyes blinked slowly.

"How long have you been watching me?"

We see all. We are many. Lonely amongst the Angels.

Jarvis gritted his teeth. This was an artificial intelligence. A masterpiece creation of the Zaprex Empire. Had he not already encountered the Key within the Secondary Realm, this moment would have overwhelmed him. His knees were already weakening, trembling under an invisible pressure.

"You're really a Mothership…" he whispered.

Yes. This is established. It cocked its head, scowling in disproval at his apparent feedback loop.

"But how are you here?" he insisted.

The AI's arms flapped uselessly. *Just because an Empire falls does not mean that which it leaves behind falls with it. Our tree is strong, our branches are long, our roots are deep, our mirrors are many.*

"Jarvis!"

Jarvis vaulted several feet into the air at Titus' shout and landed none too elegantly.

"By the Paladins, Weasel! Whatcha be wandering about for? Scared ma soul out of ma bones!"

Jarvis spluttered out, "I'm sorry, sir."

There was half a regrowth of skin across the skull of his master's face, and the visible half betrayed all the emotions the Hunter must have been bottling up. The fear of loss, the turmoil of missing his family, his intense need to protect. Jarvis winced, wishing he had not seen behind the man's mask.

"Yeh stupid *traki*. I thought yeh'd—what in all *jrak* is that?" Titus' dagger came inches from Tikal's neck. The broken machine stared blankly up at the Hunter, unconcerned by the weapon threatening the wires of its exposed throat. Jarvis threw up his arms.

"Master, stop! It's not an enemy. This is Tikal, an AI of one of the Cities of Gold."

"What?" Aaldryn had arrived. The prince's fanned air-gills and tail went slack in shock and he gaped at the tiny, broken corpse in front of them.

"Impossible," he choked out, though Jarvis was not sure if it was Aaldryn who spoke, or Khamsin.

Jarvis carefully wrapped his hand around Titus' tense wrist and drew his dagger away. "I know it doesn't look like much inside such a broken body, but I am positive it's telling the truth. It's an AI; it can't lie."

Titus scoffed.

"Jarvis is right. I can feel it in my head," Troq hesitantly interjected. He clung to Eloiko's arm, staring intently beyond Jarvis at the broken Zaprex corpse.

"See. Troq can sense it too. It doesn't mean us any harm."

"I don't think that's what Troq was saying." Aaldryn reached out a paw, as if to urge him away. Jarvis pulled back from the prince.

Tikal's head poked around Jarvis' side, its single antenna jiggling as it blinked large, glassy eyes, studying the new arrivals with childish curiosity.

"*Wind-god, your children scream,*" a tinny voice crackled through the city's intercom system. "*We are sorry. We cannot help them. We cannot set them free. They cannot play between our Angels as they once did.*"

Aaldryn's tail slackened. It was indeed Khamsin, now, staring out through Aaldryn's eyes, studying the tiny machine. "When the Thousand Sol-Cycle War broke out, how long did the Northern Tower hold?"

"*Until the very end.*" Tikal's hand reached up in a fist, then spread, sprinkling into the air. "*Your children did not manage to take the Tower. They took out the shield, but they failed to take the CCR. Despite receiving a death blow, Sekhmet refused to allow the Wind Elementals to suffer upon their return to the Secondary Realm. As a dying wish, Sekhmet offered them sanctuary in Utillia. This forced your hand in the final battle of the Unknown Gate. You fled, realising the Dragon for what he was—a Gaia.*"

Khamsin turned to Titus. "It is Tikal. Only Tikal would know that story. It was the City of Gold that dwelt in Utillia during the Thousand Sol-Cycle War and was manned by Sekhmet's bonding partner. Sekhmet was the Navigator of the Northern Tower. He brokered a contract that allowed my children free range within the Primary Realm. It was said to be his final act."

Titus sheathed his dagger. "A contract? It did not involve you?"

Khamsin shook his head. "No. At the time I was elsewhere."

Jarvis looked up. "Wait, if Sekhmet died, then who holds the contract with the Simoon—?" His eyes widened. "The Kattamont people themselves? That's how they control Wind Elementals? Please don't tell me that's what Mist is." He felt suddenly sick.

"Not so much the Kattamont people themselves, but whoever is the current leader, and at the moment that is the Iposti Order. And while Mist is a by-product of Wind Elemental existence within the Primary Realm, it is not anything evil, I assure you of that. The process of its creation was quite harmless, and farming it did no damage to my children. I am not sure that is still the case, though." Khamsin sighed. "I believe Mist was the reason Sekhmet brokered the contract, knowing Kattamonts and Wind Elementals could, together, create something wonderful with Utillia."

"So, what went wrong then?" Jarvis held out his hands.

"*What always goes wrong.*" Tikal skipped around them. "*Greed. Desperation. Power! More. More. More!*" it squeaked loudly, causing sparks to pop between the cracked joints of the corpse it used.

"It is possible that, centuries after the fall of the Zaprex Empire, after the rising of the burning-sea, the Kattamonts grew to forget the contract and came to fear the Simoon. They already believe the Zaprexes were the great oppressors. History has a way of becoming distorted over time." Khamsin shrugged.

"How can you be so calm about it?"

"I am old, child. I have learnt to be patient." The wind-god turned his attention to Tikal. "It is good to see you again, Tikal of Rainbows."

"*We hope you do not want to blow us up this time, Wind-God-of-the-North.*"

"No, not this time."

"*You have mellowed. Your wind is less harsh against our spires.*"

Khamsin smiled before Aaldryn returned to control. He shifted uneasily on his foot-paws, glancing at Troq and Eloiko. "Since we're all up, perhaps we should pack camp," he suggested.

"Wind God?" Eloiko asked. "I thought you were just a wind chaplain."

"Ah, not exactly." Aaldryn's ears drooped. "It's a long story."

"Don't press him, Eloiko." Troq tugged his paw. "Let's pack camp."

"No. No." Eloiko shook his head, studying the dejected Aaldryn. "Wind God…as in one of the Four Winds the Prides used to worship?"

"Well, to be fair, most in the Outer Sectors still do." Aaldryn rubbed his neck.

Eloiko's twin tails twitched and Aaldryn relented. "Fine. Yes, I am the host of Khamsin, Titan of the Northern Wind. I apologise for keeping it from you, brother."

Eloiko turned sharply. "I do believe, Troq, that I am the one who is utterly mad."

Jarvis listened to Eloiko's muttering, amused that the fire-coated, double-tailed prince was miffed to discover he was mundane after all.

"Come laddie," Titus urged.

Jarvis followed his master and behind them the broken machine skipped playfully, causing light to ripple over the surfaces of the sky-ships. Jarvis caught the slight smile upon Aaldryn's lips as the prince wrapped up his bed-roll. At least the Kattamont was having the chance to see the wonders he had always dreamt of.

Tikal twirled about, humming a happy melody.

"Whatever are we supposed ta do with it?" Titus raised an eyebrow at the swaying machine. He switched off the Mist stove, wrapping it up tightly in a bundle that he added to his hip-bags. Their world grew murkier, the darkness wrapping around them like cloak without the buzzing of the Mist flames.

Tikal landed beside Titus, poking its head under his arm. Titus yelped, overbalancing and landing on his rump. Jarvis slapped a hand over his mouth quickly, hiding his laughter under a cough.

"*We help. We guide. We are many. We are everywhere.*"

"It will save me having to help Troq recalibrate our position every couple of hours, sir," Jarvis offered.

Titus heaved himself back onto his feet. "I dunno if I trust it."

"Do you trust me, sir?"

His master turned his way, with an amused look across his tight lips. "Yes. I do."

"Then you can trust me that it doesn't mean us any harm."

The Hunter huffed and quickly donned his hood in distain. "Fine."

Jarvis beamed. He seized Tikal's cracked, three fingered hand. It was small and delicate in his grasp, so cold and lifeless despite the AI existing within the corpse. There was no Zaprex heart beating in the buzzing chest, no philepcon liquid pumping through crystal veins, flexing the silicon muscles, shifting the hull. It was dead. It moved through sheer force of old, crackling wires, barely hanging together, from a power source gradually burning out. It was still the closest thing he would get to a Zaprex, though, until he met the Key once again. Jarvis grinned, spinning the AI around, and it burst into laughter that was delightful.

"Lead the way, Tikal of Rainbows."

CHAPTER TEN

Her name was Mazeenaicka—'She-Who-Follows-Clouds'—and she became his Queen. That same sol-cycle the ash-clouds finally began to dissipate, and the blessed rays of the Sun shone upon green Pennadotian fields once more. In the seventieth and sixth sol-cycle of Disgleirio's life a prince was born, and in the tradition of his forefathers—much to the disgust of his brother—he named the boy Derwyn—'Oak Tree'—honouring the boy's mother also. Two sol-cycles passed and Mazeenaicka gave birth to a princess, whom they named Deilen or, in the Basic tongue, 'Leaves'.

They could not bring back the Dawn Ages of his ancestors, but as the sol-cycles passed and, brick by brick, Avalon's foundations grew strong once more, a Golden Age was reborn from the ash-clouds. Pennadot had a King and a Queen once more upon the Emerald Throne, and the Sun shone blessings upon the land.

Light blinded Zafiashid. She hissed at the fires burning around the fighting-pit as she stalked through the doors into the arena, styled as a sandy, rocky terrain that was supposed to mimic an island upon which two queens would clash for Pride ownership. She scoffed at the thought. The thundering roar of the crowd far above the high walls of the pit made the floor of the arena tremble. It was difficult to tell how many had come to watch the pit-fight, but it was likely to be a fair turn out, considering who she was.

Across the wide expanse, between the cauldrons of fires, stalked a Kattamont princess. She almost blended in with the dusty floor of the pit, her coat a freckled chestnut, with soft lavender air-gills frilled out in territorial greeting.

Zafiashid growled low. Nixlye should have had this fight. The young queen would have enjoyed another chance to settle her grudge with the Jezumatu Pride for their dealings in illegal prince pit-battles.

"Princess Uyrilk, it is good to see you again." Zafiashid inclined her head.

"Likewise, Queen Zafiashid. My sister is still mourning the loss of her sword arm to your princess. Cut in such a manner she can never have it replaced. *Tah.* So vicious."

Zafiashid smirked. Such a beautiful battle it had been to watch, dust thick in the pit, high-pitched yowls as blades pierced thick hide to bone. Nixlye ruthlessly hacking at the Queen of the Jezumatu Pride in a fit of vengeance. She had been one of the leeches that day, watching on in the crowd, cheering, and she could still recall the thrill it had evoked.

"Feel up to losing your own arm today?" she sneered, twirling her sword.

Uyrilk laughed. She loosened her own two blades from their sheaths and played them along the soil of the pit's floor.

"I doubt I will be losing any limbs, Zafiashid. I am not my sister."

"We shall see." Zafiashid dodged to the side, spinning on her heels as a blade twirled down. It hissed past her ear, barely missing it. As the attacking female, Uyrilk had the right to strike first and that put Zafiashid in position of defence. She skidded across the earth, rolling on her back, and lunged up a nearby rock as the princess followed her every springing movement. The crowd's noise became naught but a rushing hum overlaying the thudding of her heart and the timed heaves of her breathing as she blocked blows and lashes with her bladed tail. Uyrilk skipped back, somersaulting and landing on all fours.

Zafiashid coiled her tail back, fanning out her feathers, revealing the thin metal blades sewn into the skin and poison sacs. She clicked her tongue in disapproval at the young princess's shock.

"Tut, tut, young one, did you never hear the story? How my princesses pinned me down and tore out my tail spikes." She stalked the crouching Kattamont. "Thought it would make me weak, they did. Never guessed I would get metal ones to replace them. Found a very good Mist mechanic in the Outer Sectors."

"That is insane." Uyrilk spun her blades out in front of her. "How can you even lift your tail?"

"I do not believe in weakness!" Zafiashid scoffed.

Uyrilk hissed. She leapt. Her twin blades whistled with Mist. Zafiashid twirled away from their sudden extension, blocking the strike with her own sword. They interlocked, skidding along the sand, tails entwining.

"Come! Cub!" Zafiashid spat into the princess's face. "You are not even trying to kill me!" She could feel the restraint in the other's arm, the reluctance in the tension of her muscles as their swords swept back and forth. She growled low, going in for a charge, throwing her sword aside and slamming her weight into the younger Kattamont.

They both landed in the sand, rolling, clawing for dominance. Smacking Uyrilk's paws down, Zafiashid dislodged a short-sword and pinned it to her throat as Uyrilk's second blade met her midriff. Their eyes locked, low growls emitting down their air-gills as heavy breaths escaped their chests.

"All right, you have my attention, cub," Zafiashid murmured.

Uyrilk spat out blood. "I asked you here, Queen Zafiashid, to warn you."

She almost laughed into the deadened air between them. No one warned Queen Zafiashid, the Outcast of the Prides. The notion was ridiculous. Baring her teeth, Zafiashid leant in further. "Do not mock me, little princess." She pressed the blade she held deeper into the thick skin of the Kattamont's neck, sensing the sword against her stomach tremble as it, too, sank into flesh. The trickle of blood down her waist burnt like a pleasurable fire, igniting her skin, and her fur spiked down her spine.

"This… is the only place the Iposti…don't have any wind!"

Zafiashid sucked in a sharp breath. The soil around them was so still. The air without current. She flicked her gaze around the high walls of the arena, their immense size suddenly crushing. Somewhere above them the Iposti watched, but Uyrilk was correct, they could not interfere in the affairs of two fighting females—this was still their sacred territory, as it had been for centuries.

The risk, though, was massive.

"You are such a fool!" Zafiashid growled into the princess's face.

"You would never have heard me out otherwise, would you?"

Dragging Uyrilk upright, Zafiashid threw her against the nearest rock. "What is so wind-cursed pressing that you risked your life to tell an old outcast like me?"

Uyrilk winced at the sword once more pressed to her throat. She was a fool if she thought Zafiashid would have let down her guard at petty, nonsense words. Zafiashid fanned her air-gills at the crowd's beating feet. The arena floor was shaking, bouncing the soil beneath them. She growled, irked by the stupidity of her people, irked that she still would have been one of the leeches calling for blood if the situation were any different.

"I come from patrolling the Borders. Refugees are flooding across from Pennadot. They are over-running the Etrothaynd Islands and the Jezumatu Prides cannot cope. They speak of a plague and terrible unrest in the Land of the Arc of the Sun. I know that you are kind to Humans, Kelibs, and half-breeds—"

Zafiashid dug her claws into the princess's fur. The way it was worded, it was almost a distasteful slur, to make her sound weak. Did the queens and princesses of the Prides think of her as a chipped clay cup, ruined by her sol-cycles cast aside upon the waves of the burning-sea, made to mingle with Human scum and Kelib mongrels? If anything, the tides had mended the cracks; her motley crew filled the loneliness that had almost killed her.

She owed the Humans and Kelibs her life.

"This may be so, but why come to me? I am an outcast."

Uyrilk bit her bottom lip. Zafiashid scented blood, watching it trickle down the princess's chin. "The Silvertide and Jezumatu navies are slaughtering the refugees at the Borders. It is wrong. I cannot stop them, though. I am but one princess with one crew." Her shoulders slumped, along with her tensed muscles. Zafiashid growled at the gesture of defeat. It was one she knew well. Perhaps she herself had looked as pathetic once, kneeling in front of her own princesses, beaten into submission. She whacked the princess firmly over the head. Uyrilk yelped.

"Stand up! You have your crew behind you. I take it that means you still have at least one prince?

Uyrilk looked dazed. "Yes…"

Zafiashid snarled. "Keep him. You will need him. He is loyal to you only, and you cannot do this alone, Uyrilk. You did not forfeit your position within the Pride, did you, by coming here?"

"No." She shook her head.

What a little cub she appeared, eyes so wide, lavender air-gills strung with ridiculous beads. Zafiashid scoffed in the back of her throat at the thought that she had once looked as innocently naïve.

"Being an outcast is not glamourous, cub."

"You are a legend amongst us, Queen Zafiashid," Uyrilk murmured.

"I do not believe in such nonsense."

"It does not matter if you believe it or not; you are a legend."

Amusement rattled her air-gills and Zafiashid withdrew, inclining her head. Uyrilk dropped her blade and knelt, baring her neck. Her air-gills spread wide in a fan, yielding the fight. The crowd above them erupted into a deafening howl of fury. Zafiashid braced herself as the ground shook with their thunderous rage. Cursing, she peered through her half-lidded eyes, studying the unruly stands.

"I suppose they wanted us to fight to the death!" she shouted to Uyrilk.

"They should come down here and try it themselves, then." Uyrilk stood, picking up a stone from the arena floor which she flung up at the crowd. "Filthy cowards, the lot of you!"

Zafiashid fanned out her tail, bellowing with laughter. There was nothing as joyful as causing mayhem. The sea of noise was a melody to her ears, gorgeous in its chaos. They were pathetic herd animals, the lot of them, waiting for a true queen to lead them. She turned her eyes to the clear sky-sea through the bars of ancient coral. Zafiashid raised her arms, her grin growing wider the louder the crowd became.

Someday they would cry her name, either in fear, or in reverence.

Prince Aaldryn, Hunter Titus, Jarvis of the Plains People

CHAPTER ELEVEN

The tavern had a comfortable warmth rising from the fire-pit. The murmur of late-night patrons settled Disgleirio's nerves as he watched Derwyn contently playing on a nearby rug with his elder cousins. Ewyni and Kwyti, Selwyn's eldest sons, could not have been more different in both appearance and personality. Ewyni's obsidian tint contrasted vibrantly with Kwyti's chrysoberyl hue. Where Ewyni was patient, tolerant, and reliable, Kwyti was rambunctious, quick-tempered, but warmly charming. The two boys travelled Pennadot freely with their father, but their destinies were ones he could not envy. If anything, he thought his brother's plans cruel-hearted, condemning his children to a lifetime of imprisonment. Yet if Pennadot and the Northlands, had any hope of survival, Ewyni and Kwyti's sacrifice was required.

"Tell me, Brother, are you attempting to collect the many faces of Humans like gems on your abdicated crown?" Disgleirio glanced up as Selwyn eased into a large seat beside him, handing over a pint of honey-dew.

Selwyn laughed. "What a splendid idea!"

"How are you doing it, by the way?"

Selwyn stared at him over the rim of his pint. Slowly he lowered it and smirked. "What? Having children? Dearest little brother, you should be asking Mazeenaicka that question—"

Disgleirio rolled his eyes. "No, you idiot, how are you having Obilb and Soatrin offspring when you're obviously a Kimwyn."

Selwyn slouched back. "Oh, that's easy. It's all just a matter of programming. Once I worked out the root coding for each Human classification, it was a simple matter of installing that template pre-birth. I'm thinking of building an algorithm to make the process more random, so that it becomes a surprise!"

"What does Akinyi think of all this. I am presuming they are her sons?" The question was enough to give his brother pause, as mention of the woman he had left behind upon abdicating the throne frequently did. "She's just happy I visit from time to time. That together we've made a legacy, even if she'll never get to see that legacy grow."

Disgleirio sighed. "You're worse than Gifu."

"That is a compliment." Selwyn grinned.

At first Jarvis was not sure whether he was picking up an echo of a distant machine pinging off his receivers, or the twitching of Tikal's broken antenna. It was only when Troq's arm brushed against him that he concluded the new hum was the unfiltered noise of Troq's processing.

"Troq, you're thinking rather loudly."

Troq stirred. He stumbled, and Jarvis caught him, bubbling out a laugh. "You should probably try concentrating on what's outside your mind as well. I know what's going on in there is all very fascinating, but we don't want you falling down a hole."

Troq scratched behind an ear. "Sorry. I keep finding myself looping back on how unique Utillia is."

"I'll admit, I didn't think much of it when we first came here, but it holds more wonders than I would have ever imagined. It's been intriguing to see how Kattamonts have survived despite the collapse of the desktop grid."

Troq's eyes rapidly buzzed. "My father was a Human. There is a shortage of princes in the Major Prides, which can lead to illegal, underhanded dealings with the Outer Sectors. Hence, my existence." Troq motioned to himself.

Jarvis scrunched up his face. "Still not sure how that works. We're two entirely different species."

"Precisely!" Troq raised a paw. "Utillia should never have been capable of supporting Humans and Kelibs—"

"But it does. I know. It's crossed my mind as well." Jarvis clambered over a fallen beam, offering his hand to Troq.

"Tikal's Matrix Crystal appears to have broken out of its containment field, and it's been growing for centuries. Spreading out across Utillia, integrating the scattered Galactic Ships, and whatever else it comes across, into its system."

"I suppose it's possible this unregulated growth has turned it into a Conurbation, the next phase up from a Mothership." Jarvis paused. He glanced ahead at the corpse that guided them through the darkness of the tunnels. If Tikal had progressed a level in the AI hierarchy, it had been entirely unsanctioned, and he was not sure how he felt about that.

"Most Scavengers who are unlucky enough to get a high dose of spores from broken crystals are integrated into the system too, right? And it is only a select few who end up as Changelings," Troq offered, with far too much excitement for Jarvis' stomach. He would not have referred to the agonizing death Aaldryn described with a word as benign as 'integration', but it could be seen as such.

"Sure…" Jarvis hesitated. "Still don't know where you're going with this—"

"Those spores from the crystals have been leaking into the environmental system of Utillia for centuries, Jarvis. Centuries. You keep saying the sky-sea of Utillia is the only functioning system."

Jarvis frowned, picturing the rising turrets he had seen in the distance when he first arrived in Utillia. They had been similar to those in Pennadot—the decrepit, forgotten turrets that stood amongst groves of trees. Wynnila children knew to never go near them. He had ignored that warning and found himself a Changeling. All he had noticed about the turrets in Utillia was their status; they had appeared to be in functioning order.

"It took time, time that an AI had," Troq gestured to the eerie corpse skipping around Master Titus ahead of them. "But I think it gradually altered the environmental system, and, in doing so, it has altered everyone living in Utillia. We may all look different on the outside, but I get a feeling, on the inside, we're not that different anymore."

"But why?" Jarvis whispered.

"Why not?" The reverence in Troq's voice trilled. "It's a Mothership. Perhaps it saw this as its only option to protect us."

Were the mutations Jarvis had seen rejections of the process Troq had described, or steps forward? Was it possible that, if they survived the coming Long Night, whatever would emerge from Utillia would be an entirely unique race? It almost seemed like Tikal was becoming a Creator—no, not a Creator—something else. Jarvis drew back, scrolling through information his protector bot had stored. He thought he remembered something about Tikal's Matrix Crystal being used for ship-building. Perhaps this was simply an extension of that built-in directive. The AI was expanding itself, and, in doing so, had taken a new form entirely.

Jarvis shrugged. Troq looked happy at least, finally coming to terms with the changes altering him. Something his friend had said had stood out to him: 'time–time an AI had'. It made him wonder just how much the lonely passage of time had affected Tikal. Tikal bounced and leapt over broken glass beams, and cracked metal frames, making mockery of their efforts to climb and clamber over the ruined structures.

"You know what else I find fascinating?" Troq beamed brightly through the darkness, the glow of his altered eyes haloing his cheeks. Jarvis could just make out the shifting lines of nano-tech wiggling under the half-breed's fur. It spooked him a little. Had he looked as eerie during his own gradual transformation? He was surprised Clive had not made more off-putting remarks.

"Do inform me."

"I am so aware of time. Even down here in the darkness, I know exactly how long it's been since we last rested. When I fall asleep, I know the moment I wake up how long I have slept. It's incredible!"

Jarvis forced a smile. "I'm glad you're feeling more confident." He decided not to mention how much it frustrated him that he could calculate the time so precisely, that he could not become lost in the endless crystal expanses. A butterfly, fluttering without knowledge to the end of its lifetime, between stalks of towering metal beams, bent and aged, that was what he wished he was, but he was a pristine machine caught up in Time's precise hands. Thirteen days, six hours, and four minutes had passed and their supplies were getting awfully low.

Aaldryn joined Jarvis and Troq. "Do you think the Zaprex corpses you have placed above your tent can be controlled by the AI of Tikal as well? What if it is Tikal that is protecting you from the monsters you say rise up from the cities?"

Jarvis knitted his brow. "I suppose it is possible. I believe I met the AI back there, when I lost consciousness. I don't think I dreamt it."

He heard Aaldryn sigh, his air-gills expanding and slapping shut. "Nixlye would love this. All these wonders down here, Zaprex sky-ships, discarded machines, dying crystal chambers all stored away, never to be reached. It is like a world within a world, and I cannot bring any of it back to her."

"Don't say that." Jarvis turned, trying to smile for him, despite how strained their relationship had become. "We're going to have to make sure we get back to tell her all about it."

In the reflective light of the crystals surrounding them in endless pillars, Aaldryn's small nod was hesitant. "Yes, you are right."

Tikal's small hand slid into his and he startled at the touch. Illumed eyes blinked slowly before a childlike grin touched its fissured, metal cheeks, further cracking the splintered hull, causing blue light to leak out.

"We are almost to a safe place. Around next bend. Rest there. Yes."

Titus' cloak rippled around his feet as he stilled. "Alright, I'll scout ahead." The Hunter vanished briskly, leaving an imprint upon the dusty floor.

Tikal shook its head. Its little chest shuddered with an eerily Human sigh. *What a strange creature. He is neither here, nor is he there; his heart is someplace else.*

"He misses his family."

We miss our family, too. Tikal's large eyes widened a few sizes. *We wonder where they are.*

Jarvis rested his hand upon the AI's head. He could not say anything to such a lonely voice, echoing in his mind, so in silence they continued. The air grew gradually richer, tasting less of charred metal and more like it was filtered through a forest and rain had fallen upon sweet grass. Strips of light crossed the passage. Jarvis picked up the pace, his heart racing. Tikal started to giggle.

They burst into a giant glass chamber. It would have once been an observatory, and it had now become overrun with the largest crystal tree he had ever seen. Behind him Eloiko froze in sudden panic.

"We are so dead." He choked out, staggering back.

"No, Tikal wouldn't lead us into danger," Jarvis spluttered out. It would not—would it? Had he trusted something he should not have trusted all along?

Tikal continued to giggle. *"You silly big-cat! There are no scary things here. This is a safe place."*

"It's right. Khamsin says the air is clean." Aaldryn stepped carefully forward, holding out his paws in awe. "This is incredible." He burst into sudden laughter, and began to climb into the branches of the enormous crystal.

Jarvis stood slack-jawed, staring after the prince. This made no sense.

"But, Tikal, I thought if the crystals break out of their containment field, they spread, their spores pollute the air, the philepcon liquid within them seeps into the ground." Jarvis turned to the AI. "This crystal is huge. It's broken out of its field, a long, long time ago."

The AI laughed, hysterically, pinging like a little bell. He could only gape at the tiny machine, awed at the sound of its amusement that echoed through the chamber, bouncing off the shimmering branches of the rosy formation. It was a though he stood in a giant room of tingling chimes.

It stopped, suddenly, leaving him with Tikal's soft voice whispering into his receiver, words only he and Troq could hear.

Silly, silly child-bot. That only happens to tainted crystals. This is not a tainted crystal. It touched a single finger to its rotted-out chest. *We have tried to keep Utillia clean. The rot has been growing. Our efforts are in vain.*

"Don't say that, Tikal. I am sure that what you have done has helped greatly."

"I see." Troq gazed up through the expanding branches. "The crystals act as filters for the sky-sea."

Jarvis sucked in a sharp breath. This entire time he had been so certain the environmental system of Utillia had survived the destabilization of the desktop grid, but what if it had not? He stared at Tikal.

"You're the environmental system?" he choked out.

Tikal held out its hands. *"As one collapsed, a new one grew."*

"You're the environmental system of a whole land!"

Tikal rolled its eyes. *"This is established."*

"I just don't think you realise how incredible this is. You're sustaining an entire land," Jarvis insisted.

The decrepit corpse before them shuddered, its shoulders drooping. *"We do not grow fast enough. Not enough Mirrors. Cannot sustain more, and more, and more."*

Troq rested a paw to his chest. "But that is why you created me, right? I'm here to help. Utillia is my home."

A crooked smile distorted Tikal's face. *"Can you hear our song now?"*

Troq's eyes blinked rapidly. Curious, Jarvis raised a hand to the receiver under his temple, frowning when he could not sense any change in the gentle hum that had been a constant around Tikal. Tikal looked at him, and shook its head in his direction. He sighed, mildly disappointed. It was not for him that Tikal had led them to this place; it was for Troq.

"I can!" Troq burst out. "I can hear it. It's so…enormous—" Troq's tail curled tightly and his fur stiffened. "I think it wants access."

"Updates! Yes!" Tikal jumped around Troq, causing its empty hull to rattle. *"Update Yrva Krv. Soon you shall be operational."* The corpse jerked to an abrupt halt, causing both Jarvis and Troq to wince. It flung out its arms, turning to them. Its body sparked. *"You will be our shield against a storm!"*

Jarvis clapped a hand down on Troq's shoulder. "Have fun, my friend."

Troq shot him a playful glare. "I blame you entirely for all this."

"I know." Jarvis hopped over a low branch, urged forward by the sound of a trickling creek. His eyes widened at the sight of the clean water streaming free of the trunk of the crystal tree. It felt like an eternity since he had seen flowing water, so clear it was almost invisible to the eye. His heart leapt into his dry throat as his mind was swept back to the days in the farm, to the river that ran through their lands, and the silver glint it carried in the sunlight. Jarvis sank down beside the small creek, thrusting his hands into the smooth ribbon of water.

His skin chilled instantly and he felt a rush of static make his hair spike.

"It's so beautiful," he whispered.

"Aye, a sight to behold. Water. What every traveller wants at least once upon a journey." Titus laughed.

"It's clean?" Jarvis faced his master and the Hunter stepped over him, swinging their empty water-skins.

"Indeed."

"So Tikal's crystals even filter the water," Jarvis mused.

"Heh, really? That's what be happening here?" Titus looked up. "We have a similar system at the House of Flames, but only in the Hospital Spire; it be a separate entity to the House with its own crystal tree and its own river."

"They're in symbiosis, you mean?"

Titus shrugged. "I suppose they are."

Jarvis pursed his cracked lips. He scooped up a handful of water and splashed it over his face, shivering as it ran down his neck and pooled into the nooks of his collar bones. His hull danced with pleasure.

"Where do you think the water is coming from? We haven't seen any flowing water like this in Utillia."

"Well, once upon a time, long, long ago, before the Northlands became a mega-continent, there was once an ocean that was ruled by the Vixens. Story goes that when the Zaprexes combined the Northlands by joining all the Borders, so that they could create the rotational spin, they pushed all the water beneath us." Titus cupped his hands into a bowl shape. "The ocean now sits under the Northlands.

Old Man Denvy once described it as a fountain, but it goes around and around now."

Jarvis blinked a few times, his mind seeming to struggle to process such an absurd story. "That's impossible." He snorted.

His master flapped a hand, dismissing him. "It's just a Messenger Myth, laddie."

"What do you think could be causing the contamination of the Zaprex crystals then?" Jarvis splashed more water over his neck, happy to soak his entire tunic. Across the creek Titus was filling their water-skins. He looked up, sinking back on his heels to study the gently swaying crystal branches. Eloiko sat astride one, laughing at the sight of Aaldryn trying to clamber down from exploring the canopy.

"That be an interesting question." Titus threw a water-skin his way. Jarvis caught it.

"Ta be honest, I don' know. Yeh'd be closer ta figuring it out than I be. I'm not an expert in Zaprex thingies. I be only a grunt in the field of war, born ta fight."

"Don't say that, Master. You're so much more than that. You're a father too." Jarvis curled his legs together, sipping on his water.

"Aw, Little Weasel, that be very nice of yeh to say." Titus chuckled, and under the lip of his hood, Jarvis caught the upturning of the man's lips.

"He speaks the truth." Aaldryn dropped down from above. "Your mate and your cubs, what are they like." The prince nestled himself down beside Jarvis.

"What are they like? Hm. I can tell yeh what they were like when I left. I am unsure what they will be like when I return. I presume ma wife will be rather the same, as for ma children, they will have grown considerably." He rubbed a hand against his bristled chin. "Rosie be the eldest, be about nine sol-cycles now I reckon. He is off-with-the-fairies, likes ta dream, could never keep him grounded." Titus sighed. "Rein, my wife, is a Kelib woman. Strong, sturdy, independent. Wanted ta raise all the kids unconventional."

"Unconventional?" Jarvis frowned.

"Yah. As a family; Mum. Dad. Kids. Messengers don' do that."

"Oh, right."

"Rein be a bit like Jythal, I suppose." Titus sipped his water, wiping aside the dribble that caught on his chin. Jarvis followed his example, knowing their chance of having the refreshing, sweet nectar nearby might not come again for some time.

"I don't think I have ever heard Jythal likened to a Kelib woman before." Aaldryn grinned.

"No, don' mean it like that. Rein was blinded by bomb fragments very early in her life, but she also be a Dream Master. Managed ta keep a high status in Messenger society, unlike many who be wounded."

There was something in the way his master said the words, a thin vein of spite was carefully hidden within his tone. Were it not for his protector bot, he would not have picked up on the changing tenors. It heightened his curiosity, leaving him wondering what it was that made his master hide such anger.

"She eventually became Lower Elder, a very prestigious position within the Council. She be now Head of the Dreamers Who Dream, a group of ten and two dreamathics who help control communications upon the battle-field."

"Wow!"

"Aye. She keeps herself busy, even with our kids. We got wedded when we were wee things; I was about three and ten."

"That's younger than me," Jarvis spluttered out. "My sister was married when she was eight and fifteen! Father insisted!"

Titus clapped his rattling knees as he laughed. "Messengers don' live long, laddie. We marry very, very young. We be lucky if we make it past our second decade. I had recently become a Hunter. I was very scared she wouldna have me, like other Messengers, but she told me I were being stupid." His bony hand reached up, cupping his cheek as he sighed in recollection. "She cared only who I was, not what I looked like. I tried ta tell her that I looked like a stack o' bones, but she laughed it off. So did the rest of Squad Sixteen. Good people, yeh know."

Jarvis felt Aaldryn shift behind him and noticed his change in stance: flaccid, without true control over each flexing muscle under his fur.

"Your children, have they inherited any of your Twizel traits? I have never heard of a Shadow Elemental taking a host and then fathering children before."

Titus snapped his fingers at the wind-god. "Tah, I thought yeh might ask something like that eventually, heh. That's 'cause most Twizels take unwilling hosts; I managed ta take control of the Twizel, not the other way around. We have a partnership. Ta answer yeh question, yes, they have. Rosie, ma son, last I heard, he be quite skilled in phase shifting. Sure ta be giving his mother trouble. The twins react ta crystals, dunno if that be a good sign. They may already be able ta do more. As for the newborn, I'd have ta find out when I get back."

Khamsin clasped his paws in his lap.

"Yeh asked for Aaldryn, din yeh? Yeh wondering if any cub yeh have with Nixlye will end up with yer wind-powers?"

Khamsin glanced aside. It was the most hesitant look Jarvis had ever seen the wind-god give them. He had never expected the Titan to look so coy. "I doubt she has informed anyone of it yet."

"Wait." Jarvis leapt up. "She is expecting, and you still left? How could you?"

Titus caught his arm in mid-swing. "Whoa, laddie."

Khamsin had raised a single eyebrow in his direction. "The fate of Livila is far more important, and Aaldryn trusts Jythal and Nixlye with the Pride. That is what a Pride is, child. Your brother-in-law would have left your sister if he had been called to war, yes?"

Jarvis knitted his brow. "I suppose. It's just…not fair."

"No. It is not, child." Khamsin's lips pressed thin. "Nevertheless, I am glad for your kind words, Titus. Thank you."

Titus shrugged. "I dunno if it helps."

"I live in hope. As far I know, the Wind Titans of the South, East, and West are no more. If a mortal can give birth to elemental children, then any children we have will likely be future Titans."

"Great. Another Wind Titan." Jarvis slumped back.

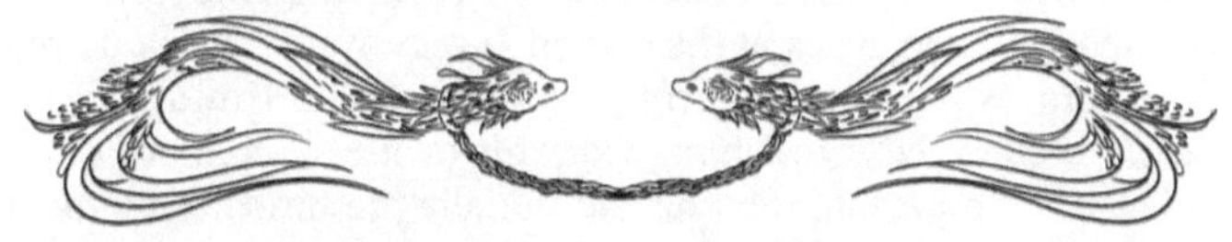

Jarvis woke with a start. He sat up, groaning at the pressure in his bladder. Titus was already packing their Mist stove into his hip-bags. Jarvis rolled around and quickly bundled up his bed, tossing it towards his other bags.

"I have to pee."

Titus's hooded head looked up. "Yeh don' do that often."

Jarvis pouted. "You don't want to know why."

His master waved a hand. "Yah, well, yeh ain't the only one here who got taken over by another entity, laddie. Aaldryn might be the most normal one out of us."

"I'm not normal." Aaldryn uncurled from his nest of blankets. "We established that Eloiko had that illustrious title."

Jarvis ducked the rations can flung at a laughing Aaldryn from a disgruntled-looking Eloiko. Troq and Tikal were completely stationary, the update still in process. Despite the several hours that had passed, Eloiko seemed reluctant to leave Troq's side.

When Jarvis returned, Titus threw his packs at him. "You left to pee to get out of packing, dincha?"

"Yeah, I totally did, sir." Jarvis smirked.

He was shoved roughly. "Come on, move yeh little totu."

With reluctance he obeyed, collecting the remainder of his gear. It was like a tickling against his neck, the sensation that Troq's update was gradually running its course. So, it was no surprise when the prince suddenly looked up and around. Eloiko, however, ended up sprawled out on his back. Tikal leapt around, the AI's manic laughter echoing through the intercom.

"Sorry!" Troq climbed down from his perch on a crystal limb.

Eloiko bounced back onto his foot-paws. "All done?"

"Yes. I should now be able to communicate with the main HUB of Tikal, and the expanded network of Galactic Ships. We need to get to work on stabilising Yrva Krv. It will require considerable work, Brother, but I believe our Pride was chosen for this."

Eloiko smiled, his air-gills expanding. He sidled up to Troq, wrapping an arm around him. "It would appear our roads diverge here, friends," he said, looking first at Aaldryn and then at Jarvis and Titus.

An odd weight dropped into Jarvis' stomach. He had known Troq could not travel with him forever, but he had enjoyed the presence of a resonating harmony similar to his own. Its absence would leave a hole—one that would once more echo the cries of his family.

Aaldryn stepped past him, unhooking two earrings. Eloiko looked momentarily taken aback at the offered jewellery as Aaldryn passed one to him, with Troq accepting the other rather timidly. Jarvis fingered the jewellery that hung from his own ear, wondering if it was far more important than he had initially presumed. Kattamont customs continued to baffle him.

Aaldryn inclined his head. His air-gills remained limp and humble around his neck.

"If the Dweller Pride is ever in need of it, my queen will be honoured to offer the same aid you have given us."

Aaldryn shifted away and Jarvis watched him move to Master Titus' side. They were waiting for him, with Tikal lingering in their shadow. He hung his head, gathering courage as he turned to the two princes.

"Get back safely, yeah," he squeaked out.

Troq grabbed his arm, fiercely gripping it. The gesture had to be Kattamont in nature, and Jarvis reached out to clasp the prince's other arm just as firmly. Troq grinned. "Thank you, Jarvis of the Plains People, for saving our Pride."

"Aww, nah." Jarvis shrugged. "I'm just the Messenger."

"Then may the Four Winds be behind you, Messenger." Troq released him. "I hope we meet again."

With a twirl of their tails, the Dweller princes vanished through the crystal branches. Jarvis tried to breathe out the tightness in his chest. Troq's dot in his optical lenses drew further away until it scattered beyond his range. He shrugged on his pack and turned away, following Tikal's laughter as the AI danced on ahead of them. Eventually they reached the end of the arching chamber. Tikal twirled and then stopped in front of an open doorway. It spread its arms into the air.

"*Up. Up, to the Moon we go,*" it sang out happily.

"Crazy little thing," Titus muttered. "Right, what is this?"

Jarvis did not even need to look through the entrance to know what it was; his optical scans had already informed him, and his heart had

sunk to his stomach. "It's an elevator shaft. Great. Another one. This is asking for trouble. It's like it's lit up with a giant neon sign saying 'DOOM.'"

Tikal started laughing.

Aaldryn looked to him, raising an eyebrow. "A what sign?"

Jarvis shrugged. "Zaprex humour."

"Can yeh see the elevator anywhere?" Titus peered through the open door, looking up and down into the murky darkness that filled the shaft like thick ink.

Jarvis joined him. He blinked, allowing his optical lenses to expand. Light flickered out from his eyes, scattering across the open void, splitting into vectors, scanning down and up the shaft. He chewed his bottom lip.

"No, actually, I can't."

His master clapped him roughly on the shoulder. "Good! That means it must have already fallen. Oi, Tikal, which way, up or down?"

"Climb up! Up! We go up! Up and out! To the Moon, to the Moon! In the magical, magical mirror machine!"

"Righty-oh…" Titus dug into his packs and tugged on thick gloves. With a leap he swung out into the shaft and landed roughly against the smooth metal surface, hanging there like a spindly spider. "Off we go then, to the Moons."

"This is still a bad idea," Jarvis grouched, activating his gravity-bubble. Aaldryn booted him through the door and he shouted as he tumbled down, until his gravity caught him, and he pinned himself to the wall, panting heavily. The prince floated beside him, wind twirling around his foot-paws. He eyed the Kattamont in fury.

"Don't do that! You know I can't actually fly, right?"

"But it is fun to watch you bounce."

"Shut up!" He sent a charge down to the tips of his fingers. The hum of metal upon metal filled him with a small amount of peace as he gradually began to follow the shadow of Titus' coat up the wall, hand over hand. Tikal and Aaldryn floated nearby, Tikal singing a sweet, warbling tune. It was exhausting, the climb, pinned to the wall, without a break. Even with the strength of his reinforced limbs, Jarvis eventually felt his muscles beginning to tremble, and sweat caused his clothes to cling to his skin.

He paused, pressing himself against the surface of the cold metal wall, fully polarising his hull, letting the magnetic pulse hold him firmly, so all muscles could go loose.

"I wish I could fly like you," he grumbled to Tikal. "It's annoying watching you both floating there."

"It's just as annoying having to slow down to keep pace with you," Aaldryn retorted. "It would be so much faster to offer you a lift. But the space is too tight. Risk a backlash." Aaldryn glanced around the shaft.

"Jarvis, get yer totu up here!"

Jarvis yelped at the urgency in his master's order. He unpinned himself from the wall and scrambled up the shaft.

"What is it, Master Titus?"

"A road block."

Jarvis studied the warped metal jammed up ahead, his breath hitching in momentary panic that it could be the mangled remains of the elevator, having gone off-line and now hanging by a cable thread, ready to fall upon them any second. How could he have missed it in his scan?

His panic subsided. It was not an elevator.

"A cave in. The air-pressure must have changed around this sector quite recently for this to have happened. This has just happened; the metal is still hot." He withdrew his hand, shaking it to soothe the burn.

"How recent?"

"A few minutes, maybe?"

"Why didna we hear it?"

"The city has an environmental system that is invisible to the eye, but we pass through its sectors all the time. It is one of the reasons why I have to keep recalibrating. For some reason, each environmental section seems to have developed its own unique behavioural pattern. It likely kept the explosion in this sector." Jarvis studied the damaged, misshapen metal. "I have a feeling it was trying to warn us not to go any further, sir."

"The environmental system is alive, now?" Titus thudded his head against the wall.

"Not in the sense of life, sir, but it is conscious of our existence down here, and since it is a Zaprex system, it must protect us. It is likely attached to Tikal's Matrix Crystal, though it may no longer realise it, nor have control over it. Tikal, what is above us?"

The Moon! The Moon!

The AI placed a hand on one of the shards of metal, going rigid as though struck by lightning. *Danger. Danger. DANGER. WARNING. CODE RED.*

Jarvis slapped his free hand over his ear in sudden pain as the world flared, his optical lenses blanking out as pixels scattered in random directions. Firewalls cracked, information flooded into his mind in a torrent. He heard distant calls from Titus and Aaldryn, but his attention was awhirl, processing the sudden influx, and his head snapped up. His eyes realigned upon the tangled mass of metal above them.

He could only see the vague outline through his scanners set on high resolution. It was huge. It was monstrous. He never wanted to see anything like it again.

"Master Titus!" Jarvis cried out as metal cracked, scattering around them. A claw, almost as wide as he was, ripped down the sides of the shaft, splitting the solid surface like parchment. A face appeared, of angular lines, fitted together in triangular pieces, and unblinking optical lenses. Red-tainted philepcon liquid oozed from split cracks in the hull of the machine. Jarvis stared into its eyes. His protector bot froze in fear. It had never felt such fear, but the raw emotion struck like a blade through his chest, slowing down his processing.

The hilt of Master Titus' broken rock blade swung into the machine's neck, barely making a dent. Debris showered around them as the machine buckled, pulling itself through the blockage, turning upon the Hunter with a deafening roar.

Jarvis' eyes widened. The machine had no gravity control.

"Aaldryn! It is falling!" he bellowed.

It was too late for his master, caught up in the tangled web of the machine's arms and legs. The shattering crack of the elevator shafts walls peeling away vibrated through the darkness as the enormous monster tumbled downward. The sudden moment of distress, witnessing his master vanish into the gloom caused Jarvis' gravity bubble to pop. He, too, plummeted.

Aaldryn snatched his wrist. Had he still been only Human, the jerk would have snapped the bone. The Kattamont prince yelped in pain as a falling metal bar pierced his side, pinning him against the elevator shaft wall. Jarvis dangled, staring down into the abyss.

"Jarvis! I can't hold on! Jarvis!"

Tikal caught him. Jarvis blinked weakly as his limbs slackened. He panted, gasping for air, shaking away the desire to drop into uncon-sciousness. Metal shards continued to cascade around them like rain. This was not a good place to be.

"Thanks, Tikal. Can you get me back up to Aaldryn?"

He would think about Master Titus later; they had to get out of danger. He had to help Aaldryn. Tikal lifted him slowly up to the dangling Kattamont, who was hissing at the metal pinning him to the wall.

"How bad is it?" Aaldryn murmured.

"Not that bad. It caught your shoulder."

Aaldryn dropped his head back, releasing a long, high-pitched whine. "Not bad, he says."

Jarvis grabbed the metal rod. "All right, what I meant to say was: at least you're going to live."

NIXLYE OF THE MISFIT PRIDE

CHAPTER TWELVE

Derwyn had grown into a young man of twenty and three sol-cycles, and atop his proud, speedy rillara, he glided along the Spider-Road like a solar flare. Deilen's laughter, as her rillara ran loops around Derwyn, trilled like a bell across the moors. Their youngest brother, Aneurin, at a modest four and ten sol-cycles, tried valiantly to keep pace on his sturdy diabond. Disgleirio watched them as he brushed down his own beast, the diabond's low rumble of pleasure at the treatment tickling his skin. The province of Istanian was beginning to thrive, with Batitic engineering aiding in the flooding of rice fields that cut into high slopes. The small town of Alya ahead was crowned by the glint of fallen Zaprex galactic-ships, around which the township had formed. His people were growing with the changing land. There was peace—

He seized his chest, staggering as his world swam. Dots scattered his vision. Beside him his diabond yowled, backing away in a frantic scamper.

The Spider-Road beneath him suddenly cracked as a crater formed around him, the null-zone bursting out of the containment field formed by his suit. Disgleirio landed roughly on his knees, vomiting blood.

"Father!" Derwyn was running towards him, Deilen paces behind. Aneurin was frozen in terror. He stretched out a hand, wanting nothing more than to be able to order Derwyn to halt, but no words came. Darkness enveloped him.

Denvy was too disturbed to speak as they scurried through the Hall of Records. From the pale faces beside him, he had little doubt that Nixlye and Jythal had both grasped what it was they had discovered. The three children at their heels could not comprehend what they had seen, but they could surely sense the tension and put together enough to realise why they had been captured.

Their childhoods had been stolen from them and, had they not escaped the tomb of the box, they would have been just as ill-fated.

Ki'b tripped. Clive caught her, and tumbled with her, giving a yelp as she landed on him. Denvy stopped to pull her quickly off the lad.

"Sorry, sorry, Clive! I'm so sorry!" Ki'b cried out.

Clive waved her off, grinning charmingly. "It's fine. I keep forgetting you're Kelib and heavier than me. I can't catch you anymore." He laughed, though clutching at his bruised chest. "I have to let you fall. Can't be chivalrous."

Denvy tweaked the boy's nose fondly. "Come along." He knelt to take their hands.

"Denvy!" Nixlye's panicked voice echoed through the library hall.

His body acted on its own accord. He felt the change in air-pressure before he heard the discharge of weapons. He swung up his water-sword, the ice shield forming in a blink. Heat of the weapon fire ripped around them, blistering the ground. The two cubs cowered against his heels. Gradually he stood as the field of ice crumbled, melting around his foot-paws and he stared through the open doorway into the chamber beyond.

Three Iposti stood in whirlwinds, but that was not what had snatched his attention, not what had fired an intense discharge of energy.

Ryojin's paper-thin thought patterns whispered past. *Denvy, please tell me your eyes aren't working and I am seeing something from your imagination.*

I am afraid that is very real, Ry.

His eyes trailed over the gleaming, metal shape behind the Iposti. Clanking with each step it took on elongated legs, the hulk towered above the Kattamonts. A single swipe of its arms would have sent them flying.

"I guess the alarms were triggered after all." Jythal conjured Rune blades into his paws.

"It would appear so," Denvy growled.

"Why aren't they attacking us?" Penny squeaked.

"We're inside a holy place," Clive responded. "They can't attack us in here. That monster thing, though, has precise aim; it won't damage any of the artefacts when it fires. It can hurt us. That is likely why they brought it." Clive removed a dagger from his belt. "The Monks in the Sun Temple were all trained in Runes, but they could not fight in the Sun Dome. We had to hire mercenaries to defend the doors there. It's a bit like that."

Surprised, Denvy looked down at the boy. He had never expected Clive to be so worldly about such things, but, then, the lad had so rarely spoken of his time at the Sun Temple where he was raised, beyond bemoaning his teachings. Perhaps the passing of time was beginning to heal the wounds.

Drawing back his water-sword, Denvy murmured to the children, "Run."

He lunged, swinging his sword high. Water surged around his foot-paws, icing into a barrier. His cubs sped past him, followed swiftly by Nixlye on her wheelchair, through the open doorway. Rune patterns scattered across the floor as Jythal's blades twisted in swift movements, capturing the attention of the Iposti as the bricks beneath them erupted into linked chains, wrapping around the machine's slender armoured legs. Jythal countered the wind blade of an Iposti with his own Rune-forged weapons. Energy surged around the Kattamont prince with each swing.

"Jythal will deal with them. Go!" Nixlye shouted.

Denvy's legs fought with furious reluctance and his stomach

twisted at the realisation that a brotherhood bond he had never noticed growing between himself and the younger prince was pulling on him to protect his brother. That bond did not want to allow him to leave Jythal to battle alone, but he had to get his cubs away and focused on that competing urge to fuel him forward. They ran between the pillars of the hall, towards the nearest corridor. The machine's whirring echo pursued them, spiking his fur. He dared to glance back, alarmed at its speed. Ki'b and Clive slammed into the doors, shoving them open. Nixlye wheeled through after the children.

"Find a way to block its path," Nixlye called back.

Denvy turned to the statues on either side of the corridor. He hewed at their legs with his water-sword. The stones shattered, and they crumbled. Dust clogged the air. He tore after Nixlye, Jythal, and the children. A thundering boom shook the corridor.

"Holy Sun!" Denvy stumbled as the floor trembled. He stared at the scorched walls behind him, the bricks melting. The machine ruptured through the choking dust, arms alight with flames. Denvy twirled his water-sword, sending forth a volley of ice. Steam filled the air as the two torrents collided.

The cubs were crying. The machine roared towards them and he could not see.

Denvy cursed. He clapped a paw against his forehead.

"Ryojin, jack me in! Now!"

Like being forced through the eyes of thousands of needles, his dreamathic mind was dragged past the yoke's barrier. He staggered against the impact.

I will not be able to keep this up, Denvy. Your body isn't immortal. It can't sustain the current as it used to. Open your eyes and deal with this!

The colours of the Secondary Realm spilled out around him in layers of unfolding data. It took him a moment to readjust, to catch the pre-echo of events not yet having transpired as information filled in Nixlye's frame. His air-gills expanded, and he snatched for Nixlye's chair, wrenching her back, away from the path of the energy blast that would have shot through her. Jarring agony spread down his spine as the binding yoke fought Ryojin's control. Denvy landed on his knees. The machine thundered past where they had stood, the ground and walls shaking at its passing. Denvy snarled at the monstrosity. He had never seen such a foul abomination, mangled together by hands that knew nothing of the beauty and sweet songs of the Zaprexes. It was a vulgar machine of sharp edges, cruel colours, and blistering heat.

Zaprexes had always been cold, like the chill touch of spring mornings—of life after bitter winter. Their world had been one of curves; even the sharp lines, when seen, had been smoothed by circles. Their clouds had never been harsh, always soft as lightly dusted pastel dawns.

Growling low in his chest Denvy bounced onto his foot-paws. Worse pain he had known than the mere cutting of his flesh. He could ignore the blood leaking from the yoke as it split his skin and soaked his fur. He had known the immense grief of centuries—alone—lost—wandering.

Never again. Never.

Ryojin. This might hurt. I apologise in advance.

He stretched out a paw, envisioning the machine vanishing. A hole, it would open beneath it, and it would drop through, into nothing. Darkness. It dribbled over his vision, the thickness of the dreamathic colours swirling together, the painting of the daydream in his mind mixing into black smudge.

Denvy! Denvy! Stop! Denvy. We can't daydream yet. Denvy! I can't stop the yoke. DENVY!

"Denvy! Stop!" Nixlye's scream ripped through Ryojin's distant dreamathic cries. "You're going to kill yourself. Stop!" Her wheelchair slammed into him. Her arms wrapped around his waist. "Stop! Please!"

He wrenched himself from the daydream. Pixels scattered. The Secondary Realm that had engulfed him dissolved like rain.

Denvy gasped. His paw clenched around his water-sword, ice crusting up his arm as he tried to draw away the raging hot pain scorching his neck. The thick smell of blood was overwhelming, and it was all his. The yoke was hissing hot and his shoulders trembled against its weight as it crushed down, making his knees buckle. Ryojin's presence had retreated, further than it had ever been. Neither of them could fight the yoke, nor break its enchantment.

I'm sorry… Ryojin's soft whisper was the barest of threads.

No. I am—

"Denvy!" Nixlye screamed.

The machine was picking itself out of the debris, clicking and whirring. Two Iposti advanced from beneath its arms.

Nixlye nocked an arrow to her bow. "New plan. I'll get the cubs; we make for the main doors. They won't let that monster-machine out of the Haven Hall into the public. Kill them. Now!"

It was a barking order from a queen. The prince in him was compelled to obey, and it was an odd emotion that swelled up within him, one of youth, that made his muscles move without their twinge of age.

Denvy snarled, activating his water-sword. His sweaty paws iced over, holding the hilt of the blade in his trembling grasp. The wind of the Iposti ripped into his skin, slicing like threads. Denvy charged into it, smashing into the nearest neutral, who met him with the same fury and they clashed into a wall. Denvy gritted his teeth. His vision kept blurring, though from lack of blood, or the eerie mind-twisting movements of the Iposti's wind elemental skills, he knew not. A wind elementalist could influence the mind, but he was a Dream Master;

even bound as he was, he would never let a mere child sway him.

A cry echoed down the corridor. It momentarily distracted him. Was it the Iposti in front of him bending his thoughts or Penny's real voice? In his peripheral vision he caught sight of Nixlye beside her wheelchair, struggling to reach her arrows as the machine loomed over her. Penny cowered against the queen's chest. Denvy's hearts slowed.

"No!" he shouted as the machine's arms swung up. If he had blinked, he would have missed it: Ki'b taking the full brunt of the strike that would have crushed her Human sister. Her dense Kelib bones absorbed the force as she snatched hold of the metal appendage, her fingers denting the plates of armour, bare feet crushing the brickwork beneath her.

"Now, Clive!" she cried.

"Ki'b! Clive!" Levelling a punch into the Iposti's chin, Denvy charged towards his cubs. A rope of wind looped around his legs, and he upturned, landing on the floor. Blood trickled from his nose and mouth. He spat it out and swiped at his eyes, trying to clear the sweat. He only worsened his vision with his bloodied paw. His water-sword? Denvy sucked in a sharp breath; where was his water-sword? The frozen blade had been torn from his skin. Nixlye's arrow flew past his ear, slamming into the Iposti's chest. Denvy scrambled to his paws, vaulting for his water-sword.

He swung it in an arc as he rolled, spreading ice along the brickwork of the floor. The machine's legs crusted over. Clive moved with sudden speed, using Ki'b's body as a ladder to thrust himself up, clapping his hands together against a dagger he flung high into the air.

Denvy blocked the burst of bright light with a paw. Clive slammed the dagger into the machine's chest with a mid-air kick. Like swatting a fly, the machine flicked Clive against the wall, its arm morphing, stabbing into the boy's stomach.

Denvy felt the world slow as the machine flung Clive aside. His small Human body rolled, smearing blood across the bricks. Penny's scream carried down the hall. Ki'b lost her grip on the machine's arm. A scattered Rune shield lit up the air nearby as bullets erupted around her. Jythal snatched her up, grabbing Penny around the neck in his jaws; he continued on all fours, planting himself in front of Clive's limp body.

Denvy staggered as wind gusted down the tight corridor. A group of Iposti closed in on them. Already they looked wounded, and he had no doubt they had encountered a backlash for using their tamed wind elementals inside the tight confines. One raised a paw, sending another volley down the corridor towards them.

"Don't!" His shout was lost as the wind cut gashes through his thick fur and he staggered backwards. They were such foolish children. He could hear their own cries as they suffered the recoil. Swinging his foot-paws over his head, he somersaulted, and sliced his water-blade into the ground. Ice sprang up, blocking the corridor and the Iposti's approach. He adjusted his wet grip on the blade, cringing against the intense burn. He turned back as Nixlye shouted for attention. She had righted herself, propped up against the wall, gripping her long bow.

"Get Clive out of here, Jythal! Go. Get to the main entrance."

The machine strode forward, undeterred, hissing steam through vents.

Denvy focused on the red glowing orb wedged into the centre of its metal chest plate, protected by sheets of crystal. Every movement it made caused the small dagger Clive had thrust into it to budge further out. Philepcon liquid trailed along the floor. Clive's Rune imprint glinted in a perfect circle upon the plates of armour. It simply needed to be finished. From down the corridor the echoing booms against the ice wall he had formed caused his ears to twitch. Iposti reinforcements had arrived. They were running out of time to flee.

"Nixlye," Denvy bellowed. "I will not be able to keep this wall up much longer. You need to go with Jythal."

Nixlye tossed aside the blanket that hung askew across her lap, and rose on her Mist-powered legs. Denvy held his breath, watching as Nixlye vaulted through the air, landing on the back of the whirring machine as it charged towards them both. Her Mist-blades slashed downwards, hewing into its armour plates with blazing hot Mist.

The machine roared past him. Denvy swung his water-sword, and iced coated the floor, wrapping around its legs. It landed, legs and arms twisted. Nixlye vaulted on her hands over its back, landing on her prosthetic feet. She looked at him, her eyes frantically wide. He wondered if she could tell he was reaching the end of his stamina.

"How do we kill it?" she screeched. "Denvy! How do we kill a Zaprex machine?"

"Take out its heart." He pounded his legs, breathing pain into them, forcing them to work, and charged forward. The machine was rising again, spitting out philepcon liquid, tainted with thick brown blood. He gagged in revulsion. Everything he had seen on the holographic screen replayed in his mind. But he had to know—he needed to see the truth for himself.

The machine spun, and a bullet tore into his arm, the hot pain so much worse than he remembered it, but it urged him on. He dropped, skidding on the ice he formed beneath himself, and arced his water-sword, smashing it up against Clive's tiny dagger with all the strength left in his trembling arms. The Rune inscription burst like a bomb. The light of a little Sun Monk erupted through the corridor.

Denvy lunged for Nixlye, landing on her, pulling her down as shrapnel rained around them.

"Rythrya! How did you do that?"

"It was Clive. He planted a Sun Rune circle in its chest. Clever boy. He knew he could never get enough power to activate it, but I could." He lifted himself off the young queen, looking back at the devastation. The walls were blackened and charred, and, in a pile of melted metal, the machine was fused to the brickwork, still twitching.

Denvy bit his lip. Beside him Nixlye cried, clutching at his arm for support. The sight of the slumped over cub lying in the cavity of the ruined machine propelled her forward.

"No! No, it isn't true, it isn't! They haven't done this. No!"

The wall of ice crumbled, sending chunks hissing across the hot, bubbling floor. Denvy staggered as another gust of wind blasted him. He growled at the Iposti appearing in a gap and flung a shard of ice. It burst through the Iposti's skull at the force of his throw.

He snatched Nixlye's hand. "Run."

"What have they done?" she cried.

"Just run!" The image was burned into his mind: a Kattamont cub's body, distorted, mangled, ruined—chained inside a suit of iron, mouth open in a constant scream. This was not what the Zaprexes had dreamed, nor imagined, nor wished. This was not their legacy; this was their nightmare—all nightmares—born into reality. He dragged Nixlye down the hall, towards the sound of Jythal's blades clashing against metal. They skidded around a corner, coming face to face with a new gathering of Iposti.

Nixlye released a scream. Her fan-tail spread in a show of vibrant pinks and purples, deadly in their sharpness, and, as she lunged into the fold of battle, metal legs lashing out, cracking bones as easily as crumbling charcoal, Denvy understood why Zafiashid so respected the youthful queen.

He searched wildly for Ki'b, Penny, and Clive, finding the two girls curled up in a corner by a statue, trying to staunch the bleeding from Clive's body. He scooped up the limp boy.

"Come. We're leaving."

"But Jythal and Nixlye?" Ki'b gasped out.

Denvy cocked his head back, watching as Nixlye dragged the last of the Iposti away from Jythal, smashing one of her metal legs into their head.

"They'll follow." Denvy rushed down stairs, his mind on the single goal of getting his cubs away from the fight. Sure enough, Nixlye and Jythal swiftly joined them, soon overtaking him, both knocking down any opposition they met as they fled.

The great doors of the Haven Hall were wide open, accepting pilgrims from the Market. It was like being absorbed by a river, plunging into the swell of the market crowd. His left arm was beginning to wane in strength, the bullet burning in his shoulder, and if Jythal's laboured breathing was anything to go by the prince was barely keeping pace. He desperately tried to think of anything but Clive in his arms. Clive who might already be dead as they wove through the markets. Nixlye stole fabrics from stalls, swiftly covering Ki'b and Penny in new shawls, wrapping herself in beautiful flowery patterns. She heaved Penny onto her back.

"Penny, dear, this is not the time to cry. We have to keep moving."

The market crowd had swelled. Denvy glanced briefly at the walls of the fighting-pit. Zafiashid's battle must have long been over for the crowds to have become so full. "Split up," he said to Nixlye. "Take Penny and Ki'b. I'll meet you at the Evergreen Tavern."

She nodded, grabbing Ki'b's hand. They broke away and were soon engulfed by the crowd. He did not even need to speak to Jythal; the prince simply vanished. Denvy blinked rapidly, trying to centre himself. He wanted to relax, to ease the tension in his shoulders, but his fur refused to calm. His hearts still raced. The horror of what he had seen lingered in every vein.

Clive lay in his arms, life barely clinging to him. Denvy hugged the child closer to his chest, whispering softly as he continued through the market.

"Please, Time Master, do not let him go. He is not ready to go. Not yet."

The sign of the Evergreen Tavern hung below a crackling mist lantern, the words painted in Pennadotian script. Denvy noted the dim light glowing from the windows, as he climbed rickety steps, haphazardly bolted together with driftwood and metal. Had it not been for Zafiashid's detailed directions, he would never have found the little tavern on the outskirts of the markets.

Cradling Clive carefully in his good arm, he manoeuvred through the evening crowd, around the outside of the building to the tradesmen's entrance. The muck of the nearby stables stung his nose. He huddled Clive closer, away from the foulness. Exhausted, he thudded a paw against the door. The wait grated on him, every moment feeling drawn out like a rope around Clive's neck, dragging his cub further into death. He startled when the door swung open to reveal a Kelib woman. She held a primed mist-gun loosely in her hand.

She studied him with a thin frown that was almost distaste. "What's your name, Traveller?"

"Krrirren," Denvy responded wearily.

She urged him inside. "You're getting blood on the doorstep. Quickly. Upstairs. The Outcast is in the last room."

"Have Nixlye and Jythal—"

The Kelib woman shook her head as she gave him a rough nudge up the creaking stairs. "I'll know to expect more of you, then. You're bleeding all over my floor. Go."

"Thank you." Carefully he made his way up the stairs. His hefty bulk was difficult to squeeze around the narrow bends, and his foot-paws barely fitted on the steps. Kovlrok's reason for choosing such a safe-house was apparent; this was not a Kattamont Tavern, it was entirely sized for Kelibs and Humans. At least the furniture and flooring would hold his weight if it could hold that of a Kelib. Finding the last room, he knocked.

"Zafiashid, it's me, Denvy."

The door creaked open, and Zafiashid's head appeared.

The queen's mouth was half open with what looked like a retort, her air-gills frilled around her head, but it died in her throat as he pounded past to the bed.

Clive was limp, his skin slick with sweat and deathly pale except for his fiery freckles. The moment he settled the boy on the bedsheets, he was aware of Jythal entering behind him, followed not long afterwards by Nixlye and the girls. They had not been far behind him after all.

Zafiashid gave a cry of shock. "Nixlye! Your wheelchair?"

Jythal shoved Denvy roughly aside and threw a pile of Rune stones, coins, and sticks into the air. They were all wounded, but Clive came first.

Denvy backed away. Zafiashid grabbed his arm. Denvy winced; it was his left arm. She was already glaring at the blood that stained his golden fur as she peeled away the stolen poncho he had used to hide the evidence. The queen's air-gills began to rattle.

"By the Winds, what happened?"

"We were attacked, in the Haven Hall," Denvy responded. "They had a… machine." That would do, for the time being. He didn't have the energy right then to explain further.

Ki'b tugged on his other arm. She was trembling, and he crouched, heaving her up. She curled against his neck, and sobbed into his air-gills. He could not face Zafiashid's searching gaze. All his attention focused upon Jythal, kneeling at the bedside, energy pooling around the ruthless wound revealing Clive's insides. It was worse than he had thought. How could he have allowed this to happen? He clamped a paw on the yoke still snug around his neck. The cursed thing; without it, tight like a vice he could not shift, this would not have happened. He growled low, rumbling his chest.

"Nixlye?" Zafiashid's tone was sharp. "The Iposti; they did this?"

The young queen walked over, throwing a blanket around Penny's shaking shoulders. She handed one up to Ki'b.

"Mother, I am not entirely sure. I never would have thought them capable of what we encountered. The Iposti are not a warring Pride. They're neutrals. A pride of neutrals could not act in such a manner."

Zafiashid frowned, her tail twitching.

"I might understand them attacking Jythal and Denvy as intruders, but how could they attack children?" Nixlye choked out.

Jythal suddenly yelped. Zafiashid was swiftest, and she did not hesitate to catch him before he slumped over. The Runes collapsed around Clive's frail body, having turned an ugly shade of black.

The doctor weakly lifted himself free of the queen's arms. "I think I drew most of the poison out. Don't touch the Runes; they're contaminated. We need to clean, stitch, and bind his wounds now."

"I'll do that." Ki'b scrambled down from Denvy's shoulder.

Jythal slumped back. "All right, then, Denvy, your turn."

Denvy shook his head. "You need to look after yourself, brother. You're in worse condition. Don't worry about me. I will survive."

The relief in the prince was immediate. He collapsed into the nearest chair, all strength seeming to drain from him. Nixlye knelt beside him, laying her head in his lap, murmuring softly to him.

Zafiashid pulled Denvy to one side. "He may not be able to tend to you, but I can. Sit. I will remove the projectile."

It took some time for all their injuries to be seen to, but, eventually, many bloodied rags, rounds of stitches, hot water, and tears from the two girls later, their wounds were finally patched up. The Kelib landlady muttered again about her floors as she tirelessly removed dirtied equipment and brought in fresh water and clean cloth, but she betrayed her concern with her repeated visits and small gestures of kindness, including leaving behind a large jug of cream. They sat around the small Mist heater lighting the dim room. Zafiashid poured the thick cream, and Denvy sighed into his mug, the warm sweetened liquid soothing his aching throat.

Zafiashid eased into her seat, her brow furrowing. They had finally gone through the long explanation of their escape and she had been silent for some time, her gaze lost in the flames of the Mist heater as she played with the handle of her mug.

"There was a child inside this machine? A Kattamont cub?"

Denvy ruffled his air-gills. "I know that, during the Dawn Age, to fly Zaprex star-gliders, one had to be jacked into the ship, and many young Changelings were trained for such a task. But they were not…melded into a machine. They drove the machine. We called them Navigators."

"Humans with golden wings," Nixlye murmured. She sat upon Jythal's lap, curled up wearily, resting her head upon the prince's chest.

"Indeed." Denvy tugged on his yoke wearily. "This is something horribly foul."

"Why would you even want to combine a child with a machine?" Zafiashid covered her mouth, looking as though she was holding down bile.

Denvy took another gulp of his drink. The liquid at least drowned out the sour taste in his own mouth.

"Two possibilities. First, you cannot operate Zaprex technology unless you are a Zaprex, or you have philepcon liquid in your veins—so you either have to be a Zaprex, or you are of the Starborn bloodlines, and there aren't many of those left running around. Thus, to activate any Zaprex technology," Denvy held out his own paws, "you must first introduce philepcon liquid into your system. The easiest time to do this is during childhood. Children's bodies are still growing; they're able to take the strain of adapting swiftly to the invasion. But here they're placing children inside the machine, replacing the matrix crystal and the processor core. So, I highly doubt whoever is doing this has access to an unlimited supply of philepcon liquid, or to Tikal's Matrix Crystal."

"Why is that?" Zafiashid frowned.

"If they had access to Tikal's Matrix Crystal they would simply grow more crystals."

"But there are tons of crystals around Utillia." Nixlye sat up straighter.

"Aye, but they are not viable any longer. They have become tainted. To create an AI, you need a Mothership. Tikal is the only Mothership in this sector—and you need a very specific set of parameters to grow an AI. As far as I know, Tikal and Troy were the only two Motherships capable of shipbuilding."

"What about all the corpses of Zaprexes here in Utillia. I hear they dig them up from time to time during scavengers' hunts. Could they be used?" Nixlye asked.

"Ah." Denvy winced. "You do not ever want to go near the Matrix Crystal of a Zaprex. Very different to an AI. While, yes, AIs were born out of Zaprexes, Zaprexes are cyborgs, and AI's are entirely crystalized. A Zaprex's Matrix Crystal will dissolve if it is not held in status. Despite what the stories say, they are not immortal beings. They are only immortal if they keep themselves in a constant harmonic state."

"Harmonic state?" Jythal's head lifted, as though he had come out of a haze.

Denvy sighed. He rubbed a paw over his aching neck. "Zaprexes came in pairs—almost always in pairs. Bonding partners, they called it. Between that pair, a transference of energy could be created. They called it a Song. It could not be heard by anyone else but that pair, and it kept their philepcon liquid flowing, their Matrix Crystal stabilized, and their hull from cracking. Zaprexes moved not using muscles as we do, but a form of liquid propulsion."

He eased back into his chair. "There are other ways to keep their philepcon liquid from drying out, but the easiest way was pairing."

"You said they almost always came in pairs?" Zafiashid poured herself another drink.

Denvy chuckled. "I can't put anything over on you. Yes. There are Negatives, Positives, and Fusion Zaprexes. The Fusion Zaprexes are the exception." He held up his paw. "They are a combination of Negatives and Positives and generate their own song. Zaprexes called them Dynasty Starters. Coming back around to AIs, can you guess where the AIs came from, now?"

Nixlye clicked her fingers. "You said AIs were born out of Zaprexes, so, if AIs are entirely crystalline beings that generate their own song, then they must have come from a Fusion Zaprex."

Denvy tipped his cup to the young queen.

"What is the second reason children would be used for these… machines?" Zafiashid stood, leaning heavily on the table.

"Children have a stronger connection to the Secondary Realm." Denvy gently stroked Ki'b's hair aside from her cheeks. She had long ago fallen asleep in his lap, curled in a ball, her face carved deeply with the lines of terror that not even sleep could take away. "This has always been the case, but more so now with the Secondary Realm fading. It is seen quite often in the House of Flames due to their population being so young." He rubbed his nose. "If you have child warriors, it is possible to tap into that flow within the Secondary Realm. It is something to keep in mind. As you get older, unless you continue practicing that connection, it gets harder to pull from."

He was unable to curb the smile that overwhelmed him as his chest expanded, his mind drifting back to the faces of the cubs he had left behind in the halls of the House of Flames. Of Zinkx and his Squad, all so young, yet each a soldier, brave-hearted and fierce. Everywhere he went, it felt as though he was leaving behind his cubs to terrible fates.

"Children have the most amazing imaginations." He tried not to choke on his words. "They can think up marvellous things."

"That may be so, but they are also innocent and open to influence." Zafiashid scooped Ki'b off his lap and carried her to the cot beside Penny.

Denvy left Jythal and Nixlye to their own whisperings. He knelt beside Clive and rested his paw across the boy's sweaty forehead. How many times had he been here before, beside a dying child? Too many times in his long life.

"Live, little one. Live."

The blackened Rune stones Jythal had used lay discarded to one side. Denvy wrinkled his nose at the sight of them. Using a sheet he plucked them up, studying them. It had not been poison—at least not the kind Kattamonts carried in their tails, nor the venom of a Batitic's fangs or a Twizel's claws. The scent was too sweet, reminding him of the blood that had filled his own mouth.

"Philepcon liquid," he whispered.

His body sagged as the weight of the situation collapsed his muscles. Jarvis had managed to merge with the protector bot, a pure matrix crystal. It was likely it had found Jarvis a compatible partner after all the lad had endured.

He could feel the taint radiating from the Rune stones. Jythal was right. It was poison. It was not going to merge with Clive—it was going to break down his body, piece by piece, like little Prince David.

Denvy blinked back tears. He had not thought of Prince David in so many sol-cycles. Not since Zinkx, wrapped in blankets, had been handed to him by a little, bloodied, wingless Batitic at the edge of Palace-Town's catacombs.

Cancer, the injured Batitic had slurred. *It might come back. It's in his cells. It is a part of him. I cannot change who he really is. I can only hide him, for a while. He will always be a White Star.*

Denvy refocused on Clive. His pulse was so faint, but at least he was breathing. At least there was life—and hope in that life. Only, what life was the lad going to awaken to, if he ever did wake at all?

A paw settled on his shoulder, stirring him from his thoughts. Zafiashid drew him up, leading him back to the small stove. He accepted a seat and sank into it. She brightened the centre Mist lantern before filling a bowl with water, pulling it closer as she dipped in a rag and took it to his matted, bloodied fur. He was finally given leave to study her as she worked diligently on cleaning him. Sheepishly, he ducked his head, ashamed he had not even enquired after her pit-fight. Things had been so frantic. Her tail bumped him, and he caught her thin smile. For whatever reason, she seemed to be enjoying fretting over him.

She had bandaged her own wounds. None of them looked serious. He had expected her to be worse off, considering the tales she had told of pit-fights. The floor groaned, stirring him. Jythal approached, carrying Nixlye in his arms. He settled her in a chair and seated himself on the floor beside her, resting his head back on the leg of the table.

"Penny is finally asleep." The prince yawned. "Exhaustion, I think."

"She will need the rest, the poor girl." Zafiashid shook her head.

Nixlye nibbled on a piece of dried meat. She sighed, sinking lower into her seat. "So, Mother, did you win?"

Denvy coughed lightly as the queen's gaze settled on him with a smirk before flicking back to the princess.

"I did, but I do not believe it was fair fight."

"Uyrilk is not an easy princess to fool into submission—" Jythal began.

"She desired to be some place we could not be overheard by the Iposti. She knew the pits were the only place this would be possible. What she had to tell me I shall only speak of when we are back on the burning-sea."

"Fair enough." Denvy purred. "How long, do you think, until we can move Clive, Jythal?"

The prince clawed a paw through his hair. "A couple of hours until the Runes I cast seal the wounds entirely."

"I do not like the idea of remaining here if we have Iposti on our tails." Zafiashid shook her head.

Denvy winced as she came near his wound and she flicked her tail against his in apology.

"We are going to have to risk moving him."

"It could kill him, Mother." Jythal sat up straighter.

"It is better than us all being killed."

Denvy growled low.

"Denvy," her paw settled on his arm, "I know you fear for his life, but, whatever this monster was, I doubt they are going to let you go now that you have seen it and slaughtered your way out of a Haven Hall."

She was right, but he did not have to admit it out loud. He amused her by folding his arms across his chest and sinking in his seat, pouting like an un-mated prince.

"I don't understand." Nixlye covered her face. "I was raised amongst the Iposti and they…were peaceful. They don't do this!"

"I am afraid, my dear," Denvy bent forward, "that everything you think you know is no longer reliable knowledge."

The *Lawless Child* looked unharmed amongst the larger trading vessels in the harbour. Denvy studied the surrounds, his stomach twisting with a weighted anxiety. A few hundred or so sand-sea sailors were milling around their vessels. Trading had not yet commenced, and the air was thick with Mist, making the drumming of the wind-mills a heavy beat in the darkness.

Denvy held Clive in a wrap against his chest, limp and hot, far too hot for a Human, but Jythal was hopeful it meant the boy was burning the toxins from his body.

They had cloaked him in skins and blankets, for though he was scorching to the touch, he shivered with fever.

Sinking back into the shadows of the harbour buildings, Denvy knelt beside Nixlye who sat upon a stack of crates.

She fiddled with her legs, cranking them to life. From above, Zafiashid and Jythal dropped into the alley beside them, causing Penny to squeak in fright.

"Five Iposti lie in wait for us," Jythal hissed. "I am not sure how we're going to get past them without alerting the harbour guards."

"But in public," Nixlye said, "they cannot be seen doing anything that opposes their Order. The best they can do is cause enough ruckus to bring down the harbour guards. Iposti keep their power based on fear in the shadows, but they have never openly harmed anyone. If they started doing that, they'd cause an uprising. The Prides wouldn't stand for it. Queens can be subjugated in the shadows, but never, ever would the Prides allow neutrals to rule openly."

Zafiashid shook her head. "I do not know if that's true anymore, Nixlye. And I'm not willing to risk our lives on the whimsical idea that they won't harm us."

Denvy nodded. "I agree."

"What do we do?" Ki'b piped up. "How do we sneak onto the *Lawless*?"

"They'd notice. Even if I used Runes, I've lost too much blood to make a strong enough cloak against the Simoon they control."

"Therefore," Zafiashid held up a paw, "I have asked Uyrilk and her prince for aid."

Denvy curled his tail around Penny and Ki'b as the air thickened with tension. Zafiashid's air-gills spread in warning.

Nixlye stood, a low snarl in her throat. "Mother, you cannot be serious."

Jythal held out an arm, separating the two queens.

"Nixlye, Mother is right. In this situation we must use the allies we have."

"You can not be defending the Jezumatu! Not after what they did to you."

"I do not defend them, my dear. I will never defend what they did to me, nor any of the princes under their care, but if what Mother says is true and Uyrilk is an ally then she may aid us in getting back to the *Lawless*. And, right now, Clive needs to be home more than our honour dictates justice."

Nixlye's tail thrashed in disgust. "Fine. I'll allow a truce. For now."

Zafiashid inclined her head and raised her paw. Denvy stepped back as another Kattamont dropped into the alley, landing beside the queen. She had the smell of a princess, not yet a queen—but she could have been; she was very close to the transformation stage, and likely that was the reason for the heightened strain she was causing her own Pride. Denvy frowned, studying the broad-shouldered, stocky, spotted-coated princess with a wary glare. From out of the shadows, a younger prince emerged, his brown coat grading into vibrant tail-feathers and air-gills of blues and yellows. He glanced towards Jythal before nodding in Denvy's direction, and he knew he had been assessed as the leader of the brotherhood within their Pride. Jythal's amusement tickled through their dreamathic nexus, and he had to admit finding himself accorded such regard was indeed laughable. He had gone from wanting nothing to do with his people to suddenly needing to learn on his foot-paws as he navigated their changing culture.

"You've caused such a stir." Uyrilk's paw rested on her Mist-pistol in a casual display of power. "Breaking into a Haven Hall. I've never heard of anything so brazen. What were you searching for, heh?"

"That is none of your Wind-Forsaken business!" Nixlye hissed.

Jythal's paw settled on her shoulder, gently tugging her back.

"Queen Nixlye." Uyrilk tipped her head to one side, her grin almost reaching her ears. "And the legendary White Prince Jythal. But… where is Prince Aaldryn? I had so been hoping to finally meet the prince who runs the burning-sea."

Jythal's paw clamped down on Nixlye's shoulder, restraining her even as she struggled. "That is not relevant, Princess," he murmured.

"The absence of your blood-brother is very relevant, I think, Jythal—"

"Do not dare to address my prince!" Nixlye snarled.

"That is the vehemence I do so adore about you, Nixlye. Will you take your revenge for your prince? Take it from me now?" Princess Uyrilk paused as her prince gently urged her back with a paw.

"Now is neither the time nor the place, and Queen Nixlye is aware you were not involved in any of the unsavoury practices of the Jezumatu Pride."

Uyrilk sniffed, shaking aside the paw.

"Doesn't stop me from wanting to rip her throat out," Nixlye growled.

"Then you cast your anger upon the wrong source." The prince shook his head. "You are not the only princess who has aided princes out of their captivity."

"I thought that was you, Lester." Jythal shifted. "You're masking your scent extremely well."

"We had a good teacher." The prince moved to clasp Jythal's paw, holding it firmly to his cheek and the scent glands therein. "It is good to see you, blood-brother."

"Likewise, if I could."

Uyrilk made a scoffing sound, though her faint smile betrayed the fakeness of the disgust in her tone. "Princes. Such bleeding hearts."

Zafiashid snorted. "We need to reach the *Lawless*, Uyrilk."

"That would be a problem with five Iposti waiting for you." The princess raised an eyebrow.

"I'm willing to grant you a favour—one favour—if you can get them to leave."

"Mother!" Nixlye gasped. "A favour! We can't be indebted to the Jezumatu!"

Denvy roused himself, speaking for the first time. "It is not the Jezumatu Zafiashid is granting a favour to; it is to Princess Uyrilk. There is a difference."

"Yes, there is." Uyrilk inclined her head in his direction. "My prince and I are acting alone in this, Queen Nixlye."

"You've gone rogue?" Jythal's ears pinned back.

"I suppose." Uyrilk shrugged. "Let's not dally any longer. The Iposti can overhear conversations, even if you have set up Runes." She glanced at Jythal. "Not that I don't believe in your skills, White Lion, but I don't trust easily anymore." She brushed past Zafiashid. "The moment you see a chance, get away."

Without another word, the princess vanished into the darkness. Denvy watched curiously as Lester and Jythal exchanged a brief parting, foreheads pressed together, and paws entangled, before Lester slipped away, trailing after his princess. He looked curiously at Nixlye, who sighed heavily.

"It's a long story, Denvy."

"I look forward to hearing it someday."

"It isn't particularly pleasant," Jythal muttered.

Zafiashid and Nixlye crouched beside the crates, watching the figures of the cloaked Iposti by the Mist lamps.

The air was tense when Uyrilk and Lester approached the gathering. Nixlye's hand curled around her bow. Denvy resisted the urge to place his own paw around hers to try and settle her nerves; doing so would cause only far more tension.

"Now we'll see if she is on our side," Nixlye murmured.

"If all queens and princesses went around killing each other how would we form alliances?" Zafiashid responded. "I would never have allowed you to live on the *Lawless Child*. It is the same thing, cub."

"It is nothing like our relationship. You are my Mother. I love you."

"We have an alliance."

Jythal sighed. "Not now. You're stressing my Runes already with the pheromones you're releasing. I am not well! Please!"

Both queens looked back at the blind doctor, their ears turned down in apology. Denvy held back his smirk, glad they could still be scolded.

"Oh! Look!" Ki'b pointed to the Iposti, Uyrilk, and her prince. "They're leaving!"

Denvy crept closer. She was correct. Uyrilk and Lester were leading four of the Iposti down the harbour, away from the *Lawless Child*.

"She must have convinced them she knew where we were."

Zafiashid looked back with a wide grin of victory.

"Well, she did just have a pit-battle with you," Jythal offered. "I suppose that helps."

"There is one remaining."

"We can deal with one." Zafiashid huffed and shifted to Denvy's side. "You take the cubs around the back of those crates and sneak onto the dingy. Jythal, go with them."

The prince nodded.

"Nixlye and I will deal with the Iposti."

The two queens slipped into the darkness. Denvy tensed. It was difficult, finding himself anxious every time Zafiashid left his sight. He knew perfectly well the queen was capable of looking after herself but remaining behind was difficult. It felt much like the times Zinkx had gone charging into battle, unheeding of his advice, and barely returned by the skin of his teeth.

Jythal rubbed up beside him. "You have not been a prince in a long time, old man."

Denvy chuckled. "No, but I have been a foster father to many children. It does feel rather similar."

Jythal crouched, allowing Penny to clamber onto his back. Denvy offered his tail to the blind healer as a guide and slowly they made their way between the crates and docked supplies. The towering crane swinging above them was empty of cargo, but still an imposing structure to behold. Denvy heard a sudden struggle and a gust of wind from above. The crane groaned. A body fell off the harbour, into the burning-sea waves. Zafiashid and Nixlye landed beside them.

"Done. Let's go. Into the dingy," Nixlye urged them.

Clambering into the small boat, Denvy settled down as Zafiashid cast them off. He studied their faces in the darkness. Jythal held Penny close, but the blind healer was beginning to wane. Nixlye was rubbing her metal legs, her gaze fixed anxiously on the blinking lights of the *Lawless Child*.

"*Jarkir*," she moaned. "My legs, they're out of Mist."

"We'll be all right. We're almost there. I can see Kovlrok's lookout light," Zafiashid said softly as she rowed with a steady beat.

The dingy bumped gently against the side of the *Lawless Child* and Zafiashid clambered up the side, vanishing over the railing. She seemed tireless, but Denvy wondered whether she, too, was on the verge of collapse. Ropes were flung over the edge and soon they were on deck, safe and warmed as crew draped duvets over their shoulders. Denvy breathed out, unaware until then that he had been holding his breath, waiting for the peace and security that the deck of the *Lawless Child* brought. He finally inhaled through his air-gills, surprised that his lungs no longer ached with the Human illness he had long been infected with.

"Are we ready to cast off?" Zafiashid asked Kovlrok.

The first-mate nodded. "Indeed, Captain."

"Good. No lanterns. No engines. We do this quickly and as silently as possible. Pick a current and follow it. I don't care where it takes us: away from this cursed place."

"As you wish." Kovlrok crossed the deck and it became a hive of activity, shadows moving in a maddening dance. Denvy took one last look back at Threnthton and the thrumming wind-mills illumed by the lights of hanging Mist lamps. His people could have been so great—but they had built their civilization not on a sea of sand, but a sea of blood.

CHAPTER THIRTEEN

Rain splattered down upon a thatched roof. It was calming. The muffled drumming rhythm reminded Disgleirio of the churning thrum that had once lulled him to sleep in the Northern Tower. He had never missed it—not until now. Suddenly the ache was intense, burrowing into him like a hot pike—a need to see Sekhmet. After all these long sol-cycles, he wanted to be a child in the arms of a fairy again.

"Father. Are you awake?" Aneurin's soft voice urged him to turn and he faced his son. White hair glowed around pale jade cheeks, rosy from wiping aside tears.

"Sorry for worrying you, Rin," Disgleirio murmured.

The boy sniffled and sank against his chest. The weight was pleasant. "Where is your brother, your sister?"

"There is a storm. They are out securing your beasts of burden in the stables." The new voice rang with an intonation only one race was known for, the curling of a tongue that dragged out vowels, making sentences slow and steady. Weakly, Disgleirio managed to rise. At the door, removing a coat heavy with rain, was a Batitic.

"Good evening, your highness. I am Skri Mazaki." Blood-red eyes studied him. "I am glad to see your episode has passed."

Episode. His gravity was collapsing. His containment suit had failed. Disgleirio touched his suit in a panic, startled to feel the revitalised life humming through it.

"You're a technomancer..." he whispered. He had thought the Dragon had killed every last one of them.

Skri smiled, passing Aneurin a warm cocoa drink.

"I am many things, your highness. Among them is an outcast. Though, I am grateful to the Twilight that I was here when your children needed aid."

Disgleirio accepted his own warm clay mug from the lone Batitic. "As am I, Skri."

For a surgery performed hanging in an elevator shaft, Jarvis thought he had done rather a decent job. He was not going to praise himself out loud, though, considering the state Aaldryn was in. His fur was slick with sweat, his air-gills slack around his neck despite his frantic panting for air. His chest expanding so rapidly under his fur had made Jarvis' fingers slip a few times, and he had been terrified his brother was dying. His brother—he felt it completely now. His anger had vanished with the prospect of losing Aaldryn. And Master Titus—he could not afford to worry about his fate just yet, but he used the pain and dread to focus himself on saving his brother first. Then he would find the man who had become a father to him.

Impressively, Aaldryn had managed to remain conscious throughout the ordeal of having the metal rod removed from his shoulder and the wound cauterised. Jarvis shook his head, trying to clear it. The screams were going to echo in his memories for a while. He felt a wave of loathing towards himself. To think he had held the actions of a Titan against his brother… He held Aaldryn firmly against the wall, his gravity-bubble expanded around them both.

"How are you feeling now?"

"Khamsin's focusing all his energies on the wound. It should be fine."

"Do you think you're well enough to move yet?"

"I think so."

"Right." Jarvis turned, peering around in the dim light. "Tikal?"

The AI appeared abruptly in front of him.

"We're going down to find Master Titus." He tried not to choke on his words. Mentioning his master's name made him panic. "Can you take Aaldryn? I don't think I'm strong enough to carry us both in my gravity-bubble."

He was, really, but he could not trust himself, not right now, while he was so emotionally unstable. He felt like an eggshell, about ready to tip over and crack, releasing all his yoke.

Tikal levelled him with an odd look of disdain. It was somewhat alarming to see it on the stoic face of the Zaprex corpse, the metal twisting around to make the lips perk and eyebrows lift. A glowing tongue stuck out at him.

Why not the wind-god? Why me?

"Khamsin is fixing Aaldryn's wound, and it's too tight in here for him to use the air currents to move us both. Please. Tikal. For me."

Tikal huffed, folding its arms stoutly across its chest. *Fine. We will make the wind-god move, but it is funny!*

The AI swept up to Aaldryn and hugged him around the middle. Jarvis backed away and gradually let himself fall. What horrors lay below them? Was Master Titus still alive? Was the monstrous machine waiting for them in the inky depths?

The change was gradual. The elevator shaft slowly opened out into a chasm. Water had so furiously rushed through the underground city it had ripped out the metal structure, forming a cave network. The air was fresher against his skin, and the temperature colder still than it had ever been, making the droplets of his tears freeze against his eyelashes. He had not even realised he was crying.

Master Titus, being technically dead, had never shown up on his life-sign sensors, but the rippling heat of the cloak he wore was an indicator he could seek out. Jarvis began scanning for the billions of swarming little nano-bots that formed the magical knit.

His feet finally pressed into damp soil. It felt foreign, to find himself upon muddy ground again. It had been so long since he had smelt mud, and it swept him back to cold, frosty mornings with his father, breaking ice on their farm's pond. He shivered, curling his fingernails into the palms of his hands, piercing the skin. The pain yanked him back into the wide, lonely chasm. Tikal gently placed Aaldryn beside a large metal beam. It looked as though it had once been the foundations of an ancient skyscraper, long worn down. They stood on the shore of an immense lake that danced with the reflections of light, glinting like stars, from the few crystals scattered about.

Other than a distant trickle of water, he was met with silence, a silence that seemed to go on forever.

Nothing stirred. Utterly nothing.

He could sense no movement, no machines, no songs. Only emptiness.

Jarvis abruptly aborted his scans; the horror of the hollowness was frightening. He had to latch onto Aaldryn's laboured breathing to ground himself to reality, using his brother as the point of focus to begin his search again.

Jarvis snapped his head around as his sensors pinged. A light flickered on the side of his lenses. He ran, lunging over rocks and debris towards the location of the smudge. The closer he drew, the clearer the outline of Master Titus' body became, pinned beneath fallen beams.

"Master! Master!" he shouted, scrambling down a boulder.

Titus weakly raised a skeletal hand.

"Stop! Don't!"

Jarvis skidded to a halt. A high-pitched screech shattered the silence. Across the darkness, two large red lenses flared to life. Clattering and clanking resounded off distant walls as a heavy metal body lifted itself out of the water of the lake. Waterfalls cascaded off its glinting hull, rippling with tainted philepcon liquid. Jarvis spun. His protector bot surged up his spine, activating with a burst of energy and his exoskeleton wrapped his skin in plates as he ran, blending into the hues of the dark underworld with his birth elemental.

Surely, now, in this immense cavern, Khamsin had enough space to be released.

He swept down beside Aaldryn.

"What do you need?"

"Get through its armour. Make me a weak spot." Aaldryn clutched at his wound.

"Right." Jarvis burst away, dashing over the rocks, dislodging them as he skittered across the cavern. He landed on the water, speeding over its surface. The machine stood to full height and it moved. He barely caught the swift action that blocked him, smashing against his arms as he swung himself up to catch the full force of the blow. It shattered against his hull and he felt his exoskeleton absorb the force.

Water erupted in a halo.

Jarvis gripped the machine's trembling arm in his own comparatively tiny hand, using all his strength to crush it and pull it apart, though he was nowhere close to matching its power. Symbols of warning spun around his optical lenses. He could feel his body weakening with every second that passed. Gritting his teeth, he sank his bladed nails deep into its armour, snarling as he split the plates, causing tainted red liquid to seep from the cracks. It was hot against his hull, and sizzled like acid, causing even more screeches of panicked warning to erupt through his skull.

Suddenly something clicked and whirred within the arm and he snapped his head up, staring at what no longer ended in fingers but a hole that burned bright orange and boiling, like a cauldron of oil. That odour. His brother-in-law; it smelt like his brother-in-law who had worked in the barracks.

A single, red line flared across his vision. Danger. He did not need the alarm to know the threat when he saw it.

"Holy Sun!" He flung himself backwards, dodging the burst of gunfire. Had his protector bot not been in control of his limbs, the memory of being struck by a single bullet would have been enough to make him freeze in terror. This was like something out of his nightmares, an exaggeration of the traumatic experience, the weapon made huge and monstrous, the bullets too numerous and fired at too fast a rate for him to dodge… except this was real. Pain sheered across his back as the weapon fire bounced off his shield. He dived behind a rock.

Heaving for air, Jarvis scratched at the back of his neck. It burned, as though fire had roasted him alive. Steam hissed from the metal. It had almost warped. The bullets had nearly made it through the armour. If he had been a fraction slower—

He hefted his blade—Master Titus had given it to him. It had been crafted from the carcass of a Fire Elemental. He was not born under the constellation of fire but that did not mean he was unable to make it hot, perhaps hot and fast enough to get through the armour of the machine. He gave it a twirl, refocusing and realigning his thoughts with the wave length of the protector bot. If the machine's movements were too fast to catch, then he had to move faster. He had to be a bullet. This cavern was large enough for him to pick up speed; he had to hope his shields would stand under a barrage of attacks. Two machines, as accurate as each other, could do so very little but strike head on.

A metal vine whipped down, cutting through the rock Jarvis hid behind. He rolled, sprang up with a burst of gravity control, and dashed across the lake, towards the furthest wall of the cavern. He heard the machine in pursuit. Bullets clattered off his armour. He dodged to one side, swinging out his blade and cutting through a crystal. With a kick he lashed out, aiming the missile at the machine as it shattered. He repeated the process with each crystal as he leapt up the wall at full speed, as far as his gravity control could take him. In mid-air he spun, activating the thrusters in his shoulders, and with a burst he propelled himself down the wall. He aimed his sword at the chest plate of the machine, ignoring the bullets that pinged off his armour. The heat was intense, warnings flaring over his optical lenses. Pain signals erupted up his spine as blood splattered, bullets finally piercing through his metal hull. Screaming, Jarvis slammed into the machine. His blade split the armour like a tiny pin. The force of the strike sent them both smashing across the debris of crystal, back into the lake. Jarvis twisted the blade in his bloodied hands, ripping it upwards, curving it around in an arch. An echo of pain filtered through his firewalls, momentarily throwing him off.

Pain—the machine felt pain. It made no sense. When he had merged with his protector bot, he had only felt its pain after the merge had been completed. What he sensed now was pain mixed with terror and—most startling of all—confusion.

He had no time to analyse any of the data.

Jarvis! Drop! Now!

Khamsin's voice reverberated in his mind. He released the hilt of his sword and collapsed into the water. Even under the surface, in the darkness, he heard the shattering clang, and watched the eruption of sparks and philepcon liquid as an enormous steel pole buried itself in the machine's abdomen. Had it hit the processor core? Master Titus had crushed the processor core of the protector bot that had attacked him, and was now merged with him—it was the only way he knew to destroy a Zaprex machine.

He burst out of the water, spluttering and coughing. The machine staggered back, emitting a low whine. Jarvis wiped at his optical lenses, cleaning them as he tried to process the blurry scene. Master Titus was perched on its shoulders, wielding a metal sheet as keenly as he had his stone blade. He thrust it between the plates of the machine's armoured neck. Jarvis turned away, gripping his skull as his firewalls were scratched and clawed at. He fought back tears. The scream was agonizing, and he could not block it out. It sounded like a child—like Ki'b. He choked on his own cry. Aaldryn held out a paw and dragged him out of the lake.

"Good work," his brother said.

Jarvis was unable to respond.

Master Titus joined them, throwing aside the metal sheet. He collapsed in a weary heap. "I am so done with all this."

In relief, Jarvis lightly touched his Master's shoulder.

"I am fine, laddie, just worn out." Titus rubbed his nose. He looked towards Tikal, hovering anxiously nearby. "Ask yeh little friend why it did not warn us about that insane piece of *fraki* sooner?"

Tikal floated closer. *"The Tainted Ones do not appear on our sensors. We cannot provide data. Something is wrong. We do not like them."*

Jarvis wiped back his hair, flicking aside water and blood. His exoskeleton was gradually beginning to liquify and seep back under his hull, growing dormant now that his heart-rate was calming, and danger averted—for now.

"Tikal is right, sir," he stammered out. "The machine did not appear on my sensors either, even when I came down here and scanned. Even now…" he looked back at the wreckage, lying silent in the lake. "It doesn't register." A shiver ran through his hull at the unnaturalness of it all. But that unnaturalness made him morbidly curious. Heaving himself up on shaking legs, Jarvis expanded his gravity-bubble and wobbled across the surface of the water, towards the machine. He sensed Tikal's presence behind him, though the AI was chattering worriedly.

Titus called out. "Jarvis! Don' yeh get too close!"

"Why do you call it a Tainted One?" Jarvis asked Tikal.

The AI was silent for a moment before responding in a slow whine. *"Sick. They are sick. We do not know when, or why, or how, but something is within them. It has made them go,"* it waved a hand around its head, *"very mad."*

"Mad?" Aaldryn inquired. The prince stood on a whirlwind above the water, still cradling his wounded arm. "That isn't really a word one would use to describe a machine, is it?"

"No." Jarvis shook his head. "Madness, insanity, sickness, those are all things that happen to fleshlings. I don't think the Zaprexes created their machines to go mad, did they Tikal?"

"We are born crystals. Crystals grow into beautiful trees if not controlled. We grow fruits of emotions if not pruned. We become mad. Emotions make you mad. I am mad, yes?"

"I wouldn't say that, Tikal. You're just a bit lonely." Jarvis smiled.

"Lonely, amongst the angels", Tikal whispered, twirling. *"So lonely, so alone…"*

"Still, I wonder. I can understand an AI growing large enough over time to gain emotions. Tikal would be really, really old, right?" He glanced at Aaldryn and the prince nodded. "But this isn't an AI." He pointed to the machine half submerged in the water. "It's rather like my protector bot—just a drone. So, what would make it go mad?" He climbed onto the machine.

Titus shouted. "I told yeh, Little Weasel, not ta get too close!"

"Tikal is right. There is something inside it."

"How do yeh know that?"

"Because I scanned it," Jarvis shouted back.

"Yeh said yeh couldn't do that." Titus had finally joined them. Jarvis looked over at his Master, bedraggled and glaring, standing on the surface of the water, arms tightly folded over his chest. The Hunter's cloak seemed to imitate his tense mood, whipping around his lanky body like a storm.

"I said it wasn't registering on my general scans. I didn't say I couldn't scan it once I knew it was there. And I think Tikal fears being contaminated itself if it does a scan of a tainted machine. I'm removed from Tikal's systems, and a hybrid. I'm a machine with the emotions of a Human, but I've managed to control the philepcon liquid within me and we've balanced each other out. We don't fight each other…"

Jarvis heaved down on the steel rod Khamsin had thrust through the weak point he had made in the armour. It loosened and glowing red philepcon liquid oozed out. Tikal squealed, spinning around, grabbing its cheeks.

"Nooooo! Don't let it touch you!"

"It's okay, Tikal. I'm protected by my hull. I'll be fine."

"It's right, though." Titus turned to Aaldryn. "You back up. We have no idea how this stuff will react to a fleshling, even one who hosts a Titan."

Aaldryn's air-gills twitched, the only sign of his irritation as he drifted back with a wave of his tail.

Titus climbed his way up to join Jarvis and aided him in easing the steel rod free of the armour plating. Jarvis studied the gaping hole, a hand subconsciously rubbing his own aching chest. He could sense his master's eyes on him even as he bent forward to grip the armour plating. Gears whirred inside his frame as enhanced muscles pulled. Plate by plate he peeled the armour back, revealing the squishy, liquid-formed insides. Jarvis swallowed back bile. Was this what he looked like inside—rows of thin, glowing fibres, vibrating with life? Titus drew a knife and hacked into the gooey, thread-like blue muscles. It took time to fight through the first few layers.

"Jarvis…" Titus paused. "This…ain't philepcon liquid anymore, laddie."

Jarvis gagged. The texture of the liquid against his skin had changed but he had refused to accept what it could be. It was like velvet and kept globing into sticky balls, smelling fouler the deeper they delved. If anything, it reminded him of the few times he had found a dead sheep on the farmlands.

"This is blood," Titus murmured.

"Oh…Sun…" Jarvis covered his mouth, only to retch as he smelt the blood on his hand. This was so much worse than the sheep torn apart by a plains lion. He coughed, gulping back the vomit as he continued to pull aside the membrane, the urge to discover what was inside the machine a sudden, maddening drive.

"No, no, no…that's impossible." Aaldryn voiced the words he wanted to say, but he could only stare at the horrible sight that faced them. Tucked within the chest cavity of the machine, naked like a babe, connected to streams of tubing, fused into the machine itself, lay a Kelib child. Jarvis sobbed. It was not Ki'b, but it could have been.

"Well," Titus sat back, wiping blood from his hands, "I think we have found out why you kids were being taken to Utillia."

"No." Jarvis dragged his fingers over his cheeks. "Anything but this." His protector bot was sparking, struggling to process the revulsion it found itself confronting. Never before would it have encountered the emotion, but now it knew the Human sensation and its disgust that such a thing was done to a living being, fusing them with the beauty of their Creators was an overwhelmingly new sensation.

The child's eyes opened suddenly, and his scream pierced the cavern.

Jarvis fell backwards off the machine. Tikal caught him before he hit the water and perched him back on the hull. Titus dived into the hole, ripping out the cords that attached the child to the cocoon, and pulled the boy into his arms. He cradled the screaming child to his chest, rocking him gently, soothing him. Jarvis curled up. Aaldryn gently touched his shoulder, and Jarvis burrowed into his lap, whimpering.

They could only sit and watch as Titus cradled and comforted the dying child, singing to him softly. He could see the life draining from his frail little body now that he had been removed from the machine. A sob escaped Jarvis' chest. How vile. How disgusting. Who had done this? Who had attached a child to a machine, and forced both to exist together as one entity, to taint each other, to scream in constant agony? Staring at the Kelib boy, he could see nothing but Ki'b.

Had he left her to a similar fate?

Titus heaved a sigh and he turned towards them. "This is troubling."

"We tell you, the Tainted Ones, we do not see them," Tikal whispered.

"It is all right, Tikal. We believe you," Aaldryn offered. "We should bury him, Titus."

"Aye." Titus stood, carrying the boy. "I would prefer to burn him to cleanse him, so he could be with his ancestors, but I don' think that would be a good idea in here. Aye, let's bury the laddie at least. Give him some respect."

Respect?

Jarvis closed his eyes at the word that echoed within his mind.

Where had respect gone?

QUEEN ZAFIASHID OF THE MISFIT PRIDE

CHAPTER FOURTEEN

Disgleirio leant against the mighty Sunstone overlooking the Last Ring of Palace-Town. Palace-Town—the name the local inhabitants of Avalon had given the great thriving city. Humans had such short memories. The recording of history was a bygone pastime left only to the Sun Monks of the order he had established, and that was all he could hope for.

He wondered if Sekhmet would have been proud of him and all he had accomplished—of his Dynasty.

Skri's cloak dragged along the stones of the battlement. The Batitic wrinkled his nose. "You may not feel the cold, your highness, but we mere mortal creatures do."

Disgleirio chuckled. "I do feel the cold. I have just lived so long I forget about it."

Skri shook his head. "I gather you wished to speak, away from the ears of your wife and children."

"Yes." Disgleirio eased down onto the wall, clasping the cold rocks with gloved hands. He could feel it, the tightening within him as his energy began its final phase.

"I am going to die soon, Skri. No. Please. Hear me out. You have kept me alive far longer than I could have hoped. I have seen my grandchildren because of you, Skri. You are the only one, other than Maze, whom I trust, and I cannot make her do this." He glanced away. "You're my best friend."

"And you are mine." Skri reached out. "Whatever it is you ask, Disgleirio, I shall do."

"When I am gone, I want you to protect what's left of me. You'll understand when it's over. And I have a brother—a Kattamont. His name is Maahes. If you can, try and find him." Disgleirio's voice broke, and he wiped at his tears. After all these sol-cycles, death was here, and he did not want to go. Was this anything like what Sekhmet had felt?

Skri bowed his head. "On my life, and the lives I have yet to sire, we shall always protect what is yours."

"You are far too noble, Skri."

"I am a Batitic. We are a noble race."

"Your feathers are fluffing from all that nobility."

The glow of the copied holographic maps illuminated the Captain's cabin as Denvy entered. He scrubbed at his weary eyes, blinking in the eerie green light. He missed the Sun. No matter how warm the Mist-Lanterns would grow, how magnificently the sails of the *Lawless Child* blazed, nothing could compare to the brightness of the Sun and its heat.

Zafiashid, deep in study of the maps, spared him a glance of greeting. Nixlye sat to the side with Jythal, trying to clean the blood stains from his white fur. Denvy clipped the door shut behind him. At the noise, Ki'b stirred from her spot by the large windows and bounced off the pillowed ledge, running towards him.

"Khwaja! How is Clive?"

"Penny is with him. He has not woken, but he is stable." Denvy gave her head a gentle pat.

Her shoulders sagged. "Jarvis was not like this; he was fine after Zaprex blood got into him."

Denvy frowned. Jarvis had been very skilled at masking the pain of his transformation from his adoptive siblings.

"I do not believe this is the same," Jythal commented from his seat, still resting his bandaged wounds. "It is an infected wound that Clive has, Mountain Flower. The poison is, perhaps, similar to a Batitic venom, paralysing its prey. I had the privilege of being raised by a Batitic, a master of his arts. Our tails are effectively very similar." He brought his tail around, flicking out its bone spikes and Ki'b carefully touched one.

Denvy chuckled. "They are similar, though there are a few rather important differences you've neglected to mention."

Jythal snorted and Denvy stumbled as he was thudded heavily by the prince's tail.

"Then do tell us, oh-wise-all-knowing-one."

"Our tails are far more colourful, heavier, and built as weapons of war, while only the Batitic males have tails; they are for balance and flight, and it is how they breed."

Nixlye choked on her drink. She covered her mouth, wiping away spittle as she stared up at him. "Seriously?"

Denvy raised an eyebrow at the young queen, amused at her ruffled disposition. "Don't presume all the bestial races are alike, my dear, simply because we are bestial."

Nixlye pouted.

"Focus, cubs." Zafiashid settled a flask of honey-dew on the map-strewn desk and leant forward, sighing through her air-gills. Denvy's ears twitched as her claws grated over the table's surface.

"These charts are unbelievable. It is no wonder the Iposti have control over the trading routes. They know the changing tides of each sector, and when the gravity will shift between the Way Stations." She pointed to a square. "Watch, here. This grid is going to merge with this one at any moment and cause a null-zone. There is a sand-ship here that will be caught up in the tide."

Nixlye wheeled over in her spare wheelchair. "But, Mother, this is in real time. That sand-ship—"

Zafiashid shook her head. "I know. The Iposti have been able to see the positions of sand-ships. It is unnerving to think about."

As Zafiashid had predicted, the null-zone appeared at the merging of the two grids and the sand-ship scattered into pixels. For a moment they stared in silence, contemplating the horror of the deaths it represented. And the implications.

Saliva was heavy in Denvy's mouth, making swallowing difficult. He inched forward, studying the hologram with a scowl. It drew him back to the memory of the Galactic-Ships he had once navigated between Lands. The shine of holograms had been a near constant in the CCRs.

"The question is how and where these maps are getting their information. It cannot be from the Towers, otherwise the Dragon's Overlords would be able to track the location. If it is from the Way Stations here in Utillia there would be sectors missing due to the collapse of the Stations, and it is unlikely they are from satellites… unless…"

"What are satellites?" Ki'b piped up.

Denvy reached out, finding his paws trembling despite how earnestly he tried to calm his racing heart. He turned the parchment hologram carefully around until the legend faced him and he flicked the keypad up, enlarging it into a workspace. Nixlye and Zafiashid stared at him, and he ignored their bewildered faces, replying as steadily to Ki'b as he could muster.

"Satellites are like iron birds high up in the sky-sea, that sing songs that other birds, down on the ground, can pick up and translate into useful information, just like these charts." Denvy tapped a few glittering squares on the map's legend, and the hologram expanded beyond the edge of the table. Nixlye wheeled back in alarm and Ki'b joined her, leaving only Jythal sitting amongst the shimmering waves of the burning-sea, confused by their movements.

Denvy looked over the rim of the holographic work station at Nixlye. The sheen of the burning-sea waves created out of the moving pixels played off her rosy fur, tinting it a brighter red. He sucked in a sharp breath.

Red—blood red—for a Messenger.

Or, perhaps, red for the warrior of the sky: Sekhmet.

"Nixlye, you told me in our dream that Tikal wanders alone amongst the Angels," Denvy whispered.

The young queen frowned. "Yes, I did, and you said that 'Angels' is not a Kattamont word."

He nodded. "It isn't. It's from the Little Blue Planet."

Nixlye mouthed the sentence back to him. "What does it mean—Angels?"

"Let's go with protectors, or guardians."

"What are you getting at, Denvy?" Zafiashid settled a hand on his shoulder.

"I think I know where these maps are receiving their intel from." He twirled his claw around, causing the hologram to shift, enveloping the cabin in a swirl of starlight, and in a circle ten spheres slowly rotated. Denvy clapped his paws together to reset the hologram to its original position on the desk. Nixlye gasped, wheeling herself up against it with a thud, almost knocking over the jug of honey-dew.

"What's going on?" Jythal stood.

Nixlye reached for his paw. "Sorry, dear."

"What are they, Denvy?" Zafiashid prowled around the desk.

"The Angels. They're Tikal's gravity stations. They were called the Angels by the Zaprexes who lived in Tikal. They kept the city in the sky-sea. I used to enjoy playing on them when I was a cub. I could defrag anywhere, and it was good practice, but I got into a lot of trouble for it when I did get caught." He chuckled. "My guess is they're still up there somewhere." He glanced at the ceiling, waving a paw. "Most likely still cloaked. These holo-maps must be getting a direct feed from the Angels. It is the only way they could be mapping the whole of Utillia's desktop grid."

"This helps us how?" Zafiashid's claw had gone back to tapping the desk.

"We should be able to triangulate the sector where Tikal will be next from the information they're relaying."

Jythal raised a paw. "Wait, you said they're Tikal's gravity stations, so shouldn't Tikal be wherever they are? Up there, in the sky-sea? We won't be able to reach it, then."

"Nixlye, love, in your dream, I told you that the Rythrya Stones looked like the top spires of Tikal?" Denvy arched an eyebrow.

"You did." She nodded.

"I believe that during the centuries that have passed, the burning-sea has risen up and the Angels have lost power. So Tikal has become submerged."

"Ah!" Jythal laughed. "I see. Even though Tikal is buried in the burning-sea, it is following the same route it would have once followed in the sky-sea. No wonder the Rythrya Stones are never in the same sector."

"This does not answer the question as to why the Iposti haven't gained access to this magical city if they have had this same information for so long." Zafiashid's arms crossed her chest.

Denvy pointed to her. "Very true, my queen, and I am sure they have tried hard to do so over the sol-cycles. However, there was only one way into the Rainbow City, and I doubt time has changed that. No sand-ship, no excavation team, would ever reach Tikal."

"But we can?" Ki'b tugged on his paw. "Clive being hurt won't be for nothing?"

"No, my dear, it won't be for nothing," Denvy assured her with a tender smile.

"Speaking of Clive, I should go and check up on him." Jythal's paw lingered on Nixlye's shoulder briefly before he left.

"Come, Ki'b," Nixlye wheeled past the young Kelib. "We need some rest also."

"But…I should stay with Clive and Penny." Her eyes misted over and she started fussing with her dress. His hearts ached. She worried too easily already for such a young child.

"Try to sleep, dear one. You'll feel better for it."

Timidly she nodded and scampered after Nixlye. Denvy watched the door close and sighed heavily, wishing that, along with the sigh, all his aches would drain out through his foot-paws into the *Lawless Child*'s wood planks. He frowned at the holographic parchments. Tikal—the Rainbow City. He had not seen the home he had forsaken in centuries, and now he seemed to be barrelling towards it, faster than he had ever thought possible.

Zafiashid pulled on a thick poncho and loaded her Mist pistol.

"Going to stand watch with Kovlrok." She wiggled her eyebrows playfully. "Just because I suddenly find myself a gorgeous, old, handsome Golden Lion doesn't mean I can abandon my First Mate."

"I like that you threw old in there," Denvy muttered. A small part of him had hoped she would stay. Her company was comforting and warm. He had been missing something and it was only since she had given him the gift of her presence that the ache of loneliness was subsiding.

She laughed and ruffled his gills playfully. "I don't know when danger might strike. Need to be prepared."

He nodded.

"You should go to your cub, dear. You are worried about him. I am sure he will sense your presence."

Clive? Yes, he was deeply troubled about the child, but he was not sure if skulking by the bedside would be useful for poor Jythal.

"I trust Jythal."

Zafiashid scoffed. "I will never understand the faith you princes place in each other."

Denvy stared at her, utterly perplexed. "No? You trust Kovlrok."

"Hardly the same."

"Well, you seemed to believe what that princess told you in the pit-fight. Enough to pin our lives on her word. That is similar, yes?"

Her lips pressed into a thin line. "It is not. No princess or queen would lie to another in a pit-fight."

He snorted. "That, my dear, is trust." He leant on the table.

"What was it she told you, by the way?"

Zafiashid took a breath. "I suppose we are far enough away now."

"One would hope."

Her tail flicked his. He rebutted with a low growl.

"There is something happening in Pennadot that is causing the

Humans and Kelibs to flee over the Border into Utillia. Apparently the Silvertide and Jezumatu Navies are slaughtering them all."

A weight heavier even than the yoke bore down upon Denvy's shoulders. The table beneath him creaked as he sagged. Zafiashid placed a paw gently to his cheek and he pressed into the comfort she offered.

"I am sorry, love. I know Pennadot is dear to you."

"I should have thought of this. Utillia has the only sky-sea that could withstand Coltarian's eruption. It is the perfect haven. Zinkx's message would have started an exodus via the Underground Messengers." He pressed his head against her chest. "What would it take for the Prides to stop?" he mumbled into the fabric of her poncho.

"Power. Strength. A uniting like the days of old." Zafiashid's arms wrapped around him and he felt the heaviness lighten, as though by the tightening of her arms she was sharing the burden. He had never been so grateful for the steadfastness of a partnership—

Was this why Zaprexes had always come in pairs? To share the weight of their responsibilities?

He sighed. "You ask a lot of an old man."

Her laughter may as well have deleted the gravity in the room.

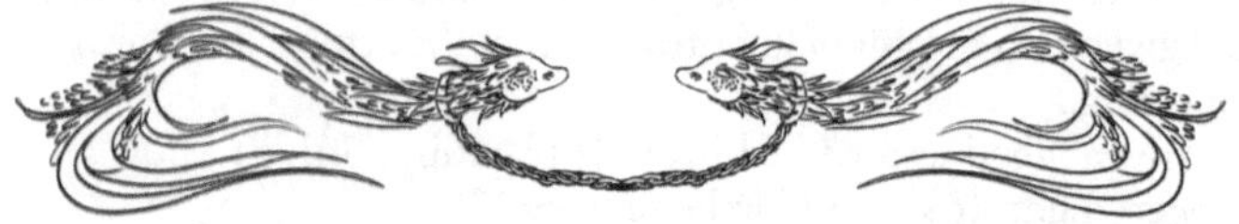

A foul odour lingered in the ventilated air; it stuck to Denvy's tongue and could not be filtered through his air-gills. He had to be dreaming again. With this smell of burning flesh, Zaprex metal, and crushed crystals scorching his nostrils it could be nothing else but a dream of his past. His foot-paws carried him down a corridor, his chest heaving in frantic sobs as he skidded on slick blood, mixed blue and red—Zaprex and Human.

Bodies lay across banisters of high walkways, some flung by weapon fire, some entirely torn apart by mighty forces of wind.

Battle.

This was the aftermath of a battle—or was he still in it?

Ryojin? Ryojin? His mental call fell in a void.

The floor beneath him shook, and he lost his balance up a set of stairs. An echoing boom vibrated through the walls. Denvy clutched the hand-railing as alarms flared. His eyes sought the doors above the stairs, crafted from large sheets of intersecting glass to form hexagons. He made a mad dash for them, thrusting one open, and bursting into the enormous domed chamber beyond. The door swung shut again, and the noise of the alarms died away.

He staggered to a halt at the shock of the sudden silence. The world was cool against his spiked fur. His air-gills settled around his neck. Wide panoramic windows encircled him, making him feel tiny where he stood upon a reflective floor that glittered with planet-light. The windows opened to the expanse of rolling black space, and the Northlands below. Denvy stared. The Northlands—not as a single continent, but as the separate islands they had once been, and the ocean that had long ago divided them.

His paw pressed against the cool surface of the window.

There was Kemet, blanketed in the horrible mushroom clouds of radiation, swirling about, captured and contained by its own sky-sea. Pennadot was still a beautiful jewel of green and gold—which meant Avalon had not yet fallen. Coltarian had not become an enormous scar. It was still a tiny volcano compared to the monster he now knew it to be.

He gave a shout as a sudden explosion erupted in front of him. He sprawled backwards. Star-gliders, glinting silver, their formations like arrow tips, wove through the onslaught of Wind Elementals.

Denvy scrambled away as a star-glider burst past the window. He briefly caught sight of the Navigator in the cockpit, before an Elemental's shifting tentacles latched onto the vessel and it shattered like glass.

"Wait…" Denvy choked out.

He knew where he was. He knew what war this was—the Thousand Sol-Cycle War. The war he had run from.

A click of a laser's charge-up caused his ears to flick upright.

"Who are you and how did you infiltrate my domain? Are you working with the Simoon?"

"Disgleirio?" he whispered. He would have known that twanging, Pennadotian drawl anywhere. Of all his adoptive siblings Disgleirio had been the closest to him in age.

The laser's tip was butted against his temple. "I know my name, Kattamont."

He held up his paws. "It's me. Maahes."

Disgleirio's mocking laughter frilled his air-gills. "Maahes? Don't be ridiculous! My sibling is barely out of cubhood. You're an old man!"

"Disgleirio, drop your weapon."

Denvy swung around at the voice. Two Zaprexes stood some distance behind the young Starborn Human. All three looked at him in confusion. Only one of the Zaprexes was physically within the domed room. The other was a holographic display, floating above the surface of the floor. They were so small, so delicate, and appeared utterly defeated. His hearts raced at the sight of them both, almost together, but not quite—the Two Irrational Zaprexes, their people had called them, hilariously beloved for their long-distance books. He knew them simply as his creators—no—he had always considered them his parents. They had given him life, and they had raised him, therefore was he not their child? A child of Sekhmet and Nefertem.

It was Sekhmet who had spoken, and who now walked with a slight limp, reaching Disgleirio and snatching the weapon out of the Starborn boy's grasp. The Zaprex flung it away in disgust. It had always been easy to spot Sekhmet amongst the Zaprex Pantheon if ever Denvy had become lost during trips to Kemet. Sekhmet was the most delicate of the Original Zaprexes, and glowed with a purple ether, gliding through the air like swimming in thick water.

Nefertem—The Mad—was stark and sharp as a deadly blade, with eyes like the keenest weapon a Zaprex could forge. So strange amongst the curves and smoothness of the Zaprex environments. Even as a hologram, the scientist commanded the deepest respect.

"It is an invader, Gibo," Disgleirio insisted.

"Look closer, Disgleirio." Nefertem drifted forward. "Feel the Secondary Realm around him."

His eyes shifted to Disgleirio, taking in the shimmering halo that wrapped around his glowing white curls, and the crystal sheen of his eyes. Everything about him would be echoed in two little princes who would one day walk Livila. He was being studied, not through the Primary Realm, but in a gaze far deeper, calculating who he was in the resonating song that lingered within his programming.

Suddenly the young Starborn launched into his arms. Denvy staggered as he compensated for the weight. "Maahes! Maahes! We thought we lost you. We thought you were gone when Sez-hat never reported back."

"How long has it been?" He glanced down at the swirling clouds encasing Kemet.

"You have been missing four months." Sekhmet floated up, grasping his cheeks tightly and pressed a kiss to his forehead.

"Four months," he murmured. "Only four months."

He was correct, then; Avalon had not yet fallen. That had happened in the final days, when Hazanin's plan to seal the Dragon within the Secondary Realm had been implemented. A faint beeping drew him from his thoughts of turmoil and Disgleirio untangled himself from his arms. He glanced at a device strapped to the silver suit that coated him.

"I have to return to my pressure chamber." He hugged Denvy tightly around the middle once more. "I am glad to know you survive, brother. I am so happy there is hope for our future."

Denvy's chest swelled.

"You are that hope, little brother, more so than I," Denvy said.

Disgleirio laughed as he twirled away. "What can a dying star do in a war? You are the Ageless One. I'm just a black hole."

A black hole. His hearts felt as though they had plunged into one, vanishing into the depths of despair as he watched the boy vanish through the doors. He opened his mouth but a gentle hand on his shoulder silenced him. Pain was all he saw in Sekhmet's pale blue eyes, a festering pain from the absence of songs. Kemet's destruction was still raw—every Zaprex that had been linked to the cities in Kemet would have felt the sudden deaths of their siblings in that single, horrifying moment.

"I am so sorry, Gibo. I am so sorry I ran. I am so sorry I forgot."

A flickering smile touched Sekhmet's lips. "I see." The Zaprex looked back at Nefertem's lingering hologram. "You did a marvellous job, dear, with your programming of our children."

Sekhmet lifted Denvy's paws and squeezed firmly. "You really are the Dream Master of the Ways."

Nefertem drifted over. "You cannot stay here, Maahes. You are disrupting the continuum. You risk creating a splinter in the time-stream. You need to wake up."

Denvy slumped, allowing the window behind him to catch his weight. "But you die. You all die and I just…live…"

"Oh, sweet child." Nefertem sighed. "The events that are happening here have already transpired. You have defragged into them like a stray, lingering thought. You cannot influence the past, Maahes, when you are simply an echo of the future. You are not of Hazanin and Osiris' ilk. You are my creation; you are simply an observer."

Sekhmet's laughter tugged at his hearts. "But you are also *mine*. I named you Maahes for a reason. You are a god of war, as was I. It is time to wake up, Maahes, and be the god of war we designed you to be."

Denvy breathed out deeply. The two Zaprexes, illumed by the light of the half-planet behind him, had long since passed into history— forgotten by most who dwelt upon the Northlands that they had fought to salvage. "I wish I could have saved you."

"You are of the future, child. Save us then." Nefertem reached forth, a holographic hand splintering as light danced through the shards of information. "We've forgiven you for running away. Son, it is time to wake up—wake up and stop dreaming. It is time for you to live."

◉ • ◉ • ◉ • ◉ • ◉

Jythal stirred from his heavy and dreamless slumber.
Dreamless…he was sure there was a reason why he had not dreamt. Muscles that had been tight the day prior now ached with a burning sensation under his fur, making his neck feathers spike from the discomfort. He crinkled his nose. Stiff bandages coated in his own herbal remedies stuck to his arms and chest, tugging on his pelt, reminding him he should have asked Nixlye to shave the wounded areas before applying the sticking substances. The rush of attending to Clive had been far more important than his own cuts and bruises.

"As long as nothing festers," he muttered.

Still, the smell of blood and medicine assaulted his sensitive nose, spinning his head, disorientating his already black world. He squeezed his claws into the tender wood of his arm chair. Tea—what he desperately needed, right now, to clear the room of foul smells, and clear his head, was tea. Straight liquorice tea. Usually he only mixed the roots with other herbs, its taste so sweet it overpowered even the sourest of flavours, but today he could do with the thirst-quenching crispness coating his throat. He sniffed, catching the softest hint of Nixlye's hot ginger aroma. Aaldryn had always compared her to rose oil. It was something that puzzled him. How did Aaldryn identify their mate with a sweetened scent when Jythal knew her by such a spice? It was possible that Kattamonts scented differently, but perhaps it was simply due to his lack of sight. All he really knew of his mate was the fierceness of her crisp mind, the crunch of her stiff tail-feathers brushing together, and how her coat melted into his paws when they mated. Strange that even amongst all the unpleasant odours assaulting him he had picked out hers to focus on. Something was different; the ginger bite had shifted.

Was that a slight tinge of honey?

He stiffened, drawing a claw over the wooden arm of his chair. He had made divots in the timber with his fidgeting, dozens of nonsensical runes, even some medical notes scrawled out beneath the chair itself. This time, though, he found himself carving out the date as a warm tear latched onto an eyelash. He blinked it away. He would make himself his liquorice tea, but for his mate it would seem raspberry leaves were in order. Aaldryn would be returning to a larger pride than he had left.

Renewed strength surged through his legs and he moved to rise from the armchair, pausing in momentary alarm as he carelessly shifted the heavy weight of Ki'b in his lap. He laughed softly. "Oh, right…last night…" Ki'b slumbered on in his lap, her breathing evenly timed and peaceful. Jythal carefully traced her face, running his paws over her cheeks and pointed ears. She had such sweet features. He could almost craft an image of what she might look like from the shadowed haziness of his blindness. She was round, like the smooth edges of the stones she always carried with her, and as heavy as the rocks of the soil, but her smell was wooden. He had only known dead wood, and he hoped that someday he would discover that Ki'b smelt how he imagined a forest of Pennadot would smell—murky and damp, bursting with too much water that dripped off every surface.

With a sigh he settled back into his chair, letting his air-gills fold down in a restful calm.

A titter of laughter made his ears twitch and he raised an eyebrow. "Awake, are you, love?"

Bedsheets rustled and wood creaked as his mate moved around.

He heard her grunt as she pulled herself up.

"I fell asleep. I am sorry." He yawned. He could barely recall collapsing into the chair. Rune healing was exhausting even when he was at full strength, and tending to Clive had been more extensive than he had realised. He had not had the energy left to make it into the bed.

"Did you put Ki'b on my lap?"

"Hm, oh yes. She could not get comfortable in the bed. Her worry for Clive was very intense."

"That is not surprising. Female Kelibs are very strongly tied to those they consider family."

"I think she makes a wonderful addition to our Pride." It was the dreamathic link between them that allowed the colours to spread through his mind, like leaking ink on a parchment—swells of honey, mixed with melancholy violet flowers. While he could not pick up her thoughts, he could guess where the colours were leading—did she know she was pregnant? The violet swirls always indicated her mind shifting towards his blood-brother.

"I think so, too," Jythal replied. "Though she is young, it pains me to consider what she has already suffered."

The colours and scents of his mate's mind were the closest he came to seeing, and he was grateful for them—when they were not angry or sorrowful colours that scraped at the walls of his mind or grew into vicious nightmares.

"All misfit-born suffer at some time. It is what makes us stronger," Nixlye murmured.

"Your thoughts dwell on Aaldryn."

"I miss him. I miss Khamsin's wind. Does that make me weak?"

"No, my queen." Jythal shifted carefully, easing Ki'b into his arms. He took the measured steps towards the bed, bumping into it with his knees to feel its position before he settled Ki'b onto the blankets. He reached for Nixlye's hands, his paws curling around her Human fingers, and he raised them, kissing them gently.

"I miss him, too."

Nixlye's voice warbled. "I am selfish. He is your blood-brother; your bond is a strong one. I am glad of that. I did worry something awful about you two not getting along with each other."

"Princes will always seek to form brotherhoods, my dear. We can't help it." He stood, releasing her hand. He sent out a soft, invisible pulse of runic energy through the cabin, sensing the responding echo of each of the Rune stones he had positioned around the room. He directed himself to the stove and kettle. A small smile touched his lips as he felt for the cupboard above, tracing the runes carved into the wooden tea and spice holders. Everything he had marked with runes, everything within the cabin, down to the fabric of Nixlye and Ki'b's clothing, he had marked so he always knew their positions if he opened a channel to the Secondary Realm.

Ki'b was convinced he had memorised the whole cabin, and it was amusing to hear her laughter whenever he produced something she was unaware of. Truthfully, he despised leaving the comfort and safety of the rooms he had filled with runes, their cabin and his doctor's quarters. Aaldryn had been lenient as an alpha, allowing him to mark everything in such a manner. Marking was a sign of ownership and thus usually frowned upon between brothers. Jythal sighed heavily. They had a very strange brotherhood.

Where was Aaldryn now? And little Jarvis—were they still together? Jythal paused from spooning out raspberry leaves, his whole body turning towards Nixlye.

"Nixlye, you're very sorrowful this morning and you're projecting it at me."

"Oh! I am so sorry!" The colours of her mind swirled with shame. "There is just so much to think about. Mother fighting the Jezumatu Princess and not killing her!"

"You really do need to get over what they did to me." Jythal set the kettle down, perhaps a little too sharply, for he heard her sharp gasp.

"How can I? They made you into a pit-fighter when you are anything but one. Your paws are for healing, for tea-brewing, and love-making. Aaldryn would have been a better choice for a pit-fighter and even he would have despised it."

"Yes, pit-fighting isn't something princes tend to enjoy. We're not really into killing each other, since there aren't that many of us to go around."

"I enjoy it…"

"You are a queen, love."

"Mother enjoys it."

"You are born to fight. Princes do not fight unless we meet in territorial battles. That is why it is fun for some princesses and queens to watch us pit-fight, because it is so unusual. That's all it was, Nixlye, a foul display of our collapsing culture. I cannot blame them for that."

"But you should."

"No, I won't. It is not in my nature to hold grudges."

He carried the tea tray towards her, setting it over her lap. As he sat on the bedside, he pressed a paw gently to Ki'b's cheek. She was cool. He frowned, reaching for a nearby blanket, and wrapped it around her, tucking it neatly under her chin.

The colours flooding into his mind from Nixlye had turned into angry swells of red and blinding hot whites.

"So, if you ever met the Jezumatu Queen you would not take revenge?"

"Never said I would not take revenge; I said am not holding a grudge for what they did to me. It is far too burdensome." He reached out, brushing aside her hair, managing to cup her cheek. "Besides, love, I am grateful for the Jezumatu, as they did bring us together. I would not have a queen such as you, a brotherhood with Aaldryn, and a beautiful home like the *Lawless Child* without the hardships I endured. I would endure them all again for this family." He gently gave Ki'b a pat. "And our Pride is expanding day by day."

The reds and whites of anger had faded, replaced by sweet lavenders and pinks he had come to equate with Nixlye's settled mind—added with the new flavour of honey.

Nixlye drew a breath. "If the raspberry tea is anything to guess by, we are expecting a cub of our own?"

Jythal laughed. "I would like to say that all that love-making I am apparently so good at paid off, but, if my dates are correct, I believe this one is Aaldryn's."

Nixlye's free hand pulled him closer. "He'll be so happy."

Jythal bumped their foreheads together. "Unbelievably so."

Her fingers knitted through his air-gills.

He clasped her wrist. "Ah, no, no, I'm drinking my tea."

"But Jyth—"

"Tea."

"You and your tea—"

The sand-ship lurched to one side abruptly. Grav-cannon. Jythal's reaction was instinctive, snatching hold of Ki'b before she tumbled from the covers and across the floor. The cabin groaned around him as wood and metal bent against themselves.

He tensed, waiting for the realignment of their gravity engines. Ki'b rolled into him, clutching his arm. He cursed his lack of sight as a sudden weightlessness beset them. His tea—his tea was going everywhere.

"Silvertide!" Nixlye growled.

He hissed in response. It had to be. Only the Silvertide Pride had such advanced weaponry that entirely negated gravity. It felt almost like passing into a null-zone, except that he could still sense the Secondary Realm—grav-cannons, at least, did not cut him off from his Runes.

They landed roughly as the world turned and their magnets realigned with a gut-wrenching sensation.

Nixlye crawled off him. He heard the slap of her hands as she hit the floor, and scooted herself over to her wheelchair. He made his way to the door, ripping it open to hear a crew man shout out, "All hands-on deck! We're being pinned down by four nolats."

Nixlye shoved him out the door, the wheels of her chair scraping sharply as she headed down the corridor, yelling back over her shoulder, "I'll oversee the crew on the cannons. You head topside. Mother will need you if we're boarded."

"What about me?" Ki'b grabbed his leg, twisting her small hands into his fur.

"Stay close."

Breathing out steadied his nerves. He summoned his blades. Ki'b's footsteps fell in line with his own. Escaping the Jezumatu Pride had been difficult enough—they had no hope of defeating four nolats of the Silvertide Pride. This was not a fight they could win. It was a fight they had already lost.

◉ • ◉ • ◉ • ◉ • ◉

The Mist sails were ablaze, rippling like fire had ignited them. Denvy ducked as an arrow whizzed past his ear. He swung his water-sword, slicing through a Silvertide sailor's arm, searching for Zafiashid in the chaos. Grav-cannon fire bounced off their crackling shields, which were barely holding, if the yellow-tinted lightning dancing across the air was anything to go by. They had not seen the approach of the Silvertide Navy on the charts they had stolen. They must have had some form of cloaking—that had to be it. That was how they ruled the burning-sea.

Denvy cursed as the deck under him rolled to one side. Two of their crew were cut down and he reached out, yelling for them. A Silvertide neutral spun in his direction. He snarled low in his chest, frilling out his air-gills, and he charged into the fray of battle, tail thrashing.

Jythal landed beside him, blocking the swing from an opposing Kattamont. The white lion's second blade sliced keenly through the Silvertide's throat, and with a thrust of a foot-paw he sent the limp body overboard. Jythal moved at lightning speed, into the battle, his movements as elegant as a dancer, despite the shuddering of the deck as two nolats continued to pull closer. The light of their Mist shields danced in Denvy's vision.

"Cannon fire!" Kovlrok's voice bellowed out across the deck.

Denvy jerked.

The Silvertide nolats had bridged the gap. The noise was deafening. Metal and wood splintered as the sides of the *Lawless Child* burst open in an eruption of Mist-powered cannon fire emitted from the Silvertide's nolats. The *Lawless Child* groaned. Above, reinforcements from the Silvertide Navy swung onto their splintered deck. Jythal's runes ignited, blistering the air, shooting through some of the neutrals. Others landed roughly, cutting through their crew. Jythal was surrounded.

Denvy slammed against the mast. The results of the carnage drained into the rivets of the *Lawless Child*'s deck, staining his foot-paws. He could not stop this.

But we can. Ryojin's soft dreamathic colours intruded through the bombardment of noise. Denvy clutched at the yoke.

Denvy. No. Maahes. We can stop this.

The yoke's weight pressed down against his shoulders, swinging back and forth with his movements. It had become second nature to adapt to it. Denvy gritted his teeth. He was beyond this; he was beyond allowing a curse to dictate his life.

Ryojin, jack me in.

Denvy seized the small gem Nixlye had given him upon his arrival and his mind focused; like a clear pond suddenly dispelling all ripples, he was plunged deep into its watery depths without disruption. Ryojin's paw was outstretched, the hazy apparition of data that forged the young prince grinning at him wildly. He was not the mammoth generators of the Zaprex's great sky-ships, but he was a focal point, a doorway into the Data-Stream.

Denvy ignored the searing pain, the sensation of blood trickling down his neck. It was all there, lingering so softly, a whisper against his mind. The web he had once navigated so naturally was frayed beyond recognition, and it sickened him. He—the first of the programs, the Dreamer of Ways—had been created for the singular purpose of protecting the Data-Ways, and it lay in ruins.

Ryojin tugged him roughly.

Blocks.

More blocks. They streamed past constant blocks.

The web was sealed. There was no key to unlock it. Places once open to him were closed, and, in the distance, the pain lingered, horrible and sharp, of the still burning remains of Kemet.

It's like a festering wound, Maahes.

Leave it, Ryojin. Don't ever enter it. It's the epicentre of ruin. It is Osiris.

Ryojin recoiled. *This is what you are running from?*

I am not running. Not anymore.

He had a destination; gleaned from the maps lying in Zafiashid's cabin. He needed to only activate the song. The song felt so distant, echoing down through the ages, evoking the most horrid of images, but Denvy fought back the panic, the gasping breaths, and grabbed hold of the frail melody. He heaved, ripping the energy through Ryojin, and their bodies dispersed, merging with the song, and all pain vanished as the *Lawless Child* defragmented in a sudden, loud crack.

TIKAL OF RAINBOWS

CHAPTER FIFTEEN

The Dream Stone was a weight in Skri's heart that he wished he did not have to bear. It was all that remained of the Great White Star of Pennadot's Golden Age. There had been no body to embalm and bury in the catacombs of Palace-Town. One morning he had awoken to the panic of a missing King and he knew in his heart that his friend had gone. His foot-claws had taken him on a journey across the Plains of Rannamon, through the ocean of blood-red flowers until he reached a crater in the earth.

His technomancy had led him to the Dream Stone in the centre of the huge hole. His knees had given way. His body had shaken, and the cries had torn from him as he cradled the precious carcass of his beloved king and friend. This was it? This was the end of the man who had given him a home after his people had cast him out?

Disgleirio had lifted Pennadot out of the ash-cloud of war and drawn her back into the sunlight. He had deserved so much more than to end his life alone.

"But he was not alone..." Skri whispered. "He was so loved."

Curling his claw around the Dream Stone, Skri shouldered his pack. He cocked a smile as he swept away into the rising mist. He had a Dream Master to find, a promise to fulfil, and then a city to guard until his final breath left him.

"My children, until eternity's end, will forever protect our home, Disgleirio."

Jarvis relished the wondrous sight of starlight scattered across a drapery of deep blues. The metal of his hull shimmered in reflection as he stood atop the high peak of a skyscraper. Stars danced to the tune of the Great Song, forever trapped in the melody that created them. He sucked in a deep breath, delighting in the feeling of being free of the underground. The air had a foul, toxic odour to it and that was disheartening, but it was at least new air, and not the air of a dying environmental system choking itself to death. Jarvis flipped himself upright, wind brushing his skin. He pulled back his hair, tugging it into a bun as he wandered to the edge of the skyscraper and leant on the railing. Even further above him, the faintly ebbing light of a receiver on a long, thin pole, beamed out into the darkness, across the expanses that now covered the distance between the Border and Coltarian.

The Border and the Black Wall—their next obstacles. He was not looking forward to either of them, not least the frightening wonders of Coltarian that lay beyond the thick, charred, jagged cliffs of the Black Wall. The sky-sea at that point was sickening to look upon, thick and poisonous, swirling back and forth in a constant storm. Sparks of lightning played over the horizon, reminding him of threads in a tapestry of energy. How were they to move through Coltarian without dying from exposure to the horrific environment?

A tail wrapped around his shoulder, tugging him against Aaldryn's chest. He looked up at his brother and smiled. He was aware of how much the Kattamont relied upon the sensation of touch, but it had taken him time to accept it. A Human would not consider a Kattamont's fur to be anything more special than that of a mundane beast, like a plains lion, but it was a foolish lack of awareness, and he knew now why Kelib poachers so desired Kattamont pelts. Their fur was as much a vital part of their physiology as their air-gills and tail-feathers, composed of millions of tiny receptors that magnified the sense of touch. Aaldryn could detect so much from the changes in the air against his fur. It never had been Khamsin. Kattamonts, it seemed, were always seeking contact with each other, and whatever was around them.

Which explained their exquisite furnishings. How he missed the wonderful beds on the *Lawless Child*, and the divine clouds in the Dwellers' village.

Humans in Pennadot had families, but not Prides—not in the manner of Kattamonts. He would have someday grown up, moved on from his father's farm and lived easily on his own, but a Kattamont had no such luxury. Jarvis closed his eyes, picturing the faces of his parents, his sister, and brother-in-law. So crystal clear in his mind thanks to the philepcon liquid of the protector bot. Forever they would be preserved in his memories. Forever his mother's kind touch on his forehead would linger, and his father's strong hands on his shoulders would be recalled in an instant. His sister's laughter would toll like a bell and his brother-in-law's scent of weapon oils would never dull. Though Humans were not like Kattamonts, they still loved just as much, cherished as deeply in their own way.

He sniffed, rubbing away a tear. It was strange. Parts of him felt Human, parts felt machine, and parts of him felt Kattamont. He was a Changeling of many species.

"You should try and get back to Nixlye and Jythal. You've been away from the *Lawless Child* for almost two sol-cycles—"

The prince's chest rumbled a warm, deep purr.

"Khamsin has a reason for entering Coltarian, too, remember, and I am his vessel. And as Alpha of the Misfit Pride it would be ill of me to leave you on this quest. Nixlye would be very displeased with me."

Jarvis frowned. Nope, he would never understand Kattamonts.

"Come on." Aaldryn drew him away from the edge of the skyscraper and the dancing stars. "Titus is having a fit about something. You need to calm him down."

Groaning, Jarvis followed the prince. Master Titus had not been in the best state of mind since drawing closer to the Border, though he could not blame him. They were returning to the war ground of the Messengers and if even half the stories Khwaja Denvy had told inside the box were true then they were entering a dreadful place.

They jogged down the stairs, back into the coolness of the skyscraper's interior. Tikal swept up to him and Jarvis reached out to gently pat the machine's head.

He is broken, Tikal whined.

"Who is broken? Master Titus or Aaldryn?" Jarvis quipped.

Aaldryn snorted, rolling his aching shoulder. "I'm doing fine, thanks."

The Shadowed One.

"Ah. Master Titus."

He is hitting walls. He is yelling at nothing. He is broken. Yes?

Jarvis laughed. "Nah. He's annoyed about something." Waving the machine aside Jarvis quickly made a beeline for the hunched figure, crouched beside a heavy chest. Supplies were spread out around Titus' ankles and Jarvis glanced over them briefly. Many were oddities he had never seen before, and even his protector bot was baffled. Messenger tech, then? As interested as he was at new things to poke, figuring out the problem was far more important.

"Master, what's wrong?" He tried not to sound exasperated. They had finally reached the Border. He had expected some jubilation, not a moping sack.

"Wrong?" Titus slammed the lid of the chest. The force rattled the whole room. "I'll tell yeh what be wrong, laddie. This Messenger Outpost has been raided! Someone has already been through this area and no one has been back ta restock, that be what's wrong!" Titus lashed out, kicking the chest. "I just be…gah…how could they not check! They know how important this Outpost be ta stranded Messengers like us. *Jarkir!* I'm going ta strangle our so-called High Elder when I get back. He won' know how ta speak after I ring his little neck."

Jarvis stepped aside from the furious man as he swept past, throwing a shimmering package in Aaldryn's direction. The prince caught it with his good paw.

"Perhaps, sir, they've had more pressing matters to attend to. Like the Obelisks collapsing?"

"No matter what, laddie, yeh don' let Outposts go without supplies. They be a vital part of saving lives. If we'd come here in need of medical aid, none be here."

Aaldryn unfolded the odd, shining fabric from the package Titus had flung at him and held it out, raising a curious eyebrow. "What is this?"

"It be a battle-suit. Protects yeh from lava and toxic stuff." Titus took it from the prince, running a finger down the spine and Jarvis grinned, clapping his hands as the fabric became putty in his master's hands. He switched on his optical lenses, scanning the strange goo.

"Awesome! A nano-bot suit. How did you make them? That technology should have died out with the Zaprexes. I mean, it's like your cloak, but your cloak must be from before the Dawn Age, right?"

"Ma cloak is where the House first harvested the nanos, but now only the High Medic and a few of her Healers know how to grow and harvest the nanos to create the suits. It be a dying art." Titus flicked the liquid back out and it reformed into a solid shape. He handed it to Aaldryn. "Yeh are gonna need it on. I doubt even Khamsin will be able ta protect yeh in the Plains of Blazing Fire. We're entering the domain of Prometheus of Fire, not of Khamsin of the Northern Wind."

Aaldryn frowned. "What about Jarvis?"

Titus looked down at Jarvis, and huffed loudly. "I was worried, but Tikal says it has a solution."

"Really?" Jarvis turned to the floating Zaprex corpse buzzing around a selection of crystal panels. It glanced up and blinked at him with large globular eyes.

"Yes?"

"Yeh said yeh can help Jarvis with crossing Coltarian?" Titus tapped the floor. His irritation was still thick in the air. Jarvis blew a rasp, sending his Master a tart glare. It simply would not help if the Hunter caused Tikal to retreat into itself. The AI was already convinced his Master was erratic.

"Yes. We can." Tikal twirled towards them and landed on its delicate feet, causing the floor to ignite in swirling patterns. Titus yelped, backing away from the colours. Jarvis bit his lip, holding in his laughter at the evidence of the poor man's highly-strung nerves.

"Little Protector needs an upgrade."

"An upgrade? Like a system upgrade or a hardware upgrade?" Jarvis scratched the back of his neck.

"Hardware." Tikal gripped its chest-plate between faintly glowing cracks. Before Jarvis could intervene, the machine peeled apart the metal hull, revealing the shimmering insides of the ancient Zaprex corpse. The fluid network spanned out of the Matrix Crystal, into run down, aged mechanisms, still moving the worn-out hull of the Zaprex carcass that the AI inhabited.

Jarvis shivered.

This had once been an actual Zaprex. It should not have so easily slipped his mind. He was staring right into the beating heart of a Zaprex's core. All that had once made it a cyborg was gone. The tin remained.

Tikal pointed to a crystal branch, arching away from the larger matrix.

"This one. It upgrades the exoskeleton." It moved its fingers to his chest, jutting him sharply enough to make him step backwards. *"You put it in your processor core. You grow stronger. Yes. Stronger."*

"I can't take that, Tikal. It will kill you." Tampering with a Matrix Crystal? His protector bot was in a state of utter panic. It had never come across a situation like this. Until recently, it hadn't even known it was possible to grow to become a hybrid; the choice it had made to merge with him had led them both here, to a point where they faced defiling a Creator.

He calmed his racing heart, focusing on Tikal's cracked face. The unblinking, illumed eyes were soothing. Titus thought them frightening and alien, but, to Jarvis, they were like the bog-lights over the moors, something familiar from home here in a place so very far away and foreign.

The AI stared at him blankly, as if he had said something ridiculous. *"Kill us? No. We are not this body, silly little protector bot. We told you, we are many mirrors. This is but one mirror. You take this. You grow stronger. Upgrade. We show you how."*

He knew it would keep insisting until he accepted. It had made up its mind. Likely it had decided on this from the moment it had encountered them.

Jarvis sagged, unable to find the strength to face either Aaldryn or his Master. If he met their eyes he knew his resolve would falter. "Could you please…leave…" He bowed his head. "This is a private thing. I need some time alone."

Aaldryn's tail brushed his back. It was warm. He had the prince's strength always nearby to rely on. "Of course, brother."

Titus placed a hand on his shoulder and squeezed in reassurance as though passing strength into him. They left through a side door and it hissed shut, leaving him alone with the AI, who now spoke only in his receiver.

It is all right, Jarvis:_of_the_Plains_People. *You will have magnificent wings someday.*

Jarvis shook his head. "You say the oddest things, Tikal." He could not control the tremble of his hand as he reached into the chest cavity of the machine. Energy crackled up his arm, making him wince at the sharp sparks. As gently as he could, he wrapped his fingers around the crystal branch. It was immensely overwhelming, as his firewalls crumbled around his mind. His lips parted in a gasp. He was spinning, whirling through connections, millions of branches, spread so far across the face of Utillia he could never hope to keep track of them.

Everything abruptly halted. His mind was suspended before an immense, bright sphere, like the Sun, with curtains of light unfolding to envelope his fragile, tiny body.

"Tikal?" he choked out.

Beyond his mind, his hand wrenched back, snatching the crystal out and the connection ended. The light blinked out. Jarvis landed on his knees, sucking in gasps of air. Sweat crowned his brow. He stared down at the warm, beating crystal in his hand. It bled philepcon liquid through his fingers, smelling of fine, sweet treats from a market fair.

Tikal folded Jarvis' fingers around it, squeezing tightly. *We are lost.*

"You're not lost, Tikal." He gripped the machine as its grey limbs slumped back, the whirring of its insides fading. He shifted the small body into his lap, cradling it as the light within its chest slowly died. "I found you, Tikal. I found you."

The AI's eyes dimmed as they sought his, and the hand against his cheek slipped away.

Survive little protector bot. Find your wings. Like the Humans_of_ Old. *We will watch you take back the sky-sea. You will fly amongst our Angels once more.*

Jarvis bowed his head as the metal hull he held fell limp. "Goodbye, Tikal."

◉•◉•◉•◉•◉

Jarvis rested his head back against the wall, curling his hand to his chest. It was working, the upgrade. He could feel the new threads of the crystal beginning to weave their way into his own Matrix Crystal and integrate into his processor core, installing new programs that he was having to sift through. It was paralysing. Though his body had already begun to alter from the inside out—his skin no longer the flesh of a Human; it moved like water over shimmering metal, and he could create his exoskeleton armour in battle; his once dull brown eyes glinted like precious opals, reflecting his birth elemental gift—that had been an external experience, until now. He had never looked inside himself.

He had never opened himself up.

Never thought much about the change within.

Until now.

Placing the new crystal into his chest required exposing the Matrix Crystal, which meant opening his chest cavity. He had almost been unable to do it, the Human within him balking at the very notion. Yet he had stood there, in front of the reflective glass, facing his inhumanity. Why had he wept such scorching hot tears? He had known from the moment he had fought the protector bot and lost, that the philepcon liquid within him was altering his physiology.

Jarvis groaned, curling his knees against his chest. He wiped his wet cheeks.

A solid thump startled him, and Titus slid down to join him. An arm wrapped around his shoulder and he was tugged firmly against his Master. Bony ribs pressed into his hyper-sensitive hull. He did not mind it, instead, he burrowed deeper into the man's skinny frame.

"Yeh be all right, Weasel?"

"Am I a monster?" he whispered.

Titus shook his head. "Nay, Sonny Jon. Jarvis of the Plains People still be there. Just because yeh body changes don' mean yeh change yerself. It frightened me too, yeh know. It still does." Titus drew up a gloved hand, wiggling the fingers. He sighed, thudding his head back against the wall. "That feeling, it never really goes away. The pain. The frustration. Being different. But yeh're gonna be fine. Even when we think we have no strength left," Titus made a fist, "we still find the strength ta keep moving forward. Why? Cause we be Messengers, laddie, and Messengers, no matter what, always keep moving forward!"

Jarvis nodded into his master's shoulder. "So, I guess this is it then. We're ready to go."

"Aye. That we be." Titus heaved himself to his feet. Jarvis followed him through a doorway and down a glass passage, revealing the unnerving view of the Border before them.

Aaldryn rose from his position by an entrance. There was a weariness in his manner. Their travel was beginning to take a toll on them all, draining their bodies of resources. Despite that, there was a lustre in Aaldryn's eyes, a deep hunger only a scholar and seeker of wonders could have. If it had been any other situation and if Titus had not felt so tense beside him he would have laughed at the sight of the Kattamont in the tight silver battle-suit that covered his body from his foot-paws to his neck all the way down to his fan-tail. Eventually, he presumed, it would cover his whole face and the mask attached to the prince's hip-bags would fit neatly over his eyes.

How was he supposed to breathe? What happened to his air-gills? Likely the battle-suit was smart enough to adapt to any race. Jarvis scooted up beside him, feeling Aaldryn's tail drape protectively across his shoulders.

"Yeah, nope, that doesn't feel the same with that suit on." Jarvis pulled a face. "I feel like I have an eel down my back."

"Imagine how I feel. Eels all over me," Aaldryn muttered.

Titus clipped on his hip-bags and threw a few packs to Jarvis, who quickly strapped on the new supplies.

"Right, this be our last haven for some time, laddies. We be entering a war-zone. Yeh need ta listen to ma every command. I say run, yeh run, I say drop, yeh drop. Do yeh understand?"

"Yes, sir." Jarvis nodded.

Titus waved a hand over the activation pad of the door. It wheezed open, revealing the outside world. The Border between Utillia and Coltarian's Black Wall faced them. Jarvis shrunk deeper into his torn scarf as a hollow, foul air breathed past him. Black stones, like none he had ever seen in Pennadot, crunched beneath his boots as he exited the pure world of the Zaprex Way Station. He looked back longingly at the door as it sealed shut. His chest ached. Already he missed the glow of the crystals, the song of slumbering AIs, and the beautiful shine of metal upon metal. And Troq. Would he ever see him again? Tikal would take care of Troq. He felt a pang of jealousy. He did not care that unknown dangers lurked in the underground cities of Utillia's burning-sea—he wanted to wander them forever; he wanted to be lost with Tikal forever.

He let out a slow breath as he dragged himself after Titus and Aaldryn, down through the charred rocks, towards the edge of the Border and the cliffs that emptied into oblivion. The deep emptiness sat as a pit in his stomach as he stared at the never-ending crack in the surface of the world.

"I am a long way from the farms of my forefathers now."

Aaldryn's hand rested on his head, ruffling his hair. "I am sure your ancestors are proud."

"My father, perhaps. My mother would prefer me to be in bed by Sun down." Jarvis wiggled his eyebrows.

Titus came to a halt beside a rickety-looking contraption. Jarvis watched as his Master walked around the base of the strange twisted steel device, muttering to himself. He peered over the edge of the cliff, testing a thick wire that draped over the lonesome drop.

"Thank the Paladins; the hook's still attached." Titus held up a fist in a victory salute.

Jarvis' eyes widened. The surface of the device glinted with a polished lustre, untouched by the weather, despite the sol-cycles it must have been left untended in the harsh landscape. Rocks had piled up around it until its platform had merged with the cliff-face itself. Was he looking at a Messenger-designed ballista? His father had once taken him to the Lord of the Province's castle and left him with his brother-in-law's brothers, all of whom were province guards for the lord. They had spent the day showing him the fortifications of the castle, the catapults, the siege towers, and the ballistae. He had wondered at the time why they needed such things when Pennadot was in a time of peace, but his father had later explained as they dallied on the way home, that their Province Lord was in a silent war with the neighbouring province, ruled by the Province Lord's sister. While no battles had yet been fought, there was always the possibility that it could happen. It had been one of his father's many lessons, teaching him how fragile their peace truly was.

"Master, what is that?"

"I'll show yeh, if yeh step back." Titus shooed him aside and jumped onto the back of the device, grabbing a large wheel. He began to crank. Gears and cogs whirred to life inside.

Jarvis gaped as the large wire hanging over the edge of the cliff slowly began to move, creeping back into the stomach of the weapon that went deep into the earth itself. The sound of the cranking echoed down the empty canyon.

Aaldryn murmured beside him, "We really are on the edge of Utillia. You can even feel the ground shifting."

His words drew Jarvis' attention away from watching Titus. The ground shifting? Was that the background noise he had been filtering out since they had left the safety of the Zaprex Way Station? He glanced back at the glossy doors high above them, and the silver glint of the skyscraper protruding from the jagged rocks, like blades catching the starlight. His scans had indicated that across the vast chasm of the Border there was another Way Station built into the Black Wall—but it was possible that they had once been the same building and the Border had ripped the base apart.

The rumbling noise he was choosing not to hear was likely the gradual separation of the two tectonic plates. Now that Aaldryn had alerted him to it, despite his programming tuning it out, his sensors were picking up the vibrations and he could feel the eerie chill across his hull.

"This is creepy."

"Yes. Khamsin says there is no wind here, nothing at all. Nothing. This is a dead zone."

"That's even scarier."

Titus let out a sudden whoop. "Got it!"

Jarvis watched in fascination as his Master swung onto the back of the massive launcher and took the aiming device. Circles clicked together as Titus spun them, turning towards the Black Wall in the distance, across the canyon of the Border.

"Cover yer ears, laddies," Titus called out.

It was the only warning he gave them before the weapon fired. Jarvis landed on his rump as the ground rippled. A wave of light expanded from the weapon's crystal energy source and Jarvis clutched at his chest as his protector bot reacted violently to the sudden danger, activating his exoskeleton. In awe he watched as a long arrow carried a wire in a high arc across the canyon. The echoing boom of it striking the cliff on the other side vibrated back as the weapon's noise died down.

"Holy Sun on High!" Jarvis crawled to his feet, deactivating his exoskeleton.

"Told yeh to cover yer ears, laddie." Titus leapt off.

"You could have warned me. That thing is Zaprex!"

"Aww, kinda. It's Messenger tech. We're not as fancy as the Zaprexes. We back-rig their junk in a bit tidier a fashion than Kattamonts do, though."

Aaldryn touched the long wire, stretched across the expanse of the Border. "So, this is how Messengers cross the Border from Utillia. I have always wondered."

"Aye. This cannon and zip-line was installed a few centuries ago. 'Twas actually the brain-child of one of ma ancestors—Titus Timothy Telvon the First! Whom I am, of course, named after." Titus handed a metal loop to them both, hooking his own over the wire and slipping his foot into it. "Right, so, it be pretty basic. Put the metal over the wire, put yer foot into that little footie-hole and leap off the edge of the cliff. There be a cave on the other side. Aim for that."

Jarvis stared down at the contraption in his grasp. Was he serious? It was a flimsy piece of steel.

"Ah, I have a question. What if this metal breaks, or the wire breaks, or the arrow-hook on the other side breaks out of the Black Wall? Or we miss the cave?"

"Then yeh die." Titus shrugged. "So, don' die."

"Did I ever mention how mad Messengers are?" Jarvis shouted as Titus leapt off the cliff. The reply he received was a loud hoot.

Jarvis clapped a hand over his face and groaned. "This is insane."

Aaldryn urged him to the edge. "Picture it as flying. You have your golden wings back, Human. You'll be fine."

"This is the Border! Do you know the distance? Because this is huge! The speed we will be going is immense. It will be impossible to stop. Not every Messenger has gravity control! Aaldryn, I can't. No. You can't make me do this."

"Come, come, it will be fine. Khamsin will be watching over you."

"I feel so much better with the idea of an interfering old wind-god looking after me," he grumbled.

Aaldryn laughed, ruffling his hair. He had almost forgotten how annoying that was. Hooking his foot into the metal ring, Jarvis panted heavily. He could do this. He was a Human who would find his wings.

This is for you, Tikal.

He launched himself from the cliff edge with a mighty swing. Air ripped past him. He could barely keep his eyes open until a protective shield filmed over his face and the stinging sensation vanished. The world became clearer. A grin captured his lips behind his mask and laughter ripped free of his lungs.

Flying. He was flying!

It was over. The abrupt halt he had expected never came. Instead he gradually eased to a stop before the cave entrance and his Master appeared with more supplies strapped to his back, looking extremely chuffed. Jarvis leapt from the zip-line, storming up to Titus.

He hit his master's chest. "I can't believe you didn't tell me there was a gravity cushion!"

Titus laughed and tweaked his nose. "Come on, yeh enjoyed it."

Jarvis pulled away with a scowl. "That doesn't matter. I thought I was going to go splat."

"Splat? Nah, there be a big generator from the Zaprex Way Station up here. That be why we put the zip-line here—ta make use of the gravity cushion. Thought yer little protector brain would have noticed that." Titus flicked his forehead.

Overhead, Aaldryn flew past and leapt free, landing with an elegant roll.

"By the Rythrya! That was a whirl." He laughed.

"Couldn't you have simply flown over?" Jarvis arched an eyebrow. He was more irate than he should have been, he knew it, but he could not help it. His Master had tricked him into feeling scared and it was humiliating.

"Nope." Aaldryn popped his lips. "Told you, this place is a dead zone. No wind, no elemental presence, nothing. Khamsin has no power here. There is no Secondary Realm." He peered over the edge of the Border. "The Unknown Realm."

Jarvis opened his mouth, wanting to yell at him that he had trusted Khamsin to catch him if he had fallen off the zip-line, but the words of the prince caught him off guard. "The Unknown Realm? The last of the three realms of existence? The realm the Titans were cast into by the Dragon? We're in it?"

Aaldryn shook his head. "No, but Khamsin thinks it's seeping up from the cracks in the Borders."

Jarvis joined Aaldryn by the edge of the cliff. It was a sheer drop into the murky darkness. Pieces of earth broke away from the great continental plates slowly tearing apart.

"Not much is known about the Unknown Realm—"

Jarvis snorted. "Yes. Hence the *name.*"

He was squatted over the back of his head.

"But we do know it is a place where Elementals cannot exist, hence the Dragon's decision to cast the Titans into it."

"Yah. It's called Space." Titus flung the wire over the canyon edge. They watched as it swung away, echoing a loud boom, sending dust and debris into the air as it hit the other side, left there for another Messenger to crank up someday. Jarvis shivered at the eerie claw that trailed up his spine. Would they be the last Messengers to ever travel in this manner with this era coming to an end?

"Space?" Jarvis murmured. The word had meaning to his protector bot.

"Yah, you know, Space. Out there, with the stars…and stuff?" His Master flapped his hands. "Elementals are beings of the Secondary Realm. They exist to create nature. When formed of the world they become a part of it. They cannot exist outside of this solar system, or their particular sector."

"Solar system?"

"Oh, *jarkir*, don' tell me yeh don't know what a *traki* solar system is?"

Jarvis pouted. "I know what it is. The information is there. It is just difficult for me to comprehend. I suppose, though, it does make sense that a wind-god would not be found in a vacuum, but, hey, aren't the stars supposed to be elementals?"

Aaldryn peered up, following his gaze to the dancing stars in the sky-sea above them. "That has always been the legend. Even Khamsin says they're elementals.

"How interesting. Contradicting information in my data-base." He grinned. "So Master Titus, where to from here?"

"Up." Titus dusted off his pants. He motioned with a tip of his head towards the carved pillars, imposing monuments chiselled out of the rocky surface of the Black Wall. Beyond them, steps began to rise in the long journey up, becoming lost in the high, toxic clouds swirling in the sky-sea. Aaldryn whistled loudly as they walked.

"Welcome, laddies, to the Pass of Stairs. 'Twas carved out by the Thyrrhos long ago. There be a number of their entrances into Coltarian along the Black Wall. Another be the Pass of Fire at Mount Odeaian, but that be commandeered by Twizels now. However, it can be snuck through. There be also the Pass of Osiris. Take a guess why it's called that!" Titus laughed. He twirled on his heel and started up the stairs. "This one be a long, long way up, laddies. Maybe it be a good thing it be only us, heh. Khwaja Denvy always did hate climbing."

Aaldryn laughed from behind. "Little weasel legs." Jarvis yelped as Aaldryn heaved him up around the waist, aiding him up the first, enormous step.

"Shut up, Kattamont," Jarvis griped as Aaldryn moved past on all fours, easily leaping up the carved out, black rocks. He glared after him in envy. If that was how it was going to be, well, he was a Zaprex hybrid, he would not let a bunch of stairs defeat him.

The climb was gruelling. His legs fought against his forward momentum, until it was not only his ankles and legs that became bloated, but his hands and fingers stiffened with unfathomable pain. Each step he conquered he thanked the Sun above that Clive, Penny, and Ki'b had not taken the journey with them. There would have been no way his adoptive siblings would have managed the scorching heat already bleeding through the Black Wall, nor the steep vertical height of the cliff, and the possible fall into the nothingness of the Border. Despite the rests they took beside cool water bubbling out of little icy pools, that Master Titus explained were put there by someone called Eros—an Ice-hybrid Elemental—he felt no sense of respite. Exhaustion heaped upon his shoulders, heavier and heavier with each step. The icy water was welcome, though, when his ability to regulate his temperature finally faltered; the boiling heat radiating from the Black Wall had overpowered his systems. He wished his Master had not told him it was only going to get so much worse.

Ten days—he calculated—it took them ten days to scale the Black Wall and the Pass of Stairs. Which, he supposed, was an improvement, considering the months they had spent underground. Standing on the rim of the caldera, Jarvis slackened his aching limbs, all energy draining out of him through his feet, as though the earth sapped what remaining strength he had. The sight that greeted them beyond the Black Wall was one he had never expected to witness. Bards had told tales of the volcanic land over the Western Border of Pennadot, where the legendary and terrifying Messengers did battle. They had spoken of the Messengers' ruthlessness and always warned the little children of the villages to go straight to bed at night, lest a Messenger snatch them away for being naughty. And this was the horrible, nightmarish place those children would be banished to.

Now, here he was, upon the precipice of the war-torn battleground and all he could do was shed tears. This was a graveyard of brethren he had never met, and yet the connection was there. He knew them through the stories Khwaja Denvy had told, and by travelling day by day with his Master.

His gaze shifted from the burnt, blackened horizon, littered with rivers of red and yellow, towards his Master, standing atop a rock, his cloak rippling around him. He looked like a thin, charred twig, all that might remain after a fire had ripped through a wheat field. Everything about his Master's happy, free, and relaxed nature had shifted over the course of the days' climbing, until he had become a tense, melancholy character whom Jarvis felt he did not know.

Was it this place—did it change people?

Would it change him too?

Ash crushed beneath his feet as he walked, approaching the Hunter. Black eyes shifted his way. Titus jumped down from his perch. While his smile was forlorn, it was still warm, and Jarvis accepted the hand that settled on his head. It was comforting in its the heavy pressure.

"What do yeh think, Little Weasel?"

"It's bigger than I thought."

Titus bellowed an abrupt laugh. "Oh, aye, aye. Coltarian has been getting bigger over the centuries. That be one of the reasons the Zaprexes built the Obelisk System in the first place, or so they say. Best keep the Fire Lord bound otherwise it'll consume the whole *traki* world!"

"You give my sibling too much credit," Khamsin grumbled.

Jarvis looked up at Aaldryn. The wind-god within his brother was scanning the horizon with a firm scowl. He upturned his nose, crinkling Aaldryn's gentle features. "I can already smell Prometheus' stink."

"You really don't get along with your siblings, do you?" Jarvis teased.

"Wind and Fire is a bad combination." Khamsin shook Aaldryn's head. "Or good, depending on the situation."

"Oh, I know. I have seen firestorms take over the wheat provinces. Terrible sight, but also incredible."

Titus whistled. "Sheesh, laddie, yeh got around."

"My father wanted me to be the best farmer I could be, so I would travel with my brother-in-law and sister every Summer and Spring, from when I was able to walk. They took the Spider Road with the Pilgrim Caravans. Father always said the best farmer was a farmer who knew the land he toiled upon." It was nice, he mused, to speak of his family and not feel the grating ache in his stomach or the burning in his chest. The pain of their loss still lingered, but a strange acceptance had settled.

"So, what are the Obelisks?" He looked up at Titus.

"See those big silver spikes?" His Master reached out a hand and he followed its direction, zooming in with his optical lenses, catching sight of the nearest glittering spire in the distance. Jarvis rubbed the heat blur from his eyes and looked up again. He was not seeing things, they were real.

"Those? But they must be huge! They're bigger than…mountains! They touch the sky-sea. No, they go into the sky-sea. Look how the storms swirl around them." Jarvis jumped, stretching his arms high. They were adequately named. He had seen the carved obelisk shrines of golden limestone honouring the Spider Road, but they had never been so big. His brother-in-law had once told him a story of seeing the great stone obelisk gates of Tempath but even they could not have compared to the towering silver pinnacles stretching into the sky-sea, blackened smoky clouds dancing around their tips, lightning crackling down their glistening sides.

"Aye, they are. There be ten of them, in a grid, around Coltarian. Or, there were…" Titus sighed.

"Chains for an Elemental Lord. For Coltarian to erupt, those chains must be breaking," Khamsin murmured.

Jarvis scrubbed at his face. He could not even comprehend the force capable of knocking down one of the enormous Obelisks. "They're Zaprex. They should be unbreakable."

Khamsin chuckled, flapping Aaldryn's tail about friskily. "Oh, dear child, even Zaprex technology can be broken. You should know that from what you have already seen. It has its weaknesses, too."

Jarvis bowed his head, looking away from the wind-god. "I know. I know. I just don't like thinking about it."

"Ah, well, laddie, take a look over there." Titus knelt beside him, directing his gaze once more to what he had first thought was an oddly tinted river of ice. Considering Coltarian was the Land of Ice and Fire, supposed to be living in a constant balance, he had simply presumed that was what it was. "That be the Ivory Path. It is where we want ta go. It is the only habitable place in all Coltarian. The Zaprexes created it. It's a long road through Coltarian. Well, sorta like a road." Titus twisted his face. "It be like this lush, beautiful forest, raised above the lava plains."

"The story was that the Zaprex Set built it for his bonding partner Ma'at, for he loved to wander beautiful gardens as he wrote his tomes. They, and their offspring, dwelt in Icarus, for it was the Library of the Zaprexes' knowledge," Khamsin added, his expression withdrawn as though he was not gazing into the distance, but into the past he had long ago lived.

"Icarus?" Jarvis frowned, feeling files shifting in his mind, being sorted through, searching for the word in his data-base. His optical lenses fizzed, and he winced as access was denied, causing his screens to blank out. He clapped his head, clearing his optical lenses, resetting the display panels. He was not going to go looking into those folders again anytime soon.

"*Icarus:_Wings_of_Golden_Sun, House_of_Flames* is its full mothership title," Khamsin offered. "A very formidable enemy. One I am grateful I never had to go up against. If it had been functional during the Thousand Sol-Cycle War it is possible the Zaprexes may not have lost Kemet to the Dragon."

"Wait." Jarvis twisted towards Titus. "Wait! Wait! Hold it. The House of Flames is one of the Cities of Gold and no one thought to mention this?"

His Master shrugged. "It has long been speculated that it is possible, but, thus far, no evidence has been found that the House of Flames we dwell in is actually the House of Flames of legend. Even Prometheus doubts it. Don' get yer hopes up, laddie."

Jarvis bounced on the balls of his heels. They might have had a fire-god to cross, but the sudden excitement bubbling up from within him was uncontainable and washed away all exhaustion from his limbs. It was almost as though they had already made it and they were there, he had done it, he had reached the House of Flames and found the Key.

Titus' hand suddenly clapped down on his head and he shook himself free of his daze, facing the laughter of both his Master and Aaldryn.

"Come on, little bouncing Weasel, enough with yer daydreaming. We got a long way ta go." Titus strode off and Jarvis jogged to keep up with him, unable to stop grinning.

A new land full of fresh adventures lay ahead.

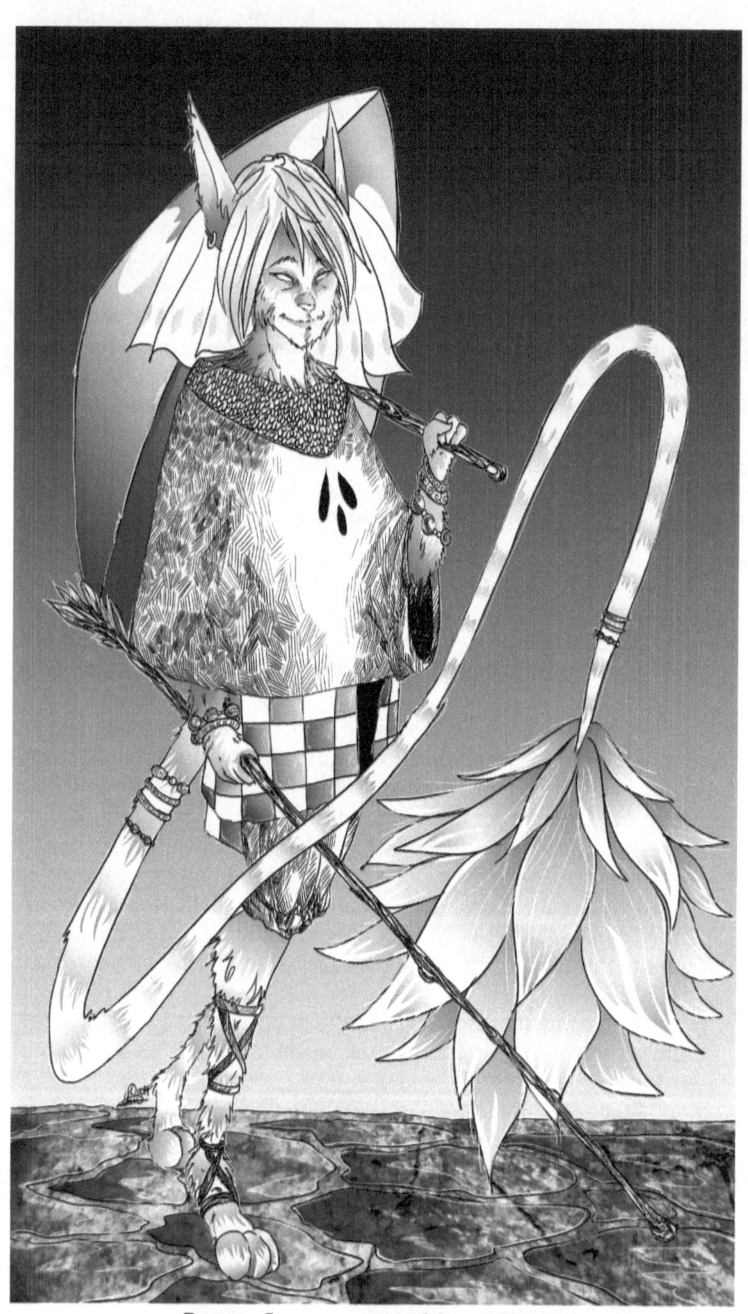

PRINCE JYTHAL OF THE MISFIT PRIDE

CHAPTER SIXTEEN

Silence. Nixlye winced. She had never realised how eerie silence was, how it could impact her ears so painfully. The world around her was blurry. Bits of splintered wood and metal rained around her, larger pieces cracking from the ceiling. A heavy thud vibrated beside her, and still silence ruled. Gradually, though, a ringing pierced her ears, painful and sharp, and the world began to put itself together, section by section. They had been in a burning-sea battle with the Silvertide Navy. Two—maybe more—nolats had broadsided them. She could not recall whether the grav-cannons had managed to tip the *Lawless Child*, but it had seemed their intention had been not to sink them but to board them.

She frowned.

The Silvertide Pride always did like to do their killing close range. She had learnt that much from Mother and Aaldryn.

With trembling arms, she lifted herself off the floor. The armaments of the *Lawless Child* lay scattered around her, along with the crew. Some were still alive; she could hear them groaning. Quickly she reached for her metal legs and started cranking. Mist leaked between the plates, fuelling the limbs until they wheezed to life and shakily she heaved herself upright. Intense pain flared against the stubs and she fought back a swell of nausea and steadied herself.

"We need a light! Someone get us a light!" she bellowed.

"Princess, you have to come and see this," someone shouted back through the haze. "You're not gonna believe it."

She was handed a Mist lantern, and she shifted past a body, crushed by a fallen beam. Others lay scattered. The damage was extensive, and moans and cries of pain echoed through the cabin. She watched as crew members moved about, tending to the fallen. She joined the young half-breed Kattamont who had called for her. He was clutching a bleeding gash across his torso but was foolishly ignoring it as he peered out of the porthole.

The silence returned suddenly as she was struck by the sheer impossibility of what lay before her. Nixlye barked out, "Get the wounded down to the galley!" Mist hissing with each step, she sped towards the stairs to the upper-deck, clasping the railing when she wobbled weakly on her feet. Topside deck was littered with the chaotic ruins of the battle. Her heart leapt to her throat. The Mist shields remained active, but their sails were limp, the engines dead—they were adrift amongst the dunes. She stumbled towards the railing, landing against it, staring out over the burning-sea. It was not her eyesight playing tricks. She was not in some dreamscape. She really was gazing upon the crystal rainbow spires of the legendary Rythrya Stones. They were so close she could almost reach out and touch them. The lonely song they cast out across the sand-dune waves tingled up her spine, into her mind, calling to her with an ebb and flow akin to the tossing of the burning-sea.

"Nixlye! Nixlye!" Ki'b's voice broke her daze. Nixlye turned, catching the girl as she stumbled.

"Ki'b?" Nixlye knelt, feeling Ki'b over. Tacky blood caked her neck and shoulders. "Are you hurt?"

Ki'b shook her head. "No. I'm fine. Jythal got hurt a little, but he keeps insisting he is all right. He is helping Mother round up the prisoners. I am going to see if Clive and Penny need me."

"Be careful." Nixlye released her and she dashed off quickly.

With a whine of her legs, Nixlye moved through the carnage. Tears dampened her cheeks. She could fight in the pits, kill any princess or queen in a death match, but to see their crew dead and dying pained her and twisted her insides in a vice. They were part of the Misfit Pride, and no one harmed their Pride.

She came across Denvy, slumped over dislodged crates like a discarded sack. Her eyes widened at the sight of him, his shoulders soaked in blood as though a cape were draped across his golden fur, his limbs hung as though weighted with lead. But, in his paws, he clasped the gradually crumbling remains of the yoke she had always known him to bear. She increased her pace, rushing to his side.

"Denvy!" She dropped to her knees. "You did this? You moved the *Lawless?* You could have killed yourself!" The rawness of his neck was agonising to see now. Without the yoke hiding the damage the festering wound was obvious. It smelt of pus and yeast. She doubted fur would ever again grow upon the skin that had so long been cursed.

His gentle, warm gaze settled upon her and he smiled wearily, letting the metal slip from his grasp. It clanked down hard upon the deck.

"We had to do something. Besides, there is no such thing as a curse."

"You foolish, foolish old man."

His bloodied paws rested gently on her head. "You keep dreaming of fairy-castles and we will help you find them. All of them."

Nixlye buried herself in his lap until the shaking of her shoulders eased and the tears stopped flowing. Her ears tweaked back, and she rubbed her eyes, lifting away.

"Sorry," she murmured, glancing at Zafiashid.

"Should I be worried you are stealing another prince from under my nose?"

Nixlye stood, glancing aside. "No, Mother. This one is far too old for me."

Zafiashid snorted. Her brow creased in concern, and her paw rested upon Denvy's shoulder, as though she was convincing herself the golden lion was still breathing.

"What are you doing with the prisoners, Mother?"

"I was considering throwing them overboard. Letting them drown."

Denvy lifted his head. "Oh, you can't do that."

Zafiashid held up a paw. "They are Silvertides. My own kin. That is all that saves them from walking the plank. They came here, slaughtered our Pride; they should feel my wrath, but I see no need for further death. Not in the presence of the blessed Rythrya Stones." She turned sharply. "They get a dingy and a week's supply of food and water. Then they can fight it out."

Nixlye cringed. "I think letting them walk the plank would be more merciful. One of the neutrals is likely to morph into a queen due to the close confines. That is simply cruel. They'll eat each other alive."

"Cruel is killing my crew."

"They at least have a chance of finding an island," Denvy interjected. "Perhaps the currents will be kind to them."

Zafiashid stalked away. "You are a giant cub with a bleeding heart."

"That is a compliment, dear."

"It was not supposed to be one! You will get yourself killed!"

Denvy's gaze returned to the yoke as it finally disintegrated. His frown deepened the lines around his eyes. "I suppose she is right. I am not immortal anymore."

"It might return now that thing is gone," Nixlye said.

He heaved a sigh. "That is possible, but, for now, I find myself in the oddest predicament. I have never before been a program without a backup system." He arched an eyebrow, and suddenly chuckled.

"Care to share your amusement?"

"Someday."

Nixlye took his arm. "Come, we should find Jythal and see if he can stop the bleeding from your neck."

Denvy nodded. He lumbered upright. Carefully they picked their way over the deck, towards the dozen Mist lanterns held by members of the crew. Wounded lay on makeshift stretchers, Jythal moving between them diligently. He turned at their approach, setting down his bloodied tools. Nixlye's chest expanded sharply as he stepped over a stretcher and she was enfolded in his long arms, hoisted off the deck, and crushed against him. Her prince was trembling, each breath rattling through his air-gills. Nixlye dangled limply, curling her fingers into his back fur. In public, Jythal so rarely expressed his need to feel her, to know she was nearby. Without his sight, touch had become his grounding knowledge of the world. The panic in his grip gradually subsided, his muscles loosening.

"Sorry," he murmured. "I should never have left you."

"Nonsense." She rubbed his cheek. "I am fine. A little rattled."

His paw settled on her waist.

"I am sure the cub is fine too," she assured him. "Ki'b said you were hurt?"

"Not terribly." Carefully he settled her onto her metal feet. "Brother Denvy?"

"The yoke, it came off. Jythal, the skin is awful…" Her voice trailed off as Jythal shifted past her, his attention drawn to his fellow prince. He grasped Denvy's arm solidly and helped him down onto a nearby barrel.

"By the Winds," Jythal muttered as he gently felt the flesh. "I am surprised it didn't severe your throat."

The old prince's claws were digging into his knees, the only indication of the pain Jythal's touch, though tender, caused him. "I suppose it was getting tired of me, heh?" Denvy joked.

Shaking his head, Jythal tugged out bandages from his hip-bags. "This will have to do until I can shave and wash the infected skin away."

"I will survive. Lived this long, haven't I?"

Nixlye laughed.

"Where are we?" Jythal tipped his head in her direction as he worked. "I can hear the most beautiful tune. The crew keep telling me they see the Rythrya Stones?" The hope she heard in his voice was heartbreaking.

"They're incredible, love. They're like everything Aaldryn ever described the buried cities to be, but so much more. They glow with starlight and sing a song with the wind."

His air-gills spread wide. "The voices, then, what are they?"

The question was directed at Denvy, and she looked his way. "It is Tikal's Matrix Crystal, singing to us. You are both dreamathic; you are hearing Tikal resonating. I am flummoxed as to how it is still so strong; indeed, I am still surprised how so much of the Zaprex technology here in Utillia seems to be functioning. Other than the desktop grid, however. Even that managed to be sustained in a power-saving mode."

"Any idea how we have been able to maintain this state?" Nixlye rubbed her ears. Despite knowing the song was dreamathic, it was still disconcerting, feeling as though it was coming from her own ears.

"A few thoughts, and I do hope I am right. If I am, then we may have a chance to unite the Prides." Denvy felt the bandages as Jythal pulled away.

"No one has done that in centuries." Jythal lowered himself beside one of his patients, opening his doctor's kit, feeling for the right container.

"Now is as good a time to try as any." Denvy shrugged, only to wince at the action.

Jythal lifted the arm of a wounded Kattamont and slowly began to wrap a gash. "What did you do? I honestly thought we were ended."

Denvy looked at the sky-sea, the dancing stars far above them. Nixlye wondered if he was searching for the invisible Angels he knew must have been somewhere above them, but his gaze was far too distant even for that—as though he was looking even further, perhaps into his memories of a lifetime beyond her comprehension. "With the maps validating the existence of the Angels, I knew that Tikal still existed—and where. Your dreams are not only an echo of the past rippling back. I am the server-god of the Data-Ways, or I was when the Data-Ways existed. I defragmented us."

Nixlye wrinkled her nose at the odd word.

"I was created with the ability to move over vast distances through the Secondary Realm, without the need of a defragmentation station." He spread his paws.

Denvy motioned to the Rythrya Stones. "I had been intending to take us inside Tikal. The only way to access the Rainbow City is through defragmentation."

Nixlye breathed out an unsteady breath. He had been aiming to take them inside the great formations? Her heart was aflutter at the thought.

Jythal wiped blood from his paws. "Why didn't we get in?"

Denvy rubbed wearily at his eyes. "Tikal blocked me. Not for malicious reasons—I think I ran into a firewall and we bounced back. It happens sometimes when an AI is picky about what they let inside."

Nixlye drifted to the railing of the *Lawless Child* and leant upon it. Her fur was hackling, unable to contain the excitement building within. Her tail lashed back and forth. "Well, no harm done. I would not be able to see the Rythrya Stones up close if we had gone all the way in. To think that what we have thought all these centuries to be the cause of the currents in Utillia were actually the spires of one of the Cities of Gold."

Denvy's chuckle made her arch around. "They are the source of the currents, only not in the manner you think, my dear."

Nixlye clapped her hands together. "We should gather the crew. Many will be confused. Then we should attempt this defragmentation again." She clicked her tongue around the word. "Do you feel up to that, Denvy?"

"I don't think so, Nixlye," Jythal spoke up. "I know you are excited, but he has just survived an incredible ordeal."

"We should not remain here. I will try," Denvy cut in.

Jythal sighed heavily, his air-gills rattling. "Fine! But I am washing your wounds out first. No. Stay right there. Stay!"

Nixlye grinned as she walked away, listening to the grumbling protests of Denvy and the frustrated hissing of her prince. With the light of the Rythrya Stones igniting hope within her, she could not help but believe all would be well.

CHAPTER SEVENTEEN

Skri blinked rapidly, lifting a claw as the defragmentation settled around him, revealing the lonesome Zaprex Way Station. The several centuries that had passed since the Thousand Sol-Cycle War had barely made an impact upon the pristine Way Station. He stepped down from the defragmentation station, swaying slightly. The sooner he found Maahes and sealed the Data-Stream, the easier he would rest but, for now, a well-aimed conduction at the station's controls shattered the crystals.

The lights died away as he moved towards an opening torn in the Way Station's wall. The floor against his foot-claws unsteadied him. It was alien. It rejected him. It wanted to cast him, and the Dream Stone he carried, far away.

"I am here to stay, for a while at least..." he murmured as he hiked his way up a small rise. The Way Station, it seemed, had long been buried by fallen rubble—a blessing he would praise the Sun for. He paused on the edge of the rise, cool wind scampering past his ankles.

"Well. Well. Well. If it isn't Eldorado. We'd wondered where you fell." He leant wearily on his staff, grinning mockingly at the enormous mountain range in the distance, their tips shaved off by the upturned saucer wedged into the depths of the earth. "I think you'll make a perfect new home." Skri donned his travel hood.

The Midlands were bathed in the light of a foreign Sun, but no matter how far he travelled or where his foot-claws took him, his Sun would forever be a White Star.

The lava pools surrounding their camp were surprisingly beautiful. Jarvis watched the bubbling hot liquid dance about, contemplating what it would be like to swim in the cauldrons. Khwaja Denvy had told stories about young Messenger children who did just that in their battle-suits. What sort of children dared to swim in lava like it was water? He winced at the sharp pain emanating from his shoulder blades where Master Titus was carefully warping the metal of his outer hull with the red-hot tip of a blade. They had made camp under the protection of a large black glass formation, creating a small cave. The air inside was clear enough for Aaldryn to remove his mask, and they had decided to rest for a few hours, giving his Master time to perform what he referred to as a Messenger Network Tattoo. They did not have ink, only blades, and so it was scarification rather than a tattoo like those he had seen flaunted by Kelibs and Soatrins. It would be similar to the one Khwaja Denvy had carved into Ki'b's arm. At least he had something connecting him to her now.

Aaldryn's had been a simple matter of shaving off fur to get to his thick hide. He had protested, but finally relented, on the promise they would not laugh at this bald patch.

Jarvis had been a whole other problem. His exoskeleton had been taking a serious beating. His hair, his skin, everything that made him look remotely Human was gone—scorched off by the heat of the plains, leaving him as a glossy exterior. His body was metal now. It required intense heat to be shaped and so Master Titus had dragged him down to the lava pools and silently set to chiselling into his shoulder like a sword smith to a blade. Worse still, he had to program himself not to automatically heal the damage being done to his hull. He did not want to know what he looked like—some hideous, eerie, boy-machine? It was nice that the lava pools did not show reflections.

Jarvis looked up as basalt crunched beneath Aaldryn's foot-paws and his brother eased down beside him, handing over a rations pack. They were living off Messenger stores, strange food that was either very dry or a gooey bar. Aaldryn was having the hardest time consuming them, the Kattamont's disgusted face amusing every time he took a bite.

"Thanks." Jarvis nibbled his half of the ration bar. If anything, it tasted like powdered sugar, the type his mother had used to sweeten bread, condensed into a single slab. It was not appealing against his already dry mouth.

From atop the Black Wall, the Plains of Blazing Fire had looked flat and smooth, with rivers of molten rock snaking through blackened earth, forming large plates that shifted and groaned. How wrong that impression had been—the plains were anything but flat. They had travelled over terrain crinkled like a tossed blanket, covered in blasted glass towering high in formations carved out by scorching, howling, toxic wind. Every so often they would encounter ice.

Ice. Somehow there was ice amongst bubbling lava. Miles of dirty glaciers, piles of snow that Titus swore at him for touching and he quickly realised why when his metal hull had started hissing. His Master had doused his hand with some of their precious water supply and clapped him roughly over the head.

"Toxic water, laddie. Toxic snow! We don' wanna be around when the acid rain hits. That's the worst."

He had been baffled. "Why is it snowing? Why is there ice? It should be impossible. It's so hot!"

Khamsin had been the one to respond to his confusion. "This is a land of Elementals. It is ruled by the Fire Lord, and likely my sibling Eros has been trying her very best to keep the Fire Lord balanced. We used to exist as a balance in nature. Even the Zaprexes understood our function. The Dragon, sadly, does not care."

Jarvis sighed. He winced again as, behind him, his Master hammered into his hull. He glanced over at Aaldryn. He could see the prince's face properly without the mask he had been wearing for days. The silver suit covered the whole of his body like a second skin, even coating his feathers in a protective film against the filthy air and sizzling heat. How he envied him.

A hiss rippled down his spine as his body flushed itself with cool philepcon liquid from his Matrix Crystal and he breathed out a sigh of relief as his aching limbs eased slightly. He was burning through his energy reserves keeping his hull from warping, but he was surviving thanks to the upgrade Tikal had provided, which was allowing for a much faster production of philepcon liquid usually not allocated to a protector bot. He had to wonder if this made him more Zaprex now that he technically had a piece of a Zaprex in him.

"There we go." Titus finally pulled away.

"Have you finished it?"

"Aye." Titus set aside his tools. "All done. That took longer than I thought. Yeh had thick skin there, laddie." His head was given a fond pat—no hair to ruffle; at least that was a small blessing.

Jarvis felt his shoulder, running his fingers over the carved metal. It felt like a circle, but he could not make out the other runes within it. He knew they had meaning, though.

Titus motioned with the pack of rations in his hand over the horizon. "See that bit yonder, near that Obelisk and between those two shiny sapphire things that are glowing?"

Jarvis squinted at the blurry distance. His optical lenses had such a hard time functioning in the heat. The area was surrounded by another smaller caldera.

"That be once called Phebes but, after the Battle of Phebes, Commander Zinkx had it renamed The Neutral Zone. We are heading there to get onto the Ivory Path. We can find aid there, and won't be attacked by Twizels. If we are attacked there by anything else, help always arrives."

"Why?" Jarvis looked back.

Titus rubbed the bridge of his nose. "It be a long story, but the Messenger Tattoo I gave yeh both is part of it."

"So it's like a brotherhood?" Aaldryn enquired.

"That be it, yes, it's a brotherhood. Squad Sixteen is a protected Squadron. If we can make it to the Neutral Zone, I have contacts who can help get us to the Ivory Path."

"Do you mean other Hunters, like you?" Jarvis asked.

Titus' chuckle was the only reply he received.

Jarvis shook his head, fingering the Map piece hanging around his neck. His stomach was twisting into knots. He had not expected Coltarian to be such a foreign land. He realised now that each time he passed over a Border he was entering an entirely new, separate environment. Walking the pathways of Coltarian, he finally understood why the Zaprexes had found it necessary to chain the Titan of Fire. This land was frightening, and whoever ruled it—

They had to be just as frightening.

This was the land that would destroy the Northlands if it erupted.

Whatever was the Dragon planning to do with a world that was burned by a fire-god?

"Master Titus, how long will it take to evacuate all the Messengers in the House of Flames?"

"Pretty fast if the Guilds are working tagether."

"And if they're not."

"Oh, I don' wanna know. Let's just hope our message got through, yeah? I don' wanna talk to the Council. Bleh. Bleh. Get some rest, both of yeh. I'll take watch." Titus stood, stretching.

"I can watch, if you prefer," Aaldryn offered.

"Nah, laddie. I know what ta look for. This be my terrain." Titus winked.

It was the same thing his Master said every time Aaldryn offered to keep watch and Aaldryn, once again, accepted without issue. Jarvis narrowed his eyes, irritated at being dismissed. He was dragged down by Aaldryn's tail as it slunk around him and he curled up beside the prince. His eyes followed his Master as he climbed up the glass formation that protected them from view, lit by the light of the lava pools. The Hunter sat upon it like a bird of prey, watching the eerie, red-stained horizon. Jarvis would have kept watching, but sleep came far too quickly.

Titus leant against the pommel of his broken giant rock blade and steepled his fingers. He missed his sword; he was going to miss it even more soon. Coltarian was as he remembered it. A land in constant movement, groaning and cracking in a mantra. One day a mountain might be on the horizon, another it could become a valley. Yet every Messenger born seemed to know how to run the Plains of Blazing Fire with an innate ability, as though the memories of all those who had come before them were bred into their very being.

He held out a thin hand to the horizon. Somewhere, far beyond his vision, he could picture Second Base rising out of a basin of molten gold. There, his wife and children waited for him—they were so close. And so far.

"I am so sorry, Rein, my love. I miss yeh so much. I do hope yeh can forgive me."

Gradually he stood, his limbs protesting the movement. He laughed and slapped his knees. "Oh, *tah*, come on, yeh old Twizel, we've got more ta do yet. Don' yeh give up on me now."

His gaze shifted to the red plains and the tainted smudge at the skyline. Few would have been able to tell the difference between the twirling storms of the sky-sea and the horde of a Twizel swarm—but he was a Hunter; he knew Twizels.

Titus pressed his lips together. "Figure the one I let get away would come back ta bite me. When he has a swarm behind him, no less. What a coward." He spat, swinging the hilt of his blade. "Ah, well, guess it be a fair fight now."

He leapt down from his perch and ducked into the small cave where Aaldryn and Jarvis slept, curled together in a protective cocoon. He knelt beside them, studying them in slumber. Without his skin, Jarvis reflected the glow of the lava pools nearby, and the shine was beautiful, almost crystalline in the way it refracted into rainbows. Did the lad know how magical he appeared? He reached out, gently tracing the patterns of the philepcon liquid beneath the metal—the alien blood that could have killed the boy, but instead had accepted him and changed him. He was the stuff of legends now; Messengers would tell great tales of the young Changeling who had run the Plains of Blazing Fire.

"Don' worry, laddie, yeh skin will grow back. We have that in common." He chuckled.

Wind gently brushed against his cheeks. Khamsin was ever present. He smiled in gratitude to the wind-god as he shook the lads awake.

"Time for me ta show yeh how to run the Plains like real Messengers."

Jarvis yawned. "You mean that what we've been doing hasn't been real?"

"Nope. Now it gets serious." Titus gave Jarvis' head a firm pat, just as Zinkx had always done before a battle. Jarvis' mechanical eyes were still wide, so full of endearing trust. It reminded him of how he had felt about Zinkx—nothing but admiration and awe. Which made him wonder: had his old commander experienced the same sickening dread in his stomach as he did now? A building sense of failure, of never truly being good enough. Titus forced back the emotions, compelling a smile to his lips, watching as Jarvis mirrored him.

"Let's run the Plains!" Jarvis cheered.

The other feeling, deep in Titus' chest, threatened to bring tears to his eyes—pride.

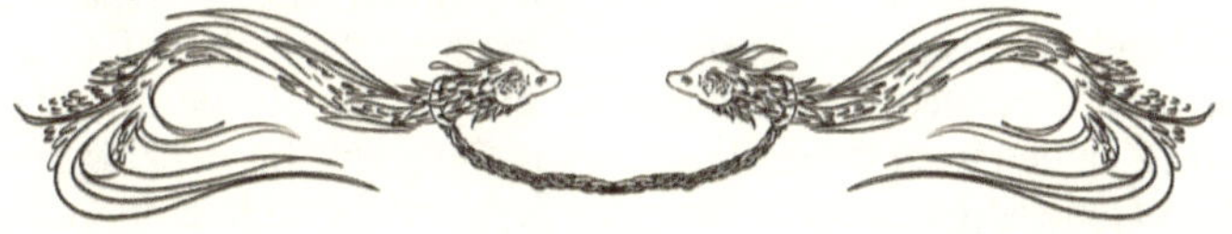

Even with his Changeling abilities, Jarvis could barely keep pace with Master Titus as they ran over the cracked earth, scaled boulders, and jumped rivers of lava. At times Jarvis felt as though he was flying across the surface of the boiling landscape, the world blurring around him. Hours—they ran for hours—without halt, and soon he knew why.

His Master kept looking back, frequently enough for him to cast back his own gaze and focus his optical lenses on the shadow pursing them. It grew closer; the harder Titus pushed them, the faster they ran, the clearer it became in his vision.

Twizels. They were being pursued by Twizels, and they were not gaining any ground.

His chest burned. Was it panic, horror, fear, or excitement? He could not tell. It was all jumbled together in his mind as he dashed after Titus towards the glistening Obelisk in the distance. The monument grew larger as the hours rolled onward but remained an unobtainable goal. His mind drifted, carrying itself back to the wagon box, and Khwaja Denvy's voice in the darkness. The old Kattamont's stories of Commander Zinkx and Squad Sixteen running the Plains, chased by Twizels—now he understood that exhaustion, and still moving, the pain and still running. Jarvis lunged down a boulder, skidding across basalt. Aaldryn flew over him, landing elegantly on another rock formation, only to daintily take flight once more. He glided over the entrance into a canyon. Jarvis wanted to smile. He was out of the wagon box and inside of Khwaja Denvy's stories; this was where he had always wanted to be, but it was altogether suddenly very terrifying.

Master Titus studied the canyon ahead of them.

"Lava Trench. We should move quickly through it. Lava tends to clear a path through the trenches. It's only a small one. Khamsin! Can you keep watch from above?"

Khamsin made a signal with Aaldryn's paw before vanishing up a cliff and Jarvis quickly followed Titus into the depths of the canyon. The air was easier to breathe and Jarvis was grateful for the brief respite. Titus slowed his pace, enough to allow him time to drink. Ahead of them, the glitter of the Obelisk through the yellow haze was a constant guide.

"How far to the Neutral Zone from here?"

"From the Obelisk, about another two days."

"What?"

"We'll make it, laddie." Titus forced a smile. A smile Jarvis could not trust. "I've been in worse situations—"

"Titus!" Khamsin's call was all the warning they had. Jarvis snapped his head up. His optical lenses flared, catching the flashes off to the side and he reacted, throwing himself into a roll across the ground as bullets rained from above. They were nothing like the cracking pop, pop of the Zaprex machine within the depths of the underground city.

This was worse, his mind quickly decided. It was like black sludge being fired out of a hollow barrel at such a speed he could not see it. His optical lenses were unable to gauge where the attack was coming from, and he could not even anticipate the next outcome. He landed roughly on all fours, panting heavily.

Jarvis stared at the boiling bullets behind him, melting into the soil. If they had hit him, what would they have done? They gave off a sickly smell, coating his mouth with the odour. The butchers in the market square, on a hot Summer's day, the meat too old—his mother had always refused to buy the foul-smelling meat. His stomach twisted with the memories. Sparks scattered down his limbs as his insides seized. Titus snatched him up roughly, dragging him away as another round of fire danced off the rocks. The earth shook, cracks forming in the crust as the soil bloated and lava surged through. Jarvis clutched at his head, an intense pressure building in his skull.

"*Traki!*" Titus swore.

Streams of red flame erupted around them. Titus swung the hilt of his broken giant stone blade in an arc, using the pommel to slice through something invisible. Jarvis cringed back against a hot rock as a screech echoed down the canyon walls. Khamsin smacked down beside him, sending a volley of sharp rocks into the air, twirling them into a vortex, in the same direction that Master Titus had struck.

Jarvis rubbed at his eyes. A distortion appeared. Something was ripping itself between the layers of the Realms. Titus had grabbed his shoulder again. On the canyon walls, Twizels swarmed over the edges, screeching and chattering. Jarvis' eyes centred on the massive, lumbering creature bursting into the Primary Realm like a diseased piece of flesh. It floated above the earth, swirling tentacles surging around a body that was nearly all mouth, muscles, and plates of blackened armour. It was enormous, filling the expanse of the canyon.

"Graa-crel!" Titus twisted away. "That fiend would send something I can't fight on my own. We're not battling it. Run!"

"Wha...what?" Jarvis yelped as he was dragged away. The protector bot within him was protesting; it wanted to fight. Surely, he could bring it down, like he had brought down the insane machine? "But it's stuck in the canyon!"

Titus shouted over the screeches of the Twizels, "Yeh don' fight Graa-crel's without a Squad. Go. Go. I don' know how many the High Class brought with it." He shoved Jarvis aside as a tentacle whipped past them. Titus smashed his hilt down, slicing through the rippling flesh. The Hunter was knocked flat as another coiling arm smacked him to the canyon wall. Jarvis skidded to a halt. Titus landed on all fours, spitting out blackened blood. He snatched a grenade from his belt, ripping the pin out with his teeth. He threw it down the canyon and bolted, heaving Jarvis off his feet and lugging him down the winding lava tunnel.

Khamsin skidded up beside them. "They've blocked off the other side."

Titus swore.

"You're a Titan! Make a whirl-wind, Khamsin!" Jarvis shouted.

"I am not risking creating a chain reaction in Coltarian while it is unstable. I told you, Elementals work on balance."

"Sun curse your balance!" Jarvis yelled. He winced as alarms flared around his lenses. The Primary Realm split beside Master Titus revealing the hawk-like shape of the Ki'rayh his Master had told him—had assured him—was dead, gone, forever. Yet there it was, and it smashed the Hunter into the crack and the magma below.

His protector bot activated, all weapons systems bursting online. Screaming, Jarvis ran at the Ki'rayh, aiming his laser as the beast's head reared up, staring at him with red-tinted eyes and a horrible, manic grin of fetid teeth.

The hilt of his master's broken blade suddenly swung up, hacking off one of the Ki'rayh's talons. The Hunter emerged from the lava, skeletal form hissing steam as he walked across the shaking ground, making imprints in the crust as though he weighed more than his thin frame suggested. He planted himself protectively before Jarvis and Aaldryn. Gradually he removed his rippling cloak. Jarvis winced as the weight of the precious garment fell over him.

"Khamsin, get them out of here," Titus murmured.

"No. Master, I can fight—"

Khamsin grabbed him, running through the horde of Twizels. Jarvis screamed and struggled as Master Titus' broken sword met the talons of the Ki'rayh. He was suddenly submerged in magma, dragged under the surface of the crust by Khamsin. The shock of the intense heat against his hull flung his systems into a panic. He stared up, out of the open crack they had plunged through. Twizels surged around the gap. Khamsin hauled him even further down, into the depths of the fiery ocean.

No. He needed to fight. He had to go back. He had to get to his Master. He fought the current, and Khamsin's grip.

Child. If you respect him as your Master, then obey his last command, and live. Khamsin's voice echoed in his mind. *Remember the Key, and your mission.*

Jarvis stared at the diminishing split in the crust, stretching out his hand.

Goodbye, Father.

Jarvis shivered. He could not stop. His body refused to feel warm despite the boiling surrounds of the Plains bubbling with cooking rocks. A blinking light to the side of his optical lens warned of an error in his thermal balancing system, likely due to the long and frantic swim through the lava sea below the Plains. His fingers twisted around the hilt of his blade as basalt cracked behind him.

He knew it was Aaldryn, but his systems were on high alert. Everything felt over-powered, panicky, and running on a level of horror that he could not tone down.

Aaldryn knelt, settling Master Titus' thick nano-cloak back over his shoulders. He had not noticed it had slipped off. Jarvis snuggled into it, seeking comfort from the lingering waxy, oil-lantern scent of the Hunter. He had cried into exhaustion; there was little he could have done to stop himself even if he had wanted to. It was as though the emotional dam he had bottled up inside since the slaughter of his family had burst, rushing out. His stomach was queasy, vision blurry, and his legs simply refused to function despite how much the protector bot wanted to drag their body back onto the battle-field and tear through every single Twizel.

He looked up, squinting at Aaldryn standing on a boulder, his tail flicking about in agitation. The prince's gaze was turned to the Obelisk that took up their horizon. The silver structure looked as though it had grown out of the crust, merging with the landscape, though more likely it was the Plains that had morphed round the turret over the centuries. On wobbly legs Jarvis picked himself up, stumbling over to Aaldryn's side.

"What did you find," he croaked out.

"I think we have made it into the Neutral Zone."

The sick feeling in the stomach grew. So close. Master Titus could have made it. They could have—

Aaldryn's paw rested on his head. "You cannot think like that, child." It was Khamsin, not his brother, who spoke. "Banish such thoughts from your mind."

Khamsin lifted Aaldryn's paw, pointing beyond the Obelisk. "Do you see that glow, those flashes of light?"

Jarvis frowned. He focused his optical lenses. The distance was too great, and the haze in the air too much to clear, but there was something going on over the ridges. Every so often he caught the echoing boom along with the flashes. He might have thought it thunder and lightning, but it was nothing like the storms in Pennadot.

"What is it?"

"I think it is a battle." Khamsin frowned.

A battle. Jarvis curled his toes. Messengers were dying. The chill of his philepcon liquid caused him to shiver once more and he burrowed deeper into Master Titus' cloak, his fingers wrapping around the Map piece loose on the chain about his neck.

It was him and Aaldryn now. And Khamsin, he acknowledged reluctantly. They had to reach the House of Flames. They had to make the Messengers believe they needed to evacuate. Perhaps they would believe Khamsin—a Titan's words had weight, right?

"Do not worry, little brother. All we have to do is head for the Ivory Path. We shall be fine." Aaldryn leapt down from his perch.

Jarvis nibbled his lip. The sick feeling kept growing. He was not sure if they would be fine without Master Titus. This land was cruel and unforgiving. What if Aaldryn—

Jarvis shook his head against a sharp invasion of pain. He staggered backwards, tumbling off the boulder, landing in a skid on his back. He clutched at his skull. Something was drilling into his mind. His protector bot was screaming, sending panicked streams of energy through his body. The drilling stopped abruptly.

He blinked. The world swam. Aaldryn's worried voice echoed in the swaying pixels. Jarvis stared ahead. It was not possible. It could not be. He had felt this presence before, so heavy, so immense and crushing he had thought it would swallow him whole.

Jarvis sucked in a breath, stretching out his arms, scrambling away from something—nothing—anything. His firewall shattered. His head smacked to one side and he landed against the stones, blue blood smearing down his cheek and neck.

"Jarvis! Rythrya! Jarvis! What is going on?"

It was inside of him, consuming his systems. Massive and monstrous, boiling his philepcon liquid, filled with the intense desire to consume and destroy.

It was so hungry.

Jarvis clutched at his chest, clawing for the metal plates that opened to his Matrix Crystal.

"I can't let him out. I can't. I can't let him free."

Aaldryn's paws snatched up his hands. "Jarvis!"

"Dragon. He's…he's…"

The prince's eyes widened. He flung Jarvis over his shoulder and in a surge of wind the Kattamont was running across the plains. Jarvis clutched at his skull, opening his mouth in a silent scream. It was like his father's house was shattering all over again, the bricks of the wall bursting apart in front of him. Only this time it was his mind; the bricks were the protector bot within him, scattering into dust as the invader entered where it was not welcome.

He struggled, fighting Aaldryn's grip.

"Let go of me! Let me go!"

"Jarvis, stop."

"Release me, you insolent—"

Aaldryn's grip tightened. "Jarvis, you have got to fight him."

He was kicking, screaming, tearing at Aaldryn, and he was doing so without control over himself; it was as though he was an observer, standing above himself, watching with detachment. Aaldryn did not release him, even when his air-gills ripped, and blood soaked his battle-suit. Jarvis looked up, through the blackened haze, staring at the Obelisk. His limbs struggled with renewed intensity, a sudden, horrified, frantic rush as though the being within him knew something about the Obelisk he did not. Aaldryn's grip around him tightened. But it was the Titan who was holding back the Dragon, pinning him to the cold, steel wall of the Obelisk.

"Come on, Jarvis, give me your hand, lad."

He wanted to. He really wanted to. He fought the thing controlling his arm and willed his hand into Aaldryn's paw. The Kattamont slapped his hand down upon the activation pad.

"Come on." Khamsin snarled out. "Work!"

It had to open. Jarvis sobbed. It had to recognize his protector bot.

Moments passed. He heard himself laughing. It was a horrible cackle, only to be broken off by the wheeze of the long-disused, ancient door mechanisms easing open. Aaldryn snagged him around the middle and stared into his eyes.

"Die. Monster."

Aaldryn flung him through the open doorway.

He heard himself scream.

Skri Mazaki

CHAPTER EIGHTEEN

Should a grandfather say that he had favourites? He adored all his children, and all his grandchildren, and soon a great-grandchild. None could say that his bloodline was lacking for strong blood. Skri sank back in his couch, watching as young Rynk tried, with earnest effort written across his face, to conduct the flames within the fire to his will. The Lost Batitic Bloodlines he had discovered in the Midlands were extraordinary in their traditions, having made an exodus from Sin'musk'qu during the worshiping of Tahhak due to their refusal to sacrifice their offspring to the Great Devourer. Integrating himself into their society had been...interesting—it had been interesting.

Rynk finally sat back on the rug, his long ears going limp in despair. "I just can't do it, Grand-papa."

Skri slid forward in his seat. "Have you ever considered that you are not affiliated with fire?"

"But I was born under the constellation of fire, Grand-Papa."

Skri arched an eyebrow. "Perhaps not. Perhaps you were destined for something greater—"

"Father!" The doors of his office were flung open and Rion, his eldest, burst through, panting heavily. He sagged against the wooden pillars, clutching at his chest.

"Rion?"

"Father! We just uncovered Eldorado's HUB. You need to see this. You're not going to believe it."

It was the strangest sensation, gradually awakening within a body, feeling muscles pull, eyelids flutter, and a heartbeat vibrate within a chest. Breathing was, at first, disconcerting, before it naturally became a welcome relief, helping to orient him in the strange eeriness of the new and alien environment that was the body encasing him.

Skin. He rubbed a hand against an arm. How incredibly wonderful to feel skin—and not just dead flesh but to be encased in something that lived. He was no longer just energy in a cage of numbers. He was back in a realm of randomness—a realm without control—a realm ready for his control.

Weakly, he blinked. His eyes were faulty, but slowly the blurriness faded, and he focused on wood. He was in a cabin and it was rocking from side to side, the swaying motion soothing. It was rustic and lovely, with herbs dangling from a low ceiling as though they were knitted and knotted to chase away sickness. Turning his head slightly, he spotted an Obilb girl, reading a book. She was fiddling with a glittering necklace that sometimes found its way into her mouth. He smiled at the sight, though he was not sure why.

He shifted, lifting an arm that slipped out of the heavy blanket covering him. There was a hot warmth emanating from the side of his chest—a wound; that explained his weakness.

This body was feeble. It had been sick, but—he was alive.

He choked suddenly. Tears overwhelmed him. It had worked; Zilon had done it. That foolish minion, with all his conniving plans, had finally achieved the impossible. He was alive—physical. He was no longer disembodied. His chest constricted involuntarily as the tears continued to flow down his cheeks.

He was free.

His shackles gone.

Hazanin had lost the game.

The girl was suddenly by his side, grabbing his hand and clutching it to her chest.

"Clive! Oh, Clive, you're awake. It's fine. You're all right. Jythal was there. He was so quick with healing you. We thought…no…no… you're fine."

"Clive?" he whispered. "Is that my name?"

The girl frowned. "You don't remember?"

No, he did not, and that was troubling. The mind of the child was almost impossible to search through. His lips parted in a frustrated hiss as he sighted a cap hanging on a nearby rack. A Sun Monk? Had the boy been training as a Sun Monk? No wonder he was already beginning to seal his memories and personality away; the vile little Human had been well taught.

Oh, well. He would have to make do.

"No. I don't remember. Where are we?" He wobbled his lips.

The girl smiled and brushed back his hair. He should have been repulsed by how near she was, by her gritty, coal stench, and the slickness of her sweat, but something about her was comforting to the newness of his tiny body. After his virtual cage of nothingness her touches were soothing. "We're in Utillia. We're safe again. I'm sure that your memories will come back. Mayhap the fever made you forget a bit. That happens sometimes—"

The door creaked open and he tensed. Another girl entered. Kelib. He narrowed his eyes. She was young, perhaps three and ten, but Kelib women were dangerous, no matter their age. They knew him. But she had no soil under her bare feet. Perhaps he was still safe from her. She seemed anxious about something. Blood stained the wool of her dress; he could scent the spice of battle on her, and it showed in her eyes. For a child she appeared jaded. He sank deeper into the bed. Something else was wrong, and it had nothing to do with him. He was free—Zilon had fulfilled his contract. Not entirely as he had wished it, but, still, it was fulfilled.

"Penny, Khwaja Denvy is asking everyone to come top deck. He is moving the *Lawless Child* again."

"I can't go. Clive is awake." The Obilb girl sniffed.

"No, I will come, too." He moved under the covers. The sweet Kelib girl, with her honey eyes and doe lips, had mentioned Denvy. Surely she could not mean Denvy, the Dream Master of the Northlands?

"Clive!" He was suddenly assaulted by her heavy weight as she wrapped her arms around him, smothering him with the smell of earth and rain. His instinct was to pull away, but the boy was her friend and, for now, he had to be that boy.

"We missed you!" She snuggled into his shoulder.

He tugged away gently, smiling.

"He can't remember things, Ki'b!" As though she were a storm child, filtering away sunrays, Penny moved between them, her arm blocking Ki'b. He raised an eyebrow, catching the tension between the girls. The stances they took, the shifting glances. How very strange. Had the boy noticed it as well and tried to regulate them, or had he let them be?

"Oh…" Ki'b shuffled off the bed, turning moue. She rubbed at her clothing, and it was only then that he realised that, unlike Penny, she was dressed entirely in alien attire. He had already been mildly impressed by the scent of battle on her, but he found himself intrigued that a Kelib woman had fallen into a Kattamont Pride while so young.

"I am sorry, Clive." She played a bare toe over the floor.

"Was there a fight?" he enquired.

She nodded and wiped aside a tear. "Jythal was hurt, but he is all right. Khwaja Denvy—oh, oh, it is wonderful, Clive: he got rid of the yoke binding him. It was so brave of him!"

"You could have been killed!" Penny snapped. "You're so stupid, following Jythal around."

"They are my Pride. I fight with them. I am a princess," Ki'b snapped.

"We are your family!"

Ki'b turned away, her shoulders sagging. It seemed this was not the first time this argument had arisen. "Come on, Khwaja Denvy needs us."

He shuffled out of the bed, looking towards Penny. "We should go when summoned by an elder. It is honourable." If the boy who hosted him now had indeed been a Sun Monk, he would likely have shown respect to his elders.

Ki'b smiled at him before ducking out the door. Penny helped him into a thick coat. "The Long Night is very cold now." She added as she left.

He stood, staring down at himself. There was no mirror in the room. He tugged on a curl of hair and pulled it down, staring at its bright red tinge. His lips spread with mirth.

"Oh, the irony, heh, Hazanin?" The Dragon sneered. "Now that I am a real boy, I wonder what sort of chaos and ruin I will bring with me."

Denvy could not take his eyes off the sprawling crystal spires looming out of the sand-dune waves. They sent glittering rainbows across the burning-sea from the glow of starlight. It was breathtaking, and everything he recalled the tips of Tikal's vast network of glossy, endless prisms to be. The city had been nearly invisible in the sky-sea, capable of blending into whatever environment it found itself within—for that had been its skill; it had been a mirror that shone the world back upon itself.

"I cannot allow the Dragon to get a hold of you, Tikal," Denvy murmured. "He may have taken Utillia, but he will never sit upon your throne. I will make sure of that."

Zafiashid's scent tickled his nose. Her paw settled on his arm. Denvy looked down. She was worn, skin around her eyes sunken against bone, and new wounds had been added over old. He had never enquired as to how she had faired in the fight with her old Pride, figuring it was a private affair she would speak of if ever she felt the need to do so.

Her lips reached his as her paw cupped the back of his neck. It was the gathering of strength as a pair, the comfortable silence of companionship he had never found until now. Denvy purred low in his chest, hugging the queen to him.

"Thank you."

"The crew is waiting."

He nodded. Accepting her paw, he let her lead him across the ruined deck towards the remaining members of their small pride. Trusting eyes fell upon him, all so hopeful under the light of their Rythrya Guiding Stones. Zafiashid rested her paw on his shoulder. Denvy sighed through his aching air-gills. This was it—he was finally going to face his past; it was going to merge with his present.

Zafiashid addressed the crew. "As you may have gathered, we were attacked by the Silvertide Navy. And somehow we were transported away. You all know the stories of the Zaprexes and their ability to travel vast distances in their sky-ships. The *Lawless Child*, herself, is built out of the skeleton of such a ship."

She moved elegantly, sweeping between the burning-sea sailors, her tail curling around ankles in reassurance, pressing against other tails, making contact where it mattered. Zafiashid pointed to the Rythrya Stones. "We have lost loved ones, and we would all have been slaughtered by the claws of the Iposti's leash-kittens if not for the gift the Zaprexes gave to us." Her voice rose above the breaking of the sand-dune waves upon the hull of the *Lawless Child*.

"The Iposti have been leading our people down a terrible path. All of us here are the result of their treachery amongst the Prides. We are misfits. We are the outcasts of the burning-sea. But no more! We will become the grains in this ocean that change the direction of the currents! Do you trust me?" She swept about, spreading her air-gills in a glorious fan of colours.

Kovlrok stepped forward. "Always, Captain!"

Zafiashid nodded. Denvy breathed in deeply as she returned to him. He felt the eyes of the crew turn his way. Though his queen relished being the centre of attention, he would never grow accustomed to it.

"As you know," Zafiashid continued, "Denvy and his cubs have become a part of our Pride. If you trust me, then I want you to trust your prince and the words he shall speak to you." She inclined her head, shifting to one side.

Denvy studied the faces of the crew, many of whom still nursed their wounds from the battle, wrapped and tended to, but all beyond ready for a meal and a long rest. However, they were proud to be summoned by their queen, to listen to her words. They were what Messengers had once been—so very hopeful.

He settled his ruffled fur. "I do not know how much of the tales remain of the era before the Thousand Sol-Cycle War, but I was told that when the Zaprexes reached Livila it was a world in great strife. It was collapsing, and they could not resist their mandate to aid in healing it. As difficult as it may be for you to believe, I was one of the programs built during the Dawn Age. I was known as Maahes, Dream Master of the Ways. These days I am simply referred to as an Ancient One."

Soft murmurs stirred amongst the crew.

"My purpose was to control the defragmentation stations across Livila. My programming allowed me to move through the Data-Ways, a weblike network across our world, and throughout the universe beyond." He tugged on an ear. "But I have never tried to go that far." Denvy eased onto his foot-paws. "My home was Utillia, and therefore my creators thought it suitable to make me a Kattamont. I lived in Tikal, the Rainbow City, until the Thousand Sol-Cycle Wars. I want you all to know that I was there, and I was frightened. I was so frightened that I ran, and I have been running ever since. But, indeed, no more!" he echoed Zafiashid. He curled a paw into a fist. "We have been given an opportunity to save the Northlands from the same evil that consumed Livila during the Thousand Sol-Cycle Wars. The evil that rose up and destroyed all the Zaprexes had worked so hard to build. We owe it to them to do everything we can to preserve their legacy, for we are their legacy! We, who are the misfits, born of their crystals, are their children. And, therefore," he pointed to the Rythrya Stones, "we own everything buried under the burning-sea!"

Zafiashid leapt onto a crate, raising her paw to the sky-sea. "I say we take it all back! We, the Children of the Fairies, will rise out of the burning-sea and seize Utillia as ours." She let out a roar. "Who is with me?"

A cheer thundered across the deck. Denvy blinked away tears. Zafiashid was beautiful, standing above them, her black coat glinting silver in the light of the Mist sails. She was a true queen; he could not comprehend why the Silvertide Pride had cast her aside when she would have led them to victory.

Zafiashid bounded down, resting a paw on his shoulder. "Take us away, my love."

He nodded.

The weight of the yoke upon his shoulders was simply a fabrication. It had been there for so long he had become accustomed to it. Now, without it, he felt lopsided. But his mind—oh, his mind was free. He could sense Jythal and Nixlye's colours, heighted by the gems they wore. Jythal's mind was grey; so curious, since the prince had not been blind at birth. But perhaps he had begun to lose the memories of colour. Nixlye was all neon sparks that burst in fireworks. He could hardly bear to remain near her for more than a few moments; her mind was so vastly different to her calm demeanour.

A deep sense of loss that was not his own welled over him. Ryojin's grief caused his chest to clench tight and he closed his eyes.

I am so sorry. I never felt your pain. To be so close to those you love, and yet so far away.

My Father always told me that time healed all wounds, but I do not think I have that luxury. It is fine, Maahes. I am just grateful for the chance to aid them. Are you ready?

Yes. I do believe I finally am.

The engines of the *Lawless Child* surged beneath him as he picked up the energy, threading it through the Secondary Realm. The network surrounding him was frayed, sections still missing entirely, some blocked to him by firewalls he would need time to decode. The songs that had once led to other sectors of Livila were burning hot, blazing a red of warning. He dared not go near them. Did it mean those had been lost to the Dragon—or simply that they were unreachable?

What if he tried to defragment to them? Would he be distorted and lost forever within the Secondary Realm?

Denvy shrank back, away from the terrors, towards the warmth that called to him, the happy, bubbly, welcoming glee radiating from a single song. He reached for it, letting it fill his mind with the co-ordinates for the defragmentation. His body thrummed with energy and he opened his eyes. Surrounding him in a swirl of data, the *Lawless Child* was piecing itself together, pixel by pixel. In the middle of the defragmentation, rainbow light, intense and sharp coiled around them, hugging the sand-ship. This was true peace, this moment in suspended time, between locations. He had forgotten what it was like to be a Navigator, to watch defragmentation as it happened.

"Hello, Maahes."

Denvy blinked. He turned.

Standing behind him, a white-skinned Zaprex hovered inches above the deck, pearl eyes unblinking. No antennae poked out of the glittering strands of transparent hair. Denvy crinkled a smile. It was an AI.

"Tikal."

"We welcome you home."

"I am sorry, Tikal, for running away."

"It matters not what was done; it matters only what is done now."

Suddenly the defragmentation stopped. The swirling data froze. The world around him turned a slow, burning red of warning. Denvy's eyes widened as, from Tikal's small form, whips of energy expanded outward from the AI's bare back. He barely saw it. It flickered in the corner of his eye before everything crashed down around him—a sight that chilled him: a shadowed, willowy form standing on the deck, consuming the frozen data.

"You cannot come in." Tikal's voice had lost its sing-song quality.

Pain flared. He had hit the firewall again.

Denvy sat up abruptly.

He was surrounded by blankets and the protective walls of Zafiashid's cabin, her singing voice gentle in his ears. The tune cut off sharply and the bed jolted, her paws wrapped around his chest as her head nuzzled into the curve of his shoulder.

"It did not work," he muttered.

She stroked his mane.

"No. Nixlye explained the firewall. I wish you had told me it would cause you to collapse for a few days."

"A few days! No! No!" Denvy scrambled free of the covers. Zafiashid pulled aside in confusion as he stumbled around, grabbing clothing. "This is not good!"

"Denvy! Honestly, you're exhausted. The yoke was only barely removed. I should never have let you—"

"The Dragon!" He whipped about, grabbing her shoulders. "He is on your ship!"

Her eyes widened at his words, air-gills spreading in a vicious show. Without the yoke he could now sense every twist of her emotions; they relayed through his mind in a flare of colour, spreading across the canvas of his awareness in icy blues of panic he would not have expected from the stoic queen.

"He could not have become flesh," she whispered.

Zafiashid curled against his chest. He wrapped an arm around her waist, pulling her close. His queen was terrified, and he felt just as scared as he curled himself around her, seeking her comfort.

"I don't know how but I will find out," he growled.

They moved swiftly through the corridors, throwing open the doors to topside. Denvy blinked back the light of the Mist sails. He searched the deck. They were anchored near one of the largest spires of the Rythrya Stones, and the currents were gentle. Crew members moused about, fixing the damaged hull. He ignored well-wishers as he dashed past, heading directly for Jythal.

The blind healer was bearing a tray of tea, setting it on a table beside Nixlye and Ki'b. Ki'b squealed in delight at the sight of him. The warmth of her voice should have brushed away the chill wrapped around his hearts, but, for once, he ignored her.

"Jythal, have you sensed anything out of order the past few days?"

Jythal's eyebrows lifted. It was so slight, the twist of the prince's paw movement, but Denvy caught it: the shine of a monk Rune glittering on the surface of Jythal's skin. It faded swiftly. Denvy's breath caught in his throat. His mind wanted to deny it.

"Nothing? Nothing at all unusual has happened?' He turned sharply to Nixlye and Ki'b.

Zafiashid grabbed his shoulder. "Denvy, you are frightening Ki'b."

And he was. His dear little Mountain Flower was hugging Nixlye tightly, staring at him as though she had never seen him before. He started to reach for her, to reassure her all was well, but his paw was suddenly grabbed by a squealing Penny.

She launched into his arms.

"Khwaja Denvy! You're awake. Thank the Sun. Clive said you would wake soon."

He stood, arms slack, startled at the girl who so rarely showed such exuberant emotions, even around him. "Clive's awake?" he choked out.

"Oh, yes." Penny laughed. "He is feeling so much better. He forgot things for a while but after Jythal did some Runes, he's able to think better."

"Aww, come on, Petunia, I can speak for myself."

"Clive! Don't call me that." Penny spun around and ran for Clive as he came towards them. The reaction was instant. Denvy felt his paw clench around his water-sword, the elemental within activating, and the blade surged to life. He heard shouts from the crew and sensed Zafiashid step forward, along with Jythal. Confusion from the minds around him was crowding his own thoughts until Ryojin blanketed everything.

We cannot allow it to escape, Denvy.

"Penny, step away from him."

The girl's eyes were wide, her bare feet trembling as her hands played with the necklace he had crafted for her. She almost stepped towards him, but gradually her lips narrowed, and a hardened, sorrowed gaze looked up at him. Oh, when? When had he lost her?

Clive's happy, relaxed stance changed so naturally; it was frightening how quickly the shift swept over the boy. Denvy shivered as the child he loved, with a smile as bright as sunshine, smirked cruelly and eyes blackened into tarry ink. His limbs moved like those of a slackened puppet as he spun about playfully.

"Ah, well," he spread his hands, "it was so much fun while it lasted. I would try and argue with you, Old Dreamer, but I guess you're not as blind as the other Ancient Ones! Funny, you know, I just killed one of your siblings. Hmm, mmm, who knew Snake tasted so divine?"

Denvy snarled. "You lie!"

"Now, what good would lying do?"

Denvy stepped forward, spreading air-gills and fan-tail. Around him the crew were beginning to mobilise; despite their confusion, their weapons were drawn, following their queen and princes. It was only Ki'b's cries that echoed in his skull, restraining his foot-paws.

"I am not the only one who can see you in there, Dragon." He spat.

A whisper spread through the crew. Such a legendary word— Dragon. So much power it held.

A swirling rip of energy tore across the planks of the deck. Clive flew backwards. Jythal was a lightning bolt, running in a circle around the boy before he could heave himself back onto his feet. Glittering Runes formed in a pattern, glowing ropes whirled into the air, wrapping around the boy. Jythal skidded back beside Zafiashid, twirling his Rune blades.

The Dragon cackled. "The blind one. I should have seen that coming." He spat out blood and studied the Runes shining on the planks. "You seriously think this is going to keep me trapped?" he mocked them. "I am the Dragon. You all belong to me!"

Penny suddenly ran.

Denvy made a dive for her. She dodged his outstretched paw and kept running.

"Clive, please, please stop it!"

The Dragon's gaze shifted to her, his snarl falling away, growing soft and childish. Denvy sucked in a sharp breath. It was almost a Human look of affection, warm and tender that rested upon Penny. Despite his restraints, the Dragon stretched out a hand, ignoring the hissing of his skin as he did so. "Come on, Penny, let's go home. I know how much you miss your father."

"Penny. No! Don't!" Denvy swung his blade.

Fire erupted around the Dragon. It met the surge of water. Steam burst across the deck. A thundering crack sent them all backwards and Denvy rolled. He heaved himself onto his foot-paws, running under the burning sails, through the rising steam. The Dragon's arms were wrapped protectively around Penny, his body encased in rippling flames. The beast looked towards him, smiled and mouthed:

"I am free."

Ki'b rushed past him suddenly, screaming.

"Penny! Stop! Penny! No. No. Penny!"

With a forceful swing the Dragon leapt overboard, taking Penny with him. Ki'b slammed into the railing, her arms outstretched. "Penny! Clive!"

CHAPTER NINETEEN

The excavation of Eldorado had been a project his bloodline had begun after he had joined the Kyrmrn Council. A small village had grown around the skirts of Mt. Hrurn under the looming shadow of the ancient Zaprex City that was wedged into the mountainside. That village, over the sol-cycles, had gradually swelled in size the more prosperous the land allocated to his bloodline had become. Being the only Batitic with working knowledge of Zaprex technology had provided him with something to offer, and thus he and his bloodline were esteemed for their knowledge. His eldest, Rion, had long been the Mrin of Lyrnnon—their city—but it was Rion's wife who continued to oversee the excavation of Eldorado. Carrying Rynk in his arms, Skri followed the glow of Rion's conductor through the winding passages.
"Is it Maahes?" Rynk questioned his father. "Did you really find him? Did you really, really find the Dream Master of the Ways?"
The stories the kitten had been fed had ignited within him. Skri had to chuckle at the excitement in his squeaky little voice.
"I am not sure, Rynk." Rion paused by an airlock, activating it with a wave. "Now, you are not to touch anything. You're only in here because your Grand-Papa is so very fond of you."
Rynk's neck-feathers fluffed and he huddled deeper into Skri's chest. Through the airlock, Rion's wife, Fyrnra, stood bathed in the light of several conducted lanterns set up on dulled crystal terminals. It was, indeed, the HUB chamber to Eldorado's power core. If they could figure out what powered the City of Gold—the possibilities were endless. He stopped in mid-walk, staring at the hibernation chamber set to one side of the HUB.
Rynk slid down from his suddenly limp arms. Rion anxiously ushered him away.
"Father..."
"Impossible," he choked out. "Disgleirio..."

Jarvis stared at the blurry lights of the medical bay. It was peaceful. The bed he lay upon acted like a cocoon, encased as it was within an alcove in the wall. Shimmering starlight patterns surrounded him on all sides. It was surprisingly comfortable, despite having no blankets or pillows. Though, considering he had been sleeping on rocks for months, anything was an improvement. His head felt like a sledge-hammer had been taken to it. The protector bot was slowly at work, reassembling what he could only describe as walls that had been shattered into thousands of pieces. He felt like an assaulted city, completely ransacked. A sharp pain pierced his optical lenses when he shifted his eyes. At least he had managed to clear away the blue screen that had terrified him for hours as his processor core rebooted.

Everything was limp and heavy; his philepcon liquid vibrated with a sorrowful song of grief and fear—grief for Master Titus, fear for the touch of the Dragon…The monster had almost—

He let out a whine.

If Aaldryn had not figured out that getting him inside the superior Zaprex shielding would force the Dragon out, and if they had been further away from the Obelisk, he dreaded to think of what he would have become.

It was at least cool inside the Obelisk. The air was fresh and ventilated, and the environmental system was fully functional.

Aaldryn sat beside him patiently. The prince had taken off the lava-suit in the safety of the Obelisk, and he looked happy to be free of it. His tail kept dancing about with a frisky beat.

"You thirsty?" Aaldryn glanced up from the holo-pad he was reading.

"A little, yeah," Jarvis croaked out.

Aaldryn carefully cradled his head, lifting him gently, and pressed a smooth cup of cool water to his lips. He gulped the liquid down. Water had never tasted so sweet and precious, lavishing the knives that coated his throat.

"What are you looking at?"

Aaldryn sat back and held out the holo-pad. "Found the schematics of this place while you were out and had a bit of a look around. I think I found the communal eating hall."

"Really?" Jarvis squinted at him.

"Feel up to walking?"

Jarvis winced. "I can't really move."

"Yeah, that looks painful." Aaldryn indicated Jarvis' raw skin which had started to regrow over his metal hull. "Khamsin thinks you should wear this." He handed him the lava suit. "The nano-whatsits will help to speed the healing process." Aaldryn grinned as Jarvis grimaced.

His limbs protested every movement, but he gradually forced them to comply and slip into the suit. Aaldryn turned, offering his back. "Hop on. Lying around here moping won't do you any good. Let's explore." Jarvis' chin rested wearily upon the Kattamont's shoulder as the prince's arms tucked under his legs.

"Now you're the one who feels like an eel," Aaldryn added.

Jarvis snorted. "You just wanted to get rid of the thing."

He was reminded of the days his brother-in-law had carried him, in the same fashion, on their long Summer journeys down the Spider Road.

He sniffled and huddled closer to the warmth of Aaldryn's fur. "Thanks, Aaldryn."

"It's fine, Jarvis. It's what blood-brothers are for."

"Blood-brother?"

Aaldryn laughed as he headed through the medical bay door. "I think we have both experienced enough together for you to have earnt your place in our brotherhood several times over."

He had no idea what to say, so he simply hid himself in Aaldryn's air-gills and watched as the interior of the Obelisk was awakened by the presence of the philepcon liquid in his veins. Nothing around them felt sharp, despite the hexagon patterns that linked all the walls and doors like puzzle pieces. The walls themselves were filled with slow-moving lava, swirling about in tubes that formed intricate designs. He did not need to focus hard to feel the energy being channelled through the structure of the building. It twanged in the air with a great intensity.

"They really are like chains," Aaldryn muttered. They both peered over the edge of the walkway hanging mid-air over a vast drop into bubbling lava, and yet the heat was tempered; Jarvis could not feel its touch even on the exposed raw skin of his face and hands.

"I wonder how deep we are buried into the earth." Aaldryn said.

"What does Khamsin think about his sibling being chained like this? He was pretty upset about his children being slaves. Isn't this the same?" Jarvis knew they were both avoiding talking about it—the Dragon. Perhaps even Khamsin was avoiding it. The possibility of what had happened was a daunting one; it choked him up even considering it.

Khamsin spoke through Aaldryn, wearily. "Prometheus is this land, this volcano. It used to be our ruler—Chorus, the Zaprexes called him—who kept Prometheus bound, but after the First Elemental War, when Chorus was dispersed, Prometheus felt free to give fire to those who needed it. That perhaps, was Prometheus' greatest undoing—"

Jarvis interrupted, "The First Elemental War? Meaning there was a Second?"

"We Elementals have fought several times."

"So much for your *balance*."

"It is for the balance that we have fought. There is one thing that Prometheus did right, though, in giving fire to mortal kind."

"What was that?"

"Prometheus came to understand love. By having someone to protect, Prometheus' fire burned brighter for it."

Jarvis felt Aaldryn's shoulders sag. "Unfortunately, I learnt this lesson far too late."

He tightened his arms around the prince's neck. "You're getting there, you old wind-bag."

They came upon what Jarvis thought was a hangar, but the doors were unresponsive to any commands, which proved disheartening considering the pristine hawkships sitting in their docks. The defragmentation station on the observation deck proved just as useless. Nothing but rudimentary systems were responding to his protector bot. They gave up trying and headed to the communal eating area. It was grander than any of the province lords' Gathering Halls he had visited with his father and brother-in-law. They had always felt cramped, even with their high thatched ceilings and wall hangings. It seemed Zaprexes adored space, light, and curves. Waterfalls of lava overflowed into designs across the floor beneath sheets of transparent crystal.

Aaldryn set him down on a floating chair beside a table that ignited a bright blue at his presence. A hologram sprang to life across the surface. Several dainty little Zaprexes waved cheerfully before showing a selection of items.

Jarvis started laughing and Aaldryn raised an eyebrow. "I'm guessing you know what this is? Because it took me forever to get you a glass of water."

"Okay. Ah. Imagine we're at a tavern or a bar, right? But instead of a pretty waiter serving us food from a grungy cook in some dirty kitchen, we get to select our food from this table and it will be defragged here."

"But where do they make it?" Aaldryn looked around.

"It's possible they don't actually make it. I think the song for all these food items is already stored in the buffer of the Obelisk's defragmentation machine and it converts Secondary Realm energy into food."

Aaldryn stared at him for a long time.

"I think Khamsin had a minor black out," Aaldryn croaked eventually, his arms trembling as he sank into a seat.

Jarvis swiped the dancing Zaprexes aside. "Wait, you didn't know any of this?"

"No!" Aaldryn dragged a claw through his air-gills. "The Secondary Realm was once home to the Elementals. It was where they resided; the field worked in harmony with Livila. After it began collapsing they had no idea how to fix it. Only when the Zaprexes built their Towers were the Elementals able to start bridging the gap between the Secondary and Primary Realms."

Jarvis shrugged. "Everyone has this really high opinion of the Zaprexes. Including me, I will admit. I am sure they came here to heal this planet, as that is a mandate of theirs, but I also think that there was a small part of their collective consciousness that saw this raw energy field and wanted to know what it was and what they could do with it."

Aaldryn bowed his head.

"I suppose they paid for it."

"They did. Is Khamsin upset?"

"Not really. The Batitics do a similar thing with their conducting, and Jythal's Runes are also another form of manipulating the Secondary Realm. I think, living apart as they did, Elementals never realised how integrated the Secondary and Primary Realms were.

They should have interacted more with the Primary. Perhaps then the Dragon would not have fooled them so easily."

Jarvis swept the hologram back, humming low in his throat. He wanted to say they should not live with regret, but his aching heart kept accessing the last frame he had of Master Titus—forever frozen in his memory. A little dancing Zaprex pointed to an item on the menu and he smiled sadly at it, selecting the suggestion. In a scattering of light surging together in the centre of the table, something resembling a damper bun, stuffed with meat and the rare vegetable he had seen in the markets…lettuce? Was that lettuce? He grabbed at the plate. The smell was making his mouth water. Another holographic Zaprex pushed a drink towards him before twittering a laugh and vanishing into pixels.

Aaldryn was pulling faces at the unreadable menu.

"It translates to 'hamburger and potato chips.'"

Aaldryn scoffed. "What is a hamburger?"

"Don't mock it; it tastes amazing. Here, I'll order you one. You'll love it!"

Jarvis bonked his head against the hangar door. Nothing was working. He was getting beyond infuriated with himself. If he was a Zaprex hybrid then why was nothing working for him? Why could he not make the defragmentation machine work, or even get this door open? Longingly he stared through the glass panels at the rows of hawkships. His stomach kept twisting with the gut-wrenching feeling that he would fail to reach the House of Flames in time. The fear that the Key was already there, and in grave danger, had crept its way into his mind and it would not leave him. Even when he slept, he dreamt of the precious little Zaprex screaming his name in agony as the Dragon tore the cyborg limb from limb. Where had such terrible images come from? The data-banks of the protector bot? Whatever their source, they were clear and realistic enough for him to fear their possibility.

He slid down the door, hugging his knees. "I am going to fail Master Titus," he moaned.

"You will fail him with that attitude." Aaldryn looked up from the terminal he was working at. He sat perched on a chair, his tail swirling about with excitement. Everything was wonderful to the Kattamont prince, everything in the Obelisk was brilliant and fantastic, nothing seemed to dull his spirit of exploration. Jarvis blew a long rasp.

He slumped even further down, curling up on the floor, tracing the lava patterns in the tiles.

He sat up abruptly.

"Holy Sun!"

The defragmentation station was activating. He flicked through the onslaught of data filling his optical lenses as he scrambled to his feet. "Someone just punched right through! That's incredible!" He grabbed Aaldryn, dragging him off his seat. "Hurry! Run!"

"What's going on?" Aaldryn yelped.

Jarvis lunged down the stairs and around corners, with Aaldryn in pursuit. He had thought the defragmentation station to be sealed off entirely, impossible to use. But this meant there was hope. His protector bot purred with excitement.

They halted, panting, at the observation deck. The intense glow of the defragmentation station was fading, the starlight patterns swirling around were gradually pulling back into their stationary positions. Jarvis strained to hear the song, but it was too late; it was gone and all that remained were two Humans sprawled out upon the station's circle.

He gasped. One of them emitted a radiating glow that marked him as a Starborn. The Prince of Pennadot—it had to be. The protector bot had instantly recorded the change in the environmental system of the Obelisk as it adapted to the new presence.

His stomach flipped in panic. What in all the Holy Sun was he doing here?

"That's the Prince of Pennadot!" he hissed to Aaldryn.

His blood-brother crouched down in the shadows beside him. "As in Human royalty?"

"Yes."

"This may be a problem."

"You think!"

"No, I mean, one of them is wounded. I can smell blood…and something else."

"Oh." Jarvis blinked rapidly, refocusing on the new arrivals. They were beginning to stir. Aaldryn was right. One of them was wounded, the female, and quite badly if his scans were anything to go by. The Starborn was also damaged, but to a lesser degree. What had happened to them?

"You had better go in there and do something, Jarvis. They may not even know what a Kattamont looks like, being Imperial Humans. I wouldn't want to frighten them—least of all the female."

"Why?" Jarvis frowned, studying the woman as she crouched anxiously beside the Starborn, unheeding of her own dangerous wound.

"She's a Mahvash Assassin. One of the river children," Khamsin replied.

"An Elemental?"

Khamsin shook Aaldryn's head. "No. The Cor River is a server-god, like your Khwaja Denvy. He controls the water-ways of Pennadot and his children are the many rivers. Consider them a Zaprex imitation of Elementals. Be careful, she won't trust easily."

Jarvis nodded. He got to his feet. "Right, watch the lady," he whispered back as he crept down the corridor, keeping low in the shadows as he ducked past the windows. Coming to the door, he hesitated and took the precaution of activating the battle-suit's mask. Air breathed past him into the observation deck as he triggered the door's opening mechanism. The conversation of the two Humans cut off at his appearance. He wondered what he looked like to them, standing in the white suit that hugged him like a second skin. He registered a spike in their heart rates, so did they see him as a threat? Perhaps he appeared to be one of the mythological protectors that dwelt within Zaprex holy places. The thought amused him, considering the philepcon liquid that flowed through him and what it had once belonged to. Yet he felt no desire to defend the Obelisk from the two Humans before him. They were not enemies of his Creators. They were in a terrible state, stinking of months' old blood, maggoty flesh, and burnt air. Fire had scorched part of their clothing, and, somehow, the woman smelt of poison, much like that of Aaldryn's tail spikes.

The Starborn stepped forward, blood leaking from one of his wounds. "Please, we mean you nor this place any harm," the man's voice cracked. It was so hoarse. "We come seeking protection from the Dragon. That is all."

The poetic irony struck him, and Jarvis found laughter slipping from his lips. "Then we are here for the same reason." He drifted into range of the Starborn prince's illuming halo. His scans revealed no airborne contaminants that might pose a threat to him. Raising a hand, he released his mask with a pop. The skin-tight liquid covering his features came away, revealing him to the two Imperials. He heard the woman's sharp intake of breath.

"Are you a Messenger?" The Mahvash Assassin inched forward.

He scanned her. She had weapons stashed under her ruined clothes, but most interesting was the armour adhering to her skin, made of a very particular alloy. She was a metal elementalist then. He would have thought that being the daughter of rivers she would have been born under the stars of water. But it made her even more dangerous; she did not need to be near him to attack him.

He shook his head, approaching them with feigned confidence. "All those who oppose the Dragon are Messengers, but, in the sense of being raised in the House of Flames, no, I am not. My name is Jarvis Alderti, of the Plains People."

He barely caught it, the flicker of recognition crossing the Starborn prince's features, as though his name was somehow familiar. Beneath the tight suit, the Map piece around his neck was being pressed into his tender flesh. He reached in and pulled it free, rubbing a thumb over its smooth surface. "I once hailed from the farming regions around Daru'th. That was a long time ago now. Another life." He moved across to the terminals surrounding the sealed panoramic windows and slid his fingers over the surfaces, activating keys. The room came to life, swirling patterns of lights down the dark walls and across the floors in polygon shapes. Now that it was no longer the glow of the Starborn lighting the room, he breathed a little easier. The man's eyes strayed to the Map piece around his neck, as though he had seen it before. "Needless to say, I was a little surprised when the defragmentation station of his turret came to life. I have been trying to get it to work since I arrived."

"Defragmentation station?" the woman murmured.

"Travel through the Secondary Realm," the Starborn answered her.

"You think that is what you did, by jumping into the waterfall?" Jarvis raised an eyebrow.

"Probably. Though I doubt it would have the ability to control my destination. I must have been drawn to the first possible…what did you call it?" The prince glanced at him.

"Defragmentation station."

"Yes, that."

"Daniel! We could have ended up anywhere."

"Anywhere was better than where we were. Did you want to be dinner for the Dragon? He looked a little angry about not getting my body—"

"Daniel!"

Jarvis frowned. The Dragon had wanted this Starborn Human for a host? Was that what had happened when his mind had been invaded? But that made no sense—that had happened a week ago. Why had they only arrived now? He stared blankly at the Starborn and the woman who had smothered his mouth with her hands to stop him saying anything further. Jarvis' mind was spinning with the amazing possibilities of what could have transpired. Had they been trapped in the buffer of the defragmentation station and only appeared when safe? Or, even more incredible, what if the Mahvash woman's wounds had been worse and the defragmentation station had only released them when she was stable enough to survive?

He suddenly recalled why the woman was so worried. She thought he did not know who the Starborn was. She must have been confounded by her ordeal. He started laughing.

The two Imperials gaped at him.

"Milady, do not bother. I know who he is. He is lit up like the Sun itself. The Prince of Pennadot." He spat out a long string of curses that would have made Master Titus proud. "How the *traki* am I supposed to look after you? Here! In this place?" He threw out his arms. "Let us not mention the current problem of Coltarian about to erupt in our faces. You are a massive power source that could keep one of the Cities of Gold flying." Jarvis rubbed at his temple. He eyed the illumed man critically. Like many Kimwyns he was tall, far taller than Jarvis knew he himself would ever grow as a Wynnila. But he looked as though he had not played the role of an Imperial for a long time, with his white hair scruffy and chin an unshaven mess. What he could see of his clothes beneath foul stains of bodily fluids seemed similar to those worn by the caravan folk of the Spider Road—thick woollen gowns dyed in traditional Pennadotian symbols. Had the royal been in hiding?

"Although, considering our situation, you could prove rather useful." Jarvis glanced around their current prison. The Prince of Pennadot had managed to employ a defragmentation station that had been deactivated—what more could he do?

"You are trying to reach the House of Flames, aren't you?" the Starborn asked suddenly.

Jarvis felt every one of his defence systems trigger and he swung back to face the couple. "How do you—?"

The Starborn lifted his hands. "I know Sam. The Key. You are wearing one of his Map pieces. You have to reach the House of Flames to give it to him, right?"

Jarvis curled his fingers protectively around the Map. "Yes. That is my task. However, I am stuck here because the Dragon tried to invade my mind. The shields in the walls protected me. I was lucky I was close enough to this place to get in." He said it, feeling guilty for leaving out the part about Aaldryn. If he had been alone he would never have made it; he owned his life to his blood-brother. "I doubt others were as lucky as I was at the time of that…whatever it was."

"The conduction?" The Mahvash joined the conversation. "The Dragon is flesh. He consumed Jarid, one of our friends."

Jarvis jutted a thumb at the prince. "Is this Jarid a Starborn like him?"

"No." She shook her head. "But he is a paladin."

Jarvis glanced away. "Ah, a Silverblood. Interesting. Just like Master Titus was. Still, it wouldn't have been enough." He shrugged. "The Dragon needs the constant energy of a Starborn; you folk are walking miniature suns. Just plug you into a grid and let you rip…" He blew a rasp.

"So, what are we looking at? What does this mean?"

"Well." Jarvis scrubbed a hand through the new growth of hair that was proving highly irritating. "If my mind being invaded is any indication then I surmise that, without you, the Dragon was forced to compromise at the last minute. It is likely he had had a backup plan for a while now, in case he did not get a hold of you. I should know; I was a part of that plan. It would have been his fall-back, and he would have implemented that."

"So, Jarid sacrificed himself for nothing?" The Mahvash Assassin clutched at her bloodied robes. It seemed whoever this Jarid was, he had been dear to the couple.

"No." The prince shook his head. "I am not the Dragon. It would have been worse if he had my body, right?"

For a reason he could not understand, the Prince of Pennadot was looking to him for reassurance. "Depends on what the fall-back plan was. If there are others out there like me, who can hold the Dragon's mind, then Sun help us all…"

"Why?"

Jarvis turned away. "It would have been easier to kill one target than many. No offense, your highness, but were you the Dragon, royal or not, I would gut you." He had to speak the truth. It did not seem the Starborn was fussed about his words.

"None taken. It is not like I would feel it."

"No. No, we must hope that Jarid is alive in there. That he is fighting that foul beast even now," the Mahvash insisted.

"Your Lady is correct, your highness. If anything, if the Dragon was forced to compromise, then it is possible that he spread himself thinner." Jarvis managed a small smile.

"Like a Hydra," the woman murmured.

Jarvis glanced her way. "A serpent with many heads. I suppose that description would suffice, yes." He rubbed his chin. "Those who are now his hosts may have a chance to overcome him, rather like someone who has been consumed by a Twizel. Like…my Master…" He winced, gritting his teeth, bowing his head. "He would have known what to say and do right now."

Why—why had Master Titus gone and died? He lashed out at the nearest chair, feeling a sudden spike of anger flood through his systems. Was it anger, though, or grief that he had not yet expressed? It was so hard to tell the difference between the anger and the stabbing pain of loss. He wished he could file the emotions, but they kept resurfacing themselves. There was no deleting grief.

He half tuned in to the Imperials' discussion about leaving to find someone and he could not help but feel amused. At least they could get him out of his slump. They had no idea where they were. It was hilarious.

He coughed lightly to regain their attention.

"Sorry, Imperials, but I'm afraid you will not be going anywhere." He gestured with one hand while he pressed the other against the wall behind the glass desks. He flicked several switches, ordering the shields of the observation deck to rise. Hexagon by hexagon they lifted away to reveal the world beyond. Coltarian in all her glory. The surging, constant storm of the sky-sea, crackling with lightning that struck the ground in magnificent bolts. Threads of lava weaving between the plates of the charred crust, scattered with volcanos spewing ash in a constant halo. It was a terrifying sight to anyone who had lived in a land of green and gold.

"This is Coltarian, your majesties: the land of Fire and Ice." He turned to the couple as they held each other, and smirked. "Welcome to the Messengers' War."

The Starborn prince stepped forward as though in a trance. He bumped into the terminals, causing them to light up in a stream of holograms springing to life. Jarvis held in his laughter; it was wrong of him to find amusement in this moment, seeing their horrified faces. Something else was going on that he did not know anything about. He had no knowledge of their story—just as they did not know about Master Titus.

"How?" The royal choked out. "How are we ever supposed to get back now?"

Jarvis approached him, settling a hand on his arm. "If you cannot go back, your highness, then I suggest you try going forward. It is what Messengers do."

CHAPTER TWENTY

It was not Disgleirio. Disgleirio was dead. All that remained of his friend hung around Skri's neck. The weight of the Dream Stone had never felt heavier as he stared at the frozen Starborn Human contained within the hibernation chamber.

Fyrnra's voice startled him so much that he jolted upright. She looked at him with anxious eyes. "Sorry, Father."

"No. No. I was far away. I didn't hear you—what did you say?"

"I don't think this is Eldorado."

She had spoken to him often of her thoughts on this matter, that nothing they had unearthed revealed the structure to be one of the Cities of Gold and he was inclined to believe her hypothesis—he simply did not know what else structure could be. Disgleirio had spoken only of the Cities of Gold and the Towers, and he knew this was not a Tower. "Father, I know it's ludicrous, but I think this place predates the Zaprexes' arrival on Livila."

"It is ludicrous, but I have learnt that there is nothing that is impossible when dealing with Zaprexes." He rested a claw upon the cool surface of the hibernation chamber. The Starborn man had elements of Disgleirio, but, upon closer inspection, it was easier to see variations. This man's skin-tone was not that of a Kimwyn, despite his Starborn glow.

"But you are a descendent..." Skri murmured. "And, therefore, you fall under my family's protection."

A Starborn, slumbering away in the darkness, blissfully unaware of the passage of time—or was he? There was something in his expression that ached in Skri's chest—pain, loneliness, grief.

"This man is out of time, and place."

"Should we wake him?"

"Goodness, no!" Skri jerked towards her. "We are not waking him. Not until we know what this place is, and who he is. Do I make myself clear?"

The deck of the *Lawless Child* was lonesome. The space was welcome. The emptiness filled Denvy's mind with a vacantness he could fall into. Sleep was impossible; his dreams were troubled and he loathed forcing Ryojin through the pain of nursing him in his tender, raw state. It was eerie—the sudden newness of being removed from the yoke. He was not even sure whether he was dreaming now; it was becoming difficult to tell when he felt so empty inside. He was beginning to rely too much on Ryojin to reassure him that he had not accidently wandered into a dreamscape.

The soft wind carried a song that drifted through the Rythrya Stones, like wind-chimes on a tavern window. He leant lazily on the railings. It was easy to see why the spires of Tikal had become so mythical to his people. If sand-sea sailors had sighted them from afar, or if they had risen upon sand-ships unawares, they would have been a dramatic sight. How many of the misfit children of the burning-sea had dreams of Tikal's spires, like those Nixlye had? Had Tikal been trying to draw the misfit children to it for centuries?

Denvy clenched his fists.

If Tikal had been drawing in the vagabonds, then so had the Dragon. His precious cubs had been misfit children and he had not even known. He shook his head. It was difficult to clear his mind of the horrible sight of the Kattamont child caged in a machine—and if only he had not taken his cubs into the Haven Hall, Clive would never have become infected. The Dragon would not have consumed him.

Yet he had become so accustomed to children in war.

Denvy scrubbed at his air-gills.

"How did you escape, Dragon? I thought you needed a Starborn body? Hazanin was adamant about that."

He paused, his ears twitching rearward as he picked up the sharp sound of metal heels clicking on the deck.

"You seem to have forgotten much of what I taught you, my son."

He had to turn, his whole being compelled to do so. In a soft glow, backlit by a flutter of wings crafted from blue, chaotic energy, Nefertem stood like an elegant, delicate butterfly. The creator of the server-gods was studying him with a cocked eyebrow. Whether it was a look of disproval or amusement, he could not be sure.

"Gifu? Am I dreaming again?"

"You are always dreaming, Maahes. It is what you do." Nefertem skipped onto a crate, joining him at the railing and the view of the Rythrya Stones.

"How? Why?"

"How am I here? The Data-Stream is a flow of energy surrounding Livila, created by the rotation of the planet, and it flows through all of us. The Song of Eternity." Nefertem pulled out a pipe, filling it from a pouch and lighting it with a spark from a flick of his finger. "As I am still a part of you, you are patterned after me. You were my first creation, my first born, so to speak…"

"So, I am technically talking to myself," Denvy grumbled. "Wonderful. The first sign of insanity."

"Well, perhaps. Or I could be a manifestation of the remainder of my program left within the Data-Stream that is waiting for the cycle to begin again, being channelled through you due to our connection. But…it is more likely that you are talking to yourself and going mad."

Denvy rolled his eyes. "I am fairy-born. I am already mad. It was your title after all, Gifu—the Mad Scientist."

Nefertem clicked his tongue in disproval. "Don't be so snarky. Besides, it is about time you had some cubs, heh. Spread those mad genes of yours around."

"The Dragon has become flesh. There will be war. Hardly the time for cubs." His thoughts flashed to Clive and Penny—oh, darling Penny, what had he done wrong?

"There is always war, Maahes. Whatever era you live in, there will be signs of war, or death, or horrors unimaginable. Do not allow fear to stop you living." Nefertem turned away. "Tikal needs a Navigator and Utillia needs Maahes, the Gold Lion."

Denvy wrapped his digits around the worn, warm wood of the railing. "No, Utillia needs a Sun."

The Zaprex ghost twittered a sudden laugh. "Oh? A Sun? The Age of the Black Sun, indeed."

"Wait, Gifu!" Denvy stretched out a paw to the departing Zaprex. "The Dragon, how did he free himself? I thought he needed a Starborn."

"Ah, thinking in absolutes. You and Hazanin always had that in common. I should never have let him be your tutor. You keep forgetting the reason I built you. The Era of the Elementals had ended, Maahes. Why did I need to build the server-gods?"

"Balance." Denvy stopped dead. "He balanced himself out over many hosts."

The apparition faded into the darkness. "You have your answer. Now, what are you going to do about it?"

What was he going to do? He would not panic. He would not fear the Dragon, not this time. Denvy looked at the Rythrya Stones, their glow so soft, and the wind a welcoming brush through his mane and air-gills.

"Time to go," he whispered as he released his mind, catching the song of defragmentation. Surrounding his foot-paws the merge spread out in a wave of pixels, and around him the *Lawless Child* began to scatter.

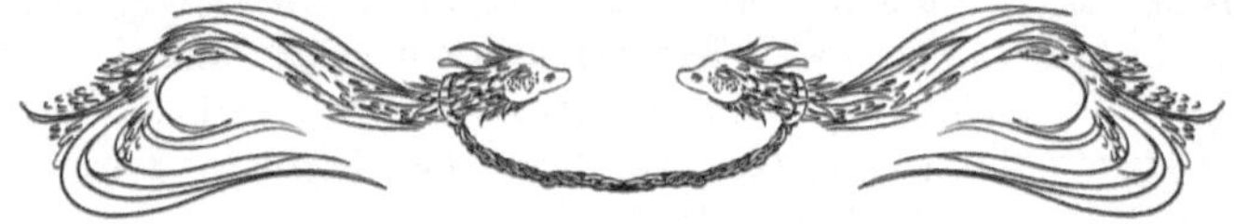

Ki'b heaved another shuddering sob. Her pillow was wet, but the tears would not stop. No matter how her puffy cheeks ached, or how her throat burned from gasping through her mouth because her nose was blocked, she could not find the will to cease, for it had all been her fault. Her siblings, all of them, even Jarvis, were all gone, because of her.

Ki'b curled into the covers, clutching at her throbbing chest. Everything was so sore. It was like she was being sat on, and it was impossible to push away the feeling of guilt.

Coolness settled over her temple, water dribbled down her hot cheeks. Her stuffy nose began to clear as the scent of fresh leaf oil tickled her nostrils. Ki'b whimpered as the bed shifted. Jythal stroked her hair aside and she buried herself deeper into the pillows.

"Oh, come now, Little Mountain Flower…"

Easily she was plucked, like the flower they called her, and lifted into Jythal's lap, settled against his cool fur. His air-gills rustled as though they were mimicking trees and she dived into his shoulder, wanting to hide amongst branches as she sobbed.

"It's my fault."

"My little princess, whatever makes you think that?"

"If…I had talked to…Penny more…and to Clive…maybe…the Dragon wouldn't have…" She covered her eyes. She could not bear to see the doctor, or the little cabin she had come to love like a Family Hall. "I shouldn't ever have left Penny! I knew she wanted to go home! I knew she hated it here, but I had no idea she…"

"…that she would go with the Dragon?" Jythal added softly.

She could only nod. The thought was still so very horrible.

"I do not think she believes he is the Dragon, dear," Nixlye said, wheeling up to the bed. "I think she hopes she is still with Clive. Maybe that she can bring him back here, to you—you are still her family."

Ki'b looked down at her hands. The queen was right. She was supposed to be Penny's sister. But she had never really tried to be close to Penny—which is why it was all her fault!

"I had Jarvis, and then you." Jythal's arms wrapped around her as she spoke. "Penny and Clive must have felt like outsiders. Even Clive had his Runes. Penny had nothing—only Clive to speak to. I never meant to shut her out! I just…never understood her. I don't think…I ever tried. So…it is my fault!"

"No, no, sweet one." Nixlye covered her in a blanket. "You are a child in a war. You would never harm your sister. She will need you more now."

Ki'b hiccupped. "What am I supposed to do?"

"You are a princess; you will fight this Dragon." Nixlye gripped her trembling hands.

"Even if that means I have to fight Clive?" Ki'b squeezed her eyes shut. She did not think she could do that. Clive's smile was so easy to picture in the darkness. He had been so bright, so happy, always ready to make her laugh. He had been the one in the horrible box who had never, ever let the Twizels take their hope away.

"You will do it for Penny." Jythal lifted her off his lap as he stood. He moved across to the kitchen, reaching for the tea-pot. "When the time comes, Ki'b, you will find the strength is there, inside you, to save your sister."

She nodded weakly, curling her toes. She could only trust they were right, since she felt so alone and empty. Ki'b shook her head, trying to free it of the scary darkness. Jarvis would want her to be brave. Jarvis did not know about Clive and Penny—she had to make sure they were back before Jarvis came home.

She lifted her chin. "I can do it."

"That's my princess." Nixlye tweaked her cheek fondly. The queen spun her wheelchair, frowning at a clattering sound from outside the cabin door. Ki'b tensed. Not again. Was it the Silvertide Pride, returning to fight them?

Nixlye opened the door. Ki'b joined her, watching as crew members ran past. They did not look scared; their faces were bright with excitement and wonder.

Nixlye hailed the nearest one, "What is going on, sailor?"

"You don't know? Prince Denvy moved us again. Look out the window—we're inside the Rythrya Stones!"

Ki'b heard tea cups shattering and suddenly Jythal was at the door. Nixlye heaved her onto her lap and they careered down the corridor, closely followed by the blind doctor. Her chest rose, capturing the excitement of the two Kattamonts. What had Khwaja Denvy done now?

Nixlye burst out topside. Awed shouts filled her ears. She spun her wheelchair around, unable to believe what she was taking in. She was not dreaming; Ki'b's heavy weight was still pressed against her chest and, surrounding her, the crew was as mesmerised as she was.

This was real.

"By the Four Winds…" she murmured, tears gathering under her lashes. "Is this what Pennadot looks like?"

On all sides of the *Lawless Child*, a forest—something she had only ever seen images of in the tomes of the Haven Hall libraries—enveloped countless platforms that hovered within the crystal spire. The air was crisp, hackling her fur with its chill. It tickled her lashes, akin to Mist, but so much thicker, like she could drink it with her lungs. There was too much green, every shade she could have dreamed of, amongst the leaves shimmering in light as bright as day, reflected down upon them from mirrors. She could not fathom where the source of the glow came from, but it flood-lit the dewy forest.

"It's like we're inside an eternal spring morning after the rain." Ki'b slipped off her lap.

Spring, rain—they were unknown words, they had no meaning to Nixlye, but Ki'b said them with such wonder and longing they must have been something magnificent.

She rolled to the edge of the *Lawless Child*, her heart jumping into her throat. "Oh, Aaldryn, how I wish…" Nixlye clutched her hands to her chest.

They were surrounded by the most stunning of alien vessels, hovering amongst them as though they too were simply docked with the silent, slumbering sky-ships. Some she had heard Aaldryn describe from his dives deep into the burning-sea, but others, in docks throughout the forest cascading down around them, were beyond anything her prince had mentioned. He had spoken of them dying, torn apart, warped by time, damaged by war or deeper horrors. These were fresh, new, shining, and bright with pulsing life.

Yet her mind could sense the eeriness of emptiness surrounding her.

The interior world they were in was asleep.

There was no noise.

No song.

Just silence.

Even the crew, despite their heightened excitement, were only whispering. It was as though they too could sense that they stood within a place that was in deep rest.

"Nixlye…" Jythal's sorrowful voice stirred her. She squeezed her eyes shut at his agonised tone. It tore at her, that she could see such vibrant wonders and relish the splendour, but he could not.

"Is it beautiful?" he added.

She reached for his paw. "It is beyond our dreams, my love, beyond all our hopes. I wish, oh, I wish you could see it."

He brushed her face, feeling her smile, touching her eyes, her ears, and finally falling back to her lips. "I can see it; your face says it all."

"Khwaja Denvy!" Ki'b's feet thumped over the deck. Nixlye bounced in her wheelchair as Ki'b tore past. She spun her wheels around, catching sight of the girl launching herself into the prince's arms, burrowing into his chest. Jythal pushed her chair gently, urging her forward to join them.

"Is this your home, Khwaja?" Ki'b pulled away from Denvy's fur.

Denvy hoisted Ki'b onto his shoulder. "Yes, this was my home and it will be again."

"You…you…fool-hardy old man!"

Nixlye winced at Zafiashid's thundering Ching roar. The queen charged across the deck, the crew dispersing swiftly lest they be caught up in her fury.

"What possessed you to try something that has already harmed you twice!"

Denvy stood his ground against her assault as she barrelled into his chest, her air-gills spread in a dangerous display. "Technically, I was only knocked out once; the first time actually took out the yoke around my neck. I'd say that was a good thing, wouldn't you?"

Zafiashid's fan-tail rattled. "I just know I will regret falling in love with you, you insufferable idiot. You will make me worry worse than any cub."

Denvy settled a paw on her shoulder and pressed a kiss to her forehead. "This is more than likely true, yes."

Zafiashid growled out a long sigh, folding her arms across her chest. Nixlye hid her smirk behind a paw as Denvy settled Ki'b onto the deck. "We need to find the Central Control Room. Hopefully I can still remember where it is." He furrowed his brow.

Zafiashid stalled him. "The crew—I cannot leave them here."

"I can assure you, they are safer here than they have ever been anywhere else." Denvy hoisted himself over the edge of the *Lawless Child*, grabbing hold of a rope. "Tikal will tell them if they are doing anything wrong."

Nixlye laughed as he vanished over the railing. His glee was catching, like a cub encountering the wonders of Mist for the first time, dashing about with a lantern as it turned on and off in the darkness. "He's like a cub on an adventure."

"Hopefully he remembers his age before he breaks a knee," Zafiashid grumbled under her breath. "Well, don't just stand there—let's go after him."

They met Denvy on the surface after Nixlye's wheelchair had been lowered by the crew, and it was only then that the true sense of enormity and vastness of the environment settled over her. Never had she seen the under hull of the *Lawless Child* in such a manner, and there she was, sitting beside their sand-ship as it floated amongst alien sky-ships. Some of the vessels were small and delicate, perhaps fitting one or two crew members, others dwarfed even the biggest sand-ships she had ever seen. Denvy spoke in soft tones as he described the slumbering vessels, calling some of them by name.

They reached the end of something akin to a harbour. It was the only word that sprang to mind, though it felt inadequate and she was left wondering what Aaldryn would have said. Would he even believe she was here, wandering the corridors of a fairy-castle?

They followed Denvy deeper into the city, through empty halls of reflective glass that carried the light, spreading rainbows from jewel-encrusted ceilings and pillars. Every so often they caught sight of a delicate figure dancing in the reflections, smiling and laughing at them.

Between Denvy and Zafiashid, Ki'b clung to both their paws, her little bare feet making ripples on the floor.

"The city has a drum-beat. Like the trees in Pennadot," Ki'b piped up hesitantly.

"I am not surprised you feel it." Denvy nodded. "The AIs in the

Cities of Gold were often referred to as Crystal Trees, due to how magnificently large they would grow and the formations they would take. Here—we'll get a good view of Tikal, right… about… now…"

The door opened, folding in on itself. Ki'b gave a loud squeal and pulled free, running into a circular chamber with windows opening onto a vast drop, and a seemingly endless ceiling. Ki'b slapped herself against the glass, pressing her face to it in uncontained glee. Nixlye wheeled in, twirling her chair around the empty room. They were suspended high in the branches of an immense crystal tree, tinted in yellow and blue hues. Cascading waterfalls gushed from somewhere far above them, and the thundering roar must have been deafening, but within the chamber there was silence, save for their own voices.

"It's beautiful," Zafiashid startled her with the sudden admission. It was not often the outcast queen admitted that anything affected her.

"Oh, you have not seen the half of it. Tikal, you can wake up now," Denvy ordered.

The room emitted a pulse. Patterns spread out across the floor in squares, running back and forth beneath their paws. Sheets of glass rose up in rows and, like liquid drops, dozens of chairs joined them. A single main throne dropped from the ceiling, landing like a raindrop in a puddle. Denvy came to stand beside it, motioning to Zafiashid.

"Captain, I believe this is yours."

Zafiashid propped a paw on her hip. "Hilarious."

Giggles echoed around the chamber. Zafiashid and Jythal tensed, both shifting their stances, readying for battle, as a swell of tiny flakes merged beside Denvy, forming a tiny white creature.

Nixlye grabbed Jythal's paw. "A Zaprex!" she choked out. The most she had ever known of them had come from texts in the Iposti Archives, and old files Aaldryn had dug up for her to translate. She had dreamt of them, but this was beyond her imagining.

Denvy shook his head.

"No, this is the avatar of Tikal, the artificial intelligence of this city. They choose to appear somewhat similar to our Creators. Zaprexes tend to have a skin coating that is turquoise, or aqua, sometimes even deep emerald. Most AIs have pale metal tones and they do not have antennae. Tikal has always been fond of glass skin, in keeping with its desktop theme."

"We are shiny," the hologram chimed.

Jythal laughed suddenly. Nixlye had never heard such a laugh from him, and she thought she knew all the variations of his laughter. This one was pure, childish delight. He covered his mouth in shock.

"Sorry. Ah…I can feel the vibration in the air through my air-gills. I can almost…well, I can see it."

"We try to calibrate for all peoples. We would not be very useful if we could not make ourselves known to everyone. You would hit walls.

That would damage you, yes? We make sure you are not harmed. We are AI. We protect all."

"Interesting. So this is who you have been referring to?" Zafiashid turned to Denvy. "This is the great treasure of the Zaprexes that Utillia has hidden all these centuries. This is what I have searched for…" She smiled, crouching before the AI. "I am Zafiashid, Outcast of the Silvertide Pride and Queen of the Misfits, Captain of the *Lawless Child*. It is an honour to meet you, Tikal."

Tikal's white eyes blinked. "You are Mother of Aaldryn, the host of North Wind Khamsin." The hologram turned to Ki'b. "You are Ki'b, bonding-partner of Jarvis. We like Jarvis. We promised to tell you Jarvis is all right."

"Aaldryn!" Nixlye wheeled forward. "You've seen Aaldryn and Jarvis!"

Ki'b bounced. "Where are they?"

The AI stared eerily at a point between them both. "We are many. We see much. Our mirrors are everywhere."

"Tikal, they have asked you where you saw Aaldryn and Jarvis," Denvy urged softly.

"Passed beyond our mirrors, into the Land of the Fire Lord."

"Coltarian. They made it, then." Denvy sighed.

Nixlye sank back into her chair. Jythal knelt beside Ki'b hugging her to his chest.

"At least we know they got through Utillia," Nixlye tried to reassure Ki'b, but her words were more for her own sake. If she spoke them aloud, maybe she would believe herself that Jarvis and Aaldryn were alive and well.

Denvy was frowning, his focus still on Tikal, and the AI hologram shifted with a guilty-looking back and forth movement, refusing to meet the prince's eyes.

"Tikal, you did not answer my question. Where did you see Aaldryn and Jarvis?"

The AI made a dramatic motion with its arms, causing a blur of pixels. "Not enough time. Never enough time!"

"Tikal." Denvy arched an eyebrow.

"Establishing connection: *Yrva Krv*."

"Wait…what?" Denvy stepped back as a shimmer of an image darkened the room like a curtain falling from the ceiling. With equally as much confusion as Denvy was displaying, a young half-breed prince peered back at them, tapping at something off to the side.

Nixlye gripped the arms of her chair, breathing in sharply. "Aaldryn?"

It was not her prince, but the similarities were unmistakeable. The Silvertide Pride's glinting silver fur and sleek build was unique amongst Kattamonts, but she had never expected to see a half-breed of the staunchly puritan Pride.

She caught the brief look of shock that rippled Zafiashid's air-gills before the queen quickly stifled the emotion behind a stern frown.

"Is this working? Hello? Hello?" There was a lag to the audio, and the image of the half-breed prince flickered.

"Greetings, young prince," Denvy replied. "You're coming through with a bit of a lag and some static, but we can hear you. I am Denvy Maahes, Prince of the Misfit Pride."

"This is really working? You're at the HUB?"

Denvy's air-gills frilled out in surprise. "You know of the HUB?"

"Of course. I've been getting commands and upgrades from the HUB, but no direct communications. I do apologise. Yrva Krv is in need of considerable repairs and I'm not entirely equipped for such tasks. I am Troq, the third prince of the Dwellers' Pride. I'm getting a lot of static interference, but I gather that's Queen Zafiashid?"

Denvy glanced at Zafiashid and she stepped forward.

"I am."

Troq touched his chest, revealing a hand eerily like Nixlye's own, humanlike and slender. *"I am sure my appearance raises many questions for you, Queen Zafiashid, and I promise in due time we will have that discussion."*

She nodded. "We shall."

Nixlye felt her shoulders relax. Mother did not look like she was about to immediately run off on a single-pawed campaign to destroy the Silvertide Pride, though such a confrontation was most likely coming.

"My Alpha and I escorted your son and his companions as far as we could through Yrva Krv. Tikal informed me that they had reached the Border between Utillia and Coltarian. I am happy to tell you they were still in good health."

Jythal's paw caught her hand and Nixlye clasped it tightly.

"Then there is still hope that the message that Jarvis and Titus carry will reach the House of Flames. We shall have Messengers coming to Utillia from the West and Pennadotians from the South." Denvy scrubbed a paw through his mane.

"Kattamonts are not known to share land; we barely tolerate each other in Prides. Denvy, we are the worse race anyone could ask refuge from. We are territorial, and some Prides are xenophobic." Jythal reached protectively for Ki'b. "We've kept our distance from that sort of trouble, but, I assure you, I have witnessed it."

"I do not doubt you." Denvy shook his head. "With the Dragon amongst us now, there is no telling what he will stir up in the burning-sea."

"It is likely he already has the Iposti on his side," Nixlye spat out. She did not mean to be so vicious, but her mind instantly returned to the Haven Hall, and the sight of the cub fused with the machine. Her body chilled. Would she have ended up inside one of those horrible things if she had not left the convent?

"What makes you say that?" Ki'b worried her hands against her dress.

"Clive was wounded by that ghastly machine inside the Haven Hall and it was then that he…well…" Nixlye let her put the pieces together.

I do not know what terrors you have witnessed, princess, but, though the Iposti's roots go deep in Utillia, I can assure you Tikal has been at work far longer. It has been creating us—its Mirrors—for these troubling days ahead.

His voice was not rough like Aaldryn's, with the uncultured twang of sol-cycles sailing the outer sectors, so the tears that threatened to escape the corners of her eyes were overwhelming. It was simply the face, so like her mate's, speaking words of comfort that triggered the tightness in her chest.

"You're a Changeling," Denvy surmised.

Troq nodded, his sharp movements once more blurring the screen. *"Queen Zafiashid, my Alpha stands with you."*

The static image scattered, leaving a vacantness within the chamber. Denvy scratched his chin, looking down at Tikal's delicate hologram. "You've been hard at work, I see."

"Not enough time. Not enough mirrors." Tikal's warbling tone echoed through the chamber. "The Tainted Ones are many. Too many."

"But this means we have allies," Jythal offered. "That is a lot more than we could have asked for."

Zafiashid turned to the hologram. "You have done well."

Tikal grinned. "We kill Gaia. You kill Tainted Ones."

Denvy clapped his paws together, drawing attention away from the disturbingly manic AI. "There is little we can do now about the Dragon, but we can do something about the refugees."

"We can?" Zafiashid scoffed.

"My dear, you set a task: to unite the Prides—No, do not snort at me." The old gold lion twirled on his heel and threw open his arms. "Let us raise this old bucket out of the burning-sea."

"You are mad!"

The grin he threw back at Zafiashid was manic. "Perhaps I am, but why not? This is a city. It must be filled with inhabitants."

"Oh, I never said it was a bad idea, simply that you are mad."

"It is in my genes, I'm afraid."

Nixlye followed Denvy in her chair. "Of what I know about Zaprex machines, you need an energy source. The turrets are fuelled by their connection to the Secondary Realm; that is why they are failing gradually. Surely if the turrets are failing, then a City of Gold cannot be fuelled by the Secondary Realm. We cannot use it."

Denvy tweaked her nose fondly. "Ah, ever observant, Nixlye." He ran his paw over a terminal. "You are correct. Do you, by any chance, happen to know the Myth of the Seven Falling Stars?" He cocked his head towards her.

"Of course. The way the Iposti tell it, the Zaprexes were the Great Invaders who came to Livila and brought ruin to our old world. The Seven Stars fell across Livila in a blinding light, bringing with them the Ninth and Tenth races: the Zaprexes and the Humans."

"Very good." Denvy moved around her, fiddling with the holographic screens. "What they didn't tell you is that the Seven Stars, travelling together, were known as Atum-Ra, the Migration Conurbation. It broke into seven sections when it arrived."

"Like Tikal?" Ki'b wrapped her arms around the dainty AI, only to fall flat on her face as she phased through the illusion of light. The hologram stepped to one side and stared down at her as she pouted, rubbing her nose.

"We apologise, fleshling. We were not prepared for your physical contact. We shall endeavour to create a solid form for you to interact with in the future."

Ki'b looked up at Denvy. "It's not really here?"

Denvy smiled. "It is a creation of light, love."

"We are Tikal." Tikal offered her a hand. "We are many."

She carefully took it, smiling when it gripped her fingers and easily heaved her onto her feet.

Denvy turned to Nixlye. "Have you figured out why it speaks in plurals?"

She had been curious about that, but it was least odd thing that surrounded them. "I presumed it was normal."

"Tikal was the youngest of the AIs grown out of Atum-Ra's great Matrix Crystal. It was created as a shield and cloaking device, hence the rainbows. It was the only AI given its own power source that could be controlled without Starborn Humans, who controlled the other cities. It needed to be a self-sustaining system, in the event that something happened to the other AIs and their pilots."

Denvy flicked his paws over a few buttons and stepped back, his grin widening as the floor beneath them began to ripple. "You asked once what it was that created the currents of the burning-sea. Well, now you know..."

Nixlye was too busy trying not to shout in alarm as the floor became completely transparent. It was as though she was sitting in mid-air upon her wheelchair, suspended amongst the branches of the crystal tree, and, below them, the source of all light. It was beyond words—beyond her comprehension. She would never again be able to refer to anything else as beautiful again now that she had seen the wonder of the swirling, shining sun spinning slowly amongst the branches beneath them.

Ki'b clung to Jythal. "What is it?"

"It is a star." Denvy placed his paws behind his back. "Captured many eons ago in another universe, very different to our own universe. The Zaprexes contained it here within Tikal's Matrix Crystal. They call it a star-drive. Each of the Cities of Gold had one, but Tikal's was unique."

"There is a reason it can't be controlled by a Starborn, isn't there," Jythal offered. "Otherwise the Zaprexes would have installed the same system."

"I will have to admit the Zaprexes had a terrible habit of making everything similar. But this star, though it looks small here, was once a giant. Its energy levels had to be enough to fuel the shields to protect the Migration Conurbation through the Multiverse. Back then the Starborn Humans were unable to control such power."

"What if the Dragon got a hold of this?" Zafiashid gripped his arm.

"It is quite possible that is why he has been here in Utillia. Though it is highly unlikely he would ever gain entry without me or a Zaprex. Tikal is the only City of Gold that has no doors. It can only be accessed through defragmentation."

Jythal raised a paw. "This is all really lovely, but I can't see any of this, so I have a question. Why does it refer to itself in the plural?"

"Mirrors." Denvy chuckled.

"Mirrors?" Jythal frowned.

"What is in a mirror?"

"I wouldn't know."

"A reflection of yourself," Nixlye answered, turning her wheelchair about. "The whole city is covered in mirrors; the windows, the crystals, the ceiling and floors, every surface shiny and reflective. The city is a reflection of itself," she added before her prince could grow frustrated at his inability to see what it was they were talking about.

Denvy nodded. "Somewhere, amongst all these reflections is Tikal's split personality. I have only spoken to it a few times when I was a cub, but it was a frightening force to behold. It is all the rage and fury of that star down there, contained in a soft fluttering voice."

"How will we know the difference?' Nixlye hesitantly glanced towards the hologram standing innocently beside Ki'b.

"It will never refer to itself in the plural, and you may find yourself in a room that is upside down rather suddenly. Do not be alarmed. It does not mean you any harm."

"Who does it mean harm to?" Zafiashid asked.

Tikal started laughing. "Gaians."

Denvy spread his paws. "Everyone, please, take a seat."

Nixlye gave the arms of her chair a pat. "I am already sitting."

"Tikal, could you please strap Nixlye's chair down." Denvy pointed to her and Tikal's hologram vanished and reappeared beside her in a flash.

"Your chair is insufficient. We shall get you a new one soon. For now, please remain within this zone." A square lit up around her chair.

Jythal felt for a seat beside her and Ki'b leapt into his lap, snuggling against his chest. Nixlye raised an eyebrow at the sight of Zafiashid slipping into the throne, swinging one leg over the other, regal in her silver coat that gleamed in the light from the star below. Denvy's chair rose to meet him and he was so at ease in it. This was clearly where he belonged, surrounding by the shine of holographic screens and the twittering laughter of the AI that danced around them.

Denvy settled his paws upon the glass terminal and breathed in deeply.

"Hold on."

She gripped Jythal's paw. The star beneath them surged with a sudden burst of light. From the corner of her eye she caught sight of a halo of gold forming around Denvy's head, but it barely mattered; the world rumbled, and her stomach lurched into her throat.

The sides of the spire they were situated within began to let in light as sand pulled away.

Nixlye's heart raced. They were lifting. The city was surging out of the burning-sea. Her fist clenched around Jythal's paw.

Reality was far better than dreams.

CHAPTER TWENTY-ONE

The absence of the Dream Stone from around Skri's neck terrified him far more than he ever wanted to admit. Rynk had grown into such a fine young Batitic; sending the lad and his young family back to Pennadot—into the unknown—had pained him. His grandson had always known that to him would fall the burden of returning to the Northlands, to bear the weight of the Mazaki name, and carry the Dream Stone. He felt he had sent his beloved grandson to his death. Skri dropped his head back against the cool surface of the hibernation chamber.

He was old. So old. Yet still he lingered, as though he had not yet finished something Disgleirio had asked of him.

"Maahes. I never found Maahes," he murmured. "I wonder where you are...Maahes..."

Skri sighed. He always found himself returning to the silence of the HUB where the unknown Starborn slumbered. The presence of his energy was comforting, reminding him of Disgleirio.

A soft glow permeated the edge of the HUB, breaking through the blur of his tears. Skri wiped at his eyes, staring at the approaching scattering of light.

"Hello. Skri? That is your name, yes?"

A hologram stood before him. He had only seen pictures of Zaprexes, delicate little creatures, so perfect in their design. Being suddenly confronted with one was so alarming he scrambled away.

The hologram held out its hands. "No. Please. I mean you no harm."

"Who are you?"

"Atomic Horus." The hologram bowed. "H.O.R.U.S. Horticultural Orbital Rotational Utility Station."

Skri clawed back his hair. "So, not Eldorado."

The hologram grinned. "The Cities of Gold? You're talking about my children." It held out its small hand to him. "Come, Skri, we have a lot of work to do."

"I am far too old for this."

"Nonsense, you're practically a child!" Horus tittered.

Skri motioned to the hibernation chamber.

"Who is he?"

Horus glanced back. "A man out of his time. He is old."

The Dragon clawed at the planks of the sand-ship, arms straining as his thin, weak chest heaved for air. He had spent hours struggling to keep himself and Penny above the tossing waves of the painfully hot aptly-named burning-sea. His body was raw. Blood oozed where sand had shaven his skin. He cursed the old Dream Master, he cursed Hazanin and Zilon, and everyone he could think of for putting him in such a pathetic predicament.

Who had placed him in such a weak body, that he could not even summon enough strength to save himself? It was disgusting!

Kattamont claws snagged his wrists, heaving him up and over the railing of the sand-ship. "We've got yeh, lad. We've got yeh."

He staggered, landing on his knees upon the surface of the rocking deck, vomiting bucketloads of sand. Water—thank the Blackness—water; he gulped it down greedily. A mortal body was so weak. Casting the cup aside, he scrubbed at his eyes, staring around the crew that surrounded him. His gaze fell on Penny, lying limp on the deck. A Kattamont knelt over her.

His chest sized with sudden panic. She was not moving. Her green sphere and the numerals that indicated her life-time no longer glowed above her head. He could feel no energy within her. Had he eaten her in his own attempt to survive?

"No. No!" He scrambled for her, confusion muffling his thoughts. He should not feel such emotions attached to this little Human child, but he could not control himself as he knelt over her.

"Penny!" He shook her shoulders. Her head rolled. This was not right. He had not kept her afloat for so many hours only for her to be dead. He did not allow people to die. They needed his permission to die! Burning rage surged through him. He slapped a hand against her chest, pulling energy from the Secondary Realm, tearing it out, and with a thrust he shoved it into her. The pulse of life flushed back through her. The green sphere flashed alight over her head, and the numerals spun forward, filling with time. The Dragon sat back on his heels, tension releasing from his shoulders. Good. Osiris had not yet dispersed her data. He had acted quickly enough.

Her eyes fluttered open and she looked up at him. Suddenly she overwhelmed him with a hug. Relief crept up his spine at her touch and he shrugged it aside. She was the first person he had seen when he woke from his imprisonment; like a babe he had simply imprinted on her. "You saved me."

"We will keep surviving." He gripped her hand and looked up. A female Kattamont approached—from the manner of her walk, she had to be a princess. She did not kneel to reach their height but stared down at them through her frilled air-gills. The Dragon licked his dry lips. He wanted to stand, but his legs were watery. For now, he would let himself be looked down upon—just for now.

"Why were you in the burning-sea, Humans?"

"We were cast overboard, along with some other prisoners. They drowned, but we managed to keep afloat by hugging each other." The Dragon gingerly touched his raw skin.

"I see. By any chance where you cast overboard by the Captain of the *Lawless Child?*"

"Yes!" Penny almost shouted. "Yes, we were. It was terrible!"

"We have been following the trail of the *Lawless Child* for many days now. It vanished out of thin air during a battle with the Silvertide Navy. It is only through the grace of the Iposti with us that we managed to track them here."

The princess' gaze shifted to the Rythrya Stones in the distance. The Dragon frowned. So, there was an Iposti on board. He was not sure whether this helped or complicated matters.

The deck suddenly jolted, provoking shouts of alarm from the crew. The Dragon dragged Penny upright, grinning wildly. It was not possible, was it? The thick surges of power through the Secondary Realm—was it really? Oh, the Dream Master was so fantastic, so brilliant! He had thought the fool might turn tail and run, but, no, he had decided to embrace his past. Landing against the railing of the sand-ship, the Dragon stretched out his hands. He wanted to be nearer to the singing of the spires as the sand-dune waves rolled away from them, rippling towards their sand-ship. The burning-sea tossed in a mighty distortion. More spires appeared, climbing higher into the sky-sea, shining with brilliance, casting light through the Long Night.

The City of Tikal rose above them, raining down sand. The power of its star-drive crackled across his skin. How hungry he was, how much he wanted to consume this. He laughed, waving madly. "Oh, Denvy! You are tempting me!"

He breathed out, settling his trembling body.

Penny's hand clasped his. She had to yell over the roar. "Clive, what is that?"

He pressed his lips to her ear, shouting back. "That is Khwaja Denvy's fairy castle."

He laughed, turning her about in a twirl. "Come on, we've got to go and find my Overlord. She's been hard at work here." He touched his chest thoughtfully. "I guess I have to thank her for this body. I do so hate thanking Overlords." His face twisted in mild disgust.

"But, Clive…what about my home?"

He kissed her cheek. "Don't worry, Penny. I am going to need my army to take back Tempath for you. I promise to make you the new Lady of Tempath. Then you will never have to worry about leaving your home again. We shall even erect a statue of your father. How does that sound?"

She fiddled with the necklace around her neck. "All right."

"Good." He looked around at the crew as they gaped at the risen city of Tikal. "First order of business. How do you think we should take over this sand-ship?"

Penny pulled out a hidden dagger from her apron. "Well, if I kill the princess, doesn't that make me one?"

He grinned. She was, quite possibly, his most wonderful accidental discovery of a little mortal. "You are so beautiful." For once, he realised, he actually meant his usually twisted words.

Sketches & Art

The following pages contain sketches, scribbles, works-in-progress and art — some I did for this book but discarded, other's are just random character design work.
Thought it might be fun to include them here.
Enjoy! KL

This was my sketch for the origonal illustration of Auldryn but I ended up liking the sketch more than the final piece.

This is the "original sketch" for the Jarvis/Khamsin illustration. I was pretty upset the others didn't workout to my liking, because I really liked this one.

This is the only illustration out of my original "plans" that actually sorta worked out, so I thought I would include it here. Yes, Khamsin's scales took FOREVER and I did three whole illustrations with him in them before I scrapped this style. GAH.

This is an illustration of Jythal and Nixlye that I ended up disliking after finishing — which is a shame — as it was a bit of a tricky feat.
So, here it is, even though I don't like it at all.

Sam sketches. Cause he brightens up a page.

I believe I was getting bored of drawing young-adult Skyeola and went back to Book one Skyeola.

The king who wanders
I love drawing silhouettes!
It is a great way to begin concepts,
and form interesting characters.

This is one of my favorite sketches of Jarvis.
It captures his personality in a glance.
I haven't been able to do it again. I'm just that sort of artist.

This is the original sketch of the Denvy Illustration in this book.

My original concept draft of Disgleirio.
I always have the most fun doing these.

Another concept draft of <u>Disgleirio</u> — just in a more formal Palace attire.

My very first sketch of Disgleirio.

Skri

My first sketch of skri.

Sometimes I just have to
go back to where it all
began and sketch some
Zinkt and Shanty <3

These are the only designs I have of Prometheus
and Eros — sadly I can't print them in colour here.
Someday I'll get around to updating them.
For many years I couldn't draw how I envisioned
the Fire Elementals, but, eventually I reached a point
where I hashed out something near enough.
Human Height

When I started writing Book 3 of <u>Chronicles</u>, I was struggling considerably with feeling the "naturalness" of the characters. Its odd, when you've "known" characters for years, and years, and then suddenly start writing them but everything just feels wrong. So, I did what I usually do to help, I drew them. Everything started falling into place after that.

Hah, I just wanted to add this here because I was just really happy that I actually drew a Twizel.
I don't like scary things...so...terrible at drawing my own nightmares. ^^;

About the Author

Kylie Leane lives in a sweet cottage home in the beautiful hills of Adelaide, South Australia, with her dimensional hopping pet cat, Aislinn Dreamer. When she is not travelling to different worlds, recording historical events, she spends a considerable amount of time at the local café writing, she also enjoys illustrating cute little green aliens. In her spare time, she loves watching Anime, reading old-timey sci-fi books, gardening, and going for long walks.

Having been raised with a love of old classic Science Fiction thanks to her Dad, Kylie adores all things spacey and science and she acquired a bountiful amount of creativity thanks to her very resourceful Mum.

Kylie started writing *Chronicles of the Children* when she was about ten, coming up with the idea for the story in the back seat of the car on a long drive with the family. Despite being dyslexic, she taught herself how to write and (sorta) spell through her stories. She is hopeless at grammar though.

Kylie was diagnosed with chronic pain when she was nineteen, and now tries to live life day to day. She's come to realise that she is going to be in pain anyway, so she may as well live her life to the best of her abilities. She had always found strength in the world of imagination and story-telling, and uses her weaving of tales and characters as a way to cope with the daily battle of pain.

She has a great desire to share her stories with the world and to spend her life encouraging others to use their own gifts. To let them know that even though they might have their own limitations, through their own imagination and their uniqueness everyone has a truly marvelous and incredible strength living inside them.

Kylie really loves hearing from people, so if you ever happen to be online feel free to drop her a hello—she has a website—and an email:

authorkylie.com

authorkyileleane@gmail.com

THE LONELY BARD